CHAIN OF ILLUSIONS

A BRINGER AND THE BANE NOVEL

Also by Boone Brux

Shield of Fire: Book One of The Bringer and the Bane

Kiss of the Betrayer: Book Two of The Bringer and the Bane

Suddenly Beautiful

Tweet: Love Knows No Bounds Anthology

CHAIN OF ILLUSIONS

A BRINGER AND THE BANE NOVEL

BOONE BRUX

Entangled Publishing, LLC
2614 South Timberline Road
Suite 109
Fort Collins, CO 80525
Visit our website at www.entangledpublishing.com.

Edited by Erin Molta
Cover design by Heather Howland

Ebook ISBN 978-1-62266-036-0
Print ISBN 978-1-62266-037-7

Manufactured in the United States of America

First Edition November 2013

PROLOGUE

A thousand years ago fire scorched the earth and the rivers of Inness ran red with the blood of humans, Bringers, and the soul-sucking Demon Bane...

The Bringers, an ancient race of powerful people from Bael, fought a war against the demons called the Bane. The Bringers were victorious over the Bane, freeing humans from the demons' deadly grasp. Though the Bringers won the war, the Bane were not so easily defeated. Vile, a power-thirsty demon, claimed the Bane throne. Gathering forces deep within the icy caverns of the Shadow World, he bided his time until he could rise up against the Bringers again.

In order to keep both Bael and Inness safe, the Mystic Arch between the two worlds was sealed. A few hundred Bringers—Shields who were protectors, healing Redeemers, and Tells who were endowed with the *Knowing* were left on Inness to protect the humans from the threat of the Demon Bane.

For a millennia humans lived in peace. The legends of the Bringers and the Bane fell into myth. Truth became lost and stories of the Bringers valor and the Demon Bane's treachery became nothing more than tales to be spun around the campfire.

Still the Bringers watched and protected, ever vigilant. But like a brewing storm, the Bane's return was heralded by nothing more than a quiet breeze. One by one, Vile assassinated the Bringers who had stayed on Inness, until only one remained—Rhys Blackwell.

Believing he was the only full-blooded Bringer left, Rhys scoured Inness for humans whose bloodline had been mixed with the Bringers. Together they formed a rebel band of mixed-blood soldiers whose goal was to subdue the Bane threat that was spreading across the lands.

When their fight seemed desperate, a new hope appeared on the horizon. In search of the kidnapped Bringer King, full-blooded Bringers emerged from beyond the Mystic Arch. Joining forces with Rhys and his followers, the group strengthened the Bringers' fight against the Demon Bane. In a fortunate twist they discovered the bodies of several of their brethren frozen deep within the Shadow World. One body saved was that of Rell Kendal.

Set upon by the demons thirteen years ago, Rell had been transformed to a demon and forced to live among the monsters that had stolen her life. Fearful that her younger sister would meet the same fate, Rell saved Jade and secretly raised her within the caverns of the Shadow World. But as the years passed, the taint of the Bane threatened to steal what was left of Rell's humanity.

With the arrival of the full-blooded Bringers came the revelation that transforming Rell back to human might be possible. Captured and held in a Bringer cell Rell learned that one of her captors is the man she had helped escape from the Bane prison—the man she loved, Siban.

CHAPTER ONE

Siban lifted his chin toward the gray sky and inhaled. Crisp air filled his lungs, clearing his head. The time had come for him to take his place among his people, the Bringers. Past time, actually. They needed him in the fight against the Demon Bane—a fight the Bringers seemed to be losing.

He exhaled and walked to the closest outbuilding. His hand hovered on the cold metal of the door handle, his determination wavering. Could he go through with the ceremony that would finally bring him to full power as a Bringer? Perhaps if he hadn't seen Luc's conversion firsthand, hadn't watched the blade drive into his friend's chest, and hadn't felt the life draining from Luc, he wouldn't feel so anxious now. But there was no turning back. Hopefully he'd be able to control the power that came with being a Bringer Tell. Endowed with the *Knowing,* he would sense things more strongly. Would know truth from a lie. Saints willing, the darkness that still tainted his soul from his years of imprisonment in the Demon Bane's Shadow World wouldn't grow stronger as well.

Chilly wind whipped his hair, bringing with it the smell of fall and the hint of snow. The sky echoed his mood. For a year he'd been dealing with the dark memories of being held captive the only way he knew how—alone. But now he'd found Rell again and she needed him to be strong. He'd been the one to change her mind about being put to death by one of the immortal daggers of the Bringers. As the only weapons that could vanquish a Demon Bane, it was the only way to kill her, but Siban wouldn't let that happen. For too long he'd grieved the loss of her. Nothing would stop him from helping her survive the *healing* that would transform her from a Demon Bane back into her human form—and into a Bringer.

Inside the building waited the other full-blooded Bringer warriors, newly transformed and ancient, planning to face down Vile, the Demon Bane's King, and his efforts to overrun Inness with his Bane. No longer could Siban avoid his destiny—or his past.

He yanked on the door but the wind beat it closed again, as if sensing his apprehension. He pulled again, this time opening it and slipping inside. A cloud of warmth and the smell of lavender and sage enveloped him. All eyes turned toward Siban, the Bringers' conversation halting. He closed the door behind him and exhaled softly, stilling his urge to turn around and walk back out. Dozens of candles lined the wall and burned on every available surface, lending a calming, golden glow to the room. But the ambiance did very little to reassure him about the impending pain he was about to experience.

"You came." Rhys Blackwell, his best friend, approached and held out his hand. "I was afraid you'd change your mind."

For years Rhys had thought he was the only full-blooded Bringer left after his parent's had been assassinated by Vile. He'd roamed Inness, protecting humans against the Bane and building a small army of mixed-blooded Bringers, those whose bloodlines had been diluted by humans. Thankfully, Rhys had recognized Siban for what he was and had taken him in, even though he was tainted by the Bane's evil darkness. Since then Siban's loyalty had never wavered. He gripped Rhys's forearm in a show of solidarity. "And miss all the fun?"

"My apologies for doubting you." Rhys laughed and released Siban's arm. "Come, Gregory has everything prepared."

Gregory, the King of the Bringers, met Siban halfway, a smile creasing his face and brightening his eyes to the color of liquid silver. "You look like a man facing his own execution."

"It feels a bit like that, yeah." Siban scanned the room. Most of the faces he recognized, but there were a few new Bringers he hadn't been introduced to yet. That could wait until he was through the transformation. Siban nodded and exhaled. "All right then, let's get this over with."

"Of course." Gregory placed a hand on Siban's shoulder and guided him toward a long wooden slab in the center of the room.

A smaller table had been erected about four feet from where he was to lay. A white sheet covered it. Siban stopped and stared at the form pressed against the cloth. The outline was of a woman—Rell's human form lying in perfect repose.

"We thought your transformation would be easier if you remembered what you were fighting for," Ravyn said from beside him.

"Thank you." He glanced at her. Ravyn watched him with understanding. She'd already gone through the transformation to become a Bringer and understood the risk. He looked back at the body on the table, refraining from voicing the fact that the person on the table was a stranger to him. His Rell was a Demon Bane with smooth green skin, leathery wings, and small delicate horns. He released a heavy breath, pushing aside the dark thought that he might not be able to accept her as a human. It had been the *demon* who risked so much to help him escape the Shadow World. Would the human female be different from the demon he'd fallen in love with? "I'm ready."

"Remove your shirt." Gregory turned to examine the immortal dagger lying on a small table.

Siban slipped his tunic off and handed it to Ravyn. Shivers from the chilled air ghosted across his skin. When Gregory lifted the dagger, Siban's heart began to pound. *I can do this.*

Ravyn spread a linen blanket over the wooden slab and placed a small pillow at the head. "Lie down, please." She patted the table. "I promise we'll take good care of you."

Without replying, he slid onto the table and rested his head against the stiff pillow. The blanket did little to cushion the hard wood pressing against his back, though he doubted he would have been able to relax. Unsure where to place his hands, he interlocked his fingers and rested them against his bare abdomen. He shifted his shoulders, trying to find a more comfortable position and ignoring the awkwardness of being everybody's focus.

Four Bringers he didn't know approached, each carrying two small sacks. In evenly spaced positions they emptied the contents of the bags onto the table.

Cloves, lavender, and a piney scent rose up around the edge of the table. Siban swallowed and stared at the ceiling. He mentally counted the dark beams above, forcing himself not to watch the Bringers working around him. Another shudder rippled through his body. Three months ago, allowing somebody to cut or stab him would have been unthinkable. The nightmares from his time among the demons still haunted him. He pushed away the dark thoughts, unwilling to give them power over him. After having been tortured with everything from talons to shards of rusty metal while in Vile's prison, Siban's consent to be brought to full power was a testament to his devotion to Rell.

It helped that *he'd* made the choice and that Gregory's

action would be done with gentleness not malice. Still, when the man turned toward Siban bearing the knife, it took all of his self-discipline not to hurl his body from the table and flee the room.

A low, healing chant kindled to Siban's left. The song flowing around him was one of the most beautiful Siban had ever heard. Clear and pitched surprisingly low, the notes resonated along his body and sent tingles skittering along his skin. Another voice joined the melody, deeper in tone.

The light in the room shifted, altering Siban's sight. Ribbons of blue and white drifted from the Bringers, encircling them like lace, binding each together. The lyrical composition surrounded him and burrowed under his skin, winding its way to what felt like his soul.

More soft voices mixed with the song, and the light from the ribbons grew stronger, pulsing inside him and creating a halo of light around the table.

Ravyn and Rell's sister, Jade, joined the circle and each placed their hands on one of his shoulders. When Rhys and Ravyn had brought their friend Luc Le Daun to full power, Siban had held his legs down in a similar manner. Luc had fought them, almost escaping their hold. Siban wondered how Ravyn and Jade expected to keep him restrained if his control broke.

The two women joined the chant and instantly warmth flowed into his body. Streams of light spiraled from their hands and entered his shoulders at the point where they touched. Tension eased from his muscles, the mantra lulling him into a relaxed state. Even when Gregory approached, fear did not grip Siban.

"In death there is life," Gregory said, circling the blade in front of him in a looping pattern. "In sacrifice, return." Heat traveled down Siban's torso and his eyes remained steady

on the king. "All barriers destroyed and evil be spurned."
Gregory lowered the knife and laid the blade against Siban's
chest, directly over his heart. Despite the relaxing chant, he
couldn't help but tense when the cold metal touched his skin.
"No hindrance remain, from our blood be renewed." Gregory
dragged the edge downward, lacerating Siban with a shallow
slice. In an effort not to cry out, he bit down on his lower lip.
The metallic taste of blood coated his tongue. "That which was
taken, settle in those who Bring true."

Fire danced along the cut and Siban braced himself, waiting
for Gregory to plunge the dagger in his heart as they had
done with Luc. Instead of stabbing him, Gregory set the knife
between two piles of herbs on the wooden platform and placed
his hands next to Ravyn's. Again the king spoke, but they were
words Siban did not understand.

The heat burning along the slice spread across his chest,
eating up every inch of Siban's body. Searing pain ignited his
organs as if incinerating him from the inside out. He gasped for
breath, but couldn't inhale as wave after wave of pain gripped
him.

The chant around him grew louder and more hands pressed
against his legs and arms. His muscles convulsed. It was as if his
very soul was being pulled from his body through his chest. He
choked against the tightening at his throat. His mouth opened
in an effort to suck in air, but none could pass.

The words grew louder and above the unified chant he
heard Ravyn's voice. Separate from the other Redeemers, she
spoke the Bringer's ancient language. Her words demanded
and coaxed the darkness from inside him. His vision blurred
and his head pounded as the need for air became desperate.

Ravyn placed her hands on his forehead and raised her
voice, shouting, "*Avec mea!*"

From Siban's throat rose a white vapor. It hovered a foot

above his mouth and then descended to cover his face. The sensation of being branded scorched the skin under his lower lip. After a few seconds, the white vapor evaporated completely. Siban gasped, drinking in the cool, perfumed air, and collapsed against the table. All traces of pain and the ribbons of healing light disappeared. The blood pounded in his ears, and his heart raced. He waited, expecting another wave of agony, but none came.

Gregory stared down at him and then smiled. He touched his index finger against the skin directly below Siban's lower lip. "A Tell."

The spot burned and Siban flinched away, pressing the back of his hand to the area and trying to numb the sting, knowing he now bore a the single black line of the Tell. "Are you finished?"

"Did you want something more?" Gregory smirked. "Perhaps you would have preferred I plunge the dagger into your heart?"

Siban's craned his head to look at Ravyn. "Expected, not preferred."

Ravyn cleared her throat. "It seems actually stabbing somebody in the heart isn't required to bring a person to full power."

"That would have been nice to know." Luc scowled at her and rubbed his chest.

She shrugged. "Sorry. If it's any consolation, I did it to myself as well."

Siban struggled to sit up, spreading the herbs along the edge of the table and knocking some of them to the ground. He looked at his chest. A thin red line stretched from his sternum to his left side, but there was no blood. "What was that white smoke? I felt like I was choking."

"Think of it as a net that encased your powers. Due to generations of Bringers breeding with humans, the Bringer essence within us becomes bound. The ceremony severs that bond." He pointed to Siban's cut. "It will be healed by morning and the only evidence of the ceremony will be your Tell mark." Gregory placed a hand on Siban's shoulder. "How do you feel?"

How did he feel? It was difficult to put into words. New vitality hummed through his body, as if a million tiny sparks had snapped against his skin, leaving their tingling reminder. Even his head felt clear, unfettered from the nightmares and dark thoughts that had been his constant companion since his imprisonment in the Shadow World. "Better."

"You are a master of the understated," Rhys said, handing Siban his shirt.

"Thank you." Siban slid the tunic over his head and shook his chin-length curls from his eyes. "When will you heal Rell?"

"Tonight." Gregory placed the dagger back on the table. "That will give you time to rest. She will need all of our strength."

"I will be there." Nothing would keep him from Rell's side.

"Good." The king faced him. "I don't foresee her transformation to be as easy as yours."

"I'll give her whatever strength I have." He scooted from the table. His legs quivered, and he grabbed the edge of the wood in an effort not to stumble. Gregory reached for him, but Siban waved him away and straightened. "I'm all right."

"Then come to the house and eat." Willa, Rell's mother, stepped from the shadows. Her white-blond hair glimmered in the candlelight and her eyes sparkled with determination. "We're all going to need to fortify ourselves if we plan on saving my daughter."

Though he wasn't the least bit hungry, under no circumstance would Siban contradict Willa once she'd made a command. The woman was fire and ice mixed into a tiny, unassuming package. He was fairly certain Willa would have gone into the bowels of the Shadow World herself to bring back her daughter's body if

Luc and Jade hadn't beaten her to it. Such fierce loyalty was a trait he understood and respected.

He nodded. "I am coming, my lady."

· · ·

The wind beat against the thick, murky glass of the window, its low howl like a consoling friend. Rell dragged her talon through the dirt on the floor, circling the point in an endless design of interconnecting loops. Though the Bringers had provided her with a comfortable bed and blankets to warm her against the nip in the air, she preferred to feel the cold. Material comforts were something she hadn't had since she was a human and using them now somehow poked at her like a lie.

The cell the Bringers had constructed for her sat in the center of the room, out of reach of the stone walls, which had been warded to keep her in. The iron bars pressed against her back and wings like an icy reminder that though the Bringers were trying to help her, she was still subject to their decision of whether she would live or die.

"You look like a giant bird," said a child's voice from near the door.

Rell dragged her eyes away from her mindless scrawling and leveled her gaze on the small boy. Hayden, she'd thought she'd heard the human woman call him. His blue eyes were round and his brown hair tousled from the wind. Dirt smudged his face and the faint scent of fear mixed with unrepressed curiosity emanated from him. He'd been a regular visitor, though Rell suspected his mother didn't know. "What kind of bird?"

"A love bird." Hayden scooted forward a few inches, his pants scraping against the dirt floor. "Like the pretty green one in the painting in Lord Le Daun's library."

She cocked a brow. "You think I'm pretty?"

His head bobbed up and down. "Sometimes the light from the fire makes your skin sparkle, like jewels. And sometimes, like now, your eyes turn bright green."

"My eyes turn green?"

He nodded again. Except for her reflection in the hot pools in the cavern of the Shadow World, where she'd raised Jade, Rell had never seen her demon reflection. Always she'd assumed her eyes were yellow, like the other Bane. The boy's words pushed the darkness that threatened to steal through her soul back to a tolerable level. His unguarded innocence and honesty encompassed her like the warm blankets she refused to use.

"Thank you." Besides Siban, nobody but the boy had ever made her feel like she wasn't an abomination. Even Jade's tireless struggle to help keep Rell's humanity had been mired in the fact that Rell was a Demon Bane and not a normal sister. Every struggle they'd overcome, every move they had made had hinged on her being Bane. Rell's time with Icarus, the Demon King's son, had been based on the fact that the two of them were different from the other demons. It seemed that even among her kind, she did not fit in. "I think you would like flying."

Hayden's eyes widened. "Can you take me one day?"

She gave him a sad smile. He was so trusting, which would mean his death if he'd been talking to any demon other than her. "I don't think we'll get the chance, Hayden. The others are going to try and make me better tonight—human again."

A frown creased his small face. "Will you still have your wings?"

Rell shook her head.

His scowl increased. "I like you the way you are."

"Thank you." A knot formed in her throat. "Perhaps when I am human we can hunt together. It's not the same as flying, but it would still be fun."

That idea seemed to placate him, but before he could answer the door swung open, bringing with it a blast of cold air and Siban. The boy scooted backward and pressed his back against the wall. Hayden stared up at Siban, the wonder in his eyes now replaced with fear.

"Does your mother know you're here, boy?"

Hayden shook his head.

"Best run along to the house. There are warm biscuits and honey in the library."

Hayden rose and skirted Siban's large body but stopped at the door, turning back to Rell. "You promise we'll go hunting?"

Her lips tightened into a smile and she nodded, unable to speak the promise she might not be able to keep. The healing the Bringers were to attempt on her had never been done before—by any of them. There was no guarantee she would survive the transition. The one consoling thought was that at least she would be free of the oppressive darkness inside her that constantly demanded she give in to its will.

Siban pulled the door closed behind Hayden and turned to face her. "It's time."

She pushed up from the floor of the cage and stood, ignoring the quiver in her legs that was more from nerves than fatigue or cold. "I'm ready."

He approached the cage and wrapped his hands around the bars. "Everything is going to be all right, Rell. I'll be there with you through the healing." His troubled hazel gaze held hers. "We've already been through so much." His voice cracked slightly. "When this is over, we'll be able to start a new life."

Together was left unspoken. There was no need. From the first time they'd met, their paths had been joined. She'd secretly cared for him in the Shadow World, tending his wounds after Sha-hera and Vile had tortured him for information about the

Bringers. She'd fed him when, trying to break his will, they
had left him to starve. She'd given him the comfort of her
companionship, which she'd needed just as much as he had.

"I hope you're right, Siban." Rell approached the door of
the cell. "But if something goes wrong…"

"It won't." His jaw clenched and unclenched. "I refuse to
lose you again."

She nodded, unwilling to shatter his fragile conviction to
save her. "What now?"

"I'll need to carry you to the healing room. The floors and
walls are still warded, as are the grounds. You'll be burned and
drawn back to the Shadow World if you touch anything."

Her sister, Jade, and Ravyn, had been thorough in marking
the area around Rell's cell. The wards left the walls and the
floor inside her prison free of magic. Even though escape would
have been impossible, Rell had not even been tempted. There
was nothing left for her in the world of the Demon Bane. There
never had been.

Being reunited with Siban had eradicated Rell's urge to
flee and given her a small spark of hope that she really could
be human again. Though, if they were successful in the healing,
she doubted she would emerge as the same woman who had
lost her soul to the Demon Bane thirteen years ago.

Dark thoughts pressed down on her. "I'll warn you," she
said, trying to lighten the mood, "I think I've put on weight with
the rich food my mother has been feeding me."

He smiled. "It's fortunate I've been brought to full power
then. My new strength will come in handy."

Rell cocked her head and scanned his body from head to
toe. "I knew there was something different about you. I thought
perhaps you'd bathed."

"A bath?" He harrumphed and pointed to his Tell tattoo.
"I've just gained the mythical powers of our people and you

compare it to bathing?" He reached inside the pocket at the front of his tunic and pulled out the key to her cell. "I can see I'll never suffer from an inflated ego with you around."

A small laugh slipped from Rell, taking her by surprise. It had been a long time since she'd actually felt anything close to happiness. Interesting that the only times she could remember had been with Siban.

The key scraped against the lock, and the metal grated as the large bolt slid into its casing. He pulled the door open and stepped inside, slipping the key back into his pocket. "Your carriage awaits, my lady."

Rell folded her wings tightly against her back and took a step toward him, stopping an inch away. He was ruggedly handsome. His features spoke of a heritage from the sand people, darker skin and sculpted cheekbones and chin. But what she liked best about Siban were his hazel eyes. Though he was a man of few words, his eyes spoke volumes.

She tilted her head. "Siban?" Her voice came out as a whisper. "Will you kiss me one last time—as Rell?"

Perhaps with the feel of his lips on hers she'd make it through the healing. If not, she'd cross through the Veil knowing he'd truly cared for her for who she had been—a Demon Bane.

He lifted his hand and caressed her lower lip with his thumb. "And I will kiss you every day for the rest of your life when this is complete."

His head lowered to hers and his lips gently brushing against her mouth. Strong arms enveloped Rell, dragging her against his hard body. He dwarfed her, making her feel safe and giving her a sense that he could indeed chase the darkness from her soul.

CHAPTER TWO

Siban lifted Rell's tiny, warm body and cradled her against him. The Bane taint bit into his skin but he made no show of the irritation. Now at full power, the bite was stronger than he was used to, but he endured it without complaint. She wound her arms around his neck and rested her head against his shoulders. Nothing would stop him from saving her—nothing.

He maneuvered her out of the cell and strode across the room. Before opening the door, he stopped and turned to face her prison. "This is the last time you will ever have to be in here."

She gave a slight nod and threaded her talons through his hair. With no more words, he turned and kicked the door open. The wind caught the wood, slamming it against the outside wall. She shivered in his arms, and he pulled her more tightly to him.

The partial moon was bright, its glow lighting the path back to the manor. Wind rustled through the trees, causing their branches to sway in a slow dance. Leaves rubbed against each other. Their movement created a swooshing sound that rose and fell with the force of the breeze.

The healing house stood closer to the manor, far inside the

warded boundaries the Bringers had erected. Siban decided on the direct path across the grass, his mind sifting through what was about to happen. It took a minute before he realized the biting irritation, a Bringer's alert that there was a demon near, had increased. His steps slowed. The sensation was different than Rell's, stronger, more caustic.

"What is it?" She lifted her head and looked around the dark grounds.

"Can you feel that?" He didn't know if the Bane could sense each other. The Bringers had never had the chance to question a demon. Always they'd just dispatched the creatures back to the Shadow World. "I think there is another demon close by."

Rell was silent for a second and then looked at him. "Icarus. I recognize his presence."

A twinge of jealousy pinched Siban. She and the son of the Demon King had formed a relationship during their quest to lure Jade and Luc into the Shadow World. Siban couldn't help but wonder what that bond had entailed.

He scanned the trees, turning in a slow circle. Not used to his new Tell abilities, he forced his awareness outward in an attempt to locate the powerful demon. His senses sped across the ground like a psychic blanket, perceiving a thousand different details about the night. The wind, the life force of insects, and plants registered but did not disrupt the wholeness of his inquiry. The immense amount of information rushed through him, pounding along every nerve of his body. In an effort to cope, he stilled his mind and relinquished control over his Tell powers. They would guide him.

Even before he'd been brought to full power, he'd been able to sense when something was true or a lie. Now the intensity of his abilities nearly swamped him. His Tell slithered toward the demon. At the tree line, it began to vibrate, sending information and warning back to him.

"Yes, it's Icarus," he said. Instantly Siban understood the situation. Curiosity, and even a sense of hope, emanated from the pulsing darkness. He let his awareness linger on the demon, trying to absorb and understand all he felt. The information was an undefinable mass of impressions and darkness, but the demon didn't feel angry.

"Will he attack?" Tension flowed through Rell's body, her posture growing stiff in his hold.

"No, I think he's waiting to see how you fair with the healing."

She settled against him again. "Oh," was all she said.

Icarus's discovery that the Bringers had found Rell's human body had led the demon to confront Jade, Luc, and Ravyn's sister, Meran, after Rell's capture. Bold in a way no other Bringer had ever dared to be with Icarus, Meran had approached and touched the demon. What surprised everybody was that Icarus hadn't attacked, hadn't stolen her away when he could have so easily picked her up and flown into the night.

Later Meran had divulged to the rest of the Bringers what she'd sensed when she'd made contact with Icarus. "He is searching for something. The darkness inside him is like nothing I've ever felt. He is at odds with his father, Vile, and he knows all is not as he's been told." After another deep breath, she'd said, "He's been banished from the Shadow World."

That was all she had shared with them, but Siban suspected there was more. One could not touch the Bane darkness and remain unaffected.

Turning his thoughts back to Rell's healing, Siban continued toward the healing house, his strides eating up the ground. The quicker they converted her back to human, the safer she would be from Icarus's influence.

They entered the room and Siban's step slowed. He was

surprised to see even more Bringers assembled. One woman, he knew instantly, though he'd never met her—Ravyn and Meran's oldest sister Juna. Expected to arrive days prior, unforeseen circumstances had delayed her appearance. Beside her stood a fairly young-looking man. His dark auburn hair glinted copper in the candlelight and Siban couldn't help noticing that he appeared trail-weary. A few days' growth shadowed his chin and though his eyes were bright, dark circles puddled beneath them.

Siban sent up a prayer of thanks to the Saints that Juna had reached the manor in time for Rell's healing. The three sisters, Ravyn, Meran, and Juna, were the Trilation. Three Bringers to battle the darkness and open or prevent the opening of the Abyss of Souls. They were also powerful Oracles and might be the extra measure of guidance Rell would need to pass from demon back to human.

Rell's arms tightened around his neck. The crowd stepped back to allow them to pass. A few of the Bringers rubbed their arms, no doubt against the gnawing of the Bane taint Rell caused.

"Welcome, Rell." King Gregory greeted them from halfway across the room. "We'll try to make you as comfortable as possible."

She peered at him, as if weighing how much she could trust him and then said, "Thank you."

The urge to clutch the small demon to him, and never release her, overwhelmed Siban. This might be the last time he held her—the last time he'd see her alive. But he pushed his personal needs aside and set her on her feet. Uncertainty plagued him. Rell had only seen her human body once and it had been during the chaotic night of her capture. How would she react to seeing her body in its suspended, death-like state? Siban stepped back when Jade approached.

...

Rell had been at odds with her sister since the day she'd been captured. She waited for Jade to speak. The glow of the candles illuminated her face. No malice or anger registered there, giving Rell a measure of comfort. Instead of words of reassurance, Jade reached for her hand and intertwined their fingers, pulling Rell toward the line of Bringers standing several feet away. They parted to reveal a table she hadn't noticed when they'd first arrived.

Rell's heart beat faster, the realization of what lay beneath the white shroud taking hold. She stopped, tugging Jade to a halt.

Her sister turned. "Don't you want to see her?"

Jade's question confirmed what Rell had suspected. Though her sister had fought and sacrificed to keep Rell's humanity intact, she'd always viewed her as something other than Esmeralda, her human sister. Rell stiffened her spine, refusing to show that the thought stung.

Her gaze drifted back to the shrouded figure. Did she want to see her body? Would it change anything? Whether or not it did, she needed to see. "Yes."

Not releasing her hand, Jade pulled her forward until they stood next to the table. Two Bringers, one woman, one man, gently folded back the cover to reveal the porcelain features of the girl she'd once been.

Rell untwined her fingers from Jade's and took a step closer, angling her body so she could view the face more clearly. Esmeralda, her old body, looked as if she were sleeping, though the coloring of the skin was more pallid than it had been when she'd been full of life. She reached and touched the cheek with the knuckle of her finger, making sure not to prick the skin with her talon. The soft flesh gave way under her caress but felt unnaturally cold.

Rell pulled her hand away, paused to take one final look, and then turned away. "I am ready."

Having her body revealed had made no difference in her resolve to go through with the healing. The driving force was no longer just to be human, but to be with Siban and possibly repay the Demon Bane for all they had taken from her. She would do whatever it took.

Of her own accord, she walked to the large wooden slab and climbed onto it, dangling her legs over the side.

Siban moved to stand in front of her. "Are you all right?"

She nodded.

His voice dropped to a whisper. "I am here, fighting for you. Never doubt that."

She nodded again and turned to place her feet on the wood. Siban rubbed her hand and stepped aside when Jade once again approached. Perhaps it was her possible impending death or being with Siban that had abated some of the darkness from her soul, but Rell wished that no animosity existed between her, Jade, and Willa. But the words wouldn't come. She needn't have worried. Once again Jade took the lead in making things right.

"I love you." There was no waver in her sister's declaration. "Mother and I will be here for you during and after the healing—no matter what happens."

"I love you, too." Rell reached for her hand and squeezed. "Thank you for everything."

Willa moved forward with hesitant steps. Rell hadn't spoken to her mother since she'd been captured; the anger and shame of keeping Willa's existence a secret from Jade had fed the darkness. There were so many lies and misconceptions between them, but now, as Rell faced her uncertain future, all her hostility slipped away. Though she couldn't bring herself to ask for her mother's touch, a comfort she desired more than she would admit to even herself, she did need to make recompense of some kind. She looked at Willa. "I'm sorry."

Without hesitation, her mother swooped in and wrapped Rell in a warm hug. "Just get through this so we can be a family again."

The embrace stirred the sensation of memories long forgotten. *Love. Safety. Home.* Rell wrapped her free arm around Willa in a tentative hug. She closed her eyes and breathed in the scent of her mother. She smelled like the cooking fire, fresh air, and the herbs that permeated the healing room.

Rell let her arm slide back to her side when her mother released her. Instead of stepping back, the woman cupped Rell's cheeks in her hands and looked at her. The blue eyes she remembered from when she was a child searched her face as if taking in every detail. "You are beautiful."

A foreign sensation tingled along her nose and burned behind her eyes. Rell blinked away the irritation and looked at Jade, unsure how to respond to her mother's compliment.

Jade's brow furrowed and she reached to tilt Rell's chin toward her. "Your eyes are green."

Three of the Bringer women moved forward and poked their heads between Jade and Willa, peering at Rell as if she was a puzzle they were trying to figure out.

"Extraordinary," said the older of the three.

The one named Ravyn grinned at Rell. "I think Siban has been a very good influence on you."

She gave Ravyn a hint of a smile. "This we agree on, Bringer."

"If you're ready, Rell, I think we should get started." The king gripped the arm of the first Bringer who had spoken and gently pulled her away.

Her sister and mother released her and stepped back from

the table, their expressions strained impressions of hopefulness. Ravyn took her place in the circle of Bringers.

One small woman remained, smiling at Rell. She resembled Ravyn and the woman Gregory had pulled away, but was lighter in coloring. "My name is Meran. I am a Redeemer, which means I will help you through your transformation. If you lie back on the table, we can prepare you."

The darkness inside Rell screamed not to submit to the Bringers. As if sensing her battle, Siban moved forward to stand directly opposite Meran and lay his hand against Rell's back. "It's all right. I'm going to help you through this, and I'll be here when it's over."

Warmth spread along her skin, easing the tension and the impulse to resist the Bringers' help. She held his gaze, drinking in the strength of his words and presence. Shifting her position, Rell reclined to lay flat on the table and settled into the curved opening between her wings. They cradled her, cushioning her head where they crisscrossed at their tips.

"We will need to restrain you," said the Redeemer.

The urge to fight the Bringers reared up inside Rell again. Her lips pulled back in a silent snarl, and she bared her fangs in warning.

"It's for your own well-being and the safety of those performing the healing. We don't know what to expect." Perhaps to strengthen the truth in her words, Meran gently laid her hand on her wrist. "Will you allow this?"

A tingle of heat trickled across the skin where the woman touched, soothing Rell's alarm like a comforting balm. Letting her snarl slipped away, she inhaled and breathed out her resistance to the request of being bound. "Siban may bind me."

The healer looked at him and he gave a single nod. Before stepping away, Meran reached under the table and brought up three, thick leather straps, one at Rell's chest, one at her hips, and the last at her ankle. Siban mimicked her, producing the same straps on the opposite side of the slab, where he stood.

As he secured the first set of straps across her chest, Rell's anxiety resurfaced. Though she could still move her arms from the elbow down, the tight binding immobilized her upper arms and chest.

A wave of terror gripped her mind when Siban tugged on the second set of straps, drawing her hips and forearms firmly against the table. She kept her breathing steady and stared at the dark rafters of the ceiling. The wind buffeted the front door, pounding it in a steady beat—matching her heart.

Slowly turning her head, she looked at her mother. Willa's clutched hands were fisted against her lips, her eyes trained on her daughter. She lowered her hands and mouthed, "I love you."

The straps pulled tight around Rell's ankles, but she didn't look away from the woman, so desperately needing the reassurance only her mother could give. Everything would be all right. It had to be. For the first time since being turned into a demon, Rell truly *wanted* to live.

Half the Bringers moved forward to form an arc around the left side of the table on which Esmeralda's body lay and the other half did the same to Rell's right, creating a complete circle around the two tables. They joined hands. The deep voice of the Bringer King began a low, melodic chant. Rell's eyes slid shut, and she focused on the beautiful words, trying to relax. The unknown was sometimes the hardest to endure, but soon the healing would be over.

The smooth alto voice of the Bringer standing at Rell's head joined the king's chant, harmonizing. Tremors rippled along Rell's muscles and her body gave a single jerk. One at a time each Bringer joined the chant, their voices traveling around the circle and merging until Rell was surrounded by the song.

Tightness formed in her chest and squeezed, the sensation quickly crossing from discomfort to pain. Rell's eyelids popped open and she gasped. Air trickled in and out of her with each labored breath she attempted. It felt as if a giant snake slithered through her organs and vessels inside her body. Rell struggled to keep control and not cry out when the blackness glided up her neck and behind her eyes, attempting to steal her sight.

The oppressive presence sifted through her mind, taunting Rell for her foolish belief that the Bringers would be her salvation. She tried to block out the mocking darkness but could feel her will weakening. A whimper slipped between her tightly pressed lips.

The sizzle of burning herbs hissed to the right of her head and the scent of sage enveloped her. Wind hammered the door against the wood frame, its howl filtering through the cracks with a mournful wail.

Still the Bringers continued, relentless with the healing song that caused the Bane presence to roil inside her. The shadowy manifestation filled her head, attempting to block out the words of salvation from her mind. The chant grew muffled and the words that she was desperately trying to hold onto faded to an indistinguishable drone. With nothing for Rell to focus on, the loneliness her sister had battled so hard to keep at bay slipped forward. The darkness inside Rell slithered around the part of her soul that was still good—the part that still wanted a human life—and tightened.

A chill invaded her body. Driving so deep it felt as if it was buried in her bones. She shivered. A wave of hopelessness swamped her. A cry pushed from Rell's lips. She was unable to control the anguish coursing through her. She would not make it through the transition from demon to human. Nothing could possibly win against the all-encompassing bleakness.

Her body shook violently, as if wanting to levitate from the wooden platform she lay on. Helpless to aid those who called to her, centuries of souls bound by the same darkness tried to lay claim to her eternal soul. Tormented screams erupted in Rell's mind. The cries of dark souls screeching to be set free shoved Rell toward the brink of insanity.

Just when she thought all was lost, warmth registered against Rell's thighs and shoulders. Like grasping for a branch while being swept along a cold, raging river, she focused on the spreading heat, drawing strength from its power. Feminine voices broke past the screams and the dark barrier, reaching for her soul. One voice rose above the rest—Ravyn. With a chant ancient and powerful, she burned a trail through the blackness, lighting a way for the others.

In Rell's mind, a spiral of fire ignited the Demon Bane's hold on her and blazed a path down the coiling snake that imprisoned her. The beast writhed and squeezed tighter, unwilling to release Rell's soul. The table on which she lay began to shake, beating violently against the ground. Though strapped to the table, her body trembled against the force of each punishing strike. A new presence attacked the dense blackness and pelted it with white light. The snake screamed. Its rage lashed out like a barbed whip.

A third figure appeared, walking through the turmoil to where Rell's soul lay helplessly restrained within the coils of her black prison. Golden threads spiraled from the third Bringer. Each thread wove its way between the coils of the snake and wrapped around Rell. Warmth and loved filled her.

The Bringer's glowing touch cleared the doubt and chaos from Rell's mind. She directed her soul toward the light and latched on. The black snake yanked, turning the battle between dark and light into a tug-of-war. Again the two other Bringers attacked, pummeling the snake with fire and white light. Its hold loosened. The golden tendrils heaved one final time and dragged Rell's soul from the Bane body.

Silence enveloped her. The sound of the wind beating at the door and the chanting was no more. Rell floated toward the ceiling and hovered above her demon form, which now lay lifeless. Three golden ropes wound around her thighs and neck. The lines connected Rell's soul to the three Bringer women standing below her.

Now free of the demon, the darkness's hold vanished. A sensation of freedom overtook her. There was no more pain, no sadness, no regret. She wanted to stay like this forever.

The three women skirted the large table, where Rell had laid in her demon form, and moved toward her human body. She glided with them until she hovered above her small human form. The urge to yank free from the golden ropes seized Rell. There would be discomfort and weakness once she was human again. Only Siban's hopeful face weakened her resistance. The freedom her battle-weary soul was experiencing would have to wait until it was *her* time to pass through the Veil. This was not the day.

With a different chant, the women slowly lowered her soul until it hovered mere inches above Esmeralda. Six more Bringers stepped forward and laid their hands on the motionless flesh of her human body. A new heaviness moved along Rell's soul, pressing her down—down—down.

Blackness encompassed her. The chant from a single Bringer woman filled her ears. Rell didn't understand the words, but they welcomed her. Though bereft of her soul's lost freedom, the chant ignited hope inside her. Had she made it?

The singing dimmed and finally stopped. A firm hand pressed against her forehead.

"Rell?" Whether from the woman's voice or the touch during their battle to free her soul, she recognized the Bringer who had possessed the golden tendrils that saved her. "Can you hear me?"

Her eyelids felt like iron weights, and it took all of Rell's effort to open them. She blinked several times trying to bring the room into focus. Three sets of pale blue eyes stared down at her with concern.

Then Siban was there, crowding in to bend over her and clutch her hand. "Are you all right? Can you hear me?"

She opened her mouth to speak but no words came out. Her throat felt dry and raspy, her breathing labored. The smallest action took a great amount of effort. Tremors rippled through her body as her sluggish blood started pumping more quickly through her veins. She wiggled her toes, which sent a cold push of blood up and into her heart, causing her to shudder and convulse again.

King Gregory moved to Rell's side, gazed upon her for a few seconds, and then nodded to somebody beyond her vision. Her mother and sister stepped forward.

"This will be over in a few seconds." Jade lifted the thin fabric of the chemise Rell wore to just below her breasts. "You'll be much stronger after Gregory brings you to full power."

Unable to speak, Rell watched the man raise a dagger. Her heart beat faster. If not for Jade's words of assurance, Rell would have believed Gregory was about to kill her, and the weakness of her body would have prevented her from stopping him.

"In death there is life." He made a sign in the air above Rell's body with the knife. "In sacrifice, return."

More voices joined the chant. Again the hiss of herbs and their scent wafted around her. The three women who had returned her soul to her body laid their hands along different parts of Rell's legs and torso. Warmth flooded her.

"All barriers destroyed and evil be spurned." Gregory pressed the cold blade against the bare skin next to her heart.

"No hindrance remain, from our blood be renewed." Without warning, he made a shallow cut. The pain stung along her upper rib but was nothing compared to what she'd already been through. "That which was taken, settle in those who Bring true."

Like a torch touched to dry timber, her body exploded as if on fire. Heat raced through every vessel, filling it with strength and burning away the cold chill of death. Rell gasped and arched away from the table but firm hands held her down. Siban's low whispers helped keep her rooted in the present when her body and mind threatened to shatter into a thousand fiery sparks.

The sensation of choking pulled at her throat. She gasped, her eyes growing wide as panic gripped her. A white vapor spilled from her mouth and hovered above her face briefly before descending to cover her. A searing sting burned just below her bottom lip and the cloud evaporated, leaving her alert, but not completely free of pain.

Willa's hand smoothed back her hair. Rell exhaled heavily and let her body relax against the table. Her throat still burned from thirteen years of inactivity.

"Water." The word rasped from her.

Within seconds, a goblet of water appeared before her. Willa and Siban helped her to a sitting position and Jade held the edge of the goblet to her lips. The cool liquid soothed her burning throat. Rell coughed when her reflex to swallow threatened to rebel. Another sip—each cell of her body absorbing the first trace of drink in more than a decade.

She brought a shaking hand to her mouth and wiped. "Thank you."

Nobody spoke, all eyes trained on her as if expecting her to do something—anything.

The woman named Meran approached. "How do you feel?"

Her emotions were too chaotic and contradictory. Happy that she'd made it through the healing. Grateful for a chance to live her human life again. Yet bereft over losing the nearly indestructible demon body that had protected her soul. Rell sighed. "Human again."

Every person in the room seemed to relax, the tension melting into joyous chatter. What she said was true. She did feel human. Her muscles quivered with weakness and Rell couldn't help but lament the loss of the strength her demon form had possessed. The skin she wore felt awkward and foreign. It was smooth and soft, so unlike the taut, thick hide of the Bane. Though her hair cascaded down her back, there was no burden of the small, weighty horns. But the thing she tried hardest not to miss was her wings. Now earthbound, she would no longer know the freedom of flight.

She looked at Meran. "I felt you during the struggle. You helped me."

The young woman's smile held a hint of the ethereal, as if she knew more than most and was among them for a higher purpose. Rell recognized Meran's strength. She'd experienced it firsthand. Never would she underestimate this petite Bringer.

"I'm a Redeemer. It's my duty to save souls—sometimes from the brink of the Abyss." She indicated Ravyn and the other Bringer woman. "My sisters Ravyn and Juna were there too. We are the Trilation. Three to battle the darkness." She shrugged. "You were our first successful attempt."

"I'm very happy you succeeded." Rell glanced at the other sisters. "I owe you my life."

"You owe us nothing," Gregory said. "It is us who owe you. This is a great day for the Bringers. We would not have known if the conversion would be successful without your cooperation. You were strong as a Bane and will be even stronger as a Bringer."

She *had* been a strong Bane, but not nearly the strongest. His praise left a hollow feeling in the pit of her stomach. The line of Bringers blocked her view of the other table. "What happened to my demon form?"

The quick glances exchanged between some of the Bringers were not lost on her.

"Come." Siban held out his hand. "We will say good-bye to her together."

She hesitated only a second before accepting his hand. With an arm around her waist, he helped her stand. The Bringers parted to reveal the table on which she'd lain at the beginning of her healing. Her steps shuffled forward until she stood at the edge of the wooden slab.

As if created by a master sculpture, her demon form appeared to be only sleeping. No longer the pearlescent green, the skin had turned gray. When Rell reached out to touch a talon, the claw crumbled to ash. She jerked away. Like a row of children's blocks that had been lined up and then pushed over, the ripple moved along the demon body.

First the hand she'd touched, then the arm and shoulder. The ash dropped and lay in neatly formed piles. Rell didn't move, only watched as the body that had been *her* for thirteen years, disintegrated into gray powder. She wanted to scoop it up, to try and stop its destruction. Logically, there was no reason to want the reminder of all she'd been through, but the demon body had been a part of her—had protected her in a ruthless world.

When the last trace of her Bane form had fallen to ash, Rell turned away and looked at Gregory. "What now?"

He inhaled and scanned the crowd of Bringers. "Now we train." He paused. "We have more Bringers to save."

CHAPTER THREE

Rell stared at herself in the mirror. The black wool-and-leather pants and tunic Ravyn had given her hung loose on her thin frame, but she liked the ease of movement that the clothes allowed her.

It had been three days since she'd retaken her human body — three days to become accustomed to its weaknesses. When she'd first been shown her image, she'd looked about sixteen. Meran had told her she would change until she matched her present age and then grow older almost imperceptibly from there on. Rell appeared to be around eighteen years old now. Still fresh-faced, but she no longer possessed the childlike roundness.

She smoothed her hand over her cheek. Even though she appeared nearly the same as the day she had been taken, the face that stared back at her was practically a stranger. Soon she would look her full twenty-eight years. She sighed, a twinge of vanity pinching her. Most women had the luxury of aging gradually. She would gain ten years within the next month. At least from that point on she would have centuries to grow used to her appearance.

Her finger traced the single black line running from her

lower lip to the dip above her chin. The stark Tell tattoo lay dark against her still slightly gaunt complexion. Though she looked young, her soul felt old.

A knock sounded at her bedroom door and Jade peeked inside. "Good morning."

Rell turned from the mirror and smiled. "Good morning."

"You're up early." Her sister strode across the room and wrapped Rell in a brief hug. "How are you feeling?"

It was a question Rell had been asked a hundred times over the last three days and one not easily answered. Physically she was getting stronger. Her coordination was back and her spirits as good as could be expected, but there were nuances she dared not share with the rest of the Bringers—a heaviness that still stirred within her soul.

She shrugged. "Better—stronger. I think I'm finally getting used to being human again."

Jade perched on the edge of the bed. "Is it very different from being a Bane?"

"Yes, but it's difficult to describe." Rell joined her sister on the bed, wondering how much she should share. Already she'd put Jade through so much. The last thing she wanted was for her to worry even more. It was difficult enough with Siban never more than ten feet away, hovering over her like a mother hen. "The body of a Demon Bane possesses so much power, but it's dark and there was very little remorse for the things I did." The concern in her sister's expression spurred Rell on. "But I don't feel that anymore. When I think of the emotions I had as a demon, I have a hard time reconciling them with my new life. Most Bane are reactionary." She paused. "Except for Icarus—and Vile. Their actions are very deliberate."

"Gregory explained a bit about the Bane before you were returned to your human form." Jade shifted to face her more fully. "He said that the demons who can steal souls and command the forces are Spoils, the original Bane. There are also Deceivers and Enticers, but these demons can't steal souls. The rest are human who have been converted and are really just mindless soldiers."

Rell nodded. "That makes sense. I wonder what Sha-hera is."

"I've seen her and her army nearly lure an entire shipload of men to their death. I suspect the Captain of the Succubus army is an Enticer." Jade shook her head. "She is one nasty piece of work."

"And deadly." Rell gave an exaggerated shudder. Though she'd tried to stay out of the succubus's way in the Shadow World, encounters with Sha-hera had still been too frequent. Close to Vile and at odds with Icarus, Sha-hera had set herself between father and son, hoping to grab Icarus's power when Icarus was banished.

A comfortable silence stretched between them. Since her transformation, Rell had spent very little time alone with her sister and there were still things that needed to be said— apologies to be made. "Jade." She covered her sister's hand with hers. "I wanted to tell you that I'm sorry for everything I put you through."

Shame over so many betrayals swamped her. Not only had she kept the truth about their mother still being alive a secret, but she'd helped Icarus lure Luc and Jade into the Shadow World. Memories of those dark days threatened to crack Rell's will.

Her sister's expression softened. "You don't have to apologize—"

"Yes I do," Rell said, cutting her off. "I *need* to say these things so you know that I understand what I did." Jade's lips tightened into a thin line, but she didn't reply, only gave a single nod. "After I'd been turned into a Demon Bane, I was more scared than I had ever been in my life. My mind was not right, battling to accept what I'd become and the loss of my family and my human life. I remember thinking that if I couldn't accept my demon form, there was no possible way mother would accept me." She swallowed down the memories of those first chaotic hours. "You were still a child, innocent and accepting. I needed somebody to see that I was still Esmeralda."

"I understand." Jade gripped Rell's hands and squeezed. "Don't torture yourself."

"I'm not torturing myself, and I'm not making excuses for my actions. I had no control over being turned Bane, but by taking you away from our home when I knew mother still lived, I purposefully inflicted that same life on you. I forced you to live in the Shadow World with me. It was no place for a child. Cold, lonely, and dangerous. If the demons had discovered us, you would have shared my fate." She paused. "I knew it was wrong, but after a while the thought of living alone was unbearable. I couldn't bring myself to tell you that mother was alive. For that I will always be sorry."

"I won't." Jade leveled her gaze at her. "If everything we've gone through had to happen to bring us to this point, then I'd gladly live it again—even father's death."

Her sister's answer surprised her. "Why would you say that?"

"What's happening between the Bringers and the Bane is so much bigger than us, Esmeralda." Jade's use of her human name bit at Rell like a raw sore. No longer did she feel like Esmeralda. That girl was dead. "Not only have we both lived in the Shadow World, but you were a Demon Bane. You have more to offer the Bringers than anybody alive. You know how they think and feel, what they're capable of physically." She cocked a brow. "You and Siban may be the best secret weapons in the Bringer arsenal." Jade touched her finger to the spot below her lip, indicating Rell's Tell tattoo. "And since both of you are Tells, together you may be doubly effective. None of us who grew up on this side of the Arch have yet learned our full potential, but now there are those who can teach us."

Rell thought about it. Being a demon was still fresh in her mind, but perhaps over time the memories would fade—she hoped those memories would fade. "You might be right, but the price we've paid thus far has been steep."

"And bound to grow steeper before this war is over."

Siban stuck his head into the bedroom. "Breakfast has been set in the Great Hall. Are you hungry?"

She sighed. "With the meals mother and Delphina keep feeding me, I won't stay thin for long."

"But there's no getting around it." Her sister stood and tugged Rell to her feet. "Best to eat and not have to listen to either of them harp at us."

"You're probably right."

In the hallway Siban placed a hand on her back, guiding Rell down the stairs with Jade in the lead. He'd been her constant companion, only leaving her to sleep. Though sweet, his hovering made her feel pinned in at times. Being around people, and him specifically, would take some getting used to. Hopefully Siban would realize she wasn't as delicate as he believed.

The smell of bacon and the din from the household full of Bringers reached her before they'd turned the last corner. Noise and so many people set her nerves on edge. Their flowing conversations were like webs she tried to avoid. Besides Jade's presence, her life had been isolated in the Shadow World. The ability and desire to engage in senseless chatter had been lost.

As if sensing her apprehension, Siban's arm slipped more firmly around her waist. He led her to the end of a long table. "Sit here and I'll get us food."

She eased onto the bench next to the oldest of the three Bringer sisters, Juna. She was deep in conversation with Gregory, which gave Rell a chance to observe the two of them. Where Juna's sisters emanated kindness and caring, she carried herself like a hardened warrior. Though she strongly resembled Ravyn, the older Bringer had none of her sister's carefree or compassionate demeanor.

Harsh whispers between Juna and Gregory reached Rell's ears. The two appeared to disagree about what the Bringers' next move against the Bane should be. Rell settled her gaze on Siban, but her attention was fixed completely on the conversation next to her. She wondered if Juna was King Gregory's woman. He certainly allowed her far more freedom in speaking her mind than seemed normal for a king.

"Then leave them here to train." Juna's whisper rose in volume. "I will take the others to the Shadow World. Letting the Bane get any stronger than they already are is foolish."

"You're not thinking with your head. If you go into the Shadow World, who will train the others? You'll do your mother no good if you get captured by Vile. I can't allow it." Gregory took a bite of eggs, chewed, and swallowed. "Besides, you need the others. They know the Shadow World far better than you do and none of them are yet ready for that kind of mission."

The woman bristled at his tone. "I am able to take care of myself."

He snorted and shoveled in another mouthful of eggs.

"You think I can't?" Juna placed her hands on either side of her trencher and leaned toward him, her voice coming out in an angry hiss. "After everything we've been through?"

He exhaled and set his spoon down, turning to look at her. "Your abilities are not in question. It's your logic. I will not risk your life unnecessarily. That is a promise I made to your father."

She stood and glared down at him. "I don't need your

protection anymore, Gregory. I'm not a child."

Rell watched the king, as he in turn watched his second-in-command stomp away. To the unbiased observer, his admiration for the woman was more than apparent. His silver gaze tracked to Rell, but she didn't look away.

"She's very stubborn," he said.

"She thinks you see her as a child." The words slipped out unbidden. Her brow cocked in question. "Do you?"

A smile tugged at the corner of his sculpted mouth. "What do you think?"

"No. If anything, I'd say your feelings are quite the opposite." She held his stare. "Maybe you should tell her."

He gave a bark of laughter. "And lose my edge completely. No thank you."

At that moment Siban arrived with their food, putting an end to her and Gregory's conversation. Piles of eggs, bacon, and crusty bread were stacked high on the square wooden slab. Her stomach growled in response to the delicious smells.

"I hope you're hungry." Siban slid the plate onto the table in front of her.

"Not *that* hungry." She pointed to the food. "You're planning on helping me eat this, yes?"

He gave her a sheepish grin and plucked a piece of bread from the tray. "I am."

Nearly half the slice went into Siban's mouth. Rell's eyes widened. "Maybe I should eat my portion now before it's all gone."

He chewed and smiled, making him look like a happy boy. She shook her head and picked up a piece of bacon. The savory aroma made her mouth water. After all the revolting things she'd eaten as a demon, she'd never get tired of delectable cooked meat.

Gregory rose and walked to the front of the room to stand

near the blazing hearth. The crackling fire framed his large body. His black hair gleamed from the flickering flames and his close-cut goatee lent a hard edge to his features. He was very handsome and looked every bit a king.

Rell leaned toward Siban. "I think he's sweet on the Bringer named Juna."

Siban's eyes widened, his gaze skating to Gregory. He swallowed. "He's got his work cut out for himself."

"Good morning," Gregory said, cutting off the rest of their exchange. The conversation from the other Bringers stopped and everybody turned their attention to their leader. "I thought it best to explain what to expect in the upcoming days. Please, continue to eat. I'll make this as brief as possible."

An unladylike snort issued from behind Rell. She craned her neck to see Juna leaning against a stone pillar a few yards away, arms tightly crossed in front of her chest. Rell returned her attention to the front of the room.

"Two of the Bringers from my party." The king pointed to a burly man and a statuesque woman sitting at the opposite end of the table. "Magnus and Brita, will instruct those of you from this side of the Arch on the Bringer history. It is lengthy and politically convoluted but I promise you will not be bored." Quiet laughter rippled through the room. "I have a list of tasks, training, and posts that I've delegated to each of you. This will create a flowing schedule that will make the best use of our time while we train, prepare for our upcoming mission, and provide a constant watch to the manor."

"What is our next mission?" Luc asked between mouthfuls of food.

Gregory crossed his arms and spread his legs in a more relaxed stance. "We are going to rescue the other Bringers from the Shadow World."

A low rumble of approval rolled through the crowd. Rell

glanced at Juna again. The woman appeared more alert, less angry, her gaze fixed on Gregory. A sensation of anticipation and expectation emanated from her.

Siban followed the direction she stared and he smirked. "She hopes to lead the mission."

"You feel it too?"

He nodded. "Like she bashed me over the head with it."

Rell turned back to her food. "It's going to take a while to get used to these Tell powers."

"If we ever do," he said.

"Juna will be leading the training sessions," Gregory continued. "She is my second-in-command. Please go to her with any problems and questions if I'm not available."

Rell repressed the urge to smile. The king's placation was obvious even if she hadn't been a Tell.

"After you've been trained and a plan has been developed, we will enter the Shadow World and Saints willing, rescue our own."

A single question formed in Rell's mind, one that needed to be asked. She raised her hand.

The king's gaze landed on her, his eyes widening slightly in surprise. "Yes, Rell?"

All heads turned toward her. She blocked out the wave of anxiety at being the center of attention. Siban's hand slipped onto her knee below the table, giving her encouragement. "What if the captured Bringers have been turned to Bane? How do you plan on finding their demon forms?"

Gregory inhaled and then exhaled deeply. "A very good question and one I have no answer for — yet. It may be as simple as letting the Bane know we've found the bodies." He paused. "After all, *you* came to us, which we are grateful for."

Her reply was a single nod. The memory of the night she'd arrived at the manor, ranting to see her body, was not pleasant.

The sense of losing everything and not knowing what was true or a lie had driven her to confront the Bringers. It had been the turning point not just for her, but also in the Bringers fight against the Bane. The idea that she might be an essential part of their plan had given her the strength to face what was to come later—her demons, both imagined and real.

"Are there any other questions?" Gregory waited. When nobody spoke he said, "Please finish this fine meal that has been prepared for you by Delphina and Willa, and then come to the bailey and we will begin training and delegating duties."

Conversation rose again, flowing around Rell and Siban. She continued to eat, contemplating the days to come.

"Are you all right?" His hand remained on her leg, his fingers lightly stroking just above her knee.

"I'm fine." She swallowed the last bit of eggs. "I was just thinking that it's good to have a task. Keeps my mind off what's to come."

"I think that holds true for all of us." His hand made a subtle trek upward, his fingers sliding between her thighs. "I've found that a vigorous workout clears the mind and exhilarates the body."

A thrill shot through her. She slowly turned her head and looked at him. His hazel eyes were hooded with desire, which took her by surprise because it was morning. Did people get amorous in the morning? Having been turned a Bane before experiencing the mysteries of coupling, she was oblivious to how relationships actually worked. One thing was certain, she liked the way Siban touched her and how he looked at her now. They'd kissed a couple of times, but only when she'd been a demon, and only in the most dire circumstances.

Feeling emboldened, she lowered her voice. "Perhaps that is a part of my training you should oversee."

• • •

Siban held her gaze. Rell's response surprised and delighted him. He'd been leery of pursuing the urges he'd gained once she'd been turned human, thinking perhaps she was still too delicate. Though she seemed open to his advances, he definitely needed to move forward with caution.

He wanted her in his life—always, but she'd been so young when she'd been turned and he didn't know what had happened to her during her time as a Bane. Asking seemed crass and far too personal for his comfort. Now that she was human, several possible scenarios concerned him. Perhaps he wouldn't please her or maybe she'd find another Bringer more to her liking. There was no doubt she was beautiful. He'd staked his claim the second Rell had been taken prisoner. Though other men might respect his obvious interest, she might not.

Her large green eyes searched his face. She reached and rubbed a thumb between his eyebrows. "Did I say something wrong?"

He removed his hand from her thigh and placed it on her back, running it up under her chestnut-brown hair. "No, you've made me very happy."

She tilted her head and narrowed her gaze. "You don't look happy."

"I want nothing more than to show you how much I care about you, Rell." He cupped the back of her head and gently massaged. "How much I desire you."

"But?"

"But you've been through a lot. I want you to know I'm willing to take this as slowly as you need. You must be certain that I'm the man you want."

"Siban." Her pupils dilated. "There is no doubt in my mind that you're the man I want." She paused, a smile turning up the corners of her mouth. "Both in my life and in my bed." She leaned into him and placed a gentle kiss on his lips. "Always."

Her words set his blood on fire, and he pulled her against his chest, repeating the kiss with far less restraint than she'd shown.

"There are rooms for that," Luc said from behind them.

Siban broke the kiss, turning to Luc. His friend stood with his arm around Jade, both invaders repressing obvious grins.

"As always, Luc, your timing is impeccable." Siban released Rell and stood. "Or, should I say, annoying."

Luc's grin stretched, betraying the fact that he was not the least bit repentant for his rude interruption.

Jade nudged him in the ribs with her elbow. "Now you know what I must endure, Siban."

"You have my deepest sympathy, my lady."

Rhys and Ravyn joined the group. "We're on our way to the bailey," Rhys said. "Join us?"

Rell rose and slid her hand into Siban's.

He twined his fingers with hers, pulling her closer. "Lead the way."

CHAPTER FOUR

The bailey spread in front of the manor house and several outbuildings dotted the surrounding area. An unseasonably warm breeze ruffled the grass and birds sang their early morning song, welcoming the sun's golden rays.

Rell inhaled, loving the freshness of the morning. "For so long I awoke to dampness and the smell of sulfur. Clean air is something I will never take for granted again."

Siban remembered the dank and stifling feel of the Shadow World, how it used to claw at his lungs, burning them with cold and caustic vapors. "Nor will I."

They walked to the group congregating around Juna and Gregory.

"Let's get started." Juna's face was set in a no-nonsense expression that would make most men cower. The Bringers formed a half circle in front of her, each giving her their full attention. "The first group of names I call out will go with Magnus and Brita to begin learning our history. Ravyn, Luc, Rhys, Jade, Rell, Siban, and Meran." Juna's gaze tracked down the line, picking out each one of them. "Afterward we will train. Luc, Rell, and Ravyn will join Odette and Okee for hand-to-hand combat."

Siban glanced at the blond twins. They looked too young and innocent to be powerful warriors, but over the last weeks he'd learned that all the Bringers who had come through the Mystic Arch possessed abilities he could only hope to match some day.

"Jade, Siban, Rhys, and Meran will work on controlling their Bringer powers with Brita," Juna continued. "Though your powers are different, you'll learn how to communicate and understand each other's abilities. This will become imperative in battle."

"I will stay with Rell." Siban spoke the words, leaving no room for argument.

"You and Rell are both newly brought to power and both Tells. You would be best served working with those who do not share the same abilities," Juna said.

"I will stay with Rell," he said again.

She held his gaze and after a few seconds nodded. "Jade, you will switch places with your sister." The woman squared her shoulders. "I cannot stress how important it is that you do not coddle each other." Her eyes scanned from Siban and Rell over to Luc and Jade. "You will want to spare your companion discomfort, but you need to treat them as you would any other training partner."

"Don't worry. I will make sure I push Siban and that he challenges me." Rell glanced around the circle. "There are several demons I'd like to pay back for the last thirteen years."

"I'm glad to hear that." For the first time since Siban had met her, Juna smiled. Her pale blue eyes crinkled at the corner, softening her hard edge and making her similarity in appearance to Ravyn all the more noticeable. "We've got a lot of work to do."

Siban couldn't help but compare Rell and Juna. Where

both women's sisters laughed freely, they seemed unable
to indulge in whimsy or fun. Their determination and blunt
manner gave them an air of detachment that made them seem
unapproachable.

The burly man named Magnus stepped forward. "If you
come with Brita and me, we'll start your history lesson."

Without waiting, he turned and walked toward the manor.
Brita held out her arm, indicating they should follow him. She
smiled at them with the kind of grin that warmed a person from
the inside out—the kind of smile that soothed the harshness
of the world like a healing balm. From her gentleness, Siban
would have thought her to be a Redeemer, but the line under
her lip marked her as a Tell.

He focused his attention on Magnus's back and opened his
senses. The man wore a thick red beard, which was braided on
each side of his mouth. Though unable to distinguish what kind
of Bringer Magnus was, Siban had noticed he didn't bear the
mark of the Redeemer on his palms.

A Tell. The thought came unbidden, surprising him. Would
his powers work the same on the Bane? Would he be able
to decipher if a demon had once been a Bringer? When he'd
felt Icarus the night Rell had been transformed, it had been
impossible to untangle the web of impressions. Perhaps a lesser
demon might be more easily read.

The morning meal had been cleared but the smell of food
still lingered in the air. The banging of pots emanated from the
kitchen on the other side of the Great Hall. Every so often
Delphina's laugh could be heard wafting through the open
doorway. The group settled onto the benches around the long
table. Siban sat next to Rell, wanting to keep her close. Jacob
Le Daun joined them and took his place next to Luc at the
end of the table. Magnus stood where Gregory had during the
morning meal, while Brita moved to the back of the group at

the opposite end of the table.

Magnus cleared his throat. His thumb rubbed the hilt of his sword, as if he were uncomfortable speaking to a crowd. Siban had known such men. They preferred action over talk. Rhys was such a man. That was the main reason Siban had joined the Bringers after escaping the Shadow World. He too preferred action and had neither the inclination nor ability for diplomacy.

"We will be imparting the Bringers' history to you through our own memories." Magnus pulled a short stool to the end of the table and sat. Brita mimicked his actions. "But not in a way you're probably used to. There's too much to communicate with words, so we will share our experiences with you through one of the Tell gifts—memory transference." He held out his callused hands and rested them on the table. "First we must join hands."

Each Bringer took the hand of the person sitting on either side. Siban gripped Rell and Rhys's. Rell in turn, took his and Brita's. Once the circle was complete all eyes turned back to Magnus.

But it was Brita who spoke. Though soft with a lilting quality, her voice commanded attention. "The circle must remain unbroken. When we are done sharing our information, either Magnus or I will release your hands. Then you may let go."

"I'll warn you that the experience can be somewhat… overwhelming at first. Try not to react to what you're seeing or hearing. This is the past and nothing can be done about it now."

Siban's gaze slid to Rell. "Are you sure you're up to this?"

She nodded. "Unquestionably."

Instead of reassuring him, her conviction sent a wave of apprehension through him. Though he understood her desire to be involved, vengefulness rolled from her. Experience had taught him that anger was not the best motivation. It made one careless and illogical. Suppressing his concerns, he turned back to Magnus.

"Close your eyes and concentrate on your breathing," Magnus said. "Try to relax. Brita and I will guide you."

Before Siban closed his eyes, he glanced at Rell. Her lids were pressed tightly together and her fingernails dug into his hand. "Relax."

She inhaled and blew out her breath, her shoulders dropping from her release of tension. Siban closed his eyes and focused on his breathing as Magnus had instructed. At first the surrounding noises of the crackling fire and shouts from outside drew his attention, but as he concentrated, all extraneous sounds dimmed and finally faded.

A man's face suddenly appeared in Siban's mind. He flinched. The clarity of the man's harsh features was accompanied by a feeling of discontent. Siban tried to relax, letting Magnus and Brita guide his vision. The scene pulled back to reveal the man sitting on a throne. King Harlin, Gregory's grandfather, ghosted through Siban's mind.

The image extended further until the entire lay of a Great Hall could be seen. Lines of people were being herded into groups. They were dirty and dressed in rags. Some appeared injured, and all looked hungry. Disgust that was not his own filled Siban. An underlying outrage over what was happening flowed with the images. It was as if he watched everything through somebody else's eyes.

An ornately dressed man sat at a parchment-covered table. His ample body flowed over the armless chair on which he was perched. His robes pooled around him in a sea of brocade and velvet. With a plump hand, he popped a grape into his mouth and chewed. The flesh beneath his chin wobbled with each chomp of the fruit, furthering Siban's disgust.

Obviously in charge of the slaves, the official pointed to a cluster of men, whose hands and feet were bound together with lengths of rope. "The clay pits."

Four guards nudged the slaves away from the table and toward the door. A thin man, wearing nothing but filthy, torn pants, stumbled and fell. Long white scars covered his back. Siban gritted his teeth against the anger rising inside him. He bore scars such as those from his time in the Shadow World. They had not disappeared, even after he'd been brought to full power.

An armor-clad soldier drew back his foot and kicked the felled man in the ribs. "Get up, dog."

The prisoner stumbled upright with the help of another captive. The slave's eyes were wide, but he made no protest, merely remained bent and gripping his side. His spirit was broken. Though he and Siban shared similar scars, Siban had never succumbed to the belief that all was lost. Rell had seen to that.

Again, the prisoners moved forward and shuffled through the wide entrance of the hall, disappearing beyond the memory's range.

The fat man's gaze swept over a small group of young women huddled together. Siban could hear their quiet sobs. The official seemed to derive great enjoyment from the women's fear. A leering smile stretched across his mouth and he pointed a meaty finger toward them. "Pleasure house."

Information came unbidden. Siban knew that Magnus was feeding it to them in understandable chunks. Though somewhat jolting at first, there was no doubt memory transference was highly effective. Another thought came to him.

At one time humans and Bringers were the same people. The only difference was that humans had no powers. Unable to fight against a tyrannical king, they were forced into servitude.

The image panned back to King Harlin. A second man

stood beside the throne, his assessing stare traveling hungrily over the crowd of prisoners. Something familiar registered with Siban. He scrutinized the man's face. Short-cropped hair lay dark against his skull and eyes the color of silver seemed to search for something among the gathered masses. A sensation of lust and thirst for power rippled through Siban, but he could not place why the man seemed familiar. Like other Bringers in the scene, he bore a tattoo. It wasn't one Siban had seen before—an eight-pointed star. Siban made note to ask about the unfamiliar mark.

The throne room faded and a new image appeared. Lightning flashed across a gray sky. The thunder that followed mingled with the war cries of the men and women battling on an open area of blood-spattered mud. The sounds rumbled within Siban's chest, as if he stood at the heart of the battle. The smell of rain, blood, and burning flesh assaulted his nose, causing him to recoil.

Swords clashed in endless cacophony. Fireballs whistled through the air, slamming into people and exploding. Their attack was not like the fire he'd seen the Bringers use the night of Rell's capture. Punishing and more violent, the spinning fireballs raced through the air with a power far greater than a catapult. They connected with their targets, decimating them.

The dead and injured littered the ground as the battle raged on. Their cries tugged at Siban. Rell and Rhys's grips tightened. They too obviously battled the urge to defend. A huge arch, ten men wide and twice as high, loomed in the center of the melee. Siban recognized it from the legends, the Mystic Arch. Several humans ran though the doorway, followed by the king's soldiers. Many of the escaping humans were dragged back through, but not all.

Siban's attention was drawn to a young man in the midst of battle. *Prince Arron*. Siban recognized the name instantly. He was Gregory's father, and the king who had been victorious over the Bane a thousand years ago.

Again the scene altered and Arron now sat on the throne with the crown firmly on his head. Joy ebbed around the image. A quick succession of pictures flashed through Siban's mind. King Harlin being beheaded with an immortal weapon. More, smaller battles. Once again the scenes slowed and settled on the image of the Mystic Arch. The inner area of the doorway glimmered green and blue. Humans carrying bags and pulling small carts trudged toward the entrance and then stepped through.

Sorrow accompanied the human's departure from Bael, the Bringers' homeland. But mixed with the sadness was the anticipation of starting a new life. Freedom from slavery and servitude lent a bittersweet quality to the exodus.

When the last human had passed, King Arron closed the Archway. A younger version of Brita stood beside the king, watching. He performed a ceremony that warded the passage so only the reigning king could open it, thus ensuring the human's safety from those wishing to reclaim them as slaves.

The scene pulled back and faded to darkness. Noises from the present invaded Siban's meditative state, bringing with it a flood of emotions about what he'd just witnessed. Rhys released Siban's hand. Keeping with the instructions, he released Rell's and slowly opened his eyes. The group looked at each other. Their stoic faces showed the same shock he was experiencing.

"The information we just imparted happened more than a thousand years ago, before the Thousand Year War between the Bringer and the Bane." Magnus slid his stool back and stood. He paced in front of the table, as if struggling with the memories of the past. "As you have seen, King Arron was victorious over his father. In an effort to ease the suffering of the humans, he allowed them to pass into Inness. He hoped that by giving them a world of their own, they would be free to live without persecution." Magnus stopped at the table and leaned his fists against the wood. "Are there any questions?"

The group exchanged glances. Siban, for one, had a hundred questions. He focused on the specifics of what Magnus had showed them. "So, humans originated in Bael and *were* originally Bringers but without power?"

"Yes." Brita gracefully rose from her seat. "It was not unusual to bear a child without powers, but as with many have-and-have-not situations, the greedy preyed on the weak. To not bear a mark became a badge of shame in itself. By letting those humans and their families pass through the Mystic Arch, King Arron had hoped to put an end to their suffering."

"Did it?" Rell asked.

Brita gave a delicate shrug. "For the most part. But during that same battle, King Arron's firstborn son was kidnapped. We believe it was in retaliation by those who opposed the human's exodus.

"And the child was never found?" Disbelief tinged Ravyn's question.

"No." Magnus paced at the end of the table. "Our strongest Tells assured us that the child still lived, and since Gregory can not open the portal from this side—" he stopped and looked at the group— "we've surmised that the child was secreted here, to Inness."

Brita moved around the table to stand beside Magnus. Though her action was subtle, she placed a hand on his arm. Calming waves emanated from her, flowing over Siban. Magnus's stance visibly relaxed, as did most sitting at the table.

Magnus inhaled and then exhaled deeply. "Are there any other questions about what you were shown today?"

"You mentioned this was before the Bane War," Rhys said.

"Were the Bane already on Inness?"

"We're not sure." Magnus locked his hands behind his back, his brow furrowing. "Until the human queen, Anna, implored King Arron for help that day at the Arch, we never knew of the Bane. We assume they originated in Inness. Once the Arch reopened to help Anna battle the Bane, several demons slipped through to Bael. Fortunately they were quickly dispatched."

"The man beside the king," Siban said, "Who was he?"

Brita's gaze turned hard. "King Harlin's brother, Ander."

"What happened to him?" Jade asked. "Was he also beheaded?"

"Worse." Magnus pointed to his chest. "Perhaps you noticed the eight-pointed star on his chest." The group nodded. "It's called a chaotic star and is the symbol of the Summoner. The Summoners were another clan of Bringers, but because of their dark natures, King Harlin had them rounded up and imprisoned."

"Even his own brother?" Meran asked.

"Oh yes. The Summoners were the most powerful group of Bringers. They drew their abilities from dark magic, which eventually corrupted nearly all of them." Brita slowly moved around the table, weaving her tale. "When King Harlin realized his brother had been scheming to take the crown, he created an inescapable prison and threw each of the Summoners into it—including his own mother." She paused. "The Abyss is that prison."

"His own mother?" Rell shook her head. "Were such drastic measures necessary?"

"Most definitely." Brita stopped at the opposite end of the table. "She had corrupted Ander into believing that he should be king and in so doing, he would be able to set the Summoners above all other Bringers and rule not only Bael, but other worlds that the Mystic Arch opens to." She nodded.

"Though Harlin was a tyrant when it came to dealing with the humans, he believed all empowered Bringers were equal and that no single group should rule the other."

"What a contrary king," Ravyn said. "Where is the Abyss located?"

"We don't know." Magnus's thumb stroked the hilt of his sword again and Siban realized it was an action the Tell did when distressed. "Many things were kept secret by King Harlin for reasons of security. For a long time we assumed the Abyss was in Bael, hidden from those wishing to free the Summoners."

"But now?" Instead of feeling like he understood the Bringers better, the information only raised more questions for Siban.

Brita and Magnus exchanged glances. "Now we believe it's somewhere in Inness," she said.

"But…" Ravyn turned to face Magnus and Brita. "We've always believed that Vile has been trying to open the Abyss." She shook her head. "Why would he do this?"

"There is a legend that whomever opens the prison controls the army within." A heavy sign escaped Brita. "Perhaps the Demon King is misguided in his beliefs that he will be able to control the Summoners."

"Because of his bold move to kidnap Bringers, we feel he understands some of our history. But we also believe Vile is missing vital pieces, which will render his attempts to open the Abyss unsuccessful." Magnus rubbed the back of his neck. "Fortunately for us. Let's pray that is the reality."

"What would happen if he was successful?" Luc shifted and draped his arm across Jade's shoulder.

"Death, destruction." Magnus crossed his arms over his chest. "The battle against the Bane a thousand years ago would seem like a mere skirmish."

"The power the Summoners possess is great and horrifying." Brita walked slowly around the table, spinning the tale. "Because they draw from the dark, their source is nearly endless. Always there is suffering and greed from which they feed their powers." She stopped at the opposite end of the table. "That is why when a Bringer embraces their ability as a Summoner, it is almost guaranteed they will be corrupted."

Siban slid his hand along Rell's leg, needing the contact. They had both experienced the darkness. Was that the same black force, which was void of compassion and happiness, the evil the Summoners claimed? A tiny shiver ran along his skin. He couldn't imagine voluntarily embracing such a choice and condemning himself to a life of such insatiable mercilessness.

"Both Magnus and I have battled against the Summoners," Brita continued. "And though their abilities were far greater than any of the other Bringers, I'm quite certain we only witnessed a small part of their capabilities."

"Keeping the humans from persecution had been King Arron's mission." Magnus paused. "Let's pray that saving the world from the Summoners will not be ours." His gaze shifted to the doorway of the kitchen. "Are there any more questions?" When nobody spoke, he raised his hand and waved Delphina into the Great Hall. "That's enough for today. Transferring visions is draining for the both the Tell and the receiver. Refresh yourself and meet back in the bailey for guard assignments."

Magnus turned and strode from the room with Brita gliding behind him.

"I thought you lot might be thirsty." Delphina hefted a tray laden with mugs of ale. Jacob jumped to his feet and relieved her of her burden, setting it on the table.

"Thank you, Delphina." Ravyn stood and reached for a mug. "I feel like I just ran a mile."

The group was quiet as they handed the drinks down the

line, each seemingly lost in their own thoughts of what they'd witnessed. Siban took a long drink, attempting to wash away the acrid taste the battle scene had left in his mouth.

"You look like you've seen a ghost," Delphina said.

"Good as," Luc replied. He drank deeply and wiped his mouth with the sleeve of his shirt. "But this helps, thanks."

"Are you all right?" Siban rubbed his hand up and down Rell's thigh.

She stared into her cup but glanced up at his question. All eyes were on her. "Yes, I'm fine. I'm just trying to take it all in."

"That was like nothing I've ever experienced." Jade closed her eyes and pressed the heels of her hands against her lids. "It's like the visions were burned into my mind." She lowered her hands and blinked. "Now I have more questions than before Magnus shared this information with us."

Rhys leaned forward and rested his elbows on the table. "As do I. And I believe Magnus started us out easy. At least now I understand how Queen Anna knew to go to the Mystic Arch when she needed help with the Bane."

"And if that's true, then everybody on Inness, except the Bane, originated from Bringers." Jacob paused. "Including Splinters. They seemed to have figured out a way to regain a small amount of their own powers."

"Through dark earth magic," Jade said.

"I wonder, if they had been born with Bringer powers if they would have been Summoners." Luc absently tapped his finger against the tabletop.

"Perhaps," Meran said. "That would explain why they are so adept in the dark practices."

Ravyn exhaled. "It's a lot to take in and I have a feeling we've not even scratched the surface of what we're still to learn."

Siban's nerves hummed as if he'd just come off the

battlefield. Rell covered his hand with hers. Warmth and calm spread through him. Was this part of their Tell powers? Brita had seemed to do the same for Magnus. Siban's abilities were still so new, but he looked forward to finding out how they would be helpful in battle. He glanced at her...and in more intimate situations.

Learning to control his powers was much more difficult than Siban had thought it would be. Though Brita tried to gently guide them in sending out their awareness, his seemed to have a mind of its own. Each time he released it, his powers shot forward like one of the fireballs from Magnus's vision. The majority of Siban's training was spent wrestling his Tell under control. Before being brought to full power he hadn't had a problem. His abilities had been ingrained and flowed naturally with his desires. Now it seemed that his Tell was a freethinking entity that did what it wished, despite his command. It felt foreign, resisting his persistent efforts like a cold lump of clay.

To make matters worse, none of the others seemed to be struggling with the exercises. After the fifth time that his awareness sprang forward and pelted his senses with a million bits of information, Siban turned and kicked a wooden pail filled with water. The liquid splashed in all directions and spilled across the grass.

"Be gentle with yourself, Siban." Brita approached him and laid a hand on his arm, instantly calming him. "You must work in unison with your Tell, not fight it for control."

"Perhaps you could explain that to my Tell. It's being quite uncooperative." His mouth compressed into a tight line when he looked at Rell. Her lips were pressed together in an effort not to smile. "Am I amusing you?"

She held up her hands in defense. "I didn't say anything."

"Let me help you." Brita moved to stand in front of him. "Hold out your hands." She laid hers atop his. "Now close your eyes and relax so I might guide you."

He gritted his teeth. "I feel like a child."

"I sometimes use this technique when teaching the young." Her words held no hint of mockery. "It allows them to become accustomed to how their powers move."

Quiet laughter sounded from somewhere in front of him. He opened one eye. Rhys's face was passive, but Rell had her back to him. Siban harrumphed and squeezed his eyes shut.

"Now, think of using your Tell in the same way you would float on the water. Ease onto it and drift while gently directing your course."

With a deep exhale, he envisioned himself sinking into his power and he opened his mind. It shot forward, but instead of hauling it back like a runaway horse, he rode the wave. Eventually the frantic pace slowed. His senses spread across the ground, picking up on the tiny life-forms that pulsed within the grass.

"Good," Brita said. "Now open your eyes, and focus your Tell on a specific destination."

Brita's presence was beside him, riding the wave as well. But she didn't interfere, allowing him to maintain control. A few times she nudged his attempts to keep his Tell on course.

Siban focused on the forest beyond the manor. With a single thought he projected what he desired to know. The path his Tell had taken narrowed and turned in the direction he intended. The amount of psychic information lessened and became more purposeful, as if understanding what he wanted.

When his awareness entered the first row of trees it slowed even further, creeping through the underbrush and feeding information back to Siban. The life forces from different birds and animals flitted through his mind. Puddles of water, moss growing on trees, and even the wind registered positively in his mind. All was as it should be. Nothing out of placed dwelled within the range.

"Now bring your senses back, but not in a straight path. Stop at various points. When you're finished, release them," Brita said.

She removed her hands from his. The loss of her presence quivered across the top of his Tell wave, but didn't disrupt the flow. Though not as smooth as when Brita had been guiding him, Siban was able to redirect, stop, take in the information, and then continue along a course that brought his Tell willingly back to him.

He released it and exhaled. "I did it."

Brita's smile was like a mother's kiss. "Very good. Now you know what it feels like and will be able to do it again."

Rhys slapped him on the back. "Nicely done. I wish I understood your power." He flexed his biceps. "Shields are brawn, not brain."

"I wish I understood it as well," Siban said.

Rell approached. "I'm proud of you."

"I don't suppose you were having trouble too?"

She held up her thumb and index finger. "A bit, but I was having more fun watching you get frustrated."

Brita sighed. "I can see that this group will be just like my young students."

"You think we're bad," Rhys said, "You've got Luc, Jade, and Ravyn next."

Siban smiled apologetically at Brita. "Good luck with that crew."

For the first time, Brita's expression turned dark and slightly mischievous. "Let's try this lesson again, shall we?"

Rell groaned. "My head is pounding."

"Then you need more practice." Brita walked to her and

held out her hands. "It's your turn."

Rell looked at Siban for support. He mimicked her previous action and held up his hands in defense. "Don't look at me."

"Just get the feel of your Tell. Try to guide it. Later we'll work on connecting," Brita said to Rell. She turned to Rhys. "You will be able to sense information they send directly to you, but for the most part these lessons are about learning to work with each other and to find ways to communicate or read the body language of your group."

"Understood," Rhys said.

After Rell had mastered control of her Tell powers, Brita had them send out their awareness side by side and scan the grounds in a grid formation. Though Siban was completely cognizant of Rell, Rhys's presence hovered like a shadow in the background. Trying to connect with him was like standing in a thick fog and catching glimpses of his dark form every so often. Siban focused his awareness behind him in an attempt to link more strongly with Rhys. When in battle, he would need to know where the members of his party were situated. Attempting this with only one person was difficult at best. Tracking an entire group would take considerably more training.

With great effort Siban maintained his awareness of Rhys and scanned the area ahead of him. It took several attempts to clarify the streams of information pouring into him, but eventually requests from Rell began trickling to him. Her desire to patrol a certain area crystalized. He in turn made a request and each time she responded accurately. By the end of practice, their abilities hummed in near perfect harmony.

Their knack for sensing one another's needs calmed Siban's apprehension about their journey into the Shadow World. Unlike before, he would not be alone and now possessed the skill to communicate with Rell if captured again.

His eyes cut to Rell. What would she do if faced with being

turned Bane again? He watched her pick up the small sword she'd been given and examine the blade. She appeared calmer than he'd seen her in days. Maybe their newly acquired talents gave her more confidence. He watched her slash the air with the weapon, her face set in grim determination.

He hoped she wasn't too confident as to be reckless.

CHAPTER FIVE

By the end of the day Rell's head was swimming with information and her muscles ached with fatigue. Serena had readied a bath for her in the stone tub in her chamber. More than ever, Rell appreciated the fact that Jacob Le Daun was a man of innovations. He'd taken advantage of the hot springs under Faela and had created a hand pump and pipes that opened to let the water run freely into the tub. Getting the water in appeared easy, but Rell was uncertain how they were to get the water out.

Determined to enjoy her bath, Rell piled her hair on top of her head and slid into the steaming liquid. Heat surrounded her, sinking deep into her bones. She sighed as the warmth chased away the chill that was starting to settle as her body cooled from its vigorous workout. She lay against the smooth rock and thought about everything she'd learned.

Magnus had begun their lesson at the turning point just before the Thousand Year War between the Bringers and the Bane. He and Brita had imparted so much history her mind actually hurt. Ripples skated across the surface when she stirred the steaming water with her hand. Rose petals bobbed like boats on a windswept lake. Rell tilted her head forward until the water covered her chin. The muscles in her neck stretched and slowly released their tight hold.

A knock sounded at the door. "Who is it?"

"Siban. May I come in?"

She slid lower until the cloudy water touched her earlobes. Her first thought was to call out that she was not decent, but she stayed that urge. Though today's activities had exhausted her, they'd also left her exhilarated and feeling slightly daring. "Come in."

The door opened halfway and Siban stepped inside. He stopped, his eyes taking in the scene. Without looking away, he shoved the door closed behind him. His hand fumbled for the bolt and when he found it, he slid it across. "I can come back later."

Certain he had no intention of leaving since he'd just locked them inside, Rell repressed her smile. "If you'd prefer to come back later, that's fine."

He glided forward, pulling his tunic and shirt over his head in one smooth move. "I don't prefer that, so perhaps it's better if I stay."

Her breath caught in her throat. It was all she could do not to blush like the maiden she was. After everything she'd been through, it was a miracle he could still make her feel like an innocent.

Golden skin spread across his broad chest and rippled abdomen. Even in the low flickering light of the lanterns she could see the tiny white scars she'd spent hours healing, scars given to him by Vile and Sha-hera. Rell forced herself to look at his face, not letting him know the evidence of his torture brought back the pain of the desolate days they'd spent together in the Shadow World.

A shy smile crept across her lips. She was confident he

would guide her when she no longer knew what came next. "Are you here to wash my back?"

His eyebrows lifted, he was surprised by her boldness. "That—and other things."

His words sent a flash of heat through her and she suddenly wanted nothing more than to feel his hands on her body. She sat forward and bared her back to him, giving him silent permission to approach.

Siban knelt beside the stone tub and picked up the cloth. After dipping it in the water, he squeezed out the excess and applied it to her skin. She wished she could see him. Perhaps it was her insecurity at not knowing what to do or maybe she just wanted to watch his reaction as he touched her.

Rell wrapped her arms around her legs and bent her back. The cloth skated across her skin, gently washing away the grime of the day's workout. Her eyelids slid closed and she concentrated on the exquisite sensation of Siban touching her so intimately.

His presence in her chamber with her naked and vulnerable awakened a part of her that she hadn't felt since her encounter with Icarus in the caverns of the Shadow World. But this was different—more right—more thrilling—free of the darkness and unspoken obligations.

The cloth fell into the water with a tiny splash. She opened her eyes, staring at the wall opposite. Siban's fingers replaced the rag, moving across her back, gently kneading and exploring every inch. Tiny shivers pebbled her skin when he gently blew on her shoulder.

Her quiet laugh turned to a moan of pleasure when his thumbs lightly dug into her shoulders, working the knots free. Rell relaxed her position and straightened slightly. The water still hid her breasts, keeping her modesty intact, but the desire to have Siban touch her in more intimate places was quickly growing.

She inched backward and rested her shoulders against the edge of the tub. The tips of her breasts hovered just beneath the water but could be easily seen. She held her breath, trying to contain the thrill racing through her. The pink buds bobbed into view with each movement she made. Was she being too bold? Siban's massaging fingers slowed and she knew she had not been.

She watched his fingers creep along her shoulders toward her breasts. The breath stuck in her throat and for a few seconds she didn't move. But she wanted more. With a silent invitation, she let her head fall back to rest on his shoulder, giving him complete access. Siban's lips grazed her throat and his warm breath sent tremors of pleasure down her torso and up along her neck. She needed him closer, wanted more contact with him.

The desire he stirred inside emboldened her. She turned her face toward him and offered her mouth. He captured her lips. His hands drifted down her chest and cupped her breasts, his thumbs strumming her nipples to a hard point. Sparks of intense pleasure traveled to her core. She gasped and Siban's tongue swept inside, melting away her inhibitions.

Rell twisted and wrapped her arms around his neck, pulling him as close as she could get and deepening their kiss. Heat radiated from him. The water from the bath caused her skin to slide smoothly across his chest. He groaned.

Nothing had ever felt this good—or right. She broke their kiss. "I need more."

Siban shifted and dragged her from the water as he stood. The cool air brushed her skin but did little to temper the fire he had ignited within her. The stone scraped her thighs and knees but the passion encompassing her dulled the pain. Her body pressed against the length of him, his erection straining against her stomach. Still it wasn't enough.

She lifted her leg and ran her calf and foot up his thigh. In one seamless move, Siban bent and lifted her, wrapping his arm under her rear end. Instinctively Rell encircled his waist with her legs. His hardness pressed against her sex and she gripped his shoulders, staring into his eyes and savoring the sensation. The act was so intimate it made her feel alive. He kissed her again, his mouth dominating hers.

She was vaguely aware that he carried her somewhere. It didn't matter where as long as he didn't let her go. Cold stone pressed against her back and she gasped, breaking their kiss.

He'd pinned her against the wall but continued to hold her around his waist. He stared at her, his eyes burning bright with barely contained passion. "I'm only noble to a certain point, Rell." His breaths came in short pants. "If you don't want this to continue, you're going to have to stop me now." He took a deep breath and exhaled. "This will be your last chance."

The effect she had on him was intoxicating. Such control. Such power. Such beauty. The truth was she couldn't have stopped herself if she'd wanted to, and she didn't want to. Words failed her. She twined her fingers in his hair and pulled his mouth back to hers, pouring everything she had into the kiss. He was the man that she wanted now—that she'd want forever.

Siban pressed her more firmly against the wall and reached below her bottom to work free the tie of his pants. Within seconds the smooth skin of his cock pressed against her sex. Anticipation mixed with anxiety and her eyes slid closed. Her mother had explained what happened between a man and woman—that the first time might be painful, but she didn't care. She wanted the pain—wanted to feel every second of coupling with Siban.

He released his cock and replaced it with his fingers. Her

eyes sprung open at the new sensation. The calloused tips brushed her sensitive nub, sending intense pleasure through her. In an effort not to scream, Rell bit her lip. She held his stare, letting her head rest against the wall. The need to move washed through her. Tightening her legs around Siban, she lifted her hips and lowered onto his fingers. A smile stretched across his mouth at her actions. His fingers continued to work her, sliding deep inside and then slowly pulling back out, only to repeat the slow, wonderful torture. Rell rotated her hips in small circles.

"You've plagued my dreams." Siban's voice came out harsh and labored. "I've wanted this for so long."

His finger entered her again, pumping faster and his thumb flicked her clit each time he pulled out. Tremors of pleasure skittered to her core. A whimper slipped from her.

"You like that?"

She nodded and bit her lip, gyrating her hips.

When Siban lowered his head and captured her nipple in his mouth, Rell thought she'd shatter into a million pieces. Desire spiraled downward to mingle with the yearning building between her legs.

"Please." She didn't know what she begged for, only that she needed more.

Siban replaced his fingers with the tip of his cock and slowly pushed into her, inch by gloriously agonizing inch. "Bloody hell, you're tight."

She didn't know if that was good or bad, but she didn't care as long as he didn't stop. He completed her in a way she'd never experienced, not only physically, but as if he filled the black hole that still remained in her soul. She opened her mind to him and was swamped with his desire. She sensed that he barely maintained control and that ratcheted her passion higher.

He slid into her another inch and stopped. His eyes narrowed and his breathing stuttered. "You're a virgin." He shook his head. "I didn't know—didn't think about it."

"It doesn't matter." She cupped his face. "I want this."

He shook his head again and Rell could feel his mood shifting to panic. "Not like this, Rell. Not against the wall. Not for your first time."

Irritation flared inside her. This is exactly how she wanted it, hard and passionate. It made her feel alive, like she was desired as a woman. That she was no longer an abomination to be feared. His hold slackened and from his expression she could tell he was about to pull back. But that was not acceptable. He wanted her and she wanted him. Like this, right now.

She gripped his hair and pulled. "Don't you dare stop." Her lips curled in a seductive smile. "You say you've wanted this for a long time? Well I have too. I'm not some delicate maiden, Siban. The way you touch me makes me feel alive. More alive than I've felt in years." She pulled his mouth to hers, kissing him hard before pulling away. "Use your powers and read me. I want this."

His gaze focused on the wall beside her head for a second and then slid back to her face, his expression once again darkening with desire. "I can sense your need."

"Do it." She ground her hips against him, coaxing him back into action. "Make me yours."

"It will hurt."

She tightened her grip in his hair. "I want the pain."

"I promise I will make you feel good again." He hesitated only a second before driving into her. Rell gasped at the sharp sensation that erupted inside her and drank in the experience of becoming Siban's woman. With slow, measured movements he slid in and out of her. His tongue stroked her nipple, pulling it into his mouth to suckle, and stoking the passion building between her legs. When he reached between them and massaged her clit, Rell almost exploded.

His gentle movements quickened and he thrust urgently into her. The stone scraped against her back and hips, adding to the erotic collection of feelings enveloping her. He braced his hand against the wall, continuing to plunge inside her, his panting turning into low grunts of ardor. Her awareness of him pushed her toward ecstasy.

Unable to silence her desire, she whispered his name again and again, encouraging him to continue making love to her. The junction between her legs throbbed, pulsing with each thrust. Faster and faster until finally, she shattered. He claimed her mouth, swallowing her scream. Waves of unfamiliar pleasure washed over her, the sensation reaching so deep it filled her very soul, burning away the darkness and leaving only love.

Siban pumped several more times and stiffened, moaning against her lips. He thrust again and shuddered. His body convulsed, the waves that racked him growing shallower after a minute. He pressed his head against the wall, his breathing slowly returning to normal. They stood connected, not speaking. Rell stroked his hair, savoring the feel of his hot skin against hers and the cool stone against her back.

After another minute, he buried his face in her neck. She clung to him when he shifted and kicked off one boot, and then the other. He stepped out of his pants and then carried her to the bed. The wood frame creaked when he climbed onto it and lay down. Never once did he release her, holding her as if afraid she would fly away.

Rell unwound her legs from his hips and straightened them against the dark lush duvet. A dull ache radiated at her hips from where she'd gripped him so tightly, but the rest of her body purred with life. Siban pulled back and looked at her. For several seconds he just stared, as if taking in every feature of her face. She didn't disrupt his contemplation with words, content to lie in his arms and let him look his fill.

Finally he brushed a lock of hair from her cheek and laid a hand over hers, curling his fingers around her fist. "Rell?"

"Yes, Siban."

"I want to be with you." He hesitated. "To be your man."

No teasing lurked within his eyes and she felt his sincerity as if it were her own. Though she wanted the same, she had reservations. "You hardly know me, Siban. I hardly know myself. How can you be sure that you want to be with me?"

"I have no doubts." He ran his finger along her cheek. "We are the same, you and I. We've touched the darkness and survived."

"And that's enough to know you want me as yours?" She shifted and rolled to her back, staring at the red and gold pattern of the bed's canopy. Maybe a bit of innocent Esmeralda still waited inside her. His words touched her and made her feel less like an outcast.

"I think it's all we need—for now." He plucked at the edge of the pillow sham. "What I feel for you goes beyond anything I've ever felt for another person."

She turned and looked at him. "Me, too."

"In the Shadow World you were the only thing that kept me fighting for my life. There were times I wanted to give up, but knowing all I had to do was hold on and I would see you again, got me through my darkest hours." He trailed a finger along her upper arm, sending shivers of pleasure through her. "Even when you were a Bane, I loved you. When you helped me escape, it took all my will to leave you behind, but I knew the situation was growing dangerous for you. Too often you almost got caught healing me." His fingers wrapped around her arm with a gentle but firm grip. "I spent the next year battling not only the nightmares, but how much I missed you. It was like part of my soul had been left in that prison. Then when I saw you that night on the ship, when you plucked Jade from the crow's nest, I almost didn't want to believe it was you."

Her brow furrowed. "Why?"

His grip tightened. "I couldn't bear the thought of thinking I'd found you only to be disappointed. It would have been like losing you all over again."

"It *was* me though." She turned to her side and twined her fingers with his. "And here we are."

Siban exhaled. "Yes, here we are and I don't plan on letting you go again.

More than anything she wanted to be with Siban. He understood the darkness that still affected her. She wouldn't have to explain when she woke in a cold sweat from the nightmares. He'd loved her while she was a demon. He'd love her at her worst. "Yes, Siban, I'll be with you."

Chapter Six

Night had finally fallen. Folding her wings tightly against her back, Sha-hera crept from the shelter of the trees and inched toward the closest tent. Ever since Vile had banished Icarus, he'd become more secretive, less forthcoming about his plans. Long ago she'd learned to trust her instincts when it came to the powerful demon. Even though she'd served the king faithfully for millennia, her instincts screamed that events in the Shadow World were not unfolding to her advantage. With Vile's apparent lack of action against the Bringers, she'd been forced to seek help from an outside source.

Small fires dotted the encampment and the haunting music of flutes and slow-beating drums mingled with the brisk wind rustling the leaves. She had business with the Splinters, one in particular.

Splinters were nomads, traveling in groups and stopping only long enough to bleed the locals of their gold before moving on. But to only focus on monetary gain was a great waste of their talent in Sha-hera's opinion.

The white magic of healers paled in comparison to the force of the dark skills of the Splinters. Black magic *wanted* to be used. It fed on the greed of those who pursued it. The humans who shunned the dark ways in hopes of a normal life were like sheep, souls for those with less scruples and the Bane to feed on.

Sha-hera suspected those Splinters who heralded from the line of the Summoners were capable of far greater feats than just separating men from their gold. But she would not be the one to reveal that information. Their ignorance worked best for what she needed done.

She skirted the tent and slipped through the slit at the front. Fatima sat next to a sleeping child, stitching a veil onto a beaded strip of material. A single lantern burned on a low table and the smell of jasmine permeated the air. Fatima's long auburn curls shielded her face, the gleaming locks something Sha-hera had always been envious of.

"So domestic." Sha-hera cocked her head, a sneer pulling at her lip.

Fatima jumped, stabbing her finger with the needle, and looked up. The Splinter's beauty irritated Sha-hera. The features were too perfect and innocent for a woman such as her. She glanced at the sleeping child and then back to Sha-hera, her large brown eyes wide. "What are you doing here?"

"We need to talk." The demon took a step toward the pile of lush pillows. Once, her life had held such luxuries—pillows, silks, satins, and jewels. All the riches one could have ever wanted. But that was before she'd chosen to serve Vile. Sha-hera stared down at the little girl snuggled under the woven blanket. A child—another sacrifice she'd made for her king. "Have you entered Illuma Grand?"

The woman set her sewing aside and stood, wrapping her bright orange shawl more tightly around her. "I go tomorrow." Her mouth curved in a look of disgust. "I'm to enter through his private entrance. I doubt he'll allow me beyond his chambers."

Sha-hera smiled. "I'm sure you'll think of some way to persuade him."

The Bringer fortress was impenetrable to the Bane, warded against their kind. But any human could easily breach the boundaries.

"He's not as susceptible to my dancing as the others. What if he doesn't grant me permission?"

"It would be a pity." Sha-hera squatted next to the child and stroked the blanket covering her leg. "Such a pretty girl." She let the threat hang in the air.

Fatima stiffened. "I will see it done."

"Good." Sha-hera's hand lingered on the child's leg for a second before she stood. "We must know what lies beyond the Council Chamber doors."

"You will assure Vile that I am making progress?"

"Of course." She would reveal the minimal truth. The Demon King's lack of punishment toward Icarus's treachery had been the last failure Sha-hera would endure from her king. If Vile did not wish to take this war to the Bringers, then she would do it herself. "I'm sure he'll be pleased with your efforts."

The woman's stance relaxed. "Where should I meet you next?"

"Don't vex yourself. I will find you when it suits me." Sha-hera took a step toward her and to Fatima's credit, she didn't shy away. "You and I are not so different." She ran a talon down the woman's flawless cheek. "We are unappreciated by those we serve, but I promise *I* will reward you for your loyalty." Fatima didn't move, her face a stony mask. Sha-hera lowered her hand and looked once again at the child. "If you succeed, you and your child will have my protection and want for nothing."

"What of Vile's protection?"

Sha-hera repressed the urge to laugh. There was no such thing. He did as he pleased and took what he wanted. "As far as you're concerned, we are one and the same."

"Thank you." The woman's words lacked conviction.

Tired of the conversation, Sha-hera turned and walked to the slit in the tent. "You've done well thus far, Fatima." She glanced over her shoulder. "See that you continue.

Not waiting for the Splinter's reply, she slipped into the night. Though the wind swooshed through the trees, she thought she heard Fatima's sigh of relief.

Once back in the shelter of the woods, Sha-hera stopped to contemplate her next move. Being around the Splinter dredged up memories from long ago, servicing men and gaining power the only way she knew how—with her body. Where had it gotten her? Nowhere and alone. Most of the soldiers in her succubus army had sworn loyalty to Vile, not to her. When Sha-hera wanted to continue her attacks on the Bringers, all had refused to go against Vile's orders. They were coward. Just as much sheep as the humans.

It was of no consequence now. She'd made her decision to continue the fight without her king's approval. After Fatima seduced Fromme Bagita into revealing what lay within the Council Chamber, she would have the secrets Vile refused to share with her. Perhaps those confidences would lead her to the Abyss of Souls. If that were true, she'd find a way to open it and command the army herself. When this battle was finished, Icarus would be dead and Vile would be bowing at her feet.

CHAPTER SEVEN

For Rell the next week at Lord Le Daun's manor consisted of long, grueling days of hand-to-hand combat, learning the art of conjuring energy to use as a weapon, and mastering control over her Tell. Not to mention the extensive history lessons about the Bringers. Each night she fell into bed exhausted. The restlessness inside her had abated and she finally felt like she was gaining some semblance of normalcy in her life.

Brita had taken over imparting information to them since she had been King Arron's top advisor. She'd shown them Arron's peaceful reign and Queen Anna's plea for him to open the Mystic Arch and help her people—the humans. The hardest vision to watch had been Arron's death in battle against the Bane. He'd never known that Anna was pregnant with his child, Gregory. Having now witnessed the actual events, Rell was quite certain that Gregory fought not only to complete his mother and father's vision for their people, but also to avenge both their deaths.

With so much training and the constant flow of people, the opportunity to get reacquainted with her mother had not presented itself. But guilt over keeping her and Jade's existence from their mother still plagued her

During meals Rell sensed Willa's restlessness to return to her husband and other children. The thought of her mother's other life no longer made her angry or insecure. She'd found her place within the Bringers and with Siban. When the evening meal was finished, Rell and Siban picked up the last of the dishes and carried them to the kitchen.

As she entered the room, Hayden ducked behind his mother's skirt. Obviously he hadn't gotten used to seeing her as a person yet. She couldn't blame him since she still struggled with it herself.

"Just give those to Serena," Delphina said, gesturing with a wet rag to her oldest daughter. "That the last of them?"

"Yes." She handed the young girl her dishes, noticing Serena's red hands when she took the plates. Dirty dishes were piled on the table and Delphina's hair lay slick with sweat against her forehead. Her hands were also red from the hot water and the effort to scour the pots. "Can I help you with kitchen duties?"

The older woman stopped her scrubbing and smiled. "Thank you for offering, but no."

"Are you sure?" Rell remembered the domestic work she'd done around their home before she'd been turned Bane. The tasks of cooking, cleaning, and sewing were now so foreign to her. Swordplay and her Tell powers had replaced all other duties but she still remembered how to do them. "I'd like to help."

"That's very sweet, my lady, but I enjoy the hard work. It makes me feel useful." Her smile grew determined. "It helps me remember what I've risen above, thanks to the help of the Bringers." She flicked her head, motioning to Serena, who diligently scraped the drying food into a bowl. "And it does my children good to see their ma doing honest work."

At that moment, Willa shuffled in, hauling a large bucket of water. Siban crossed the room and relieved her of the burden. "Thank you. Just set it by the fire."

Unsure how to ease into a conversation that didn't sound rehearsed, Rell said the first thing that came to her mind. "The meal was excellent, as usual."

"Thank you, sweetheart." Her mother wiped her hands on the dirty rag draped around her hips. "Delphina has been a godsend. She'll have no problem cooking for the group after I return home."

Willa's disquiet washed over Rell. "Will you be leaving soon?"

"It's been nearly three weeks. I have to return sometime." Her mother sighed and picked up the first plate. With more vigor than the dish required, she scraped the remains into a bowl. Now that the mission preparations are almost complete, it's time I make arrangements for ship's passage home." She sniffed and cleared her throat. "I'll leave after the group has left for the Shadow World."

This surprised Rell. "You won't wait until after we return?"

"No." She appeared to blink back threatening tears. "Better I receive word of your mission's success while I'm with Orvis and the children." She picked up the next plate and scraped it as if to rid herself of the unpleasant possibility that they might not return. "Whether we celebrate or grieve, I'll want to be with them."

"I understand." Finally she did comprehend the depth one person could feel for those they loved. "I will miss you."

Willa's haunted expression softened. "And I will miss you." She set the plate down. "Promise you will come to the inn immediately after the Shadow World."

Could she promise such a thing? Perhaps it was more the security in believing the Bringers *would* make it than actually keeping her word. "I promise."

Siban wrapped an arm around her waist. "We promise."

His words brought a smile to Rell's lips.

"So, it's you and my daughter, is it?" Willa crossed her arms. Delphina stopped her scrubbing, no longer pretending to ignore the conversation. "I won't ask if you love her because that much is obvious." She leveled an assessing stare at both of them. "But remember, she's still my little girl." She paused. "Which means she's stubborn."

"With all due respect, my lady, I believe we've already seen the worst of each other."

"Maybe so. Maybe so." She leaned against the wooden island in the center of the kitchen. "But trust me, someday she's going to do something or say something that will make you so angry you'll wonder what you ever saw in her."

"Thank you, Mother." Rell enunciated the word mother, not sure if she should laugh or be offended by Willa's prediction.

"Esmeralda, I loved your father more than anything in the world, but the man could get me so angry that I contemplated bashing him in the head with the fire iron when he wasn't looking." She held up a hand. "So trust me when I say, I speak from experience." Willa sighed. "I can see you don't believe me, and that's all right. But remember one thing." She addressed Siban. "Even though she lived as a Bane and experienced things that make me shudder inside, Esmeralda has only been a woman for a few weeks."

Siban tipped his head in acknowledgment. "I assure you, my lady, I only have Rell's best interest at heart."

"I'm sure you do, Siban. That's why I'm trusting you to keep her safe. I just got my daughter back." Her voice cracked with emotion. I don't know what I would do if she was taken away from me again."

He didn't say anything for a few seconds. "Likewise, my

lady."

Willa sniffed again and straightened. "Then it's settled. You both will come to Dragon's Head Inn to meet Orvis and the children. I know they are all very excited about the prospect of two new sisters."

Tears burned behind Rell's eyes. It was an odd sensation and one she'd experienced several times over the last two weeks. That was one thing about being a demon. No pesky emotions except for anger to deal with. "I can't wait."

Siban smiled and nodded.

Delphina threw down the rag. "You're going to need a new gown for when you meet your new family."

"What's wrong with what I've got on?" Rell smoothed her hand over the black tunic. Thanks to Delphina and her mother's cooking, she'd finally begun to fill it out. "They're comfortable."

"Nothing wrong with them, but don't you want to look like a lady?" A wistful expression crossed Delphina's face. "I know I would if I was ever lucky enough to meet my family." She blinked a few times and then looked at Rell. "I've got a fair bit of skill when it comes to sewing and my daughter is an artist when it comes to embellishing fabric. She used to make extra coin by selling what she made in the market on Saturdays."

Shame pinched at Rell. It was easy to believe that others hadn't suffered as greatly as she had when she was a Bane. But when Delphina spoke of her life, Rell was humbled by the woman's strength. "I'm sure she does beautiful work."

Delphina beamed at the girl, causing Serena to blush.

"Perhaps I can start making the gown while you lot are gone." The woman circumvented the island in the middle of the kitchen, wiping her hands on her apron. "I'll just need to take your measurements before you leave."

Taken aback by Delphina's generous gift, Rell struggled to find the right words. "Thank you. That's incredibly generous."

She waved a hand in the air. "It's my pleasure." She looked at Willa. "As long as your mum don't mind me taking the reins on this. I don't want to overstep my position."

"Of course I don't mind." Willa untied the dirty rag from about her waist. "Perhaps Jacob has some old gowns we can repurpose." She propped her hands on her hips and smiled at Delphina. "Or if we're really lucky, maybe he'll take us to the market to purchase everything we need. Jade told me about a little shop that carries the most amazing fabric."

Lord Le Daun's feeling for Delphina were apparent, but she was a bit more difficult to read. Unable to resist, Rell smirked and said, "I believe if you allow Delphina to ask him, you'll get everything you need."

The woman's eyes grew wide and she sputtered an incoherent retort. Willa cupped a hand over her mouth in an unsuccessful effort to hide her smile. Obviously enjoying her mother's discomfort, Serena giggled.

"Come now, Delphina," Siban said, joining in the fun. "Surely you've seen the way he looks at you?"

"Lord Le Daun is a gentleman and would never be drawn to the likes of me."

Willa's expression softened. "You mean a beautiful woman who has turned his cold manor into a home again?"

Delphina opened her mouth to reply and then closed it, her gaze drifting to the wooden island. She scratched her thumbnail against the grain and fidgeted. "He couldn't possibly fancy me." She paused, sliding a glance to her daughter. "I'm soiled."

For the first time since Rell had been turned, she felt a kinship with another female. In a rare urge to comfort, she stepped forward and took Delphina's hand. "You are no more tainted than I am."

The woman looked at her and swallowed hard. "But you didn't have no control over being turned Bane."

"And you didn't have any control over your mother selling you to a pleasure house." Whether from Delphina's emotions or her own outrage, fury rolled through Rell. "Even though life was difficult, you not only survived, but cared for your children and put their needs above your own." Rell inhaled, trying to get control of her ire. "You are not soiled."

Serena wound her arms around her mother's waist. "Mummy, you're the best person I know."

Delphina swallowed and hugged her daughter. "No, you are the best person I know, love."

"Jacob Le Daun is lucky that you are in his life." Trying to lighten the mood, Rell gave a half smile. "But I think he already realizes that."

Siban chuckled. "As a matter of fact, I think you are the only one who hasn't realized that."

"Well…" Delphina straightened away from Serena and ran her hands down the front of her skirt. "The man must be daft." She patted her hair. "I look like a scullery maid."

Willa walked around behind Delphina and untied her apron. "Now, why don't you freshen up and then go ask Jacob about buying supplies for Rell's gown. I'm fairly certain he'll say yes."

Delphina bustled out of the kitchen, muttering to herself.

"If I know Jacob," Willa said, "he'd give her the world if she asked."

Siban squeezed Rell's shoulder. "Love will do that to you."

One more day and they would leave the safety of the warded grounds and head back into the world where Rell's nightmares had originated. Knowing she would not be able to sleep much, she volunteered to take the first night watch with Siban and Meran.

The evening was unseasonably warm, the nip in the air tempered by breezes from the south. The buzz from night hoppers seesawed from the darkness, their mating song a comfort as Rell patrolled the perimeter of the warded boundaries of the manor.

This was the third watch she'd taken, but the first she'd actually done by herself. Siban's constant vigilance rarely left her time alone. She stared at the night sky, realizing how much she enjoyed and needed privacy. Once social and outgoing, she now preferred solitude.

Keeping with protocol, she guided her Tell outward to the far corner of the warded area. All was as it should be. She let it seep beyond the distance she normally extended her powers. Always she endeavored to improve her skills, to become stronger, striving to regain the level of power she had experienced as a Bane.

Her senses ghosted across an aberration, instantly drawing her attention. No taint of Bane bit against her skin, but neither had she ever felt this kind of disruption in her surroundings.

A sparkle winked at the corner of her vision. She snapped her head to the right, but the object had disappeared. Again she sent her Tell toward the area she thought she'd seen the light. Her awareness flickered across the anomaly again and then it winked out.

Straining to see beyond the dark line of trees, she prowled the edge of the perimeter. Nothing appeared out of place. Still, she couldn't shake the feeling that all was not as it seemed.

She crept along the warded barrier until she reached the opposite end. The sensation of a thousand stinging bees spread along her arms. Without warning, searing heat burned through her body and gathered in her palms. She fisted her hands, trying to control her Bringer reaction to a nearby Bane. Juna had explained what would happen when encountering demons, even going as far as saying the reaction would be swift and powerful. That seemed a bit of an understatement.

Rell stepped away from the border. Though protected by the wards, she couldn't get careless and cross onto unprotected ground. Thin spindles of lightning sparked between her fingers and palm when she clenched and unclenched her fists, trying to get control of her power.

She inhaled a calming breath. The action soothed her nerves, but also brought with it a scent of the familiar. With a slow, silent exhale, she focused her awareness several yards beyond the ward near the forest. Her Tell slithered across the ground like an encroaching fog until it found the demon. Her pulse quickened. Though he had been lurking the night of her transformation, she'd not felt him since.

"Icarus?" She took a small step forward. "I know you're there. It's me, Rell."

He glided out of the darkness, his black skin gleaming in the light of the near full moon, each muscle cut to perfection in the blue glow. His yellow eyes remained fixed on her and his strides closed the distance. He stopped a mere foot beyond the boundaries.

Silence stretched between them. His stare skated over her, taking in every inch of her human body. With caution, she opened her senses and tried to gauge his response. A chaotic consciousness filled her mind, crowding her soul. She staggered against the overwhelming force and slammed her mental shields down to block out the familiar and unwanted darkness in which the Bane dwelled. Now free from her demon form, she could no longer bear the suffocating touch of the desolation.

"You have changed." The deep bass of his voice drifted across her like warm air over her chilled skin. His words hovered somewhere between a question and a statement.

From what Rell had gleaned from conversations within

the manor, the Bringers feared Icarus the most. Besides Vile, he would eventually be the most hunted. Though she'd never voiced her thoughts to anyone, including Siban, her time spent with Icarus in the Shadow World had told her there was more to him than the soul-sucking Spoil he'd been labeled as.

"Yes." She rubbed her hands against her arms. "They found my body and healed me."

He continued to stare at her. The wind whispered in the canopy of the trees and the low song of the night hoppers began again. After several seconds he asked, "Is it…good?"

His question, so full of desperate hopefulness, tore at her heart. Tears welled in her eyes and spilled down her cheeks. She swallowed hard, pressing her lips together against the lump rising in her throat, and nodded. Another awareness skated through her, probably Siban sensing her distress. The thought that he was always with her, even during her private time, irritated Rell. She pushed his presence aside and refocused on Icarus. She understood his question, his need to know not how they'd healed her, but that they'd rid her of the darkness. "Yes." She sniffed. "It's very good, Icarus."

Though nearly imperceptible, she saw his posture relax. He attempted a smile, but only succeeded in curling one corner of his mouth, which looked more like a sneer, and exposed a white fang. "You are smaller than I thought you'd be."

A giggle threatened to trickle from her, but Rell managed to keep it suppressed. Instead she crossed her arms. "Don't underestimate me, Bane."

"Ah." He paced along the perimeter of the ward. "Bane is it? I guess it is only natural that we should now become foes."

"No." She let her arms fall to her sides. "I don't believe that." She took a step forward. "You once said that I was different, like you." She matched his pace. "What if you had once been a Bringer too?"

He stopped and peered at her. "A Bringer? Me?"

"Could it be possible?" Since her transformation, she'd thought about him often. The way his body had been warm like hers. How he had no memories beyond being a Bane. "What if Vile took your soul? What if your body is frozen in the Shadow World—like mine was."

He was silent for a long time, contemplating her words. "I have lived for a thousand years, Rell. Do you not think I'd know if Vile had hidden my human body?"

"Did you know about my body?" She wanted to believe he hadn't. "Or the other Bringers?"

He stopped suddenly and faced her. "No, I did not. It seems there is much my father has done without my knowledge. But I don't think I was ever anything other than what I am now."

His agitation ricocheted off the ward. She didn't know how far she could push him. Maybe giving him something to hope for would drive him to find the truth and help them on their quest. "Perhaps Vile is not your father." She cleared her throat. "Perhaps he's been toying with you all this time."

The darkness inside Icarus swelled at her words, beating at her. His reptilian eyes pierced her, as if assessing whether or not *she* was the one who was toying with him. The air suddenly shifted. Icarus's head snapped up, and he scanned the sky. He thrust his wings outward and crouched, but it was too late.

From above a heavy net dropped over him. Rell screamed, understanding dawning. Icarus thrashed under the weighty tangle, but couldn't get free. Like a hundred beating drums, the thump of wings sounded overhead. Three dragons dropped from the sky. Their claws gouged the earth when they settled.

Unsure what to do, Rell rushed forward, intent on protecting Icarus. The dragons shifted. Rhys, Gregory, and Luc cut off her course and tackled Icarus, taking him to the ground.

"Don't hurt him." They didn't understand—didn't know

Icarus like she did. She hurled her body at the melee but was yanked backward before she reached them. "Let me go."

Siban wrapped her in a hug she couldn't get free of. "Rell, calm down."

"Let me go." She landed a solid kick to Siban's shin but he didn't release her. She watched, helpless to make them understand that Icarus didn't mean her any harm. Tears welled and spilled down her cheeks. "He wasn't going to hurt me."

The fight bled out of her once the three Shields pinned Icarus's limbs to his body and rolled him over. They pressed him against the ground, each man struggling to hold the much stronger demon down.

More Bringers appeared, flooding around Rell and Siban to join the fight. Jade walked past her, but didn't stop to comfort Rell or even meet her eyes. Raising her hands, she spoke the chant to un-ward a small section of the barrier. Her actions could only mean one thing. They were planning on imprisoning Icarus within the boundaries.

Ravyn, Meran, and Juna strode to where Icarus now lay motionless. All the fight seemed to have left him.

"If you don't fight us, Bane, you will remain unhurt," Rhys said.

Icarus turned his head to the side and sneered at him. "It is you who should be concerned about being hurt."

Luc pulled back his arm and leveled a solid punch to the demon's jaw. Icarus's head smashed into the ground. "Just returning the favor for the time we shared in the Shadow World."

"Please, Icarus, don't fight." Rell struggled against Siban. This time he loosened his hold. With a jerk she pulled completely free of his grasp and stepped away. "Why are you doing this?"

"To protect you." Siban pointed to Icarus. "Though you refuse to see it, he is dangerous."

Rell looked from Bringer to Bringer. "You knew he would come here and you set this trap." The betrayal of being kept in the dark swamped her. She glared at Siban. "You knew and you didn't tell me?"

He didn't reply. There was no need. She knew the answer.

She swallowed back her panic. "What are you going to do with him?"

"Imprison and interrogate him." Gregory's words were blunt and held no delusions that if need be, they'd kill Icarus. "Do what we must."

"He didn't hurt me. You've got to listen to me." She took a step forward but Okee blocked her path. She glanced from him and then back to the group. "There is something different about him. Icarus is more like me than Vile."

"Impossible, there is no humanity in that beast," Siban spat. "You and he are nothing alike."

She spun to glare at him. "Just because you don't want it to be doesn't make it so. I know what I'm talking about. Why aren't you listening to me?"

"Because you're not thinking clearly." He shook his head. "What you say sounds like something you wish to believe, not something that is true."

"Wishing we could heal him isn't wrong. If he can be healed, I'll do whatever it takes." She shook her head. "Nobody deserves the punishment he's endured."

"You care for him more than you should." Siban's jealousy spilled from his tight words.

"As I would care for anybody who needed help." She lifted her chin, daring him to reprimand her further. "When did you become my decision maker?"

"I love you. That's why I protect you."

"I don't need you to take care of me. I'm not a child."

"Enough." Gregory's command sliced through their

stalemate. "This won't be solved tonight. Right now we need to get him into the cell and re-ward the walls."

More than anything, Rell wanted to rage against all of them. Frustration seized her and it was painfully apparent that even though she was no longer Bane, she still wasn't fully included with the Bringers. The fact that Siban knew and didn't tell her of their plan was the worst betrayal. Where did that leave her? Once again she had no place in the world, neither Bringer nor Bane.

Meran, Juna, and Ravyn stationed themselves at three points around the men and Icarus. Rhys, Gregory, and Luc hoisted the demon onto their shoulders but didn't proceed forward. He no longer fought against his captivity.

The three sisters extended their arms in either direction and began chanting. Words Rell didn't understand filled the night as if magnified tenfold. White light erupted from their fingertips and connected, forming a circle around the men and Icarus.

"What are they doing?" Rell's panic welled gain, certain they were hurting him.

"The light will protect him from the wards," Okee said. "He'll be safe once he's inside the cell."

At his words more threads of white light shot underneath Icarus and upward in an arch, making contact with the other side. What looked like an egg-shaped net of light surrounded but didn't touch him.

"Let's get him inside," Gregory said.

The group of men moved forward and the three sisters mirrored their pace. White light continued to surround Icarus and their words resonated through the night air. Rell turned and watched them move steadily across the ground, but she had no inclination to follow. Being in the cell herself had been bad enough. Watching another being imprisoned was more than she could stomach—no matter what the situation.

Jade raised her hands again, moving them across the space in the barrier. Her soft words hissed from her and Rell could feel the wards fall back into place. When finished, Jade turned and walked to her. With silent comfort she placed a hand on Rell's shoulder. The depth of her sister's concern seeped into Rell's skin like a warm blanket, but she was in no mood to forgive any of them for their betrayal. After a few seconds, Jade slid her hand from Rell and walked away.

"Come back to the manor," Siban said.

Even though she knew he acted out of worry, his statement sounded more like a command. She needed to be alone. The last thing she wanted was to listen to all his reasons for why she should not help Icarus. "I still have two hours left on my patrol."

For a few seconds Siban didn't say anything. His distrust scraped along her awareness, making it clear he didn't trust her.

"We'll talk when you return." He hesitated, but when she didn't reply, he nodded. "I'll see you back at the manor."

He turned and strode in the same direction as the other Bringers.

Rell pivoted and paced along the ward's borders. How could she make the Bringers listen to her—especially Siban? Why couldn't he trust her? She wasn't some witless female, who had led a sheltered life. Far from it. Daily, he hovered over her as if she'd shatter into a million pieces the minute something went wrong, but the situation tonight was something different all together. They'd used her as bait to draw Icarus to them. She stomped along the ground, letting her anger feed the dark stain on her soul. Though she knew she shouldn't, she let the rage of betrayal wash through her. She stopped and stared into the darkness. Sparks of blue light tingled at her fingertips. Cupping her hands, she let the brilliant light pool in her palms. The Bringers plan had worked and they'd gotten what they wanted at the expense of her trust.

Rell gritted her teeth and thrust the pulsating blue orbs at the ward. They passed through, unrestrained, and struck a tree beyond the ward. The trunk splintered, sending chunks of bark in all directions.

At times like this, she missed being a Bane. The ability to fly away from her problems and hide in the caverns had far greater appeal than facing this situation head on. Emotions she wasn't used to crowded inside her. Her throat tightened and she forced down a swallow. How was she supposed to do what was right—both for her own conscience and the group?

She turned and paced a course in the opposite direction, trying to tame her anger to a manageable level. Tomorrow she would talk to Gregory when Siban was not around. Perhaps she could get him to see that Icarus was more than the soul-sucking demon the Bringers believed him to be. If not, how would she live with the guilt knowing she'd been given a new life but he'd been condemned for what was the same offense—being a Bane?

CHAPTER EIGHT

Siban rubbed his face with his hands and yawned. Sleep hadn't come easily last night. Rell hadn't returned to the room before he'd fallen asleep and when he'd awoken, she was already dressed and gone. In reviewing last night's incident he felt confident that he'd acted appropriately. She was too close to the situation and wasn't thinking clearly. No matter what her feelings were for Icarus, Rell needed to learn that he couldn't be trusted under the best of circumstances. Though he had to wonder what exactly her feelings were for the demon. Her reaction had been fierce and it hadn't taken his Tell powers to know she'd felt betrayed.

The words he'd needed to smooth things over escaped him. He loved Rell, but even now she was a paradox. The dark stain of being a Bane still tainted her soul and he sensed that she hadn't fully embraced being back to her human form. Her reaction to Icarus had been intense — too intense. The safety of the Bringers trumped personal feelings. What she wanted was for him to trust her. And that was something he couldn't give her right now.

Siban rolled his head from left to right, trying to release

some of the tension that had built between his shoulder blades, and tightened the belt that held his sword around his waist. Tomorrow at dawn they would leave for the Shadow World, and though he wouldn't admit it to anybody else, it was not a journey he looked forward to.

Old nightmares had resurfaced, as if he was reliving his days of torture. In the light of day he could bury the scenes and pretend they didn't eat away at him, but how he would react once back in the place where he'd been imprisoned for nearly two years, he couldn't say. The added conflict with Rell only burdened him more.

He made his way down the staircase and into the Great Hall, stopping just inside the door. Rell sat with Meran and Gregory, speaking in low tones. Unease crept over him. As much as he wanted to, he didn't trust her when it came to Icarus. Was she trying to manipulate the other Bringers into believing the demon was different? He stiffened his spine, trying to repress the pang of jealousy pushing at him. With a deep inhale, he stuffed his emotions down and set his mask of detachment in place.

When he approached, Rell looked up, but didn't smile. "Good morning."

"Morning." He gripped the hilt of his sword. Thankfully his voice remained steady, hiding his agitated state. "Did you sleep well? You must have come in after I fell asleep."

"We have no training this morning so I didn't wake you."

The fact that her statement hadn't answered his curiosity about where she'd slept didn't escape him. He nodded. "That was kind of you, but you needn't have taken such pains."

"Come." Gregory stood and indicated his spot at the table. "I'll tell Delphina to bring you food. I have a few tasks to attend to before the day gets started."

Siban wondered if those tasks involved Icarus. Certainly

he'd interrupted a private conversation. And since none of them seemed inclined to include him, he slid onto the bench next to Rell and reached for the pitcher. "Would you like some?"

She shook her head. "No, thank you. I've already eaten."

"Anxious about tomorrow?" he asked, pouring the ale into his mug.

"We all are, I think," Meran said. "Speaking of which, I suppose I should help your mother and Delphina with provisions." She stood. "Though I doubt they'll let me do much."

"They're very territorial of the kitchen," Rell said.

Meran laughed. "That's a good way to describe them. Perhaps they'll let me peel a potato or scour a pot."

"Good luck," Rell said.

They watched her walk away. When she was out of hearing distance he turned to Rell. "You three looked cozy. What were you talking about?"

She didn't look at him. "Icarus."

"What about Icarus?" His words came out sharp, the demon's name leaving a bitter taste on his tongue.

"Meran agrees with me. We can't completely discount his interest in my transformation." She swirled her spoon in her porridge, still refusing to meet his eyes. "He may even be able to help us."

As he'd suspected, she hadn't dropped the subject. Siban snorted. "Help us? Have you gone mad?"

She did look at him then, her eyes narrowing and her mouth drawing into a thin line. "They agree."

"I'm quite certain Luc would disagree. Have you forgotten the torture he endured at the hand of Icarus? Or how about Ravyn, whom he speared with his talons? For every Bringer who supports your claim I can give you two who do not." Rell didn't reply. He slammed his fist on the table. "Is my time in the Shadow World so easily dismissed?"

"That's a cruel thing to say." She refocused on her food, her voice dropping to a whisper. "I will never forget that time."

"Then why do you insist on believing there is something more to Icarus than there is?"

"Because I need to," she hissed. Snatching up her bowl, she stood. Her eyes burned into him. "If there is a chance he was once human, he will need our help." She stepped over the bench. "Nobody should be forced to live as something they were not meant to be." She shook her head, her expression laced with what looked like disappointment. "It makes me wonder why you fought so hard to save me."

"You are not like Icarus."

"Can you be so sure?" Not waiting for him to reply, she spun and stomped toward the kitchen.

He watched her stiff-spined retreat, knowing their difference over Icarus would not be solved by Gregory's and Meran's support. The demon had caused too much devastation and showed no remorse for it. Rell and the demon were nothing alike—even if she claimed otherwise. She couldn't be. She was his Rell. Damaged, but strong. The Bane hadn't broken her and he'd be damned if he'd let Icarus weave his web of lies and draw her back into the darkness.

"You seem vexed." Delphina set a bowl of porridge in front of Siban and began clearing the dishes left by the other Bringers. "Though I suspect you have a lot on your mind with the upcoming journey."

"Yes." He dipped his spoon into the hot gruel. "We all have much to worry about these days."

He took a bite but the porridge turned sour in his stomach. No longer hungry, he stood and picked up his dish.

"I'll take that if you're finished," Delphina said. "Just pile it on the tray."

"Thank you." He did as she asked. The woman smiled at

him and then went back to collecting the empty serving dishes. In an effort to lighten his mood, he attempted small talk, something he was neither comfortable with nor good at. "How did your talk with Jacob go?"

She set a stack of bowls on the tray and beamed at him. "Couldn't have gone better. He said I could buy whatever I needed for Lady Rell's gown. Said he'd be happy to pay."

"Jacob is a generous man."

"Yes he is." She blushed slightly. "But then, everybody at the manor is. Makes each day of livin' here a gift." She hefted the tray. "Well, best get on with my chores. We've got a quest to prepare for."

"Yes we do." He tipped his head in a quick bow and walked from the hall, heading for the armory.

Inside, Magnus and another Bringer named Trace sat sharpening the weapons they had gathered from Jacob's storage and those the Bringers had brought with them.

"What can I help with?" Siban picked up the axe Luc had found in the Shadow World and examined the edge. "This blade is already sharp."

Trace motioned to the two identical daggers lying on the table where the axe had been. "Immortal weapons don't appear to need sharpening."

"That will come in handy during battle," Magnus said. "That Bane hide is thick."

"I remember." Siban set the weapon back on the table.

"Grab one of these." Magnus motioned to the pile of swords. "And a sharpening stone. They all need a good edge on them."

Remembering his own blade, Siban pulled his sword from its sheath and took a seat on a short stool. With the stone in his right hand, he ran it along the edge numerous times and then flipped it over to do the other side. After he finished, he picked up a thick dagger from the pile and did the same. Neither of the other men spoke. Each of the Bringers sharpened two knives to Siban's one. Trace's nimble fingers slid along the blades, testing each edge and then tossing it into a pile.

The three worked through the day, only stopping for the noon meal. Once all the blades had been honed, they checked the sheaths and harnesses for tears or weak stitching. Throughout the day Bringers trickled in to claim several weapons each. For his efforts, Siban developed a blister on his thumb and his back ached from hunching forward. By the evening meal, the weapons had been doled out and a small bag of provisions had been given to every person leaving on the quest. When Siban entered the Great Hall, the smell of roasting meat surrounded him. A low grumble from his stomach answered the tantalizing odor.

Most of the group was already assembled, including Rell. She sat between Jade and Ravyn, and from what he could surmise, the three were talking about the interior of the Shadow World. Siban took a seat near Rhys and was instantly presented with a heaping plate of food by Willa.

"Thank you."

"Eat up." She patted him on the shoulder. "It might be the last hot meal you have for a while."

"Cheery thought," Rhys said.

Small talk flowed around Siban but he ate in silence. The group seemed more sedate than usual, the gravity of tomorrow's trip obviously weighing on more people than just him. Halfway through the meal Gregory stood and walked to the head of the table.

"Before we retire tonight, I wanted to say a few words." He leaned a fist against the table and looked at the group. "I know I don't have to tell you how perilous tomorrow's journey will be. I think it's evident in everybody's expression." His gaze tracked to each of them. "It is imperative that we stay together as much as possible once in the Shadow World."

Siban glanced at Rell, whose eyes were fixed on the king with an intensity that belied her anxiety. Despite their disagreement, he wished he was sitting next to her so he could ease her worries.

"We don't know what to expect once we enter the Bane's domain." The king made a sweeping gesture with his hand. "Though some of us have knowledge of the interior and the workings of the demons, it is wise to expect the unexpected."

The crowd remained silent, though Siban noticed that Jade shifted to lean against Luc. He wrapped his arm protectively around her. Once again Siban looked at Rell. She sat ramrod straight and unmoving. After dinner he would go to her, let her know he was there to protect her—to give his life for her, if it came to that.

"As all of you know, one of the unexpected turns we've had already is Icarus," Gregory said.

At that Rell looked at Siban, staring at him for a second before looking away. There was no mistaking her message. She would do as she pleased—what *she* felt was right for the Bringers. He gritted his teeth, worrying about what drove her obsession to help Icarus. Was it merely her desire to right the wrongs of the Bane or did her feelings for the demon run much deeper? No matter what, protecting her was going to be more difficult than he'd expected. Trusting her even more so.

"It appears he's taken an interest in Rell's transformation. We've got him locked in the cell we used for Rell now, but at some point we're going to have to deal with him," Gregory said. "Though I'm still unsure what decision will need to be made, after consultation with Rell and Meran, we believe Icarus might be of some use to us. His actions seem more personal than spurred on by Vile's influence."

"Why do you say that?" Luc's voice held a hint of malice, understandably so.

After being lured into the Shadow World by Rell and Icarus, the demon had tried to force information from Luc by torturing him. Siban caught his eyes and gave him a nod of agreement.

"We think there might be a chance he was once human and that until Rell was transformed, Icarus was unaware of the possibility." Gregory shrugged. "This may mean nothing."

"It was my understanding that we'd finally rid ourselves of the demon once we garnered information." Luc pulled the immortal dagger from its sheath at his belt and buried the tip in the wooden tabletop. "If you will not do it—then I will."

"You have every right, Luc, but I'm asking for patience in this matter." Gregory paused. "From all of you. If Icarus *was* human, he's been Bane for far longer. I've never had direct contact with the demon, so I am not in a position to offer my opinion until I speak with him further. I do however put great stock in Meran's Tell abilities. And from what Rell has said, there are enough differences between Icarus and the other Bane to indicate several possibilities."

It would take more than the word of the two Tell women to ever convince Siban, and from Luc's stoic expression, him as well.

The decision to keep Icarus alive was foolish. He felt it clear to his bones. "Be done with him, Gregory, and spare us all a lot of trouble."

"So now you are judge and executioner?" Rell said.

"If need be." He didn't look at her, not wanting to see the anger he felt emanating from her. "I will do what it takes to keep you safe."

She didn't reply.

Their leader held up his hands to stay the argument. "I'm

not saying that we trust him or even interact with the demon. But we should not act rashly. A captured foe may be of more use than a dead one." He lowered his arms and sighed. "We'll be leaving at first light. Get some sleep. Meran and Rell, I'd like you to come with me when I speak with Icarus."

"I will come, too," Siban said. "I want to hear his words for myself."

Gregory hesitated. "Only if you remain calm and silent."

That would be easier said than done, but he needed to assess the situation for his own peace of mind. "I will try."

After a few seconds Gregory relented. "Come then."

The Bringers rose, their low conversations about the quest and the revelation about Icarus swirling around Siban. He stood and made his way to where Gregory waited. Rell approached. Words seemed awkward. It would be best to let the situation unfold instead of trying to defend his opinion that Icarus should die.

The day's heat had abated when the sun dipped below the horizon. Besides the whir of night hoppers the evening was quiet. Their footsteps swished in the grass. No one in the small group spoke, perhaps each lost in their own thoughts about how to deal with the Demon King's son Icarus. As they drew closer to where the demon was housed, the burn of the Bane intensified. Siban noticed Meran lightly brushing her hand back and forth against her arm, but Rell appeared unfazed.

Gregory stopped at the door of the same hut where Rell had been kept. His hand hovered on the handle. "I will speak first. If you have questions, keep them simple so that he is unable to weave lies within his answers."

The three of them nodded. More than hearing Icarus's explanations, Siban wanted to use his Tell to ferret out the Bane's lies. For most definitely there would be many.

The demon stood in the middle of the cage. Perhaps he'd

been expecting them. Maybe he had heard them coming. Siban was struck with how little he'd asked Rell about her time as a Bane. It was a situation he would remedy tonight.

"Good evening, Icarus." Gregory led the way into the room.

"Perhaps good for *you*, Bringer. Not for me." The Bane didn't move except for his eyes, which followed them as they moved closer to the cage. "Are you here to interrogate me or dispatch me?"

Rell stepped forward and Siban had to restrain himself from grabbing her arm and pulling her out of the demon's reach. "We'd like to ask you a few questions. We think we might be able to help you."

Icarus inched forward but stopped when Siban moved to stand beside Rell. She glared at Siban. He was headstrong with obviously no intent to stand down. But he wasn't willing to risk her safety. If Icarus got hold of her, they would be at his mercy. Siban didn't want to have to make the choice of her life or the demon's freedom.

"You needn't worry, dark one." The statement sounded too suggestive and was directed at Siban. "I wouldn't hurt Rell."

Jealousy tore at him. Even if what Icarus said was true, he knew the demon was goading him. His weakness for her was a weapon the Bane could now exploit. "Forgive me if I don't believe you."

"No, I'm sure you don't." Icarus glided to the stone wall and then turned back to face him. "I'm sure you'd like nothing more than to rid yourself of me — permanently."

A humorless smile curved Siban's lips. "Then we understand each other well, demon."

Rell scowled at him again and then turned her attention back to Icarus. "Will you answer some questions for us?"

He was silent for a few seconds. Certainly the demon would not willingly help them. The entire inquiry was foolish in Siban's opinion. To his surprise and suspicion, Icarus inhaled deeply and said. "Ask. Whether I answer or not is yet to be seen."

"Thank you." Rell turned to Gregory. "What do you wish to know?"

A grunt escaped Siban. Would the other three Bringers truly believe what the demon said? One comforting thought was that if keeping Icarus became too perilous, there was no doubt Luc would help Siban vanquish the Bane. Secure with that knowledge, he backed away from the cage, allowing Gregory to take his place.

"What is your relationship with Vile?" their leader asked.

"He is my father." The answer was curt. "And my king."

"From your tone, I surmise you've had a falling out." Gregory paced a few steps along the front of the cell. "Where do you stand now?"

The demon's eyes cut to Rell. "As I'm sure you know, I've been banished from the Shadow World."

Siban let his Tell creep forward, attempting to get a genuine sense of the demon. The biting against his skin increased. The closer his awareness inched, the more suffocating the demon's darkness became. The truth of Icarus's words emanated through the thick taint, giving Siban pause. At least that part of his story rang true.

"And does that order still stand?" Gregory stopped and gripped the iron bars of the prison. "Are you and Vile still at odds?"

"Why do you want to know how my father and I fare?" Icarus turned his back to them. "What difference does this make? I am still a Bane and you are my sworn enemy."

"We might be able to help you." Meran's soft voice seemed to snare the demon. He pivoted and leveled a look at her that hinted of hope and desperation. Like a moth drawn to a deadly flame, she approached. "We helped Rell."

"How?"

The group was silent. Coaxing information from Icarus with the suggestion of helping him was one thing. Divulging the process was quite another. Siban snorted. "You must think us fools if you believe we would tell you how we transformed her."

A genuine smile stretched across Icarus's mouth. "Yes, I would have." He crossed his arms over his chest. Muscles bulged at his shoulders and biceps. "Still, you can't expect me to give and not receive something for my cooperation."

"I suppose it's your freedom you want?" Siban said.

Icarus lifted his brows in acknowledgment.

"That's something we can't offer right now." Gregory's fingers slid from the bars. "I had hoped we could come to an understanding. What we need to know is what Vile is planning. Is he attempting to open the Abyss and for what purpose."

The smile evaporated from the Bane's face. "Yes."

His direct answer surprised Siban. The truth of it punched his awareness.

"Vile wants nothing more than to command those imprisoned within." Icarus hesitated. "An undefeatable army."

"But the Abyss is merely a prison for those Bane whom the Bringers have vanquished, correct?" Meran asked.

"You would know more of this than I, my lady." The demon's tone softened each time he spoke to her. Siban glanced at Rell, gauging her reaction to Icarus's obvious interest in Meran. "Other than my father's threats, I have never been privy to where the Abyss is hidden or what it houses."

Gregory's shoulders sagged. "Then we know nothing more than we did a few hours ago."

"I find it hard to believe the son of the Demon King wouldn't know about the Abyss," Siban said.

"Then you do not know my father. He reveals only what he

wants, gives only when it serves him."

"Like father, like son, eh?" The retort gave Siban a small measure of victory. At this point it seemed insults were the only punishment he'd be allowed to inflict on the demon.

"Less than you would think," the demon replied.

"If that is the case, then help us defeat him." Meran said, approaching. Rell stepped away from the prison. "We can try to heal you. We helped Rell and she says you are like she was."

A tightness formed in Siban's chest. What Meran promised would only bode trouble for them. The demon couldn't be trusted. Unable to listen to the ridiculous promises the three would probably offer, Siban turned and stormed out the door.

Chilled air buffeted his skin, cooling some of the gnawing itch that the Bane's presence caused. The fact that the other three couldn't see that Icarus was dangerous and not to be trusted sent a wave of panic through Siban.

He needed an ally, somebody who believed as he did.

Luc.

• • •

She should have followed Siban when he left. His frustration had nearly swamped her, but trying to convince Icarus to help them, and in return help him, had been too important to abandon. More than anything, she wanted Siban to understand why she needed to help Icarus. The thought of living with the utter desolation that infused a Bane's soul was unthinkable to her.

And it wasn't only Icarus she was thinking about. If the Bringers could figure out how to return other demons to their human bodies, they might be able to gain an upper hand over Vile. Her gratitude for being transformed was something she couldn't put into words. Wouldn't the other Bane be just as grateful to escape the darkness?

Maybe it was too much to expect Siban to understand. He'd been held prisoner in the Shadow World, even tortured, but he'd never lived with the growing malice that consumed a Bane's soul. The slow loss of her humanity and compassion had eaten away at her, day in and day out—suffocating her attempts to feel the things that gave life purpose.

Rell pressed her hand against her chest. Her heart beat rapidly under her touch. The memories of those dark days could still grip her, stealing her breath and rational thought. She swallowed hard and exhaled silently.

The door clicked behind Meran and Gregory, leaving her alone with Icarus. Siban would have never allowed it, but with the warded bars and ground, Gregory seemed confident that Icarus could not escape.

"Do you trust me, Icarus?" she said.

He wasted no time with pretending. "No, I do not trust you."

His statement hurt. For whatever reason, she'd wanted to believe they'd built a connection, no matter how tenuous.

"You look troubled." He smiled, amusement dancing in his yellow stare. It was a little startling to see genuine emotion on the demon's face. "Did you think we were friends?"

"Maybe not friends." She rubbed her arms, trying to erase some of the sting his presence caused. "But I thought there was more between us than just enemies."

He cocked his head to the side. "I believe that is true. We have a—bond. I don't trust you because I don't trust anybody." He locked his hands behind his back and slowly paced a path along the front of the cell. "To live between two worlds, neither accepted by the Bane any longer and yet loathed by the Bringers is an unsettling predicament." He stopped and looked at her. "I don't need to tell you this."

"No, you don't. That is why I wish to help you."

"And you think I should readily believe that the Bringers will welcome me with open arms?" He paused. "Have they welcomed you, Rell? Is there no doubt in your mind that all of them trust you?"

She didn't reply because she didn't like the answer. Jade still tiptoed around her, acting as if at any minute she would shatter. And Siban had made it clear that her view on the situation with Icarus was skewed. The other Bringers didn't know her well enough to trust her. How could they when their first encounter with her had been as a Bane?

"I can see the answer on your face." His voice softened. "Rell—" She looked at him. "It is far easier to do and believe what I have for a thousand years than it is to change."

Propelled by his confession, she walked the few steps to the cell and wrapped her hands around the bars. "You would never say that if you were finally free of the darkness." Tears tingled behind her eyes and her voice dropped to a whisper. "It is glorious."

When he moved toward her she didn't retreat. He stopped a few inches away. Slowly, he lifted his talon and caressed her cheek. Though it took great effort, she stayed the urge to pull away. "Why do you care so much?"

"Because..." She covered his hand with hers. "If Vile has tricked you all these centuries, you deserve to know—and be free."

He dragged his hand away from her. "I cannot be redeemed. The stain on my soul is too black."

"And if you are returned to your human form, that stain will crumble to ash and blow away along with everything else that is Bane."

She didn't tell him that the taint of the Bane was never fully gone, but she wanted to give him hope.

Turning his back on her, Icarus walked to the center of the

cell. "I will think about what you have said."

When he didn't continue, she released the bar and walked to the door. Before leaving, she said, "I do care about you, Icarus. Not what you can do for us, but for you."

With that she pushed open the door and quietly closed it behind her. She released her pent-up breath and leaned against the uneven wood of the door, trying to gain her composure. Tomorrow morning, before they left on their journey to the Shadow World, she would speak with Gregory again and tell him about their conversation. It might be enough to guarantee Icarus's safety until they returned. If they returned.

A light breeze ruffled her hair and she pushed away from the door. An owl hooted in a tree to her right. Rell extended her awareness, making sure no dangers lurked between her and the manor. Bugs whirred their songs, calling to each other, but there were no other sounds. Stars twinkled above her, giving her hope. From all she'd suffered at the hands of the Bane, maybe her suffering could be used to help those who had been captured as she had.

Her mind drifted back to Icarus. There was no guarantee that he had ever been human. Only her gut instinct and Tell hinted at the difference between him and the other Bane. She prayed that what she felt was true. The tide against the Bane would most certainly change if Icarus rallied with the Bringers.

Low voices floated from the opposite side of the manor wall. Rell stopped to listen, recognizing the two men. Siban and Luc. Their words were difficult to understand. She crept a few feet closer and pressed her body against the stone wall of the outbuilding.

"I don't trust Icarus. It's as if he has a hold over Rell."

"That bloody demon should be nowhere near the women," Luc said. "And it wouldn't surprise me if he had used his evil to bewitch her. Their relationship goes beyond my understanding."

"I thought once she was no longer demon, her loyalty would shift completely." Siban was silent for a second. "But the touch of the Bane is insidious."

"It's best we don't let that infection spread, eh?" Luc said.

"Then you're with me?" Siban's question sounded hopeful.

"After what that demon did to me, I'll take great pleasure in sending him to his comrades."

Were they planning on vanquishing Icarus? Anger rushed through Rell. Not waiting to hear more or reveal herself, she jogged to the manor and up to their room. It wasn't as if she didn't understand Siban's reasoning. He'd been tortured for two years by Vile and Sha-hera. To him, the Bane were all the same—except for her. For whatever reason, he had seen her differently, even when she had been a demon. Maybe it was the same instinct that drove her to want to believe in and help Icarus.

She shut the door behind her and walked to the center of the room. Unseeing, she stared at the cold hearth. What was she to do? Siban's and Luc's hatred of the Bane could jeopardize the opportunity to gain the upper hand in their war effort. Still, she couldn't blame either of them for the way they felt.

The door to the chamber opened and Siban came in. He stopped inside the door. "I didn't think you would be here."

"Where else would I be?" She attempted a casual tone, but failed.

"With Icarus." He closed the door behind him. Not looking at her, he crossed to the hearth and stoked the fire. When the flame had grown to a sustainable size, he turned and looked at her. "Are you tired?"

He didn't sound angry with her. Some of the tension eased from her shoulders. "No. You?"

"No." He moved to the chair and sat, reclining against the back. "Too much on my mind."

Dark circles pooled under Siban's eyes, giving him a look that went beyond fatigue. Perhaps mentally weary from his inability to let down his guard. Since she'd been transformed she'd only seen him take his ease once. It had been the first night they'd made love. From that point on he'd seemed determined to protect her no matter the cost to himself.

Fool.

Desire to forget about tonight's event won out over needing to react to Siban and Luc's threat against Icarus. She would figure out what to do later. For now she needed intimacy. Even if it was only for a few hours, she wanted to numb the despair being around Icarus had caused.

She walked to him and held out her hand. "Maybe we could find something to occupy our time."

He stared at her and after several seconds a slow smile curved the corners of his mouth. He nodded and took her hand. "Maybe we can."

CHAPTER NINE

Golden light from the fire flickered against the stone walls of their chamber. Siban wanted more than anything to feel Rell's body against his and push all thoughts of Icarus and their mission away. His smile faded. "I don't want to fight, Rell." He ran his finger along her cheek. "I just want to hold you in my arms."

"I don't want to fight either." Her fingers twined around his hand more tightly. "So let's not discuss anything but us."

"We are my favorite subject." He bent and kissed her. "I missed you today."

She scrunched up her face. "We've been together all evening."

He waved a tan finger at her. "No talk of this evening, only of today."

"Fine." She gave him a mischievous smile and walked across the room to the bed. Sitting, she wrapped her arm around the tall poster. "Siban, what did you do today?"

"Mostly sharpened weapons and repaired tack." He perched on the edge of a leather trunk and leaned forward to rest his elbows on his knees. "How about you?"

"I attempted to help cook." She rolled her eyes. "Mother kicked me out after an hour and told me to find Brita. Mainly I brushed horses, cleaned their hooves, and tried not to dwell on the fact that we're leaving for the Shadow World in the morning."

"Did it work?"

She lifted her eyebrows. "No."

For the past several days they'd had many discussions about the mission, but she had never spoken of her apprehensions about entering her former home. "It will be all right, Rell."

Her smile melted into an intense stare. More than anything it appeared she needed to believe that entering the Shadow World didn't mean she would lose everything she'd regained.

He stood and walked to her, kneeling at her feet. "I promise, we will come out of this alive, and be stronger than ever."

She cupped his face between her hands and pulled him toward her. The soft brush of her lips ghosted across his. He let her take the lead, sensing that she needed to feel in control tonight. Her kiss deepened. Siban opened his mouth, and her tongue slipped inside to stroke his.

Her hands traveled down his neck and slid along his shoulders, pushing his coat off. The garment slipped to the floor, puddling at his feet. His fingers itched to unlace the green tunic she wore, but he repressed the urge. She tugged at the ties of his tunic and lifted the shirt over his head, adding to the growing pile on the floor.

For several long seconds she stared at him, her hands traveling across his chest and drifting lower to the waist of his pants. Again she undid the tie. His erection strained against the material and the tip of his growing cock peeked out the top. She pushed his pants open and gently stroked the head. A groan escaped him and he pressed into her hand, indulging in the feel of her firm grip sliding over the sensitive tip. She searched his face, as if watching his reaction. Again she slid her hand up and back over his shaft.

His breath hitched. "That feels so good, Rell."

Her expression intensified. "Teach me how to please you."

"You already please me."

She shook her head. "Not like that." She swallowed hard. "Teach me how to pleasure you. Show me what you like."

Not wanting to be presumptuous, he asked, "You mean pleasure me other than making love?"

She nodded. "I want to learn."

He exhaled deeply. "All right."

Standing brought his erection to mouth level. As he removed his boots and pants, her gaze never left him, devouring his every movement. When he stood before her naked she reached and ran her fingers along his shaft.

Spikes of pleasure tingled along the tight skin. Her cautious exploration was torturous and wonderful. She looked up at him. "What now?"

"To pleasure me with your hand—" He wrapped his fingers around hers and drew them upward to the head of his cock. "You stroke me here." He pumped into her hand twice. "Then slide your hand downward and back up." He held out his other hand to her. Tentatively she placed hers in his. He drew it downward and cupped her hand against his tight sack. "Massage here, but gently."

With perfect pressure, she rubbed her fingers along his balls, the tip of her index finger stroking the sensitive skin just behind. Siban's head fell back to rest against his shoulders.

"Yes, just like that."

For several minutes, Rell experimented with different pressures and speeds, pumping her hand down the length of him. He gripped the bedpost, not wanting to stop her, but unsure if he could hold his climax much longer.

The innocence of her exploration only heightened the pleasure she was giving him. Without warning she stopped and looked up at him. "Can I pleasure you with my mouth?"

Bless the Saints, his knees nearly buckled. He only hoped he could contain himself long enough to teach her what she needed to know. "Yes, you can."

"And do you like it?"

"Yes." His answer came out raspy and forced. "Very much."

She smiled, her grin a little too mischievous. "Then teach me."

He fumbled for a simple explanation—one that wouldn't frighten or disgust her. "Basically everything you've done with your hand, you do with your mouth."

She paused for only a second before lowering her head to his cock and taking him into her mouth. Moist heat surrounded him, making him grow larger. Her eyes rounded and she pulled free and examined his thick shaft. "It moves, as if it's alive."

He cleared his throat. "Because what you're doing feels very good."

"Ah." She turned her attention back to his cock and took him into her mouth again.

Siban's grip tightened on the bedpost, trying to resist the urge to push into her. Her lips traveled farther along his shaft with each seesaw motion she made, until she'd taken the full length of him. The erotic view of her head moving back and forth heightened the pleasure of the experience, increasing the building sensation at the base of his cock.

When her hand cupped his sac and she took him deep once again, Siban thought he would die. Unable to control himself, he threaded his fingers through her hair and fisted it at the back of her head. With little pulses he pumped into her mouth, making sure not to choke her.

Rell slid from the bed and knelt in front of him, continuing to worship him with her mouth. Though tentative at first, her actions became bolder. Releasing his cock, she wrapped her arm around his hip and grabbed his ass, gently pushing him back and forth.

He let her take the lead, the experience of being at her mercy lending an erotic spin that drove him near the edge. Sparks of pleasure prickled at the base of his cock and he knew that he wouldn't be able to withstand the sublime torture much longer.

"Rell, I'm going to come."

He tried to pull away, but she made a sound of protest and held him tight to her mouth. The hand cupping his balls moved to grip his cock, her mouth working up and down with a rapid rhythm. After every three or four strokes she would pause at the tip and suck, and then resume the motion.

Unable to pull her free and not wanting to, Siban rode the wave of pleasure building inside him. Her hand moved down his shaft, quickly massaged his balls and continued back up to stroke him as her mouth sucked the head.

Words became impossible and he was unable to warn her when his climax hit. He gripped her head with both hands to hold her steady, pumped twice into her mouth and came. She squeaked. Instantly he released her, but she didn't pull away, but instead took every drop of him.

His body convulsed and the sensitivity around the head of his cock became excruciatingly wonderful. She released his ass but continued to gently, almost lovingly, lick him until the last shiver of pleasure had rippled through his body.

Unable to stand any longer, Siban lifted Rell from her kneeling position and fell onto the bed. Her arms went around him and he buried his face against her neck, trying to catch his breath. When finally he could speak, he pulled back. "Thank you."

"By your reaction I guess I did it correctly?"

He laughed. "I'd say you have a natural talent for it." He rolled Rell onto her back and covered her body with his. "Now it's my turn to please you."

With one hand she brushed his hair out of his face. "Not tonight."

Confused, Siban furrowed his brow. "But I want to. It's not fair that I should find my release but you don't."

"Let me give this to you." She ran her hand along his shoulder. "The best thing you could do for me tonight is hold me in your arms."

Though disappointed, an inkling of understanding trickled in. She'd assessed that by giving him release, it would allay some of his anxiety. What she needed was to feel safe. He nodded.

"Come, let's get you undressed." He slid from the bed and held out his hand. She eyed him suspiciously. "I promise I will only hold you in my arms." He arched a brow. "Unless you beg me for more." He pulled her to her feet. "Then I will be very willing to oblige you, my lady."

With slow movements he unlaced her tunic and pulled it over her head. The garment she wore underneath was like nothing he'd ever seen before. It came just below her breasts and had long ties that wrapped around her torso, causing the material to crisscross. He unwound the ties and scooped the garment from her shoulders, exposing her breasts. His fingers itched to strum the pink tips, but he resisted the urge, determined to keep his promise to her.

He knelt and lifted her right foot, pulling the soft boot free, and then repeated the action on her left. The smooth skin of her stomach and upturn of her breasts taunted him to let his fingers stray up her soft belly. Instead he untied the lace at her waist and slid her pants free. Now before him, she stood completely bare. Rell watched him as if assessing his strength of will.

Determined to prove himself, he stood and pulled back the covers. "My lady."

Rell smiled and climbed onto the bed. He followed her and wrapped her in his arms, pulling the duvet over the top of them. She snuggled against him, her firm curves pressing against him and causing his cock to tighten again, though she seemed not to notice.

"What are you thinking about?" He ran his fingers along her arm. "You seem preoccupied."

Her index finger made small loops on his chest. "I'm sorry."

His hand stopped. "Are you thinking about Icarus?"

It took a few seconds for her to reply. "Yes." She rolled to look at him. "I know you don't agree with me, Siban, but I cannot help how I feel."

"You're right, I will never agree with you when it comes to that demon." Jealousy bit at him and it took all his strength not to point out that thinking about another man, whether human or Bane, while naked in bed with her lover was the worst kind of insult. "I don't wish to talk about him."

She didn't speak for a long time and Siban could feel the tension in her pose. Though he wished he could stand united with her when it came to Icarus, his history with the Bane would not allow him to.

After several minutes Rell said, "Get some sleep. We leave early."

He swallowed his ire, not wanting to start out their journey with anger between them, and kissed her on the forehead. "Sweet dreams."

They lay wrapped in each other's arms for some time before his eyelids grew heavy. Rell's chest rose and fell with a deep and even rhythm. He tightened his hold, nestled her closer, and closed his eyes. At least for the moment she was his. Tomorrow he and Luc would save the Bringers from their own stupidity and rid them of Icarus once and for all.

. . .

The fire had died by the time Rell chanced moving out of Siban's embrace. As quietly as possible, she slipped back into her clothes and crept to the door. Sending up a little prayer for silent hinges, she pulled the door open. A tiny *squeak* froze her in her exit. She glanced at Siban, but he didn't move. Daring another few inches only, Rell squeezed her body through the narrow opening.

All the braziers in the hall had been doused, making it difficult to see in the darkness. She released her Tell and sent it out around her. Bits of information indicating the path to the stairs ricocheted back to her. On silent feet, she wound her way down the steps. A long bolt lay across the door, locking them in. She pushed against it, trying to lift it, but the wood was almost too heavy for her to lift alone. What she wouldn't have given for some of her Bane strength.

Squatting, she positioned her body under the brace and lifted, doing most of the work with her legs. The rough grain dug into her hands as the barrier lifted. Once above the iron rest she tilted the bolt and rested the end against the stone frame of the door. Inch by aching inch, she lowered it until the end touched the floor.

Tremors vibrated along her arms. She pushed the wood upright and settled it against the door's archway. After waiting a few seconds to make sure the bolt wouldn't fall and wake up the entire manor, she inched open the front door and slipped out.

Four of the Bringers were patrolling the boundaries of the grounds. She would have to keep to the shadows and hope that Gregory hadn't set an extra guard on the building where Icarus was being held.

Continuing to use her Tell, she wove her way across the yard, coming around the backside of the outbuilding. No alarm registered back along her awareness. Only the taint of Icarus scratched against her skin.

After scanning the area one more time, she slipped around the side and through the front, pulling the door closed behind her. A single torch burned on the wall opposite the cell. Deep shadows cast across the floor of the small room and the air was cooler inside than out.

Icarus reclined on the pallet that had been arranged for her while she had waited for her healing. The sight of him at ease took her aback. He slowly rose and walked to the center of the cage. They stared at each other. His eyes narrowed on her and she knew he understood her intent to free him.

He answered her silent announcement. "And how do you propose to accomplish such a feat?"

For the first time since she'd decided to help him escape did she realize she had no way of getting him from the cell to outside the wards. The grounds were warded throughout, though she wasn't sure how high up the boundaries went.

"It seems your noble deed is thwarted even before you get started."

"No." She held up a finger. "I don't accept defeat so easily."

Icarus moved forward. "And what will your lover say about you helping me."

It was a question she didn't want to answer. "That's not your concern. Now, let me concentrate."

Rell had listened to Jade speak the ancient words of the warding. If Rell could remember them correctly, perhaps she could create a path wide enough for him to pass safely through.

She knelt at the door of the cell and closed her eyes. The ancient words whispered from her. A subtle shift in the vibration of the room rippled along her skin. She pressed her hands to the dirt floor and directed her intention at the wards.

What felt like the parting of water spread out in front of her. Hopefully this was the correct way to un-ward. If not, Icarus would be burned the second he touched the ground. Her progress was slow. Each foot of floor required her complete attention. Sweat beaded on her forehead and her thighs ached from squatting and moving. She sensed Icarus's unwavering focus on her as she worked her way backward. His anticipation was palpable, goading Rell to continue.

When she reached the door, she stood and placed her hands against the wood, continuing the chant. The sensation of clearing seeped upward. Certain she'd done the best she could to clear a path, she opened the door. Before exiting, she sent her Tell outward. Again, all seemed quiet. She squatted again and laid her hands on the area just outside the door. From here Icarus would be on his own. There was nothing she could do if the ward extended over the manor, but she was positive he would take that chance.

She reentered the building and snatched the heavy cell key from the hook near the door. Thankfully, Gregory had said the ward would be powerful enough to hold the strongest demon. Still not meeting Icarus's eyes, she unlocked the door and pulled it open.

"I think I did it." Not fully trusting him, she stepped to the side, making sure she stood within the warded area. Though she helped Icarus escape, she wouldn't chance him abducting her. "But know that I can't be sure."

He took two long steps forward and stopped at the entrance of the cell. "Why are you doing this?"

Her eyes met his. "War makes enemies of those who were once friends. It changes people and makes them do what they normally would not. I choose not to look at my enemies as a group, but as individuals. Each Bringer, human, Splinter, and even Bane have their own story. If I can help you, I will."

"And what of the others?"

She took his question to mean the Bringers. "I don't plan on telling them that I helped you escape, but they may figure it out." She inhaled and released her breath. "I'm willing to take that chance."

Though the emotion flashed across his face, Rell recognized his confusion. Without further questions Icarus lifted his foot. It hovered above the ground. Rell's breath hitched in her chest, praying he wouldn't burst into flames. His foot stepped solidly on the dirt floor just outside the cell. Nothing happened.

Again the breath rushed from her.

Icarus smiled and took another step.

"Walk directly to the door. Keep your wings folded until outside. I cleared a small area outside, but I don't know how far up the wards soar."

He nodded and edged toward freedom. Paralleling his path, Rell followed him until she reached the door. Before stepping out, he turned to her. It seemed that he struggled to find the right words. Finally he straightened, tipped his head toward her. "Perhaps I will be able to return the favor one day."

With that, he stepped into the night and launched himself into the sky. Rell remained rooted in place. Doubt beat at her like a swarm of angry bees. But the decision had been made. Icarus was gone and there was no sense in second-guessing her reason or the outcome. She only prayed that she hadn't just made the biggest mistake of all their lives.

CHAPTER TEN

Their respite from the chill fall air was over. Rell's breath billowed around her face as she secured her pack to a small, spotted mare. She'd ridden when she was a young, but that was thirteen years ago and she hoped she wouldn't embarrass herself.

Last night she'd slipped back into bed with Siban none the wiser to her nocturnal activity. When she'd awoken this morning he'd been gone. She'd quickly dressed and made her way downstairs, but Siban and Luc were missing from the great hall.

Her gaze searched the grounds and froze. Both men were striding across the frost-covered grass, their expressions dark. Rell returned her attention to securing her pack and tried to act natural.

"He's gone." Luc stopped in front of Gregory.

"Who?" the king said.

"Icarus. The bloody demon escaped."

Murmurs circled the group. Rell yanked on the strap of her bag and then turned to face the crowd. Siban had stopped behind Luc and was now staring at her, his look of accusation apparent. She waited for him to call her out to the rest of the group. It was his right and she'd prepared herself for whatever consequences may befall her. But he said nothing.

"How?" Juna stomped toward the men. "The entire building and cell was warded."

"Perhaps wards aren't as effective with Icarus." Meran's gaze slid to Rell for a second and back to the crowd. "Or maybe he knows how to break them."

"That must be it," Ravyn said. "I can't imagine he would have voluntarily touched the wards and been burned just to get back to the Shadow World." She shuddered. "It's a horrible sight."

"I agree." A heavy sigh eased from Gregory. "Well, there's nothing to be done about it now. Mount up and stay vigilant. It looks like we have one more demon to worry about."

The other Bringers turned back to their tasks but Siban started on a direct path toward her. It took all her willpower not to cower on the other side of her horse. She stiffened her spine and held his glare.

Inches from her, he stopped, his face so close to hers his breath brushed her cheeks. "It was you, wasn't it?"

"What was me?" She lifted her brows and widened her eyes. Ignorance seemed like the best course of action.

"You helped him escape." He glanced around, lowering his voice even further. "Just as you helped me."

"I heard you and Luc plotting to vanquish Icarus." She pushed her face toward him. "I couldn't let you do that."

"Why, because you care for him?"

"Because he doesn't deserve to die."

His lip curled into a sneer. "So you seduced me and then betrayed me?"

She gave him a humorless smile. "I could ask the same of you. What was your plan, to kill him this morning before we left on our mission? No one would be the wiser until we returned?"

Her accusation seemed to snap him back to reason. His jaw clenched and unclenched, until he huffed out his frustration. "I only want for your safety."

"You want my safety under your conditions. Soon you'll figure out that I make my own decisions. If you can't accept that…" She left the threat hanging between them.

He looked around, making sure none of the others were listening to their exchange. "Icarus is a demon and not to be trusted."

"Just like I was."

Siban shook his head. "No, you were never like him."

She adjusted the stirrup and mounted her horse. Peering down at him, she said, "Yes, I was."

She spurred her horse forward, leaving him to stand alone. At some point he would have to start listening to her, but she was done fighting. For too long she'd been a prisoner to the darkness that grew inside the Bane. Now free, she wouldn't bow down to one man's idea of how she should feel or what she should believe. She knew what she knew and Siban either needed to start valuing her opinions or not be a part of her life.

A lump formed in her throat. He'd been her rock since her transformation and the thought of being without him sent a tiny wave of anxiety through her. But she couldn't be with a man who sought to be her keeper instead of her partner.

The dangerous reality of their mission pushed through to replace her depressing thoughts. Fears about reentering the Shadow World crowded in. It seemed no matter how hard she tried, she couldn't detangle the riot of feelings she was plagued with. As a Bane, that hadn't been a problem. Now her emotions were like leaves swirling in a windstorm, fluttering around her head.

The hollow *thump* of hoofbeats sounded behind her. Siban

pulled his mount next to hers and stopped. Neither spoke, the strained silence stretching between them. Finally, he relented. "I'm sorry. I shouldn't have accused you of seducing me for the purpose of betrayal."

She shifted in the saddle to look at him. Of all the things to apologize for, that must have felt the most honest to him. She would accept his peace offering. Though at odds over Icarus, she still loved Siban. "I never want you to think that I am in our bed for any other reason than because I want to be there."

He nodded but didn't say anything further.

"Is everybody ready?" Gregory's asked. He strolled among the Bringers, pulling on a pair of leather gloves. "The sun will be up in an hour and we need to be on our way."

Jade stomped past Rell and Siban. "I didn't think I'd ever have to get on another damn horse again."

"It won't be so bad," Luc said, following her. He glanced at Rell and winked, his outrage over Icarus's escape obviously usurped by his love's discomfort. "She still hasn't recovered from our last journey."

Rell smiled. "Just make sure she doesn't fall off."

"It wouldn't be the first time," Luc said.

"I heard that," Jade tossed over her shoulder.

The urge to snicker welled inside Rell, but she repressed the impulse in order to save her sister's pride. It comforted her to know others were nervous about this mission too—for whatever reason.

She glanced at Siban. "Thank you for not saying anything to the others about…last night."

"My intent isn't to get you in trouble."

"I know." She nodded. "It's to keep me out of trouble."

He lifted his brows at her acceptance of his concern, though she refrained from clarifying that acknowledging was not the same as submitting.

Once the Bringers had mounted, Gregory held up his hand. "We'll ride in single file to hide our numbers. Keep talking to a minimum and stay alert. We don't want to get separated. Besides the Bane, there are bands of highwaymen on these roads and in the woods. Though probably not a threat to us, we'd still like to keep our progress as incident-free as possible."

Gregory gestured the group forward, with him taking the lead. Juna walked her black mare along the line, double-checking everybody and then took her spot at the very end. Anticipation rolled through the group. Rell strengthened the barriers of her mind. With emotions high it was difficult not to feed into everybody's anxiety and excitement, but she needed to remain as focused and as calm as possible.

Willa stood on the step with Jacob, Delphina, and Delphina's children. The group waved at the departing Bringers, their expressions sullen.

Hayden's small voice called across the grounds. "Good-bye, Rell."

A knot formed in her throat. The boy had been standoffish since her conversion back to human. Only within the last day had he ventured near her, skulking around corners and hiding to watch her as she trained. Not wanting to frighten him, she'd let him take his time.

She held up her hand and waved. "Take care of everybody while we're gone, Hayden, and when I return we'll go hunting."

His wiggled free from his sister's hold and ran to the edge of the top step. "I will, Rell. I promise."

She couldn't help but smile at his serious tone. No doubt the boy would be ever vigilant while she was gone. She sent up a prayer to the Sainted Ones that she'd be able to keep her pledge to him.

The line moved forward, the horses' hooves crunching against the frosty grass and the leather from saddles and reins creaking in the cold morning air. She pulled her cloak more tightly around her shoulders and glanced back at the manor. The three adults were walking back inside, but Serena and Hayden continued to watch them.

How quiet the manor would be now that the Bringer horde was gone. Rell stared until Willa disappeared inside. They had said their good-byes this morning. If and when she returned to the manor, her mother wouldn't be there.

She shifted in her seat and focused forward, suddenly very happy that she was not staying behind. Having to wait for the return of the Bringers and helping her mother prepare for her departure home and back to her other life were tasks that would have probably driven her mad with worry and boredom.

Golden rays of the sun topped the rise of the hills, bathing the treetops in light and setting them aglow. The air seemed to grow chillier with the ascension of the sun. Nobody spoke. Besides the morning songs of the birds, only the snorting of the horses and their heavy footsteps could be heard. The quiet lulled Rell into a relaxed state. She continually scanned the surrounding woods, searching for anything out of the ordinary, but nothing seemed amiss. Not even Icarus's presence registered against her senses. She wondered if he watched from afar, purposely keeping far enough away and avoiding detection but worrying about where he was and what he was doing was a waste of time. She refocused her Tell on the area around her and pushed Icarus from her mind.

They'd been traveling for about an hour when a woman's cry shattered the quiet. Gregory held up his hand, stopping the line of horses. Jerked from her relaxed vigilance, Rell's body tensed when her Tell came upon the caustic gnawing of the Banes' presence. Gasps rippled through the group, but were quickly hushed. Gregory made a motion to dismount.

Rell untied her cloak and let it pool on the saddle before

dismounting. If she had to fight, she wanted as much freedom as possible. She placed a hand against her horse's neck, sending calming thoughts to the animal in order to keep it quiet. The horse remained still even when the woman's cry filled the air once again.

Gregory turned and pointed to Juna, Rell, and Siban, and then made a motion to move forward with him. Instantly Brita was beside Rell, taking the reins from her hand and leading her horse toward the back of the group.

Rell followed Gregory and Juna in the direction the scream had come. The blood quickened in her veins and she gave a slight start when Siban's hand touched her shoulder. His stare was intense and worried, but she was ready for this. She gave a weak smile, trying to assure him she could handle the encounter. It's what they had trained for.

The four moved in a single line, creeping through the dimly lit forest. Thick undergrowth threatened to trip Rell. She opened her mind and let her senses skate forward. Information rippled back to her, warning of the possible branches or deadfall that might cause her problems or snap and thus alert the Bane to their presence.

The urge to rub her arms was almost unbearable but she resisted by focusing on her Tell and assessing the information it was feeding her. A familiar sensation brushed against her awareness—Siban. He was with her, gliding forward and searching just as they had practiced at the manor. Together they scanned the area several yards in front of their group, foreboding growing, the closer they traveled to the scream.

Then she felt it. The black void of a demon. No, not one demon—four. She held up her arm, extending four fingers. Her companions nodded. Gregory indicated that they should spread out. She and Siban moved to the left. Juna stayed in position and Gregory moved farther to the right.

The woman screamed again, her cry originating approximately twenty yards in front of them. The grunts and laughter of the demons filtered through the trees. The Bringer group increased their pace until they reached a line of oaks ten feet from their target.

Four Demon Bane had trapped the woman. An unconscious man lay on the ground next to an overturned basket. The demons slashed at the young woman each time she lurched toward her companion. Tears streamed down her cheeks and sobbing pleas heaved from her.

Rell scanned the Bane, her focus landing on the largest of the group. Her heartbeat quickened and fire rushed through her body, pooling in the palms of her hands. She ground her teeth together in an effort to control her Bringer reaction. She knew this Bane—Nab. When she'd first been brought to the Shadow World and changed, he'd been one of the demons that had held her down. His foul breath had spilled over her like rancid soup and he'd taunted her with threats of torture and rape. Nab had sliced her gown with his talon, peeling it away from her body and had brutally groped her breasts, cutting her skin. His rough tongue had slithered along her cheek, his sharp fangs had scraped against her delicate skin.

Rage filled her and her vision shifted to a haze of red, blocking out all rationalization. Thoughts of revenge swelled inside her. Without waiting for Gregory's command, she straightened from her crouch and strode forward. Vague awareness of Siban's horror beat against her but she ignored it, letting her fury carry her forward.

It took several seconds for the Bane to notice her. She stopped just beyond the line of trees and cleared her throat, causing the demons to halt their torment of their victim. "I see you're still torturing women, Nab."

His yellow eyes narrowed and he stepped away from the

group, moving toward her. The demon wore a thick leather vest, studded with metal points. A black brand that looked like two arrows jutting from a spiral had been burned into the gray skin of the demon's forearm. He was just as repulsive as he had been thirteen years ago.

The need for vengeance spurred Rell to open her mind, letting all her Bringer powers rush through her in a giant wave. Euphoria gripped her. It was as it had been when she was a demon, powerful and unstoppable. Before Nab went three steps, she hurled a fireball at his head, purposefully missing him.

All four of the demons dove to the ground. A rush of pure joy coursed through her. "I suggest you let the lady and her companion go before I incinerate all of you."

The other three demons scrambled to their feet and started to back away.

"Stand your ground, idiots." Nab rose to his full six feet, his yellow gaze driving into her. "I've seen you before." He took a step toward her. "Where do I know you from?"

She leaned her shoulder against the tree and crossed her arms and legs. Siban's anger pounded against her. Instead of ignoring it, she let it wash over her, giving her strength. "I'm hurt that you don't remember our time together. Let me refresh your memory. Thirteen years ago."

He stared at her and she could see him trying to place her face. After a few seconds his eyes widened. He ran his black tongue along his misshapen lower lip, smacking as if about to eat something tasty. "You're that Bringer girl Gust brung in."

She smiled sweetly. "So nice of you to remember."

"But you were turned by one of Vile's private guards." His head wove from side to side like a snake. "Ain't no way that you're the same girl. Maybe she had a twin."

"No." Rell pushed away from the tree and lowered her arm to rest her hand on the hilt of her sword. "I've no twin and I've waited thirteen years to repay you for what you did to me that day in the Shadow World."

Fear flashed in Nab's eyes but he quickly recovered and laughed. "You think you're gonna to take us four on with that tiny sword and those little balls of fire?"

Juna's presence was suddenly inside her mind, commanding that she stand down. Unlike Siban, whose demands were not strong enough to breach her own desires, Juna's order left no room for argument. Like a net being cast over a swarming school of fish, Juna captured her powers and reined them in, taking with it her elevated bravado.

"Absolutely." She shrugged, acting as if she hadn't just lost her courage. "Well, me and my friends."

The three Bringers moved from between the trees to stand on either side of Rell.

Gregory pulled his sword from its sheath. "And you won't be returning to the Shadow World, demon."

Fire raced along the blade. He'd always worn the sword but Rell had never given it a second thought. Of course it would be an immortal weapon. He was the Bringer King. At least until they found his brother.

The three demons turned and ran. Juna and Siban raced after them, though as far as she knew, neither carried anything other than a mortal sword. Sensing his defeat, Nab turned and bolted in the opposite direction of his companions. Something powerful and foreign welled up inside Rell, demanding its release. The restraints Juna had put on her snapped and ancient words spilled from her lips. She lifted one hand, pointing it toward Nab. As if hitting a solid wall, the demon slammed into an invisible barrier, his body frozen in a state of fleeing.

Gregory looked at her. "How are you doing that?"

She shook her head and her hand began to quiver. "Kill him!"

He hesitated only a second and then sprinted to where Nab stood, unmoving. Gregory pulled the sword back and uttered a flurry of ancient words. Rell's body trembled from the effort of holding the demon. Though he couldn't move, Nab was fighting her, trying to send the black evil of the Bane into her mind.

She screamed as the familiar malevolence clawed at the mental shields she'd erected. With a thrust of his sword, Gregory drove the blade deep into the demon's chest and then pulled it free. Not waiting, he turned and sprinted toward Rell, scooping her around the waist as her knees buckled. Half dragging, half carrying, Gregory maneuvered her into the shelter of the trees.

Nab's screams filled her head. She slapped her hands over her ears and slid to the ground, watching the demon convulse. Siban and Juna exited the trees and stopped to take in the scene.

"Grab the woman and man and get into the trees. Hold onto something," Gregory yelled.

Without hesitation, they ran to the two people. Siban jammed his sword into his sheath and hoisted the man's arm around his shoulders, Juna did the same on the opposite side. They dragged him toward the woods.

"Come on!" With his free hand, Siban grabbed the woman's wrist and tugged her behind him.

She stumbled, but let him lead her.

A large black hole formed behind Nab. His screams ricocheted through Rell's mind, sending spikes of pain through her head. Suddenly the agony and his howls ceased. Dead silence filled the woods. She slowly sat straighter and looked around, but Gregory wouldn't let her go.

"Hold onto the tree." He shoved her hands against the rough bark.

Just as she tightened her grip the breath was sucked from her body. Gregory wrapped his arms around her and grabbed onto the tree as well. Rell coughed, trying to suck air into her lungs but it was as if no air existed. Her legs slid out from under her, drawn toward the black hole growing within the clearing. By panting she managed to get a shallow breath.

Branches and rocks rolled toward the hole. She pressed her mouth and nose against her shoulder to shield her face from the leaves and sticks flying through the air. Her body lifted from the ground. Gregory tossed his leg over hers, smashing them back down.

Nab screamed again, this time his howls were not in her head. She looked at the demon and gasped. His body was stretching and being sucked into the black void, headfirst. A roar like thunder rumbled through the clearing and the ground shook. Small trees uprooted and flew toward the black hole, smashing into Nab's body.

First his arms disappeared into the blackness, followed by his shoulders, and finally his head. All at once his legs slipped inside, and he was swallowed completely. The hole expanded and pulsed. The image reminded Rell of a huge black mouth chewing its prey. Another peal of thunder rumbled through the clearing and the black hole vanished.

Her body dropped, suddenly feeling many times heavier than it really was. Gregory's knee pressed into her stomach and she gasped, pulling in a lungful of air as cool wind swirled around her.

He rolled off her and to his knees. "Are you all right?"

Rell coughed and released her grip on the tree. Her fingers ached from clawing the bark to avoid being dragged toward the void. "Yes. I'm fine." She stumbled to her feet but rested her hands on her knees. "What was that?"

His breath came out in short pants. "That was the Abyss of Souls and from its strength I would say it's getting very full."

"The Abyss?" She straightened and stared out at the now empty clearing. "Sweet Sainted Ones, that was horrifying."

He nodded. "It is not supposed to be pleasant."

Siban raced from the trees, his footsteps pounding across the clearing. Without stopping, he barreled into Rell, sweeping her in his arms and crushing her to him. Once again the breath rushed from her body.

"Siban." Her voice squeezed from her. "I can't breathe."

He released her and held her at arm's length. "Are you all right?"

She gripped his forearms in an effort not to fall. "Yes. I'm fine."

"What were you thinking by confronting those Bane by yourself." He shook her hard. "You could have been killed."

"But I wasn't." She circled her hands under his arms, breaking his hold. He reached for her again but she sidestepped him. "I'm not a child, Siban."

His mouth compressed into a hard line and his gaze narrowed. "Your actions would prove otherwise. We were to assess the situation and work as a team."

Embarrassed by his chastisement in front of Gregory, she turned her back to Siban. "It worked out for the best. Nab is dead."

Siban turned to the king for support. "Do you agree that she was careless, Gregory?"

Rell faced their leader. She *had* been careless but hadn't been able to stop herself. That was not something she would tell Siban. They'd only been on this quest for a little more than an hour and already he was harping on her—and already she had nearly gotten herself killed.

"I'm sorry if I overstepped my place, Gregory." She inhaled slowly. "He was one of the demons who helped turn me. One I had slated for revenge."

Gregory searched her face and after a few seconds he said, "You had every right to revenge yourself, Rell, but there are unknown forces we are dealing with. Next time we encounter the Bane, I must be able to trust that you will fight as one of the group, not alone."

She nodded. "Of course. I'm sorry."

"For now there is no harm done." Siban harrumphed but Gregory and Rell ignored him. "Where are Juna and the others?"

"Across the clearing." Siban glared at Rell. "The man was still unconscious, but the woman said they were on their way back to Illuma Grand."

"Bringers?" Intent on going to assist Juna, Rell took a step, but Siban blocked her path.

"I will help Juna. Go get the others. We will need their help." He continued to scowl at her, lowering his voice. "We will speak more about this later."

Rell stepped away from Siban but didn't reply. She had been rash, but the woman had needed help. Instinct had taken over and until Juna had reined her in, she'd been more than willing to take the four demons on herself. Though she wouldn't admit it to Siban, she knew her actions had been careless.

"Guide them over to the trees just beyond." Gregory pointed across the clearing. "It seems we'll need to make a stop at Illuma Grand to safely return these two—and find out if Lord Bagita has lost even more of his Bringers."

CHAPTER ELEVEN

It took all of Siban's willpower not to rage at Rell. He couldn't believe his eyes when she'd strolled directly into the path of danger, only thinking of her need for revenge. She'd been unreachable. Her anger had swamped him as he had tried connecting and corralling her back to their mission. Between that and freeing Icarus, Siban was starting to trust her judgment less and less—no matter how much she argued that her reasoning was sound. Now she sat on her horse, her spine stiff with defiance. He'd known she still struggled with the dark stain on her soul, but this was the first time he'd seen it manifested. With the other Bringers around he'd have to wait to say his piece until they were alone. Saints help her when he did.

The unknown woman sat in front of Gregory on his horse, and Trace supported the still unconscious man in front of him. It appeared the Saints had decided to smile upon them for a brief period. No other incidents disrupted their course to Illuma Grand. Siban didn't know how he would react if Rell acted so rashly again. He stilled his anger. And to think that they'd only just begun the journey.

They entered the gates of Illuma Grand a few hours after

sunup, and already the place bustled with activity. Their arrival caused quite a stir. Riding two abreast, the line of Bringers dominated the roadway leading to the palatial structure. The people of Illuma Grand pointed, some touching their chins and whispering, obviously knowing enough about Bringers to recognize Siban and the other Tells' more visible tattoos.

The white stone entrance of the main building stretched across the grounds, its archways teeming with inhabitants as they filed out to see what the excitement was about. Gregory stopped at the wide steps and dismounted before helping the woman down from his horse.

An older woman's cry ripped through the air, drawing all attention to her. She pushed her way through the crowd and ran to the young woman who had been attacked by the Bane, enveloping her in her arms. Three men clad in gray took command of the unconscious man and carried him through the crowd and into the first archway.

Siban and the rest of the Bringers dismounted, handing their reins to several more gray-clad men, who led the horses away. Rell stood amongst the activity with her arms wrapped around her like a shield. Siban moved to stand beside her and placed an arm around her waist. Instantly she relaxed.

"What is going on here?" said a large man from the top step.

Though Siban had never met him, he recognized Fromme Bagita at once. Ornately dressed, he wore enough gold around his neck to feed a small village for a year. Though only one of the ruling Bringer Council, the man held himself like a king, which from what they'd been told, was exactly his goal. The arrogant lord had no idea that the true king was already in residence.

While Gregory removed his gloves, he climbed the steps to meet Fromme. "My group and I encountered these two young people on our journey this morning. They had been captured by four Demon Bane."

Gasps and cries of shock traveled through those assembled, intensifying the din to a dull roar. From the smug look on Gregory's face, that had been his goal. Fromme's refusal to believe that the Bane were again rising was well known.

"Calm down." Fromme waved his meaty, bejeweled fingers in the air. "I'm sure Sir Gregory is exaggerating the situation."

"He's not." The woman they had saved from the demons pushed free of the older woman's hold. "We were a mile beyond the boundaries of Illuma Grand when we were set upon by Bane." She walked to the steps and climbed the first three, turning to the crowd. "The Bane are real, and they are after Bringers." She looked up at Fromme. "They said that Liam and I would make a nice addition to King Vile's collection."

Again the outrage of the crowd swelled, sending a wave of anger and fear through Siban. He clamped down on his mental barriers, trying to block out the people's panic. The emotions lessened enough for him to concentrate on what was happening around him.

"I'm sure you're mistaken, MaryBeth." Fromme's nervous stare bounced around the crowd and leveled back at the woman. "Perhaps you and Liam were sneaking away for an intimate rendezvous."

The older woman gasped and pushed forward, glaring up at him. "How dare you sully my granddaughter's reputation. She is a good girl, and Liam is a respectable boy. He has been severely injured but instead of helping him, you cast aspersions at him." She climbed two steps. "I want to know what you're going to do about this, Lord Bagita. Too many of our people have gone missing already. What are you doing to prevent the Bane from taking more of us?"

A heavy silence fell over the crowd, all eyes turning to their supposed leader, a man, in Siban's opinion, who had an interest in nobody's welfare but his own.

A greasy smile spread across Fromme's face in an attempt to distract the crowd. "I will meet with Lord Gregory." He paused and motioned toward their party. "And the rest of his people, and I promise we will figure out a solution."

Heads bobbed up and down with approval. The people began to talk amongst themselves, tossing out theories and solutions. Gregory motioned his party forward and a path opened, allowing the Bringers to pass. Siban's hand remained at Rell's waist and she made no attempt to detach herself from his touch. His ire lessened. It was obvious she struggled with not only her powers, but also with being a part of a now highly visible group. He would not add to her anxiety by stating his piece. What she needed right now was his comfort.

Lord Bagita led them through the marble halls, the *click* of his boot heels echoing off the high walls. Siban scanned the rooms as they passed them, but nothing registered as odd. People stepped aside but continued to follow them with surprised stares.

The group followed Fromme to the far end of a wide hallway. Two giant doors that looked as if they were made of gold spanned the width of the wall. Without stopping or knocking, Fromme threw the doors wide open and strode inside, taking his place in an oversized chair that reminded Siban of a throne.

Before entering, Gregory stopped and turned to the Bringers. "I need a group to stand guard outside the room and make sure we are not interrupted." He dropped his voice to a whisper, his gaze leveling on Juna. "See what you can find out from the people about any more missing Bringers. Also I need a group to search the Council Chamber. Juna will know what to look for. You have an hour at best."

Ravyn nodded. "I'll go."

"So will I," Jade said.

"Me, too." Rell stepped forward but Siban wrapped his hand around her arm, halting her. She looked at his hold and then at his face. "Let go."

The statement was laced with determination. Not wanting to cause a scene, he released her and stepped away. Though they were lovers, he was not her keeper, and she seemed bent on reminding him of that.

. . .

Rell thought that Siban would protest, and from the way he had grabbed her, the thought had crossed his mind. He had let her go, albeit reluctantly.

Though Juna was a powerful Tell, as witnessed by the way she'd bound Rell's powers this morning, and probably didn't need her help, Rell wanted to try and make up for her carelessness earlier. Reconciling the anger she'd felt when seeing Nab and understanding the overwhelming euphoria of power when she'd released her mental shields was difficult. Now, an hour after the incident, she could see the danger she'd put herself and the group in. The Bringers fought as one and would have risked their lives if she'd gotten in trouble. She pushed back the twinge of shame and moved to stand beside Jade.

The twins, Odette and Okee, took their post on either side of the chamber, and the remaining eight Bringers filed inside. Gregory gave the women a pointed stared before closing the door behind him.

"The best thing to do would be to head directly to the Council Chamber," Ravyn said. "We can work our way up from there and speak with the people once we've done our search."

"I agree. I've tried to search the chamber twice, but somebody has always interrupted me." Juna fell in beside Ravyn as they made their trek back down the hallway. "Hopefully this time we'll turn up something."

Jade gave an unladylike snort. "We always find something interesting when we visit Illuma Grand. It's inevitable."

"That doesn't sound too reassuring." Rell looked at her sister and smirked. "Then again, you do have a talent for finding trouble."

Ravyn glanced over her shoulder. "On that point we definitely agree."

"Me?" Jade glowered at her. "I'm not the one who charged into a horde of Bane."

Rell harrumphed. There was no defending herself on that point.

They continued back into the public area of the building. The beauty of the structure struck Rell. Never had she seen ceilings that soared so high or stone polished to such a glassy shine. The one prominent contrast was the dull gray outfits nearly all the people wore. Unlike Lord Bagita's opulent display of wealth, these mixed-blooded Bringers looked more like servants.

Juna and Ravyn led the way, both obviously knowing where the Council Chamber was located. Rell strode with her eyes forward, acting as if they had every right to be there. Nobody stopped them or asked if they needed help. The four took a wide staircase that spiraled downward. Rell poked her head over the railing. The drop was more than a hundred feet below them.

"How far down are we going?" Rell asked, hopping down two steps at a time to catch up.

"All the way to the bottom," Ravyn said.

They passed niches and alcoves that housed beautiful statues and paintings. Rell let out a low whistle. "There's a lot of money lying around Illuma Grand. I'm surprised somebody hasn't stolen these pieces yet."

"They have," Juna said. "We're certain that Bagita had replicas made and sold the originals. Most of these are fakes." She lowered her voice. "He's an idiot."

Jade glanced at Rell and smiled. The more she was around Juna, the more Rell liked her. Ravyn's sister had a no-nonsense attitude and didn't engage in a lot of small talk. That was something Rell could identify with.

"The pieces he didn't deem worthy of selling are actually the most valuable. Some are priceless, brought through the Mystic Arch during the Bane War," Juna continued. "But because they're not encrusted with gold and jewels, the imbecile thinks they're worthless." She shook her head. "All the better for us. At least if they stay within these walls the relics will remain safe."

"I'm liking Lord Bagita less and less," Rell said.

"He does have that effect on people," Ravyn replied.

As they continued their trek, the crowds of people thinned until nobody but the four of them remained. At the bottom step Ravyn peeked around the corner and then motioned them forward. Heat rippled across Rell's skin, sinking into her muscles. She shook her arms.

Jade looked at her. "You feel it too?"

"What is that?" She regarded the empty outer chamber. There was nothing but low-burning braziers and stone benches set into deep alcoves. The place had a hollow feel, as if nothing living should exist within the hall. She rubbed her arms to chase away a sense of foreboding. "It doesn't feel like the rest of Illuma Grand."

"This is sacred ground." Juna turned to face them. "The original site of the Mystic Arch."

The three women glanced at each other and then back to Juna. A thought occurred to Rell. "Original site? You mean the

Mystic Arch is still there?"

"Yes, this is where we entered when Gregory opened the passage. We didn't realize Illuma Grand had been built around the Arch." Juna scowled. "It's a blessing and a curse. If we can open the portal once the heir is found, then we'll be able to bring more soldiers through safely. They won't be set upon when crossing into Inness."

"That's fortunate, and would give the Bringers an upper hand," Jade said.

"Yes, but if our reinforcements are followed through the Arch by those who oppose Gregory, they could infiltrate this stronghold and bring down the wards."

"Best we don't let them through then, eh?" Rell said.

Her sister nodded. "But this won't be an issue unless we find the heir."

"And the immortal weapons." Ravyn looked at Juna, cocking her head. "That's why we're searching the Council Chambers, isn't it."

Her sister gave a single nod. "Yes, Gregory has long suspected that the weapons were hidden near the Arch so they would be easily accessible to the Bringers who crossed. He's searched the Chamber himself many times, but has found nothing."

"There is something about the Chamber," Ravyn said. "When the Council questioned me, it felt like the room itself intensified all three of my Bringer senses."

"That's why Gregory wanted us to try. My Tell is stronger than Ravyn's, but because she is part of the Trilation, she still has the abilities. With the two of us—" Juna pointed to Rell. "And another Tell, we are more likely to pick up on the subtle vibrations the immortal weapons give off."

"What if they've been moved?" Jade asked. "Luc and I found one of the daggers in the market of Faela. What's to say that somebody hasn't removed all of them?"

"Most likely that is what's happened." Juna strode toward the two ornately carved doors. Which is probably why Gregory hasn't found anything thus far."

Before Juna could reach for the handle, one of the doors creaked open and a woman slipped out. The stinging bite, similar to that of the Bane, bit into Rell's arms. The woman's bright orange shawl instantly marked her as an enemy. The *zing* of four swords being simultaneously dragged from sheaths rang through the hall.

From her time as a Bane spent ferreting out information about Luc, Rell had become all too familiar with the black magic clans. She held the point of her blade against the woman's neck. "A Splinter." Rell pushed the tip against the woman's skin. "Now what would a black-magic bitch like you be doing inside the Bringer fortress?"

A little cry slipped from the woman. She slowly turned to face them, her large brown eyes round with fear. "Please don't kill me." Her gaze bounced between the Bringers, searching their faces and dress, taking in information. "You're full Bringers—but how? I was told none of you existed any longer."

"Surprise." Jade slid her blade along the front fold of the orange shawl, pulling it away from the woman's body. "Are you here to steal?" She paused and gave a mirthless smile. "Or are you up to more nefarious deeds."

"Please, I am here by Lord Bagita's invitation." She pressed her hand to her chest, just below where the tip of Rell's blade rested. "Please don't hurt me. I have a daughter."

Juna lowered her sword toward the woman's stomach. "Even Bagita isn't stupid enough to allow you into Illuma Grand."

The Splinter swallowed hard, her eyes glancing at Rell, whose blade still pressed into her throat. "I dance for him."

Jade looked to her companions. "Is she telling the truth?"

"Of a sort," Ravyn said, lowering her sword but not sheathing it. "But she also lies."

"It's the truth. I enter through his private chamber." Her voice wavered. "Please, I've done nothing wrong."

"Done nothing wrong? What are you doing in the Council Chamber? It is off-limits to outsiders." Still holding her blade in place, Rell took a step toward the trespasser, closing the space between them to a mere few inches. "I can feel the Bane taint on you, Splinter." She laid the edge of her blade against the woman's neck and smirked. "I should know. I used to be one. So I suggest you tell us everything, because though these two might be willing to listen to your lies…" She flicked her head toward Jade and Ravyn. "I'd just as soon cut down every rotting bit of human filth the Bane has ever touched." She stepped back and let her gaze trail down and back up the Splinter's body. "And I'm certain that includes you."

Tears spilled down the woman's cheeks and she covered her face with her hands. Juna slid a glance to Rell, smirking and giving her a nod of approval.

Perhaps she'd over done the threat a bit, but in all honesty, it was exactly how she felt.

Ravyn cleared her throat. "What's your name?"

The Splinter sniffed and lowered her hands. "Fatima."

"Why are you here—besides dancing for Bagita?" Ravyn asked.

Though soft, Ravyn's voice filled the space. Rell resisted the urge to look at her, but it was difficult because she'd laced her question with a compulsion to respond.

Fatima sniffed again and straightened. "Please, they'll kill me and take my daughter if they find out I've been caught."

"Who will?" Again Rell pressed the tip of her blade against the woman's neck.

"Sha-hera and Vile." Fatima stiffened, as if preparing to be skewered. "They promised a better life for me and my daughter if I helped them." She broke into another sob. "I will do anything to keep my child safe."

"Apparently." Rell lowered her blade and looked at her companions. "What should we do with her? She can't be trusted if she's working for the Bane."

"What is Vile's plan?" Jade rested the tip of her sword on the floor between her feet, but her hand remained firmly on the hilt. "What were you orders?"

"I was to entice Lord Bagita into showing me the Council Chamber."

"To what end?" Ravyn asked.

Fatima shrugged. "I don't know. I was supposed to search the room for weapons and markings. That's all Sha-hera said."

The four Bringers exchanged glances. If Vile was trying to access Illuma Grand, then he more than likely knew of the immortal weapons and possibly the Mystic Arch. Not wanting to give the Splinter more information, Rell didn't voice her suspicions, but instead asked, "Are there other Splinters working with the Bane?"

Fatima shook her head. "I don't know. Sha-hera comes to me when she needs something done. I've not asked about any others."

"We can't leave her here to run around Illuma Grand." Juna slid her blade into her sheath. "From what I can tell, she's spoken the truth thus far." She pinned Fatima with a stare that would have quelled most men. "Is there more you're not telling us, more of Vile's plan?"

"No." The Splinter toyed with the fringe on her shawl. "I swear that is all I've been asked to do."

Ravyn looked at her sister. "You have more experience with this. What do you suggest?"

The older Tell stared at their captive for a few seconds before speaking. "There are other options for you and your daughter."

Fear laced with hope flashed in Fatima's eyes. "What other choice do I have? They will take her."

"They will take your daughter, anyway," Rell said. Her words came out harsh. "You are a fool if you think otherwise."

Juna placed a hand on Rell's arm, instantly calming the ire building inside her. "The Bringers will help you if you pledge yourself to their service."

"How can they protect us?" Though she sounded as if she didn't believe Juna, the Splinter's stance relaxed slightly. "The Bane are powerful."

Jade leaned forward, braced against her sword. "And you think the Bringers are not?"

A fireball appeared in Ravyn's hand. The orb pulsed in her palm, sparking and roiling.

Fatima's eyes widened and she took a step backward. "Please don't hurt me."

Rell had to admit; even she was impressed by Ravyn's control. A twinge of jealousy pushed at her, but Rell quickly smothered it. Perhaps one day she'd gain such control over her powers, but never would her abilities match Ravyn's or Juna's. Ravyn and Juna were part of the Trilation.

"I won't hurt you, but you must trust us, Fatima." Ravyn sheathed her sword and slid the flaming orb to her other hand. "We *are* capable of protecting you and your daughter."

Ravyn closed her fist, extinguishing the fire. The Splinter looked at Ravyn's empty hand and then let her gaze travel over the women. "And if I don't want your protection?"

"Then you are free to go." Juna waved toward the stairs. "But you will never be allowed into Illuma Grand again. We will make sure of that."

Surprised by Juna's acquiescence, Rell bit back her retort. How could she just let the traitor go? The Splinters were dangerous and from what she'd learned from Magnus, the perfect companion for the Bane.

"You'll just let me go?" Fatima asked.

"Yes, but think hard about my proposition." Juna folded her hands in front of her body and smiled benignly at the Splinter. "I doubt you'll get such a generous offer from the Bane."

Rell was struck by her words. Spoken evenly, they definitely held a threat. The woman's years of commanding alongside Gregory emanated from her, humbling Rell and her meager pride even more.

Fatima straightened. "I will think about it." She backed away from the four Bringers. "Truly I will."

They watched her walk briskly across the marble chamber, her fleeing footsteps silent. When she was gone, Rell turned to Juna. "Why did you let her go?"

"We cannot hold her or take her with us on our journey." Juna walked to the doors to the Council Chamber. "If she does indeed seek our protection, she will be more willing to help us since we showed her mercy."

"And if she does not?" Rell followed behind her. "What if she discovered something inside?" She laid her hand against the door, halting Juna. "And she takes that information back to Sha-hera?"

A look of patience crossed Juna's face. "I am confident Fatima found nothing inside." Juna pushed the door open, walked into the room, and stopped. "To the untrained eye it is just another magnificent chamber."

Rell's breath caught. Arches soared dozens of feet above her and an intricate pattern of circles made of colored tiles graced the floor. The design was familiar to her. She pointed. "This is the same configuration Gregory made with the knife before bringing me to full power."

"Yes, it's the sacred symbol used by the king in ceremony and in private prayer." Juna pointed to the floor. "The connecting circles symbolize the waves when a single drop of water hits the surface of a lake. Like those ripples, the king's prayers flow to all the people he rules, bringing prosperity and blessings to them and the land." Her expression softened and she looked at Rell, resting her fists on her hips. "Very impressive that you recognized it."

Jade gave Rell a firm slap on the back. "You always were the observant one."

Rell snorted. "Because of your penchant for practical jokes when you were a child. Need I remind you of the time you put night hoppers in my boots."

Rell took a step forward but Jade blocked her with her arm, stopping her before she stepped inside the circle.

"You may want to skirt the edges of the stones," her sister said.

Ravyn nodded. "Agreed. No telling what might happen now that we are all at full power. Last time I stepped inside the circles I burst into flames."

Rell's brows shot up in surprise. "Good to know."

"Search the walls and see if you can sense anything unusual." Juna said, turning the conversation back to their mission. She placed her hands against the smooth stones and inched her way to the left. "Rell, use your Tell to guide you, and Jade, keep watch to make sure we have no more visitors."

Jade nodded and took up a spot at the door, peering out the crack.

Ravyn moved to the far side of the chamber, while Rell circled in the opposite direction, unsure what she was supposed to be looking for. A low hum resonated throughout the room. With a little effort Rell managed to accept the strange vibration as normal and continue her search.

"Do you feel anything?" Jade whispered from several feet away.

"Nothing so far." Rell crept along the room's boundaries and as she rounded the first curve, her hands slid across a large square tile placed in wall. Warmth seeped into her palms. The change was almost imperceptible but definitely there. "Wait."

Jade jogged to where she was standing. "Something?"

"Touch this," Rell said.

Jade laid her hand against the tile and closed her eyes. "I don't feel anything."

"It's subtle, but grew warm under my touch. Juna." Rell waved the Tell over. "I think I might have found something." Ravyn and Juna edged around the stone circle to where they stood. "Place your hand here." Both women did as Rell told them. "Do you feel it?"

"Yes." Juna's fingers traced the symbol embossed on the stone square. "This is a Bringer symbol for king. Gregory told me there are several throughout Illuma Grand." Ravyn removed her hand and Juna closed her eyes, pressing her palm flat against the symbol. "Strange that Gregory did not sense this when he searched the chamber."

"I can't feel it," Jade said, "I'm a Redeemer and he's a Shield. You said Tells are more sensitive to this. Maybe that's why."

"Perhaps." Juna opened her eyes, a look of determination crossing her face. She braced one hand against the wall, and using all her force, pushed against the tile with the other. An almost undetectable scraping sound whispered. "I think it moved. Help me." The four women placed their hand against each corner. "Ready? Push."

Though awkward and unable to give it her full strength, Rell felt and heard the square move backward. "Again."

The four shoved a second time and the stone tile scooted back another inch and stopped. A louder grinding sounded to their right and a doorway, seven blocks high and four wide, slid open. They looked at each other, each smiling triumphantly.

"Ravyn and Jade, guard the door while Rell and I check inside."

Even though Juna's reason for allowing Rell to stay was probably because she'd discovered the tile, a sense of pride swelled within her, replacing some of the uneasiness she felt over her reaction to Nab and his companions. Without objection, Ravyn and Jade skirted the room and took up posts outside the door.

Rell and Juna crept forward and peered into the dark interior of the large chamber.

"I can't see a thing." Juna stepped back out and pulled a low-burning torch from the bracket, shoving it inside the opening. Firelight danced against the walls, illuminating the first several feet. "This is it."

They inched inside, Rell taking the rear position. Rusty brackets hung bolted into the walls and the faint outline of different weapons stained the stone. Long wooden tables sat empty, but the faint shapes in the dust indicated that even more weapons had once rested there.

Rell ran her fingers over the silhouette of an axe that looked very much like the one Luc carried. "If there were weapons here, somebody has removed them."

"Not all of them." Juna held the torch higher and moved forward.

A small collection of daggers and swords lay in a heap on the ground. Rell bent and picked up a dirk. Its edge gleamed in the torchlight. She flinched when a tugging sensation pulled at her hand, causing her fingers to wrap around the hilt.

Juna dragged her sword from her hilt and replaced it with

one of the immortal weapons on the floor. Rell did the same, as well as shoving a dagger in each boot. Approximately ten weapons remained.

"Pick up as many as you can carry." Juna tossed the torch aside and began collecting the weapons. "We'll dole them out to the rest of the party."

Rell stopped and looked at Juna. "I want to thank you for helping me this morning."

Juna halted her collection and slowly stood to face her. "You're welcome, but thanks are unnecessary."

"I believe they are." Bending, Rell picked up two more swords. "I was careless."

"The power I felt from you was not that of a Bringer." In an unusual display, Juna placed a hand on her shoulder. "Maybe being a Bane has changed you somehow. I don't understand it, but I know my own struggles with being part of the Trilation." Her hand slid free. "We have no Masters to teach us about our abilities, so we do the best we can."

Her understanding gave Rell a small amount of consolation. "I suppose you're right."

Juna smiled. "I am. Now, let's get these weapons upstairs."

They finished collecting the pieces and exited. Once outside the small room, Rell stopped. "How do we close the chamber?"

"It doesn't matter. There's nothing left inside." Juna headed for the door. "Let whoever stole the rest of these know they have been found out."

When they exited the Council Chamber Jade's mouth dropped open and her eyes widened. Rell shoved a sword and dagger at her. "Here, replace your old sword and shove the smaller blade in your boot."

"Is this all there is?" Jade pulled a small dagger from her boot and tossed it aside. "I thought there would be more."

"Most of the arsenal is gone." The disgust in Juna's voice

echoed around the empty hall. "We already know some of the weapons have made it to the Shadow World as well as into the markets. No telling where the others are. This will have to do for now."

The four women sprinted up the steps, slowing when they reached the final landing.

"We still need to talk to somebody about the missing Bringers," Ravyn said, scanning the bustling area in front of them.

"Beatrice." Jade gave a small bark of excitement and held up her hand. "Beatrice," she called louder.

A redheaded woman turned, her face breaking into a wide grin when she saw Jade. She rushed forward and the two women hugged. Rell stepped back, wondering where her sister had met her obvious friend. Their relationship seemed far more than just acquaintances. Rell was struck by the realization that she hadn't really known what Jade did or where she'd gone when they were apart. The memory of the lonely life she'd subjected Jade to while Rell had been a Bane rose up again. She pushed down the guilt and refocused on their mission. There was some comfort in knowing that she was trying to right her past wrongs.

"I'd heard you arrived." Beatrice glanced around. "And that my uncle was not happy to see your group."

"I bet not," Ravyn said.

Beatrice wore the same gray garments as the other women. If she was of noble birth, her station was not defined by her clothing. "Who is your uncle?"

"Fromme Bagita." Beatrice looked back at Jade. "Do you have word of Marcus?"

Taking her by the hand, Jade pulled Beatrice toward the wall. "Yes. We found him."

"Where? Is he all right? Why haven't you brought him to me?" The joy in her expression evaporated. "Is he dead?"

"No, but the situation is grave." Jade lowered her voice. "He is being held in the Shadow World by the Demon King."

"Who is Marcus?" Rell asked.

"One of those we found—" Jade pinned her with a pointed stare. "Beyond the room where Luc and I were held."

What Jade left unsaid was that Marcus was one of the Bringers frozen in ice. Rell sifted through her memories of the people she'd seen, but there had been too many and she'd been too frightened by Sha-hera's threats to remember. She nodded and said nothing more.

Beatrice's eyes slid shut and she inhaled, as if stilling the urge to cry. The need to comfort the woman surged through Rell and without thought she placed a hand on Beatrice's arm and sent calming thoughts to her. Instantly the woman relaxed, exhaling and opening her eyes.

"We're going to try and rescue him." Jade glanced around, lowering her voice even more. "But we need your help."

"Anything." Beatrice's gaze skated over each one of the woman. "I'll do anything to help."

"We need information," Juna said. "Do you know if more of your people have gone missing?"

Beatrice nodded vigorously. "Yes, three in the past month, plus the two you rescued today."

"Damn." Jade placed a fist on her hip and rubbed her forehead with her other hand. "And what has your uncle done about it?"

A sneer curled Beatrice's full lips. "Nothing. He keeps saying they've run away, but nobody believes that. Especially after today."

"I think it's time Illuma Grand stands up to their noble leader," Rell said.

"I agree." Jade took her friend's hand in hers. "Are you up for a little revolt?"

A spark of defiance gleamed in Beatrice's eyes. "I've been waiting for the chance."

"Then gather all those willing to fight the Bane, but do it quietly. We don't want Fromme to catch wind of what's transpiring under his nose," Juna said. "Wait for word from one of us before you act. No sense in putting yourself in harm's way before we know what we're dealing with exactly."

"Whatever you do, don't underestimate your uncle," Ravyn said. "And if at any time you feel unsafe, go to Jacob Le Daun's manor. Do you know where it is?"

"Yes. I've been there before." Beatrice looked at Rell. "And Marcus?"

"Saint's willing, he'll be home soon." Rell lowered her hand. "And a few more Bane will be suffering in the Abyss."

"Cheery thought, sister." Jade placed a hand on Rell's shoulder and squeezed. "You've got a bit of a mean streak in you."

"Yes I do, but I had that before I was turned Bane."

Beatrice's eyes widened and she shook her head. "Nothing surprises me with you lot anymore." She pointed to Rell's chin. "I want that."

Rell touched the skin just below her lip. "What?"

"To be brought to full power." The woman looked at Juna, as if sensing her rank. "I'm ready to take my place in the fight."

A smile curled Juna's lip and Rell could almost sense the Tell's desire to call the troops to arms. "Successfully muster an army and I will personally guarantee that you're brought to full power."

Beatrice's eyes narrowed. "I'll hold you to that."

CHAPTER TWELVE

The doors to Fromme Bagita's office opened and the Bringer party filed out. Rell and the three women stopped at the end of the hall and waited for the group to join them.

"What's going on?" Ravyn asked.

"Fromme is being his usual charming self." Rhys scowled down at her. "Uncooperative."

Gregory halted in front of the women and the other Bringers moved in, enclosing them in a circle no person would dare breach. "Did you find anything?"

"This is all that's left." Juna took the weapons from Rell and held them out to Gregory. "We've hidden a few daggers in our boots as well."

He took the swords from her grasp and passed them around the group. His expression turned dark. "Were they in the Council Chamber?"

Juna nodded. "As was a Splinter."

His hand froze, his gaze sliding back to her. "Explain."

"It seems Vile and Sha-hera have coerced at least one Splinter into helping them search the Council Chamber." Juna gripped the hilt of her sword. The way her thumb rubbed against the ornate handle belied her nervousness. "She said she entered Illuma Grand under the guise of dancing for Lord Bagita—at his invitation, of course."

"Of course." Gregory rubbed a hand over his chin and exhaled. "More and more he becomes a liability. Now he's being manipulated like a puppet and doesn't even realize that Vile controls the strings."

"What should we do?" Luc asked.

"Beatrice is gathering those who are willing to stand against Fromme and fight the Bane," Jade said. "Her fiancé is one of the men being held in the Shadow World."

"We don't have time to deal with Fromme right now." Gregory sighed. "Hopefully, while we are gone, Bagita can't do more harm than he's already done. I say we finish this mission first and deal with him upon our return."

The group nodded, bowing to his leadership.

"Let's go." Gregory pushed through the group. "We've got Bringers to rescue."

The party fell into step, two wide, Siban taking his place next to Rell. She glanced at him. His face was expressionless, but she could feel his relief at being safely rejoined with her. She said nothing and focused forward. As they marched from the building, Rell couldn't help but feel proud that she was part of this group—thankful she had a mission to complete—proud that she'd found her place amongst her kind.

• • •

Though he didn't know exactly what had happened in the Council Chamber, Siban could see that Rell was happy about what the four women had accomplished. No doubt she had played a hand in finding the weapons. Now that Rell was armed with an immortal sword, he relaxed a bit. At least she'd have some protection against the Bane—and Icarus if need be, though he doubted Rell would use it against that demon. Now if he could get through her thick, stubborn skull that she needed to be more cautious, he'd be able to sleep at night.

The group strode through Illuma Grand as if they owned it. People skittered out of their way and once outside, Gregory called for their horses. Within minutes the party was on their way and Siban was once again refocused on the quest to rescue the Bringers from the Shadow World.

When they reached the property boundaries, Gregory slowed their pace. They thinned their line to ride single file again. Nobody spoke. There would be time for talk once they stopped for the midday meal.

Siban's gaze rested on Rell's back, the rhythmic step of his horse rocking away the pent up anxiety he'd been holding onto since the encounter with the Bane. The miles passed and by noon his stomach was protesting loudly.

At a stream, Gregory stopped them. "Go to the river two at a time and stay alert." He dismounted. "We'll be here just long enough to refresh ourselves."

Rell slid from her horse and straightened, giving a little groan. Siban dismounted and walked to her. "Sore?"

She turned to face him, grimacing unconvincingly. "Not at all."

Her sister on the other hand did not suffer her pains in silence. She hobbled past them. "I think I'd rather ride that bloody dragon again."

"That bloody dragon would be me." Luc stopped beside them. "The woman complains more than a fishwife."

"But you love her just the same." Rell leveled her glare at him. "Don't you?"

Luc rounded his eyes and gave her a sickeningly sweet smile. "More than life itself."

Siban smiled and took the reins from her. "Come on, let's

water the horses."

They made their way toward the bank and stopped, waiting for Meran and Trace to finish at the river. An uncomfortable silence stretched between them. Rell appeared unwilling to be the first to broach the subject of their conflict but Siban didn't want to continue their trek with the bad feelings between them.

"You scared me this morning when you confronted the Bane. You can't continue to be so reckless." He kept his eyes on the water and struggled for the right words. "Other lives depend on your actions."

She bit her lower lip, her eyes trained on the two people at the river. "I know."

He wasn't sure she understood the danger she'd put them in, but her admission of guilt was a start to breaking down the tension between them. "And I won't say anything to the rest of the group about you freeing Icarus."

She was quiet for a few seconds. "But you still don't believe we can convert him to our side?"

"No." He sighed. "You can't see it because you—" He searched for words that wouldn't antagonize the situation further. "Have a history with Icarus and want to believe the best."

"I don't just want to believe it, Siban. I *feel* it." Her hold tightened on the reins. "I don't understand why you can't feel it as well."

"Two years being tortured by the Bane. A lifetime of fighting the demons." He bit the inside of his cheek. The Bane had taken much more than *his* life. "Watching my family being slaughtered by the demons."

Rell's head snapped around. "The Bane killed your family?"

It was difficult to keep the memory buried. He nodded. "Killed everybody but my sister." He looked at her. "Would have been better if they had."

"Where is she?"

"An abbey near Itta." It had been nearly a year since he'd gone to see her. Seeing the once vivacious girl who now sat silently staring was more difficult than his own nightmares. "She doesn't speak. Just stares out the window." He swallowed hard. "The Sisters take good care of her and I send money to provide for her."

"I'm so sorry." Though Rell didn't touch him, her compassion wrapped around him, soothing the bitter memories. "I didn't know."

"Nobody knows. You're the first I've told."

"Why did you tell me?"

"So you'll stop jumping into the fray and trying to save the world." He looked at her. "So you'll understand everything I've already lost." He reached across the space between them and caressed her cheek. "You're the best thing that's ever happened to me, Rell." His voice cracked and he cleared his throat. "I'll do anything to keep you safe."

She blinked several times but didn't look away. "I'm not your sister, Siban. I've experienced the worst. Watched my father be killed, turned to a Bane. You can't compare me to anybody else."

If sharing his darkest memory hadn't changed her mind, he didn't know what would. "You're right, you're not my sister. There's still hope for you." He paused. "For us. I care about you and want to keep you safe."

A grimace pulled across her mouth. "None of us are really safe anymore, are we?"

"No, but you don't need to court danger."

Her spine stiffened slightly. "I promised to be more careful." She placed her hand on his arm. "I know you want to protect me. But like you said, I'm part of this group. Others are depending on us. You won't be much help if you're only focused on my safety."

He shook his head. "You can't ask me to stop worrying about you, Rell."

"And you can't ask me to ignore what I know to be true." She nodded. "But I also promise not to take unnecessary risks."

His hand slid to her waist and he pulled her to him. "If only I could believe that."

She leaned up and gave him a quick kiss on the lips. "Trust me."

"I *am* trying." He sighed. "You are as maddening as a woman as you were a demon."

"But I'm prettier now, don't you think?"

He knew she was trying to tease him out of his dark mood and with her body pressed against his it was working. "I don't know. I liked your horns quite a lot." His hand drifted downward and cupped her bottom. "Really did something for me."

She scowled. "I don't know if I should feel complimented or disturbed by that admission."

His grip tightened on her rear end and he pulled her closer, capturing her lips with his. She wound her arm around his waist and opened to his assault. Their tongues met, sliding along each other.

"Your turn," Meran said. "If you two can tear yourself away from each other."

Rell broke the kiss and stepped away, blushing. "Right."

They led their horses to the stream where they drank their fill. After a quick meal of jerky and hard cheese, the group remounted to continue their trek. Their conversation had alleviated some of Siban's worries. If Rell did as she promised and tempered her propensity to dive into danger, perhaps they'd be able to work through their differences about Icarus. At least he hoped they could.

The day turned warm, making the normally cool and

shaded forest an agreeable temperature. If the knowledge of where they were going hadn't been looming over Siban, the trip would have felt like nothing more than a pleasant journey with friends.

The hours passed with no further excitement. By nightfall they'd reached the hot pool, where Luc and Jade had camped before entering the Shadow World. Though the entrance lay only a short ways ahead, Rell and Jade had both assured the group that the Bane rarely ventured to that side of the mountain.

They quickly assembled camp within the trees, keeping the horses and their gear hidden. Sleeping by the hot pool would make them an open target for anything approaching from above. No fire was set and dinner consisted of another cold meal from their provision packs, which was filling but not particularly satisfying after the delicious meals Willa and Delphina had spoiled them with.

"I'll take first patrol," Siban said, looking pointedly at Rell. She stood. "Me too."

"Okee and Odette, you take the south entrance. Rell and Siban patrol the north toward the entrance of the Shadow World," Gregory said. "Go no further than fifty yards beyond camp. There's no need to safeguard a larger area and that should be far enough out to give us time to rally should the need arise." He turned to the group. "After your shift wake two who have not yet patrolled. The rest of you try to get some sleep." He returned his attention to Siban and Rell. "Sound an alarm if you encounter any trouble. Stick together and stay alert."

The four nodded. Rell and Siban headed into the forest while Okee and Odette walked in the opposite direction. With the mountain rising to the left of camp, only the east side remained unguarded.

"Let's patrol in an arc to catch the eastern side." Siban

wove his way through the trees.

"Good idea." Rell hopped over a fallen trunk. "There's never been much Bane activity here, but with the increase of demon attacks, we can't be too careful."

"My thoughts exactly."

They stopped approximately fifty yards from camp and walked a wide arc. Neither spoke, both sending their awareness out among the trees, using only their Tell for communication. Quickly they fell into a pattern of scanning and sending information to each other. After a while, the continuous psychic touch became more effective than speaking. Words only conveyed the message and the perceived feeling of the person, but by reading Rell's Tell, Siban picked up on not only her mood, but her intent, the vibrations of the area around them, and how she appraised what she was sensing. Though they ventured no farther than ten yards apart, he became more comfortable increasing the distance between them due to their solid connection.

Temperatures dropped, turning the evening cool. A thin layer of mist slithered across the ground, slowly spreading out in all directions from the hot pool near camp. Chirping from the night hoppers whirred below the underbrush and an owl hooted in a tree near where they patrolled.

As they started their third pass a faint anomaly registered along Siban's Tell. He stopped the same instant Rell did. She looked at him and gave a single nod. They crept closer together and stood several yards from the face of the mountain. The abnormality turned into warning, which mutated into the bite of the Bane presence.

He swore under his breath and tried to pin down the Bane's location. The demons seemed to be moving quickly, making it difficult to isolate exactly where they were. The biting grew. He squinted, straining to see into the dark, but nothing moved.

Not halfway into their shift and already they had encountered problems. If they were lucky, the Bane would pass over and not realize that a Bringer party was camped in the trees below. The decision to sound an alarm warred with waiting to see if the Bane noticed them. No doubt Odette and Okee felt the presence as well, but no alarm had gone up.

They crouched. A few seconds later the slow, heavy beat of wings thumped above them, the down stroke sounding like the deep beat against a drum. Siban sent up a prayer that the Bane would pass over and no harm would befall them—but they were not to be so lucky.

Rocks tumbled from the ledge and the scraping of talons hissed through the quiet. All forest sounds ceased, as if sensing the danger from the Bane.

"I can smell you, Bringer." A familiar voice from Siban's nightmares drifted through the trees. "Come out and play."

The urge to charge forward and slay the she-devil washed over him. Rational thought gave way to revenge. The need to pay the bitch back for the two years of torture she'd put him through choked out the caution he'd preached to Rell.

In an instant, Rell was there beside him and in his head, sending waves of love to him, reassuring him that he was not alone. His rage lessened and the realization that he would put her, and the rest of the party, in danger if he acted on his impulse slowly registered.

"You can't hide from me." Clawed feet shifted, sending more stones toppling down the side of the rock race. "I'm very good at hunting."

Hiding was the last thing Siban wanted to do and from the look on Rell's face, she had the same thought. Together they stood and walked toward Sha-hera's voice and stepped out of the trees.

The demon perched on a ledge twenty feet above them.

Two more Bane females that Siban didn't recognize stood beside her. Sha-hera's eyes rounded. "Well, well, well, now this is a surprise." She circled a finger at Rell. "But how, I wonder, did you manage to become human again?"

The succubus to Sha-hera's right glanced at her captain and back at them.

Sha-hera laughed. "Don't you recognize our little Rell?"

All three demons stared at her with renewed interest. Siban stepped forward. "How about me, demon. Do you recognize me?"

The succubus's gaze leveled on him and slowly narrowed, a smile creasing her lips. "Dark one, I wondered where you had gone." As if understanding dawned, she looked at Rell. "Of course—*she* helped you escape. I should have known." The demon slid her hand down her waist and over her stomach. "I missed you, Bringer." Her lips formed into a pout. "Nobody to toy with. Nobody to torture." She crouched. "But I'm so glad you've come back to me."

"We won't be joining you for any more—fun." Siban drew his sword. "As a matter of fact, I've been meaning to end this relationship for some time."

Rell followed suit and withdrew her blade. Sha-hera's attention fixed on the glimmering blades. "Immortal weapons. Where did you get them?"

"The only thing you should be concerned about," Rell said, "is an eternity within the Abyss." Hatred washed through her. In a flash, the steel of the sword flared with a rush of blue flame and then tempered to a glow.

Sha-hera straightened and bared her fangs. "It will not be as easy as that, Bringer. There are three of us and only two of you."

"You're mistaken." Okee stepped from between the trees, Odette by his side. Both had their weapons drawn.

The twins were strikingly beautiful, appearing far too innocent to be skilled in vanquishing demons, but the power rolling off them hinted otherwise.

Both demons accompanying Sha-hera hissed and crouched, readying themselves for retreat.

"Hold," their captain barked. Her yellow glare slid back to the four Bringers. "What do you want here?"

"Our kinsmen," Siban said. "And do not doubt, Bane, that we will get them."

Leaves rustled behind them, but already he knew it was the rest of the group. The twins must have alerted them on their way to help. One by one the members of their party stepped from the trees with weapons drawn.

Sha-hera's companions hissed and without waiting for permission, soared into the sky. Not so easily driven away, the captain stood her ground. "You do not know what you are up against, Bringers. If you believe you can free your friends, I'm afraid you will be sadly disappointed." She shook her head. "Vile will never allow it and already the other two fly to warn him of your coming."

Siban let his anger drift through him and focused its energy into his hand. Vibrations rippled down his arms and pooled in his palms. The sensation caused his hands to shake. Narrowing his focus, he concentrated on Sha-hera. When he felt somewhat in control of the roiling ball, he thrust his hands toward the demon. Like a peal of thunder, the pulsing ball hurled toward her and crashed into the rock below her feet. Stones exploded, sending chunks of rock in all directions.

Sha-hera soared into the sky, her angry screech echoing through the night. The heavy *thud* of her wings thumped several times. She swooped toward the group and again Siban heaved a pulsating orb at the demon, but this time his assault was followed by a volley of fire from Rhys, Gregory, and

Ravyn. The demon swerved, barely escaping the attack. Rocks exploded behind her when the fireballs blasted into the side of the mountain.

The group jumped backward, diving toward the trees to escape being pelted by the falling stones. Sha-hera shrieked again and turned north, disappearing into the night without further words or an attack.

Despite not dispatching the she-demon who had made his life a living nightmare for two years, a sense of satisfaction filled Siban. One day he would face that bitch and it would be a fight he planned on winning.

CHAPTER THIRTEEN

The *crunch* of Vile's footsteps as he paced the length of his chamber pounded inside Sha-hera's head. She stared at his powerful back. The black tattoos covering his blue skin undulated with the tightening of his muscles when he moved, marks of his dedication to magic's dark side.

He stopped and spun to face her. "Tell me again what your Splinter said."

For the third time she repeated Fatima's words. "Four Bringer women, bearing the mark of full power, caught her leaving the Council Chamber."

Vile lowered his chin, his thick horns tipping toward her. "And they did not so much as imprison her?"

"No, they questioned why she was there and how she'd gained access to Illuma Grand." Sha-hera bit back her resentment at being questioned as if she were a simple minion, and repeated the information. "She gave them the excuse that she was there to dance for Bagita."

His brow furrowed and he straightened. "And what excuse did she use about being in the Council Chamber?"

"That it was in her nature to explore and possibly acquire

a bauble or two that she could sell at a later date." Sha-hera shifted her weight to her other foot. Vile had been interrogating her for the last hour, asking the same questions. "Fatima assured me that they suspected nothing."

"Is that so?" Vile eased onto an oversize, ornately carved chair. "And you would believe her?"

"I made the consequences clear if she did not do as I asked." Sha-hera clasped her hands behind her back. "Fear is a powerful motivator. I see no reason not to put faith in what she said."

Vile stared at her, his talons drumming against the padded brocade arm of the chair. These were his private quarters and unlike the throne room, this chamber was luxuriously decorated. Instead of rotting food and carcasses, expensive rugs covered the floor. A plush bed took the place of the cold stone surface the slavering minions slept on, and a long table, complete with golden candelabra and books, sat to the far right of the chamber. Though expensively embellished, in Sha-hera's opinion, the room's size was too modest for a Demon King's residence.

The silk curtains and lush linens that adorned Vile's bed brought back memories of her past—memories of what she'd fought to overcome. But she knew why he chose to live like this. It was a reminder of his harsh reality and the soft life he'd lost at the hands of those who had betrayed him.

"You are incapable of seeing the bigger picture of what the Bringers are planning, Sha-hera." Vile smoothed his hand along the burnished material and curled his talons around the carved claw at the end of the chair arm. "That, my dear concubine, is why *I* am the Demon King and you still serve me."

Sha-hera clenched her jaw. After a thousand years he still wouldn't let her forget her former occupation or that she had attended him at the most base level. Only by her wits had she risen in rank among his other concubines. By virtue of her will to survive had she supported his plans to overthrow the Bringer King. She given up her soul for the chance at freedom—and still he would not let her forget.

Losing her temper would be fruitless. She needed to keep his trust so she could still have the independence to move about without his spies following her. With a silent exhale, she relaxed and donned the face of the compliant servant. It was a character she played well. "What bigger picture would that be, my king?"

"The Bringers search for their lost kinsmen. I am sure of it." He tapped his talon on the end of the chair's arm. "Several of them have already infiltrated the Shadow World on different occasions. I'm sure they'd not hesitate to do it again, especially since they know about my little menagerie and have already stolen back one of bodies."

Her breath caught in her throat. Did he suspect her part in allowing Rell's sister to leave with her human body? Sha-hera had shown Rell the frozen Bringers in hopes of drawing her support away from Icarus, but then the little demon had disappeared and Sha-hera had been unable to locate her—until tonight.

Though she'd told Vile of the Bringers, she'd kept the part of Rell being transformed back to human to herself. Bits of valuable information were rare and she'd take any opportunity to gain the upper hand. She was tired of serving without acknowledgement for her loyalty. She didn't know how she would use the information about Rell's transformation but better to plan than give up her edge.

She plastered on an innocent expression. "What missing body?"

"Bowen's daughter." His hand stilled. "Did you not know?"

Sha-hera bowed her head. "No, my king. Obviously it is

another betrayal by Icarus."

"Do you really think so?" He stood and flared his wings. "He seemed quite surprised to find that the Bringers had escaped." Vile prowled toward her and it took all of Sha-hera's will to not move. He stopped behind her, speaking into her ear. "Perhaps there is another traitor amongst my demons."

"I will ferret them out if there is." Playing guiltless seemed far wiser than confessing to her crime. "May I ask, my king, what could the Bringers do with an empty body?"

"A very good question." Vile brushed her thick braid over her shoulder and traced a pattern on the back of her neck with his talon. She tried not to shy away when the point of his claw slid over the delicate area at the base of her skull. One jab and she would crumble, unable to move. "One I plan to answer soon." He circled, stopping six inches in front of her. "Perhaps they endeavor to restore her to human form."

Sha-hera blinked, trying to hide the fact that the Bringers had indeed been successful. "I've never heard of such a thing happening. How would they do it?"

A humorless smile spread across his mouth. "That is for me to know and for you to never find out."

He turned, walking back to the chair and sat again. She cursed her stupidity. All this time she'd thought Vile had been sharing his plans and secrets with her, when actually he'd been using her—just as he had when they had been Bringers themselves.

"Gather the succubus army." Sha-hera noticed how he no longer called it *her* army. "And move all the Bringers. Take them to the Threshold."

"The Threshold?" Fear replaced her anger. The place was dangerous, even to the Bane. Time and reality defied natural law there. "But if we move the Bringers to the Threshold, you may lose them if there is a power rift."

"Better to lose them, than to let them fall into the hands of our enemies." He pinned her with a glare. "It would take more than a few Bringers armed with immortal weapons to breach the Threshold. The bodies will be safe there until I have need of them." He tipped his head toward her. "See it done."

She executed a slow, delicate bow of her head. "As you wish, my king."

She settled her face into what she hoped was an unreadable mask, but inside Sha-hera seethed. She'd become complacent as the Captain of the Succubus Army over the past centuries. Instead of remaining focused on the real battle going on right in front of her, she'd squabbled for scraps of control with Icarus, which she now saw was exactly what Vile had wanted. Divide the power and keep them off-balance. Icarus had been smarter than her, catching onto what Vile was doing long before she had. Where she thought she had bested Icarus, she'd really only served Vile's intentions.

She pulled the door shut behind her and looked at the two sentries. They were from the king's private guard, followers from the beginning of Vile's rule. "Stay alert, we may be having visitors."

The two succubi from her army, Mia and Leah, waited beyond the guards at the edge of the corridor. "Did you tell him about the Bringers?"

"Yes." Sha-hera strode down the passage leading to the war room with the two demons on her heels. "We are to move the king's prisoners to the Threshold."

Both demons stopped. Sha-hera slowed her steps, exhaling an impatient breath. She squared her shoulders and faced her comrades. "Is there a problem?"

"Vile has never allowed any demon near the Threshold." Mia exchanged a worried glance with her partner. "And the journey is treacherous."

"Is that fear I hear?" Sha-hera took a step toward them. "Trust me, if you do not do as you're told, your fate will be far worse than delivering the Bringers to the Threshold."

"Yes, Sha-hera." Mia bowed her head briefly and scooted past, followed by Leah. "We will see to the preparations."

She stared at the two demons' departing backs. They'd been her friends once, serving in the same concubine harem. For a thousand years they'd fought together, having joined Vile's cause in hopes of gaining freedom from the world of man. But a thousand years later, they were still shackled, now to the whims of the Demon King.

Though the other succubi believed themselves free from the persecutions they once faced among the Bringers, she bore no such illusion. Until she escaped Vile's control she would never truly be free. Though she did Vile's bidding, she never stopped looking for an opportunity to further her own cause. Centuries ago she'd given up her soul, so what did she have to lose now? An amusing and dangerous thought came to her. She wondered what the Demon King's son would give to know the truth about his past?

. . .

The opening into the Shadow World was located approximately ten feet above the ground on a narrow ledge. Jade led the party, with Luc next, and Rell directly behind him. The three knew the entrance better than any of the other Bringers. One at a time, they climbed to the rocky outcrop and inched into the narrow opening.

Pitch-blackness surrounded Rell and her breathing became more labored the farther she crept. Only a few weeks had passed since she'd last been to the caverns, but the situation was so very different now. How would she react when she entered her old home?

After several minutes of shuffling blindly forward, heat surrounded her, indicating they were getting close to the hot pools. The passage narrowed even further. She turned and flattened her body against the damp wall, scooting until the path edged around a curve. Rell couldn't help but wonder how Jade and Luc had managed to escape carrying her human body. There was barely enough room for one person.

A pinprick of light glowed at the end of the tunnel. Her heartbeat quickened. Icarus knew of the caverns. Would he be waiting for them? The faintest prickle of the Bane's presence skittered across her arms, but there was no indication that any demons lurked nearby. Once inside the chamber the gnawing was sure to increase. Enduring the irritation was something she didn't relish. The closer to the Bane hive they got, it would become even worse.

Jade scooted to the end of the tunnel and held up her hand. The line of followers stopped. Their shallow breathing was all that could be heard in the darkness. Rell inhaled and released the breath slowly. It took all her willpower to remain still, the need to get free of the dark confines pushing her anxiety higher.

Blue light from the glowing algae in the hot pools fell on her sister's features. She swallowed hard and her eyes were wide, searching beyond Rell's sight. If the tunnel had been wider, Rell would have pushed past and taken the lead. Putting Jade at risk, yet again, was the last thing she wanted. Instead she quelled the urge and waited, having learned her lesson this morning about barging forward.

The narrow width of the passage made her feel like she was in a tomb. No noise penetrated to where they waited. After what seemed like an eternity, Jade waved the group forward. Not having to be told twice, Rell scooted out into the chamber.

A cloud of moist air blanketed her as if welcoming her home. The hot pools gurgled a greeting she recognized all too well. The *whoosh* of warm air rising through natural vents in the floor hissed and the memory of being warmed by them flittered through Rell's mind.

Gregory motioned everyone forward. Without a word the twins jogged across the chamber to take up guard at the only other entrance into the Shadow World.

Siban slid from the opening and came to where she stood. "Are you all right?"

"Yes." She let her gaze travel upward to the dark ledge that jutted twenty feet above the ground. "I used to sit there." Next she pointed to a large, flat-topped rock. "And Jade used to sleep there." She lowered her arm and looked at him. "It's all still so familiar, but completely different."

"*You* are completely different." He took her hand. "We both are."

"It's strange being here." Jade joined them. "Now that I see the caverns again, they're not that bad, eh?"

Rell cocked a brow.

"All right." Her sister shrugged. "Maybe a little bad."

"This is where your expertise comes in." Gregory stopped in front of them. "What is the best course to the chamber where you found the Bringers?"

"Through that entrance." Rell unsheathed her sword. "It's a bit of a rocky trek, so watch your footing." She stiffened her spine. "I'll lead the way."

She could feel Siban's stare burning into the side of her head, but she ignored him. This was the one way she could help the Bringers. This was her realm.

Gregory nodded. "I will be right behind you." He turned and motioned the members of their party to gather around him. "Rell will lead us to the chamber. Okee and Odette, you take the rear guard. Juna you'll be up front with me. The rest of you fall in where you can." He held up his sword. "Stay alert and ready for battle. No telling what we might encounter the farther in we travel."

"I have a pretty good idea of what we'll encounter," Luc said.

"Exactly." Gregory looked around the group. "For what it's worth, I would happily go into battle with all of you at my side" He exhaled.

"That may be exactly what we're doing," Rhys said.

"Let's hope not." Gregory pointed to the entrance. "All right, fall out."

Rell made to move for the door, but Siban grabbed her arm and pulled her to him. His mouth covered hers and his other arm wrapped around her waist, holding her to him. The kiss was hard, his grip crushing. She twined her arms around his neck and returned the kiss with everything she had.

When they finally broke, he didn't let go, staring into her eyes. "Don't die."

She smiled. "You either."

With that he released her. She stepped back, holding his gaze, and then turned and jogged to the head of the line, taking her place in front of Gregory and Juna. Siban fell into line and withdrew his weapon.

"Whenever you're ready," Gregory said.

Rell took a deep breath, stepped through the doorway and into the tunnel that led to her darkest fears. Nothing of the terrain had changed since the last time she'd prowled these corridors. Moisture coated the walls. Trickles of water slithered to the base and disappeared into grooves that had been cut by the constant flow over millennia. Lit only by the tiny rivulets and glowing algae, her shadow barely registered against the wall.

She jammed her foot against a large rock in the middle of her path and stumbled. Gregory caught her arm, holding her upright. She righted herself and looked at him, giving the king a grateful smile. When he didn't release her arm, she turned back to him in question. In his palm he held a ball of some kind, its outline perfectly circular.

Unsure what to do, she leaned toward him and whispered, "What is it?"

"A glowb." He gently blew on the orb. She felt his warm breath against her cheek and to her surprise a tiny white light sparked at the center of the circle. He breathed on the ball again. The glow grew, lighting the passage enough so she could see the path ahead.

Taking the light, she held it in front of her with one hand, while still clutching her sword in the other. With careful steps she crept forward. The illumination was enough to keep her from stumbling again but not so bright as to impair her vision beyond the light.

They wound their way through the tunnels. The bite of the Bane grew noticeably stronger but not enough to herald a demon in the near vicinity. The corridor shifted downward, the moisture on the stones making the trek tricky to maneuver. She heard the slipping feet of the Bringers behind her, but continued on without stopping.

At the bottom of the slope, the ground evened out. Rell stopped and held her hand up, signaling the party to do the same. She pointed to a black doorway a few yards ahead of where they had halted. Gregory nodded and took the orb from her hand, slipping it back into his pocket. The tunnel dimmed. Only the drip of the water trickling down the wall and the light shuffle of feet could be heard.

Again Gregory gripped Rell's arm, holding her in place as he slid past her. Juna did the same, putting Rell third in line. Unsure what to do, she followed them, her sword at the ready. Once at the doorway, Gregory retrieved the globe again, hesitated a second, and then bent and rolled the light into the room.

Rell's breath caught in her throat. Her body tensed, expecting the Bane to attack. When nothing happened, Gregory poked his head around the corner. He raised his hand and signaled them all forward. Juna quickly followed and disappeared into the room. It took all of Rell's willpower to peel herself away from the wall and continue forward.

The glow from the orb revealed that the room was empty of demons. Rusty chains lay in a heap near a far corner, the same chains she had used to bind Luc and Jade. Rell turned away, not wanting to see the reminder of her betrayal. The large chunks of stones that had once been the torture table lay scattered across the floor. Angry at Icarus, Vile had smashed the slab with a single blow.

"Where are the Bringers?" Gregory turned to face the group.

Rell lifted her sword and pointed toward the farthest and darkest corner. "The opening is over there."

Her feet didn't want to move. A firm hand settled on her shoulder and she looked up expecting to see Siban, but it was Luc. He peered down at her. "You all right?"

It was funny that he should be asking her that question. He'd been the one tortured, imprisoned by her and Icarus. "Are you?"

"Not really."

She nodded, feeling a connection with him. He understood. "Me either."

"They've moved the immortal weapons." He walked around the tumbled chunks of stone and stopped next to a ledge, placing his hand on it. "About fifteen weapons rested here. I grabbed the axe on my way out. So the rest were probably immortal as well."

"Let's hope not everything has been moved," Juna said.

A small movement on the ceiling drew several of the Bringers attention, including Rell's. She crouched in an attack position, her sword pointed in the direction the movement came.

"Imps." Siban crept forward. He pointed to several different spots on the ceiling and his posture was somewhat relaxed. "They're all over the place and not dangerous from what I can tell."

"What are imps?" Meran stopped directly under one of the bat-looking creatures. Large black eyes stared down at her. "They're not demons?"

"I don't know exactly," Jade said. "But when I was healing Luc, they shared their life force. There wasn't much, but what they had, they gave freely."

Juna stopped next to Meran, also staring up at the creature. "How odd."

The imp cocked its head and blinked once. Meran smiled. "They're kind of adorable."

Juna snorted. "We have a very different idea of adorable."

"Let's keep moving." Gregory walked to the far corner of the chamber and pressed his hands against the wall. With a slow side step he slid along the solid structure until his hands disappeared. "I found it."

In an instant Juna was behind him. Instead of rushing to follow, Rell lingered behind and waited for Siban. This was not a place she wanted to charge into at all. But if it meant saving the Bringers she would—with his support. She noticed that Luc and Jade also hesitated. The three exchanged glances, silently mustering their courage.

Luc held out his arm, indicating Rell should lead. "Shall we?"

Siban slipped his hand into hers and gently pulled her

forward, leading the way. The blackness in the corridor pushed against her eyes. She strained to see anything, but no light penetrated the passage. The air grew noticeably colder. A shiver ran through Rell and her fingers began to ache against the metal hilt of her sword.

When they rounded a curve, blue light illuminated the end of the passage, and she could see the other Bringers waiting. Thankfully the bite from the Bane did not increase. If they were lucky, they could be in and out before the demons even knew they had been there.

As they approached the end of the line, Rell couldn't help but notice that the glow was much dimmer than it had been when Sha-hera had shown her the menagerie of frozen prisoners. A feeling of foreboding grew inside her. Siban turned and looked at her, his expression grave as well. Something wasn't right.

Leading the way, Gregory slipped beyond their sight. Each one of the Bringers followed. Siban pulled her forward and out into the icy chamber. Luc and Jade were the last to enter. They stopped, they're mouths dropping open. Rell looked around the cavern and groaned.

"Where are they?" Jade said.

Vapors from her breath circled around Rell's face as she exhaled in frustration. She released Siban's hand and walked to the first opening. At one time a young man had been held here, his features peaceful, captured in an icy prison. Now the gaping hole was dark and empty.

She slowly turned and faced the group. "Vile must have moved them."

"Sha-hera must have told him of our encounter." Ravyn said. She moved down the line, checking each prison. "Perhaps he guessed our purpose."

"No doubt," Rhys said from behind her. He walked to

the opposite side and examined the jagged ice around one of the openings. He touched a shard with his finger and quickly yanked his hand away. "It burns. Be careful."

Trace jogged the length of the chamber, disappearing into the darkness. After a minute he returned. "There's no exit down there, only the way we came in."

"We knew this wouldn't be an easy rescue." The tip of Gregory's sword rested against the frost-covered floor. "I say we continue into the Shadow World and try to find where Vile has taken them." He looked around the group. "We don't know what we're up against so I will leave the decision up to the group."

Rell looked at Siban. His eyes questioned her. More than anything, she wanted to get out of the Shadow World, but she was part of something bigger now, and the chance to face her fears and perhaps exact a little revenge would probably not be handed to her so neatly ever again.

"I'm staying." She held Siban's gaze. "The Bringer prisoners need us."

His brow furrowed for a second and then smoothed into acceptance. "I'm staying as well."

Obviously not happy about the decision, but Rell was grateful that Siban made no further protest.

"Count me in." Jade moved to stand beside her sister. "We're all in this together."

"Damn it, woman, you're going to make a hero of me yet," Luc said. He joined the line. "So what's our next move?"

Gregory smiled. "Have any of you been deeper than this chamber?"

"The farthest Rhys and I have been is the Throne Room." Ravyn looked at Rhys. "At least I think that's the farthest we've been."

"Yes, and I have no knowledge of the outlying tunnels or

chambers," he said.

"I was imprisoned somewhere, but I couldn't tell you where." Siban faced Rell. "Do you know?"

"Down a different corridor, but on this level." She could feel his hesitance at knowing the details of his captivity. In an effort to ease his agitation, she kept her description general. "It would not be big enough to hold all the prisoners. So I doubt they took them there."

Siban didn't ask any more questions and she didn't provide further details.

"Well, uh—" Jade shifted uncomfortably when everybody's gaze turned toward her. "I explored as far as the succubus army's war room once."

"What?" Rell glared at her sister. "When?"

Jade waved her hand in the air. "It was a long time ago and I never did it again."

"Why not?" Rell's stare narrowed. "You almost got caught, didn't you?"

All eyes leveled on Jade, waiting for her answer. "Maybe... by Vile."

"Sweet Sainted Ones." Rell raised her arms. "Didn't I tell you to stay in the caverns?"

"Really?" With her hands propped on her hips, Jade donned an indignant scowl. "We're going to do this now?"

Rell bit back her retort and faced Gregory. "I have also been to the war room."

A sound of protest escaped Jade. "And you're scolding me?"

"I—" Rell slowly turned and faced her sister. "Was a demon, not an innocent child with her soul still intact."

"Details." Conceding defeat, Jade relaxed. "Fine, so we can both get that far, but it's treacherous."

"She's right." Rell spoke to the entire group. "The minions

don't inhabit the lower areas, so any demons we meet are going to be the most dangerous."

Luc tossed his axe in the air, spinning it before catching it again. "Then I suggest we stay on our guard."

"Agreed." Gregory looked between Rell and Jade. "I hate to ask, but would you mind leading again?"

"I will show you the way," Rell said, cutting off any argument from her sister. "I'll use my Tell to guide us. Hopefully we'll be able to sense an attack before we're caught off guard."

"Very good. I'll be directly behind you." Gregory walked back to the passage. "All of us should scan constantly. Though the Tells' abilities are stronger, we each have the capability to perceive demons."

Rell joined Gregory near the door, once again taking her place at the front of the line. She released a heavy breath and sent up a prayer to the Sainted Ones.

Please deliver us all from the mouth of the beast.

CHAPTER FOURTEEN

The corridors were eerily quiet. Though the gnawing of the Banes' presence had intensified somewhat, it was still not as strong as it should have been. A heavy chill weighed the air, making it more difficult to breathe. The smell of wet stone mingled with the taint of sulfur, stinging Rell's nose. Her heartbeat quickened as she crept forward.

She stopped. A hidden crevice that was cut into the walls to her right could barely be seen. Once when she'd been following Icarus, she'd seen him disappear into the fissure and that was the only reason she knew the opening was there. Otherwise she would have passed by it completely unaware that it led to the upper level overlooking the war room.

When seeking Icarus's help, she'd found him lurking above, listening to Vile and the succubus army plot against the Bringers. Though she had been hidden in shadows, Rell was almost sure the Demon King had known she was there.

Again she raised her hand to halt the group. Strategically they were not in a good position. The narrow corridor gave them no outlet for escape. But then again, they'd already established that until they found the Bringers who Vile held captive, retreat really wasn't an option. She turned to Gregory and indicated the crack in the wall. His brow furrowed, obviously still not seeing the entrance in the dim light.

Without waiting for him, she slipped between the rocks, hoping the others would follow. The rough stone caught her hair and the rasp of the leather sliding against rock hissed along the narrow opening. Inch by inch she scooted farther into the gap until it opened onto a circular landing. Gregory emerged directly behind her. One by one the Bringers squeezed through the crevice and materialized into the cleared area at the base of the stairs.

With her sword, Rell pointed up the steps. Instead of letting her take the lead, Gregory motioned for Trace and Rhys to follow. The three men stole up the steps that had been carved into the rock with weapons ready. The quiet *crunch* of their footsteps sounded overly loud in the enclosed space.

Juna stood at the base of the stairs, staring up into the dark stairwell, like a dog that had been told to stay and now impatiently waited for its master's call to join them. Nobody spoke. Ravyn had positioned herself at the entrance of the rocks. It seemed each Bringer was finding their place within the group. Besides Juna, the Shields naturally took up a position of defense, where as the Tells main talent seemed to be in sensing danger and the correct path.

Rell stared up the empty stone stairwell. From what she remembered, noise from the war room traveled down the steps. Just as easily any demon in the upper level of the war room would be alerted to their presence if they weren't quiet.

Strained glances ricocheted between the Bringers as the minutes ticked by. Finally, the crunching of returning steps grew louder. The group backed up as far as possible, allowing the three men to reenter the circle.

Gregory remained on the bottom step and spoke quietly.

"The war room is empty, though there are several drawings of Illuma Grand spread out on the table. We'll deal with that information later." He gave a little shake of his head. "I think we need to continue deeper."

Every member of the party nodded in agreement, but didn't speak. Without further discussion, Gregory took the lead and disappeared into the fissure. The Bringers fell into line, waiting their turn to slide through the opening. Once back in the corridor, he motioned them forward.

Where they traveled now was unknown to any Bringers and very few demons. A dark world where only the most dangerous Bane dwelled. Rell's breath swirled around her in an icy cloud. She remembered this cold. The chill penetrated deep, burning its way into her bones. It had an unnatural feel, as if it emanated from the very heart of the world.

She rolled her shoulders, repressing the urge to shiver and glance back. Siban's warm presence radiated behind her, solid and reassuring. Their path angled downward again and the gnawing bite of the Bane increased, grating more sharply than it had with the minions. Though they still hadn't encountered any Bane, demons were definitely in the vicinity.

Tension rolled through the group, and Rell had to close the barriers of her mind so as to not be carried away by her companions' anxiety and anticipation. Again their route leveled out. A narrow corridor to their right disappeared into darkness. Chunks of debris littered the floor, giving it an unused and unwelcoming quality.

To the left, an ornate arch ascended to thirty feet above them. Rell's eyes followed the graceful curve of the entrance, surprised by the detail of the work. It was obvious that a master sculptor had created this, but whom? The Bane seemed incapable of creating anything but destruction and pain. Compared to the harsh and cold caverns of the Shadow World, this masterpiece stood in direct contrast to the Bane's brutality.

Beyond lay a wide corridor, the walls smooth not by time, but by physical effort. Lavish braziers, equally as ornate as the arch, burned with cold blue flames, giving the passage a foreboding atmosphere. A foul breeze wafted from the finished hall. Rell stepped back, bumping into Siban. His hands steadied her and for the first time, his touch did not induce calm. His wariness enveloped her, indicating that he felt the threat as well.

Despite the suspected danger, Gregory stepped under the carved arch and inched forward down the passage. The Bringers spread out to stand two wide. Odette and Okee took their positions at the rear. Rell glanced back. The twins faced each other, moving forward with a side step, which kept their backs to the wall and their eyes behind the group in case of an attack.

Rell skirted a thick metal loop secured to the walls at ankle level. Chains of rusty iron hung over the ring and lay in a disorganized pile on the floor. Every few feet another loop and more chain had been attached, as if prisoners had once lay shackled there. Rell assessed the thickness of the chain. Or perhaps something far worse had been bound here, a creature they'd not yet encountered

Statues with their arms uplifted to the sky rested within deep niches' cut into the walls. Rell halted, drawing closer to one of the figures. She'd seen something similar in the temples of the Order of the Saints. Leaning closer, she narrowed her gaze, trying to discern what was carved into the statue's chest. A star with eight arrow-tipped points that emanated outward was engraved into the stone. She turned to Siban and pointed at the design with the tip of her sword. Brita stopped next to Rell, her eyes growing wide.

"The chaotic star." The words rushed from her. The Tell's

expression sent a wave of alarm rushing through Rell. Normally Brita wore a look that instilled confidence. Now she seemed genuinely frightened. She lifted her eyes and quietly called down the corridor. "Magnus."

Magnus skirted the group and moved toward them with Gregory following. As they approached a colorful curse slipped from Magnus. Gregory's steps slowed, his eyes narrowed and his mouth tightened into a straight line. He looked at Magnus, a silent message passing between them. Gregory exhaled, his gaze traveling down the still empty corridor in the direction they'd been heading. Several of the Bringers gathered around him.

His raised the point of his sword toward the statue's chest, his voice coming out in an almost inaudible whisper. "The mark of the Summoner."

Siban muttered a curse. His hand wrapped around Rell's waist, pulling her close. She went freely and rested against him, needing his strength. The Summoners were supposed to have been imprisoned by King Harlin. Why would their statues be in the Shadow World?

Though she'd known this journey would be fraught with peril, the realization that they might be walking into a trap set by the most powerful of the Bringer groups nearly paralyzed Rell. It took all her strength to continue and not contemplate the possible loss of her soul again—or worse.

"This is not good news," Gregory said, his gaze traveling over the group. "If these statues indicate that the Summoners have joined with the Bane, we are most definitely outmatched." He exhaled. "What say you? Do we continue or turn back?"

Juna edged forward. "We continue. Until we confront Vile we will not know what we're up against."

Several of the Bringers nodded. Rell remained silent, unable to make a rational decision. She caught Jade's wide-eyed stare. It seemed Rell was not the only one questioning the foolishness of their venture, but neither she nor her sister voiced their concerns. What Jade had said in her bedroom only a few days before came back to Rell… *What's happening between the Bringers and the Bane is so much bigger than the both of u*s… Rell drew strength from her sister's words.

When nobody spoke up to dispute Juna, Gregory nodded. "So be it. We continue on."

Again he took his spot at the front of the line and proceeded forward. Before moving, Rell looked back at the statue. The urge to crush the figurine to a fine powder surged through her. From the memories Magnus had showed their group, the Summoners had defied the Bringer law. No moral code bound them. The dark magic sect had made their own rules. If the Summoners were still alive, then it was not only the small group of Bringers who were in trouble, but the fate of two worlds.

The bite of the Bane clawed at Rell's arms, which meant Bane were near. She released her Tell, letting it flow forward. Two dark voids rippled along Rell's awareness. Juna had obviously felt them too. She grabbed Gregory's arm and raised two fingers. At the end of the wide passage Gregory stopped and pressed his back against the wall, raising his sword. He flicked his head forward and made a circling motion overhead. Juna and Rell mimicked his stance.

With the ease that comes from training together, the Bringers who had accompanied Gregory through the Arch fell into two lines. They spanned the width of the corridor. The first line faced forward in the direction they'd been headed. The second line moved to the back and faced the direction in which they'd just come, ready to engage in an assault from behind. Rell, Siban, Luc, and Jade fell in behind the first line, facing forward, while Rhys, Ravyn, and Meran turned toward the back to form a second line of defense. Okee, Odette, and

Trace took the very back, reinforcing the rear. Though they would be trapped if attacked from both directions, at least their positions would allow them to take out several Bane before being overpowered.

Gregory and Juna slipped around the corner. None of the others moved. The silence stretched like a tight band between them. Blood pounded in Rell's ears and power danced along her skin, wanting to pool in her hands. She glanced behind her and noticed that Ravyn and Rhys each held fireballs in one hand and their weapons in the other.

A riot of emotions rolled through Rell. She refocused on the corner that Gregory and Juna had rounded and let the vibrating power pool in her hands. She sent her Tell forward. Two Bringers registered, their presences sending positive sensations along her awareness. Beyond them stood two dark voids—the Bane. Neither demon seemed to be aware of the approaching Bringers.

The impression emanating from both the Bane was like nothing Rell had ever experienced. It wasn't dull, like the minions, but sharp and completely focused on their task of standing guard. What they watched over, she could only imagine. Rell tried to shake off the hollowness the mental touch caused and forced her Tell to remain to take in information. If and when Gregory and Juna needed them, she would be there with her sword.

Quivers of anticipation traveled back to her. Then she sensed Siban's Tell, ghosting forward and absorbing some of Gregory and Juna's apprehension. Though she couldn't see the Bringers, Rell recognized Gregory's intent to attack. A flash of emotion spun along her path at the same time the sounds of struggle erupted around the corner.

Then Brita and Magnus rushed forward with Rhys and Ravyn in their wake. Not waiting, Rell followed. As she rounded the corner, her gaze fell on two of the biggest demons she had ever seen. Not hulking like the malformed minions, but broad and muscle bound. Their skin was marbled with intricate tattoos.

One demon had Juna pinned against the wall by her throat. From her reddening face, he was effectively choking her. Magnus's blade slid through the thick leather of the demon's vest, burying it to the hilt.

The Bane released its hold on Juna. She dropped to the floor and clutched at her neck, gasping for breath. Without hesitation, Rell sprinted forward and hooked one arm under Juna's shoulder, pulling her out of the reach of the demon. Magnus hauled his sword free and stepped back. The Bane turned, its piercing yellow eyes narrowing on him. Its body convulsed once but didn't fall. Gregory impaled the second demon with his blade, piercing its chest until the tip protruded from its back.

He yanked on the sword in an attempt to pull it free but the weapon didn't budge. The demon grabbed for him. Gregory narrowly dodged the big hands. Placing his foot on the demon's stomach, he heaved backward, finally freeing his weapon.

Both Bane convulsed several times, their bodies jerking and their yellow eyes turning milky white.

"Run!" Gregory pushed Magnus in the direction they'd come. "Grab onto something."

Siban raced forward and lifted Juna into his arms. "Come on."

Having witnessed what an immortal weapon did to the Bane in the woods yesterday morning, Rell bolted around the corner with Siban and Juna on her heels. Seconds later a thunderous roar filled the passageway.

"Grab onto the rings!" Gregory lifted Juna from Siban's arms and slid to the floor with her cradled in his lap.

Rell squatted and wrapped the chain around her wrist and up her arm before grabbing a ring. Siban and the others following suit.

The figurines within the alcoves began to vibrate. Rell yanked her foot in a second before the statue above her toppled off its perch and smashed on the ground. Shards of stone pelted her face, but she didn't have time to react.

Tremors rippled down the middle of the passage, buckling the stone tiles. For a second, Rell thought the earth would open and swallow them whole. A blazing torrent of wind whipped along the corridor, flinging debris in every direction. Rell curled into a ball, shielding her face from the wind's assault. The breath left her lungs, the wind growing in intensity and continuing to drive down the corridor.

Shrieks erupted in Rell's head, the same screams she had heard yesterday morning after Gregory had impaled the Bane. Pain ripped through her skull and she cried out. Pulling her head upward, she looked around, squinting to see the other Bringers. Rhys held onto Ravyn and her hands were pressed against her ears in obvious distress.

The shrill howls escalated and Rell's vision blurred. Sharp pain jabbed behind her eyes. She cried out, but the wind sucked the sound from her. Just when she thought she would die from the punishing screams, they stopped. The wind lessened, the last gust swirling down the corridor and around the corner. Air returned to the space and Rell drank in a deep breath. Little by little the searing spike behind her eyes eased until it was nothing but a dull ache.

Chains rattled behind her and clanked to the floor. Siban grabbed Rell and hauled her against his chest. He swiped the hair from her face. "Are you all right?"

She stared up at him but didn't have the strength to speak.

The other Bringers rose. Rhys helping Ravyn, who looked

as if she was about to be ill. Had anybody besides her and Ravyn heard the screams? Aches racked Rell's body when she tried to sit forward.

"I'm all right," she said, finally finding the ability to speak. "Help me up."

Siban bent and hoisted Rell to her feet. "Thank the Saints."

"Thank the Saints we're all still alive." She got her balance and gently pushed away from him so she could assess his injuries. "Are you hurt?"

He shook his head. "No." His gaze tracked around the corridor. "Our journey grows more perilous."

"Yes, and if this is what we've endured so far, think of those who Vile holds captive," she said.

He covered her hands with his. "From here on out, stay close to me. We'll be more safe if we work as a team."

His worry was evident in his tone, but his idea of working together was sound. "We're not alone this time, Siban. We have others to help us now."

His eyes searched her face. "A bitter blessing. With the Saints' help we'll all get out of here alive." He held out her hand and she took it.

"Please tell me that somebody else heard those screams," Meran said, stopping next to Rell.

"I did." Rell rolled her shoulders. "It's not the first time. I heard them yesterday morning as well."

"And I heard them when Rhys and I fought the Bane near Willa's inn." Ravyn gave a shudder. "Their torment has haunted me and it was something I never wished to hear again."

"What do you think it is?" Rhys asked, rubbing her shoulder.

She shrugged. "I have no idea, and I don't really want to find out. I just want it to go away."

"I don't think that will be happening." Gregory stood at the end of the hall, his arm around Juna, supporting her. "Come see what we discovered." He slowly released her, but waited a second to make sure she was all right. When Juna gave him a nod, he walked to the end of the corridor. "It's here."

"I really hope this isn't more bad news," Luc grumbled as he limped forward. "I'm getting very tired of bad news."

"I second that," Rhys said.

In a far-less-uniform group than before, they shuffled forward and followed Gregory around the corner. He stood in front of another stone arch and beneath it a wooden door cut in the same chaotic star—the symbol of the Summoner.

Gregory held his sword before him and glanced back at the group. "I say we take a peek inside."

"I was afraid you were going to say that," Meran said, wiping her palm against her pants.

Gregory grasped the iron handle of the door and pushed. The door gave a little *click*. He waited, but no noise emanated from within.

"If somebody is inside the chamber," Juna said, "I highly doubt they missed the maelstrom that just decimated the corridor."

Meran and Ravyn exchanged glances. Rell wondered if there was trouble between the siblings. From what she'd been told, they barely knew each other, having been separated as infants.

Gregory looked over his shoulder at Juna, his eyes narrowing. "Still, caution is required."

She scowled at him and tapped her toe twice. Her gaze drifted to the door and eventually Gregory turned back to face it. Watching Juna was a lesson in itself. Rell couldn't imagine how the woman hadn't come to more harm already.

"Open the door." Juna's order came out as a hiss, but there was a definite push of compulsion in her words.

Gregory's head snapped around. "Do not use that on me."

For good reason, Juna took a step backward. In the short time Rell had known him, he'd never raised his voice. The expression on his face now was enough to quell the most stubborn subordinate.

With a gentle push, Gregory eased the door open. Still no sound stirred from within. He raised his sword to a vertical position in front of his face and crept forward, inching the door open. His body leaned to take in as much of the chamber as possible, and when the space had widened enough, he slipped inside. Juna shifted from foot to foot, trying to see into the room, but didn't enter.

A shiver skittered up Rell's neck as the silence lengthened. The blackness she's lived with as a demon oozed from the room. It would take all her willpower to enter.

Finally, Gregory pushed the door open. "It's empty."

Second to enter was Juna. She surged forward and the rest of the Bringers followed behind. To Rell's surprise the chamber was sumptuously adorned. Thick brocade curtains ringed the bed and luxurious linens draped over the thick mattresses. Candelabra made of gold sat lit on an ornate table and a chair fit for a king held the center spot against the longest wall. Thick tapestries, like those she'd seen in Illuma Grand, hung from the walls. Instead of a hearth, two large round kettle braziers burned with a low white flame.

Rell held her hands over the flames, flexing her fingers and trying to return some of the warmth to their tips. "Real heat."

Jade joined her. "Ah, that's lovely."

"Is this Vile's chamber?" Rell scrutinized the room. "Surely this is not where he rests."

Everything within the chamber was a stark contrast to what Rell had experienced with the Demon King.

"If I had to guess, I'd say yes." Gregory walked to the table and examined the parchments strewn across it. He sorted through each one, shaking his head. "Yes, this is definitely his chamber." He held up a yellow sheet. "It seems he's planning on attacking Illuma Grand."

Rell stepped away from the brazier and walked across the chamber. A thick tome rested on top of a small table near the bed, the emblem of the Summoners emblazoned on the leather cover. "Gregory."

She waved him over and then stepped aside so he could look at the book. A curse slipped from between his lips when he saw the symbol. He picked up the book and opened it, his eyes growing wide. He thumbed frantically through the pages.

"What is it?" Dread rolled off him, engulfing Rell. "What does it mean?"

Gregory slowly closed the book and turned to face the members of the group. "An accounting of Vile's life."

Silence filled the room. There was more to come; Rell could feel it. His eyes searched the faces of the Bringers, coming to rest on Juna.

"Vile's journal?" Juna asked.

Gregory nodded. "It appears that the Summoners are not working with the Bane." He swallowed hard. "The Summoners *are* the Bane."

CHAPTER FIFTEEN

Nobody spoke for several seconds.

Siban let the information sift through his mind, trying to reconcile that the treacherous demons could be some of their own.

"But how can that be?" Juna crossed the room to stand beside Rell. "I thought all the Summoners were imprisoned within the Abyss."

"As did I." Gregory looked at Magnus. "None of us have ever actually seen the Abyss. King Harlin kept its location a secret and I was born after my father's death."

"King Harlin thought that the fewer people who knew where they'd imprisoned the Summoners, the less likely it would be that anybody would free them." Magnus paced the length of the room. "Once we crossed through the Arch, we suspected the Abyss was here. It appears we were right."

"When King Arron sent the humans through the Arch in hopes of finding freedom, he essentially sent them into the path of the Bane," Ravyn said.

"I'm sure he didn't know where Harlin had imprisoned the Summoners, or he would not have chosen Inness for the humans." Gregory walked across the room and held the book out to Okee. "It is of the utmost importance that this book makes it back to the manor before Vile discovers it's missing. Take Odette."

Okee accepted the book from Gregory. "I will see it done." He turned to his twin. "Come."

Odette nodded, her eyes cutting to Trace. The tall Bringer held her stare for several seconds. With a rare show of emotion, Trace walked to her. "Don't stop. Get free of the Shadow World at any cost."

Odette's blue eyes rounded. Though it looked like she wanted to say something, she merely nodded and reached to press her hand against Trace's chest. Without the fanfare of more good-byes, the two Bringers exited. Hopefully they would make it to the surface safely.

Siban contemplated Vile's journal. It could possibly tell them everything they needed to know about how the Summoners had turned to Bane. Something in that thought poked at him. What did they know about the unstable group of Summoners who were also Bringers? They were dark and unpredictable. Even King Harlin had been forced to imprison his own brother and mother. Siban's thoughts froze, the realization dawning.

"Gregory." Siban took a step forward, the blood turning to ice inside him. "I know why your great uncle Ander seemed familiar when Magnus shared his memories." He met the king's silver gaze. "Ander is Vile."

Ravyn gasped. "That's it. That's why his face was familiar but I couldn't place him."

The color drained from Gregory's face. "That's not possible. Ander was imprisoned within the Abyss, as was his mother."

"What if your grandfather didn't imprison his brother?" Juna laid a hand on Gregory's arm. "What if he escaped and came through the Arch when the humans were crossing over?"

What Juna said vibrated with truth. Siban looked at Rell. She appeared to be weighing the words as the pieces began to fall in place. Slowly Rell lifted her eyes to Gregory. "What if he was the one who kidnapped your half brother?"

Again, the possibility rang with truth, not just because Siban's Tell hummed at the statement but because it made sense. Silence blanketed the room, the logic of the situation stunning everybody into silence.

Meran, who had been quiet during the exchange, stepped forward. "Gregory, what if Ander took your brother and claimed him as his son?"

Gregory's lips tightened into an angry pinch, his head shaking as if not wanting to accept the next conclusion of what she said.

"Icarus."

A low growl rumbled from Gregory's throat. "You think Icarus is the bloody king?"

"Impossible," Magnus said.

"Why?" Rell strode to the center of the room to stand in front of Magnus. "You admitted you've never seen Ander as a Bane. You've purposely concealed your presence from Vile until it was time to fight the demons. And Gregory, you were not even born when your brother was kidnapped. There would be no way to recognize him."

"She's right," Gregory said. "My uncle has covered his tracks well. There is no way I would have recognized him, and he has been careful to not let us see him. That is why he killed the Bringers left here after the Bane war."

"That is why he didn't kill me." Bile roiled in Siban's stomach as his memories of being tortured by Vile rose up like an angry beast, threatening to devour him. "He and Sha-hera asked me the same question every day. 'Where are the other Bringers?' I had no knowledge of you at the time and refused to reveal

Rhys—but he was looking for those who could identify him."

"This changes nothing." Juna released Gregory's arm and moved closer to him, bending slightly so he would look her in the eye. "More than ever we must vanquish Vile. He means to open the Abyss, and with Icarus heir to the throne, Vile will then use *him* to open the Mystic Arch."

Siban swore. "I knew Icarus could not be trusted. He's been playing us to get information for Vile."

"No." Rell spun to face him. "He wouldn't do that."

Normally he would applaud her tenacity, but in this case it was misplaced. "Rell, he's a Demon Bane. Of course he would. And just because you want to find the good in him doesn't change the fact that he's not."

"Let's not jump to conclusions," Meran said. "I'm not convinced Icarus knows of Vile's treachery."

"I agree," said Brita. "He was impossible to read when we captured him."

Siban grunted his disagreement, but didn't argue any further."

Gregory scrubbed his face with his hands and then lowered his arms, looking like a man who just had the weight of the world placed on his shoulders. "Forget Icarus for the moment. If there are other Summoners free then our fate is truly dire. We cannot triumph in a fight against them."

"We are the Trilation." Juna straightened. "If anybody can defeat him, it is my sisters and I."

"I'm glad you're so confident," Ravyn said. "But we don't even know what that means."

"Then we'll figure it out." Juna glared at her. "But we can't give up and turn back now. Yes, the danger has increased, but so have the consequences of not defeating Vile."

"Noble words, Juna." Luc said. "but do you even know how to use this supposed awe-inspiring power?"

Juna sneered. "It will come to us. It's in our blood."

Luc rolled his eyes. "I feel much more confident now."

She opened her mouth to argue, but Gregory cut them off. "Arguing will not get us anywhere." His gaze swept the Bringers. "Who is willing to journey forward?"

Siban waited for Rell's response. When her hand lifted, his heart sank, though he couldn't fault her for wanting to continue on. After all, he was going to do the same. Siban raised his hand.

"At least when we are all killed we can say we didn't die a coward's death—a fool's death, yes—coward, no."

"Not a lot of comfort," Luc said, raising his hand.

At varying speeds all the Bringers volunteered to continue. But not before each of the couples exchanged glances, silently consulting with their partners.

"It is decided then." Gregory paused. "We move forward with our plan."

"Where do we go from here?" Siban wanted to know exactly what Gregory was planning. "We don't know where Vile is."

"The Tells can help with that." Juna walked to the door, with her sword pointed forward. "It's what you've trained for."

Rell glanced at him and then trailed Juna out the door. Hesitating only a second, Siban followed her. Time had come for him to fully embrace his Bringer powers. There could be no wavering from here on out. If he wanted to get Rell safely from the Shadow World, he'd have to become the Bringer he was meant to be and take back the life Vile had stolen from him. The Demon King and Sha-hera would pay for all they had cost him. Somehow he'd have his revenge.

The empty passage sent a wave of unease through Siban. "Why haven't the Bane come to see what the disturbance was?"

"Vile probably knows we are here," Brita said, joining them in the hall. "I wouldn't be surprised that he orchestrated this whole thing to draw us in."

"Agreed," Magnus said. "The dark powers of the Summoners are unfamiliar to those who refuse to engage in such acts. There's no telling what they are capable of."

"Then it's best to be prepared for anything," Gregory looked at Brita. "Where to now? What path does your Tell sense."

Brita took several steps in the direction the group had originally been heading. "We must continue on."

"I agree," Juna said.

A smile tugged at the corner of Siban's lips. Even during these dire times Juna made sure she had her say. Though he didn't know exactly how old she was, Siban was certain that Brita had nearly a thousand years on Juna. Being part of the Trilation may give Juna increased powers, but he doubted her Tell abilities were as finely honed as Brita's. Plus Brita had seen two violent wars and survived. Siban thought that experience, not pride, was the best teacher.

Gregory claimed his post at the front of the line and strode forward, leading them to an unknown fate, and possibly, Siban ruminated, the same nightmare Rell had freed him from a year ago. He wiped his sweating palms on his pants, repositioned his sword and took his place beside her. What had started out as an attempt to rescue the Bringers had now turned into a quest to save two worlds.

• • •

Sha-hera circled the treetops and glided downward to perch on a low branch overhanging the trail. The quiet jingle of an approaching rider tinkled through the night air. She waited until the donkey was twenty yards away and then spread her wings and floated to the ground to land in front of the animal.

The donkey reared at the presence of the predator, but

Fatima retained control, quieting the animal with soothing words and magic. Once calmed, she slid from the animal's back. "Sha-hera, you startled me."

"Yes, I'm sure I did."

"What is it?" The Splinter gripped the reins and took a few steps toward her. "Does Vile have a message for me?"

"Why else would I be here?" Sha-hera lied. She sauntered toward Fatima, closing the distance between them. Though the donkey shied away, Fatima stood her ground. Not many were brave enough to travel these roads at night, but the Splinters had their own magical protection. "He has another task for you, but you are to report only to me."

The Splinter laid her hand against the animal's neck and it instantly grew quiet.

"What are his orders?"

From Fatima's tone, Sha-hera could tell that the woman was not happy about the prospect of doing more of Vile's bidding. "You are to gather the Splinters from your clan and travel north to the Frost Lands."

"The Frost Lands? But that's nearly three weeks ride with our wagons." She lifted her chin a fraction of an inch. "For what purpose?"

"You should ask fewer questions and concentrate on the task at hand." Fatima was becoming far too inquisitive. Sha-hera contemplated her response. She needed the woman to believe the orders came from Vile, but didn't want to reveal too much of her plan. "My army and I are under orders to transport several items for Vile. He wants you and your clan to smooth the way for our arrival." She paced around Fatima and the donkey. "Keep the residents of Pillager's Peak occupied until we've accomplished our goal."

Though her explanation was true, the Splinters' presence had nothing to do with moving the Bringers. Sha-hera needed the clans' magic if indeed the Abyss rested within the Threshold. This could be her one chance to open the prison and she would not suffer a lost opportunity.

"But what about my daughter?" Fatima turned, never giving Sha-hera her back. "She is too young to make such a journey."

Sha-hera stopped in front of her. "I care not what you do with your offspring. My only concern is subduing the town so they will not notice our presence. It would be unfortunate if they were to stumble upon Vile's precious cargo." She reached out and let one of Fatima's coppery locks slide along her talon. "Are we understood?"

Several seconds passed before Fatima replied. "Yes, Sha-hera, we understand each other perfectly."

Something other than compliance laced the woman's acquiescence. As long as Fatima gathered the other Splinters, Sha-hera didn't care if she railed against her when she was out of earshot. Results were her only concern. The curl slipped from her talon and Sha-hera lowered her hand.

"Send four of your clan members to other Splinter clans in the area. They are to do as I have instructed, subduing the smaller villages surround Itta, Alba, and Faela. In turn, they should send messengers to the southern clans, instructing them to do the same. I want Splinters in every small village in the land."

"You mean to control the outlying areas?"

"No, my sweet." She gave Fatima her sweetest smile. "You are to control these villages."

"And what are we to do with the people once we accomplish this?"

She could see the Splinter trying to work out the logic of what Sha-hera was asking, perhaps even plotting how best to use the situation to her benefit. "What you do best. Bleed them of money, lure them under your spell, steal, lie, whatever it takes to subdue them."

Fatima stiffened, her jaw clenching and unclenching. She took a shallow breath. "Is there anything else?"

"No." Sha-hera shook her head. "That should be enough— for now. I shall give you further instructions once you reach Pillager's Point."

Not saying anything further, Fatima turned and remounted the donkey. With a light tap to its hindquarters, she urged the animal forward. Not looking back, Fatima continued on her previous course, spine straight and head held high.

Sha-hera watched the Splinter until the darkness swallowed her, only the tinkle of bells could still be heard. With that task out of the way, she could now concentrate on transporting the Bringers to the Threshold. For her army the journey would be arduous. Flying would be a more desirable option, but stealth was of the utmost importance and that meant moving the Bringers through the tunnels. Some of the passages had not been traveled in centuries and may very well have collapsed, but Vile's plan would not be waylaid—and neither would hers.

Sha-hera turned, preparing to take flight and froze. Icarus stood in the center of the trail, his yellow gaze peering at her through the dark. "So the banished son has taken to skulking in the woods?"

"I might ask you the same thing?" His deep voice caressed her. "What are you doing out here talking with a Splinter."

"My activities are none of your concern." Her body remained tense, expecting him to attack. "What do you want, Icarus? Are we to fight?"

"What business does Vile have in the Frost Lands?" He glided forward.

Sha-hera flared her wings, taking several steps backward. "Why don't you ask your friend, Rell?"

He stopped. "What about Rell?"

"I assume you've seen her." When he didn't answer, she continued. "I can tell by your silence you have. She's quite beautiful as a human, don't you think?" To have Icarus foil her carefully laid plan was not a risk Sha-hera was willing to take. Sending him on a wild chase would accomplish two things, keep him occupied and possibly get him sent to the Abyss if Vile caught him back in the Shadow World. What a victory. To command him as well as the entire army imprisoned inside the Abyss sent a rush of joy through Sha-hera. "As we speak, she and her friends are attempting to find the Bringers Vile has taken prisoner."

His gaze constricted, the slanted pupils of his eyes dilating. "Where?"

"The Shadow World. I'm certain Rell found many secret passages in and out of the tunnels while she was Bane." She paused. "Unfortunately for them, Vile also knows this." She crouched preparing to launch herself into the sky. "I'm feeling very generous tonight Icarus, so I'll give you one last gift."

His lip curled, exposing a white fang. "And what is that?"

"Ask Vile about who you really are." She smiled when his expression softened to surprise. "I think it's time you know."

Not giving him time to reply, she leaped into the air. He didn't follow, only watched her glide away until he too faded into the darkness.

Chapter Sixteen

The corridor stretched before them in an endless maze of twists and turns. Brita and Juna used their Tell powers to guide them in what Rell hoped was the right direction, whatever that might mean.

It had taken all her fortitude to continue with the quest. Being so deep inside the Shadow World made her skin crawl. Foreboding seemed to be her constant companion. Though she wouldn't admit it to anyone, especially Siban, she'd wished Gregory would have ordered her and Siban to take the tome back to the manor.

Having made the decision to continue, however, she doubled her determination to not fail the Bringers—even if their cause seemed hopeless. They had given her so much.

The group traveled in silence for more than an hour. The corridor changed from a polished sheen to the natural rough walls like those in the caverns. The trail narrowed, the stones once again littering the path and becoming slick with moisture.

At regular intervals, Rell switched her sword from hand to hand, trying to bring back feeling in her fingers. The temperature had dropped again and the air felt thicker, more difficult to breathe. She was tempted to remove the small pack from her back to drape the rolled up blanket around her, but freedom of movement outweighed her comfort. She needed to have full range when she swung her sword.

They turned a sharp bend. Before them the passage opened onto a wide tiled area. Far beyond that, another arch soared fifty feet high, though no walls supported the monolith. It merely framed the path.

Gregory slowed, stopping a foot from where the tiles began. There was enough area along the overlaid surface for all the Bringers to examine the path before them. Rell stood next to Meran and Siban, looking down at the perfectly symmetrical stones.

Symbols like those she'd seen at Illuma Grand were etched into the tiles. Since the ancient language was not familiar to her, Rell didn't know what, if any, significance the markings had.

Gregory knelt and gently brushed the silt from the tile directly in front of him. He examined it and then reached to brush clean the stone to the right as well. "Bringer markings." He slowly rose, his gaze fanning forward. "It's a puzzle."

"Perhaps it's a riddle of how to safely cross to the other side," Rhys said.

"Perhaps." Gregory pointed to the first line of tiles. "Clear off the first stones in the path, but be careful not to push too hard."

Each Bringer knelt and swept the silt-like dust from the squares. From what Rell could see, each symbol was different. Gregory paced along the edge, examining the markings. Brita inched in the opposite direction, her attention fixed on the floor. An intense sensation of awareness swirled around Rell. The ancient Bringer was using her Tell and from the feel of it, Brita was putting everything she had into deciphering the script.

Not having the history or experience as a Tell frustrated Rell. She glanced down the line, noticing that the others were also waiting for either Gregory or Brita to come to a conclusion.

Siban shifted next to her, squatting to trace the symbol and then standing again. He looked at her and shrugged. Obviously he was as in the dark as she was about the puzzle. That made her feel slightly better, though it didn't improve their predicament.

"The right path must be chosen or all will be lost," Brita said, stopping at the far right of the tiles.

"But what is the right path?" Juna asked. "Where do we even begin?"

Brita pointed to the last tile on the right. "That is the symbol of the first Bringer King—the beginning. Follow the path of the kings."

"Our royal lineage?" Gregory strode to where Brita stood. He peered down at the symbol and then sighed. "I hope I can remember them all."

"I know them." Juna stepped forward. "Besides, you should not be risking your life. The Bringers need you to lead this battle."

It didn't surprise Rell that Juna knew all of the Bringer kings. That seemed like something the Tell would do, learn everything she could about her people. Savvy and smart, Juna no doubt took every opportunity to give herself an edge.

"I will not let you risk death, Juna." Gregory stepped in front of the first tile, blocking her path.

Juna took a deep breath, her posture stiffening. "This is my task as second-in-command. I assume the risks, Gregory."

"No." His answer brooked no argument.

"Then who would you risk? Are any of us less valuable?" She crossed her arms over her chest. "Or do you enjoy playing the martyr?"

Gregory's jaw clenched and unclenched. For a second Rell

thought he would yell at Juna, but instead he nodded. "All right, but you will follow behind me, giving me the order of kings."

"That makes no sense." Jade said. Gregory and Juna turned to look at her, startled by her comment. "So if you make a wrong step, we lose both of you? That's an idiotic plan."

"She has a point," Ravyn agreed. "Juna, we can't risk losing one of the Trilation."

All of the Bringers were valuable. The ancients had the knowledge, the sisters were the Trilation, and there was no way Rell would put Jade in harm's way again. The answer was obvious. She would traverse the treacherous path. She straightened and walked to Gregory. "I will go." She looked at Juna. "You will guide me through the course."

"Rell, what are you doing?" Siban closed the distance between them and gripped her arm tightly, trying to pull her away from the stone. "You can't even read the symbols."

"I can help, Siban." She looked at his hand on her arm and then back to his face.

"I will cross first," Siban protested.

She shook her head. "I can do this."

He lowered his hand. She could see the emotions warring within him. He'd said he'd trust her, but this would be the ultimate test. After a second he nodded and stepped back, but his gaze stayed trained on her. "All right."

A small dose of relief washed through her, but not much. She still had to navigate the path without dying. The Saints only knew what would happen to her if she made a wrong move.

"Step on the first stone," Brita said.

Rell glanced at Siban. The sensation of his Tell swept around her, swirling like a windstorm and feeding her strength. Her thoughts became sharper. Taking a deep breath, she stepped onto the first stone. The instant her feet settled, doubt filled her mind. Why had she thought she could successfully navigate this course?

"There is something here," Siban said. "Something dark."

Brita brow furrowed. "I do not feel it."

"It's here." Rell swallowed. "You don't sense it because you have no darkness inside of you." She looked over her shoulder, giving Siban a humorless smile. "This evil is a familiar companion—to both of us."

"Then it will be up to you to guide us in helping her," Brita said to Siban. She held out her hand. "Join with me so that we can learn of the dark presence."

Siban took Brita's hand. Meran clutched his other hand. Though Juna's powers as a Tell would have been helpful, she chose to stand on the edge of the tiles and call out the next symbol that Rell should look for.

"The symbol of the second king is a branch." Juna pointed to the tile at Rell's left. "There."

She looked down. "Which one? There are two tiles with branches."

"It has leaves at the tip."

Inhaling, Rell gently pressed on the stone with her toe. When nothing happened, she added more weight until she stood fully on the tile. The breath she'd been holding whooshed from her. She scanned the next stones. "An owl, flame, crown, scepter, and a goblet."

"The scepter." Juna indicated the tile to Rell's left. "King Bartholomew."

Again Rell gingerly touched the stone before giving it her full weight. Despite the chill in the air, sweat beaded on her forehead. She glanced over her shoulder at Siban and noticed the line of Bringers with their hands joined. He smiled at her and then closed his eyes.

· · ·

The farther Rell moved onto the grid, the stronger the darkness grew. Siban opened himself to the oppressive blackness, trying to pinpoint its location. Like rotting fumes from a decaying carcass, the evil seemed to emanate from the stones themselves.

His Tell slithered across the area. Instead of recoiling from the darkness that had haunted him for the last year, he embraced it and absorbed the nuances of the malevolence. Perhaps by welcoming the obscure evil he could gain control over it.

"This is like a presence I've never felt before," said Brita.

Siban opened his eyes and looked at her. "Pray you never have to endure it again."

Rell took another step, the stone holding. A wave of blackness rose up and surrounded her. Siban felt her falter—sensed her desire to step on the stone directly in front of her. She raised her foot and shifted as if she would precede forward.

Juna paced along the edge. "Not that stone, Rell. The griffin."

"Encircle her." Though his order was brief, Brita and Meran appeared to have understood. They sent their Tells forward, encircling Rell. He sensed her hesitation. Vibrations from the other Tells intensified, sealing Rell inside their swirling barrier.

She straightened and stepped forward but to the right, settling onto the tile of the griffin. Relief stirred inside Siban, mixed with his anxiety. She was only twelve tiles forward, not even a third of the way across.

On and on the dance went, Juna shouting instructions, Rell struggling to obey, and the Bringer Tells trying to hold the darkness at bay.

After nearly an hour, Rell held up her hand. "There is one more row, and then I will be across."

The last stone had been Arron's, which meant the symbol she searched for would be Gregory's.

"Do you see a symbol of the Arch?" Gregory asked.

"Yes." She pointed to the ground. "It is directly in front of me."

"That is my symbol," Gregory said.

A feeling of wrongness rippled along Siban's Tell. "Wait." He opened his eyes. "What other symbols are there? Say them slowly."

"There's a sun to my far left."

Siban looked at Brita. She shook her head, confirming his thought. "That is not it."

"Next to it is a crown."

"No," Meran said beside him. "That is not it either."

"A lion," Rell said.

"That would be Icarus's symbol if he were king," Gregory looked at Siban. "Is it his symbol?"

"No." Siban didn't know why, but Icarus's symbol felt wrong. "What's next?"

Rell was quiet for a few seconds. "The Summoners mark."

Gregory sneered. "That is it—isn't it?"

"Yes," Brita said. "Only one as arrogant as Ander would set himself up as the next king."

"And only one too stubborn to admit they were not the heir to the throne would choose his own symbol."

"That is what Ander believes you would do," Juna said.

Gregory looked back at Siban. "You are certain it is the Summoners' symbol?"

He hesitated a second, the weight of his decision pressing down on Siban. She was so close to the end. One wrong step and she would be lost to them, but he had to begin to trust his abilities. "Yes."

Siban glanced at Brita and she gave him a reassuring smile.

"Move to the chaotic star, Rell." Juna continued to pace along the edge, her body leaning as far forward as it could without her actually stepping on the stones. "That should be your last step."

Siban sent a wave of reassurance to Rell and he thought he saw her shoulders relax. Her foot lifted and the breath froze in his throat. A prayer to the Sainted Ones slipped from his lips and he sent a wave of protection toward Rell. With the lightest touch, her foot grazed the stone. Nothing happened. She settled her foot squarely on the tile and leaned forward slightly, as if testing her weight.

If he'd told her wrong, he doubted the stone on which she stood would remain in place. Most certainly what lay underneath this puzzle of tiles was not something she could recover from—a perilous fall—or worse.

Forging ahead, Rell shifted forward to stand fully on the tile. None of the Bringers moved, each frozen, waiting for something to happen.

When nothing did, Rell hopped onto the far ledge and turned to face them. "I made it."

Weakness threatened to buckle Siban's knees. He released Brita and Meran's hands and walked to the edge of the tiled floor. "Wait there," he called to Rell. "We will follow your path." The need to make her stay made him repeat his command. "Don't move."

"I won't." Rell wrapped her arms around her torso. And though her feet remained in place, she searched the area on which she stood. She looked back at him, the single word she spoke spurring him forward. "Hurry."

Siban turned to Gregory. "Let me go next. Rell is scared and I can calm her."

Their leader hesitated for a second and then stepped back. Following the trail of cleaned-off tiles, Siban crossed the grid. When he was halfway across, an intense wave of confusion washed through him, taunting him to step away from Rell's path. He clamped down on his mental barriers, trying to block out the foreign presence that tried to sway him.

A few blocks separated him from Rell. Her expression was anxious, her hands pressed to her lips as she watched his every move. The square shifted under him slightly, but held. With a final leap, Siban jumped onto the ledge, wrapping Rell in a tight embrace.

She squeezed him as if she'd never let him go. He tilted her head back and claimed her mouth. Their tongues swirled in a powerful dance that had nothing to do with passion and everything to do with defying death.

When they finally broke apart, he crushed her to him again. "I'm proud of you."

Rell gave a humorless laugh. "Me, too." She looked into his eyes. "A dark presence tried to fill my mind and control me. I didn't think I was going to make it."

He nodded. "I felt it." He brushed a stray lock of chestnut hair from her face. "But we beat it."

She lifted on her tiptoes and kissed him again, this time more slowly—this kiss more about passion than fear.

It took another hour for the rest of the Bringers to cross the stones, but since Rell had cleared the way, there were no missteps and all arrived safely on the other side.

After Jade stepped safely onto the ledge, she launched herself at Rell, squishing her in a hug. "Did you forget that I'm the risk taker?"

"You have taken risks for far too long." Rell smiled and hugged her sister back. "It's my turn to protect you."

"I've never been so scared in my life for you." Jade released her sister and stepped away. "I think I like being the one in danger much more."

"Sorry," Rell said.

"Don't worry, Jade." Luc's arm slid around Jade's shoulder

and he gave her a little squeeze. "I'm fairly certain we're only getting started and there'll be enough danger for everybody."

Jade groaned. "Great."

"Never fear, little sister." Rell rubbed Jade's shoulder. "I'll protect you."

"I'm more worried about who is going to protect you," Jade said.

Rell smiled at Siban. "He's done a good job so far."

He shook his head, giving her a quick kiss. "She doesn't make it easy."

Luc made a face as if he'd smelled something foul. "It must run in the family."

Luc moved away to speak with Rhys. Several of the Bringers congregated around.

Juna joined them. "Well done."

"I couldn't have done it without you," Rell said.

Juna looked at Siban, a smile tugging at her lips. "Let's just say it was a united effort.

He dipped his head at her veiled compliment. Juna took a step toward the towering arch and turned back to look at them. "One obstacle down." She paused. "I wonder how many more we have to go."

Siban wondered the same thing. From his estimate, this puzzle had been fairly easy to figure out. Besides the last square, any of the ancient Bringers could have guided Rell, though probably not with as much certainty as Juna had done.

"It is good to see that we can work together for a positive end." Gregory gathered the group beneath the arch. Though there seems to be nuances some of us cannot pick up that others can." He turned and faced the path leading away from them. "Vile's illusion traps are bound to grow more complex the deeper we travel." He turned back to the group. "Remain vigilant. Help each other. Take nothing for granted."

Gregory's words unsettled Siban. On the surface of Inness, things were usually what they appeared to be. He counted on the grass being green, winter wind to blow cold, and the sun to rise each morning. In the Shadow World there were no rules. Siban latched onto that confusing bit of truth. The only way he'd be able to reason through the shifting dangers of the Shadow World was to let go of all he ever thought he knew and to open himself up to the one thing he'd been trying so hard to run from—the darkness.

CHAPTER SEVENTEEN

Thick slabs of carved stone sat stacked on top of each other to create the soaring arch. Rell's gaze followed the climbing columns that came to rest on the Summoners' star at the top of the peak, a symbol that this was *their* domain.

Before them the path narrowed to an uneven trail that skirted along the ridge of a wide gorge. Jagged rocked jutted outward from the sides of the gorge like the mouth of a dragon and then faded into blackness, hiding whatever lurked at the bottom. How far of a drop it was, Rell couldn't tell.

In single file, the Bringers shuffled forward, climbing over boulders that lay haphazardly across their path, hampering their progress greatly. Slippery frost clung to nearly everything, making each step they took and each rock they skirted even more hazardous.

Rell kicked a small stone over the ledge. Echoes of the rock as it bounced down the sloping gorge wall seemed to go on forever, eventually fading, but there was no sound of it hitting the bottom.

Their breath turned to frosty smoke once it hit the chilled air and thin clouds of vapor trailed the group. Rell blew into her folded hands and flexed her fingers, trying to coax warmth back into them. Magnus's beard looked white, the rime particularly thick across his mustache. A fine layer of crystals dusted each of their shoulders. Rell lamented leaving her long cloak with the horse, though the bulky garment would have been a hindrance while crossing the tiles.

A low rumble reverberated through the caverns. The sound droned constantly, as if below the icy surface an inferno raged. Every so often the ground shifted, shaking loose parts of the gorge walls and sending an avalanche of rocks skittering down the slopes.

"Do you hear that?" Rell cocked her head. "It's like thunder inside the caves."

Siban nodded. "Once we passed the arch I heard it. Unfortunately, I don't think that's a good sign. I suspect we're getting close to where Vile awaits."

"I sense growing peril." Rell flexed her fingers again and shoved them into her armpits. "As well as more Bane."

"Some of that Shield heat would be welcome right now." Siban took her hands in his and blew, rubbing them to get the feeling back. "I wonder how long we've been traveling."

"We've yet to stop for sleep, but I'm tired, so it could be as much as a full day already." She shook her head. "Since returning to human and then being brought to full power, I no longer know my limitations. I guess I will find out." They stopped behind Juna.

Juna spoke over her shoulder. "I think we are all receiving a lesson in endurance and forbearance."

As usual, she had claimed her place behind Gregory. Siban and Rell followed directly behind her. For a long time nobody spoke, as if each felt the stirrings of things they didn't want to alert to their passing. Constant ripples of warning spooled back to Rell whenever she sent her Tell to search yards ahead. The danger was building, drawing closer. Or was it them who closed in on the menace? Was Vile the only threat, or were there unimaginable perils awaiting their arrival?

The bite of the Bane had changed from a painful to an almost seductive scratching that left her feeling violated. She rubbed her arms, trying to chase away the chill stealing through her. She spoke to Siban's back. "Something isn't right."

"I feel it too, but I can't pinpoint what."

They rounded a corner and the trail spread out to form a wide ledge. Now instead of a single path, there were three, each branching in a different direction. Gregory approached the first corridor, peering into the darkness. "Magnus and I will scout this passage. Stay here until we return."

With swords drawn, the two men entered the opening. A couple of yards in the darkness swallowed them. The dim light of Gregory's glowb sparked and then grew. Rell watched until both men had rounded a bend and disappeared. As usual, Juna paced at the entrance, occasionally peering down the dark tunnel. The minutes ticked by and still Gregory and Magnus didn't return. Rell tried not to show her growing concern as their absence lengthened.

In an effort to divert her attention, she walked to the beginning of another trail that led in a straight, open path across the ravine. On the left the cavern wall extended upward into darkness. To her right was a straight drop to what was probably the bottom of the gorge. The trail was barely one person wide, but in her opinion, seemed by far the safest route. She stared along the skinny path. It may seem hazard-free but she was learning things were not always what they appeared.

The seductive scratch of the Bane increased. She turned and opened her mouth to say something to Siban, but Gregory appeared from the dark passage.

Juna spun and looked at him and then back down the

tunnel. "Where is Magnus?"

"Exploring another passage. He'll join us in a few minutes." Gregory walked to the trailhead and stood next to Rell. "That passage leads to a drop-off. There is no way to traverse the path." He pointed across the open trail. "It appears this is our only choice."

Instantly Rell was on alert. She stared at Gregory. Perhaps it was the way he spoke or his mannerisms, but something seemed off about him. Her Tell skated over him, trying to decipher what was different, but could not identify anything specific.

Siban inched forward, his eyes locking with hers. "Rell, come walk beside me."

His burning stare told her he felt it, too. Brita moved forward to stand beside Siban. "Perhaps we should wait until Magnus returns, Gregory." She paused. "In case we run into anymore Bane."

Gregory smirked. "They haven't been a problem for us as of yet."

"But the demon at the arch nearly killed you." Brita pressed her hands over her heart. "We must be cautious."

"But I was victorious." Gregory held his arms wide, his words confirming the deception unfolding before them. "Magnus will catch up."

Trying not to make any sudden movements, Rell took a slow step toward Siban, but Gregory's hand shot out and gripped her arm. "Where are you going?" He pulled her toward him. The familiar darkness swamped her, fastening to her like thick molasses. "I said we travel this path."

With a hard shove, he pushed Rell forward onto the path. She stumbled. Her right foot slipped over the edge but she caught herself before she fell. The suffocating presence eased somewhat. She drew in a deep breath and slowly turned to face

Gregory—or whatever was pretending to be Gregory.

He smiled, his expression sending a shiver through her. "You see, there is no danger here."

Jade glared at him. "Why did you do that?"

Before Rell could take a step back toward safety, a small rivulet of water that had been flowing down the wall shifted and streamed across the trail. It spread across her feet. She jumped backward, but the shimmering liquid followed her, covering her boots like a silvery sheet.

The sensation of the ground shifting beneath her sent a rush of panic through Rell. She stumbled toward the ledge but righted herself. "The ground is moving."

Gregory laughed, the sound maniacal and not like the man she'd come to know.

Jade made to lunge forward but Luc grabbed her arm, pulling her to a stop. "I don't think that's Gregory."

Rell struggled to keep her footing on what felt like sifting sand. No matter what she tried, she could not gain ground forward or back to safety. She clutched a jutting rocked sticking out of the cavern wall and tried to climb above the water, but it was impossible to lift her feet from the liquid. Deciding it best not to move, she clung to the wall and forced herself to remain still.

Her eyes beseeched Siban to do something. His Tell touched her, giving her comfort that everything would be all right, but she didn't relax.

Siban gripped Brita's arm and pulled her to his left. At the same time Ravyn rushed forward. Both she and Siban raised their daggers and in one smooth motion, hurled the weapons at Gregory. The blades buried deep in their supposed leader's chest. Juna cried out, as if still not understanding the situation.

Gregory's image wavered. His mouth opened and closed, his now-yellow eyes rounding in shock. He grabbed for the knives, but Siban rushed forward and yanked the immortal weapons from his chest. In an instant, Gregory transformed from Bringer to Bane. Black tattoos covered every inch of the demon's body. At the center of its chest the Summoner's symbol extended outward, the points of the star reaching across its body.

Rhys leveled a solid kick to the Bane's stomach and catapulted the demon over the edge of the trail. A high-pitched scream followed the creature's descent, the sound of its body hitting the bottom of the gorge abruptly cutting off the screech.

Again the ground shifted beneath Rell. Her grip slipped slightly. She clawed at the wall, trying to get a firmer hold on the icy rocks and pressed her cheeks against the cold stone. The silver water bubbled around her feet, its flow increasing to run across the ground and over the edge. The liquid churned and roiled up her legs.

"Siban!" She attempted a step forward but nearly lost her footing completely. "I can't move."

"Hold on." He crept toward her and extended his arm, stretching his body in an effort to reach her. "I'm coming."

Rhys gripped Siban's wrist and then latched onto Luc. One by one the Bringers formed a human chain. Again Rell tried to move toward them but the water welled up, encompassing her legs, as if its single purpose was to drive her over the edge.

A thunderous roar erupted from below her, shaking the ground more violently than before. Wind swept through the cavern, battering each one of them and pushing Siban back toward safety. One of her hands slipped free. Rell cried out, her arm swinging wildly in an attempt to grab the wall again, but the wind and water beat against her. Rocks tumbled from above, sliding downward in an avalanche of water and stones.

Again the screams she'd heard in the corridor pierced her skull, their cries even louder than before. The water surged and lifted one foot completely from the ground. Rell could hear Siban and the other Bringers yelling at her, but the cries ricocheting through her head muffled their words. Her nails scraped along the stones as the force of the water drove her toward the edge. Pain throbbed through her fingers from trying to hold on, but inch by aching inch her grip slipped free.

Time seemed to slow, all movements around her registering at once. The ground shifted and Siban lunged for her. Rell's feet gave way and suddenly she was falling.

The shrieks inside Rell's head were replaced with her own screams. Wind beat against her ears as she toppled head first into the black gorge. There was no way to save herself. Her one thought was of Siban and how they'd never gotten the chance to live a life together. She closed her eyes, waiting for her death.

Something hard slammed into her, knocking the breath from her. Intense pain speared her arms and for a second she'd thought she'd hit the sharp rocks jutting from the wall. Her body lurched, her neck snapping backward, nearly halting her in midair. A hard *thump* of wings sounded above her and she was yanked violently upward. Her stomach flipped, nearly causing her to vomit.

The realization that talons wrapped around her arms sent another wave of panic through her. Had the demon they had thrown over captured her? Her instinct to fight back reared up. But to fight and win would mean falling again. She craned her neck, trying to see what Bane held her, but the darkness and the angle at which she hung made it impossible.

Upward they flew and to her surprise, the demon dropped her, though none too gently onto the ledge a few feet from the group. Siban rushed forward, his sword drawn. He scooped Rell into his free arm, crushing her to him. Though he spoke, she couldn't understand him with her head pressed against his chest. Stunned that she wasn't dead, Rell collapsed against him, the tears coming unbidden.

The *whoosh* of wings and the heavy *crunch* of stone pulled her from her shock. She pushed away from Siban to see the Bane who had saved her. "Icarus?"

Tall and imposing, Icarus stood a few yards from where he'd dropped her. His yellow eyes glimmered in the cavern's dimness and his shoulders were squared, as if completely at odds with his noble feat. "Being human has made you rather clumsy."

Siban shoved her behind him and pointed the sword at Icarus's chest. "Do not come any closer."

"He saved me, Siban." Rell tried to step around him, but he held her in place.

"Why is he here?"

Rhys and Ravyn moved to stand on either side of Siban. Bright orbs of fire burned in the palms of their hands.

"You mean to vanquish me after I saved your friend?" Icarus's voice pulsed with anger.

Frustrated by the Bringers' reaction, Rell pushed past Siban. He reached for her, but she dodged his grasp and walked toward Icarus. "Thank you."

The demon's brows furrowed when her step didn't slow, and when she threw her arms around his broad chest his body stiffened, as if shocked by her reaction. Though he didn't return her embrace, he didn't pull away.

"Rell." Siban's voice lashed out at her. "He can't be trusted."

She released the demon and stepped back. "I think he's proven he can."

Icarus inched away from Rell. "You have also become emotional."

She nodded, still trying to reconcile what she'd just experienced. "Perhaps."

Footsteps thundered from inside the passage and Gregory

and Magnus appeared, swords held ready. Both men slid to a stop.

"What is going on here?" Gregory looked from Icarus to Juna.

"Another illusion trap." She flicked her head toward Rell. "She fell and Icarus saved her."

The stilted explanation was correct if not brief. Though Magnus's stance didn't relax, Gregory released a heavy breath and straightened.

Siban took a step forward. "Why did you save Rell? Because you owe her for your freedom?"

"Siban!" She turned and glared at him.

"Rell, what does Siban mean?" Jade asked.

Rell's eyes searched the group. All of them watched her and she could see their understanding dawn.

"It doesn't matter." Meran stepped forward. "If Icarus hadn't been here, Rell would have died."

She was grateful for Meran's words. Even though she had freed Icarus and had therefore enabled him to save her life, she couldn't fight the feeling of having betrayed the group.

Siban leveled the sword at Icarus's chest. "I find it too much of coincidence that you just happened to be here. Are you following us?"

"I am not here by chance. Sha-hera told me of your journey."

"And you rushed to our aid?" Condescension laced Siban's words."

"Siban asked you a question, demon," Rhys said, lifting the spinning ball in threat.

They stared at each other for a few seconds. Finally relenting, Icarus folded his wings behind him. "Yes"

"Why?" Ravyn asked.

"Because I wished to know what you do here," Icarus said.

Gregory moved to stand beside Siban and placed a hand

on his shoulder. "We are in your debt, Icarus."

"That is not a place you want to be, Bringer." The demon turned his head and stared into the crevasse. "Why are you here?"

Siban shrugged off Gregory's hand. The group exchanged glances and then looked to Rell. She took their response as permission for her to speak for them. "We are searching for Vile and the Bringers he's captured."

"I am unfamiliar with this place." The demon surveyed their surroundings. "I've never journeyed beyond my father's sleeping chambers. These corridors are off-limits to all but Vile and his private guard."

"I'm certain he didn't want you here." Gregory stepped forward. "We have discovered things I think you should know."

The demon turned and looked at him, his voice thick with suspicion. "What things?"

Gregory looked at Rell, giving her an encouraging nod. Perhaps their discovery was best coming from somebody Icarus knew. Where did she begin? She pointed to Gregory. "Do you know who this is?"

Icarus's eyes narrowed, his chin lowering a fraction of an inch to focus on Gregory. "I assume he is your leader."

Rell tipped her head in a nod. "Yes, he is King Arron's second son."

"And why should this concern me?"

She looked at Gregory. This was his secret to reveal, not hers. He moved to stand next to her. "I am your half brother."

Icarus didn't move. Not even a flinch or shifting of his eyes. His yellow glare bore into Gregory for several seconds until finally looking at Rell for confirmation.

"It's true, or at least we believe it to be true. You are Arron's firstborn, Icarus. We think your uncle kidnapped you when you were just an infant and brought you through the Mystic

Arch to Inness." She mimicked his posture, not moving and barely blinking. "He changed you to a Bane before you could remember your Bringer life." She swallowed hard. "And he's kept you here ever since." Silence stretched between them, but Icarus did not reply. "Do you understand what I'm saying?"

Icarus turned and walked to the edge of the ledge, peering into the darkness below. "You are saying that Vile is my uncle, not my father."

"Yes," Rell said.

"And that I am the heir to the Bringer throne." He lifted his head and stared across the gorge. "That he stole my soul and forced me to serve him for these past thousand years."

True emotion seemed to coat his words. On some small level she understood what he must be feeling, but the magnitude of realizing what he had suffered at his uncle's hands could not be fully comprehended.

"I'm so sorry, Icarus." Rell moved toward him, but Siban gripped her arm and drew her back.

She went willingly, realizing her actions were motivated by her own emotions not logic.

"We travel to confront Vile," Gregory said. "To vanquish him."

Icarus turned and faced the group. "Then you journey toward your death." His gaze drifted over each member of the group. "And I journey to mine as well. I will confront my *father*." He nearly spat the word. "We will travel together."

"A truce, then?" Gregory asked.

"A truce." Icarus gave a single nod. "Until such time as it is no longer necessary."

"We know of the darkness that dwells inside you." Meran glided forward, her eyes leveled on Icarus. "You have seen what we accomplished with Rell."

Icarus cocked his head to the side, his gaze sliding down

and back up Meran's body to stop at her face. "You offer me my humanity?"

She stopped several feet from him. "It is possible. If we can locate your human form, we might be able to transform you back to Bringer."

His laughter echoed off the cavern walls. "First I would need to possess a soul for you to save. I can assure you, Bringer, mine is beyond redemption."

"I don't believe that." She drew herself to stand straighter. "And if you do not believe, then I will hold your hope for you."

Icarus's humorless smile faded. "Who are you?"

She cleared her throat, her hand gripping the hilt of her sword. "My name is Meran."

With a great flourish, Icarus extended his wings. "I fear you will be gravely disappointed, Meran."

"Then it will be my disappointment to bear," she said.

He held her stare for a few more seconds before raising his arm and pointing to the far side of the narrow trail Rell had fallen from. "I can see a wide, flat stretch at the end of this path." He lowered his hand. "I suggest those of you who can fly do so." His yellow eyes traveled over Meran. "As a show of good faith I offer you passage, but I do not think you will accept."

Meran walked toward Icarus, stopping inches away. "Then you are wrong."

Rell could feel surprise and anxiety ripple through the group, though none seemed more surprised than Icarus. His eyes widened and what looked like a genuine smile tipped the corners of the demon's mouth.

"You are either very brave—" He wound his arm around Meran's waist and pulled her small frame against him. Her hands rested against his chest, but she didn't fight his hold. "Or very stupid, Bringer."

"I guess we'll find out, won't we—" she wrapped her arms around his neck—"Bane."

Rell's heart leaped to her throat when Icarus turned and launched himself and Meran into the air. A ripple of fear traveled back along her Tell and from the familiar touch, it was Meran who emanated the emotion. Though she'd appeared brave, the woman had put her life at risk in an attempt to anchor Icarus's trust more firmly to the group.

They watched in silence as the two glided noiselessly along the crevasse, effectively avoiding any further illusions. Once they'd alighted on the other side of the trail, Gregory spoke. "The Shields can transport the rest of the group. We'll do it in two groups."

"I can fly myself," Ravyn said. "But I don't think any will want to touch me."

Rell had to agree. Even though Ravyn was part of the Trilation, her strongest power was as a Shield. Unlike the other Shields, who transformed into dragons, Ravyn transformed into a phoenix. During training, Rell had watched her change and sweep the sky with fire. A blanket of blazing orange had streaked behind Ravyn as she flew. Impressive, but deadly.

"I will carry Jade across first and come back for whoever is left," Luc said.

A groan that sounded like it came from the deepest recesses of her soul escaped Jade. "I had really hoped we were done with flying."

"Don't worry, Jade." Rell rubbed her sister's arm. "I'm sure Luc won't toss you to the ground like I used to do."

"Yes, remind me to repay you for your gentleness once we are out of here." Jade turned to Luc. "No fancy flying. Just straight to the other side."

"Your wish is my command." Luc kissed the top of her head. "As long as you don't retch all over me."

Jade grimaced and stepped away from him, motioning the others to give him space. "I can neither confirm nor deny that I won't lose what little food I've eaten today, but I will try my best not to."

In an instant, Luc changed from human to dragon. Golden scales formed to cover every inch of his powerful body. His arms extended, growing razor-sharp talons that curled and scraped against the stone.

Rell remembered battling Luc as a dragon. He had been powerful even though he'd barely tested his wings. Now obviously much more in control, he swung his head to face Jade and growled at her.

Jade released a heavy breath and moved forward, climbing the dragon's massive leg and onto its back. She gripped the horns like she would the reins of a horse and shifted to find a solid seat. "Sweet Sainted Ones, don't let me die."

At those words, Luc dove from the ledge. His golden wings spread to catch the updraft. At first they dipped, but the air lifted them with what looked like effortless ease to glide down the gorge—though Jade's screams would suggest the ride was anything but smooth.

CHAPTER EIGHTEEN

The golden dragon landed and faced Rell, purring at her. A thrill shot through her. Not since she'd been a Bane had she been able to fly. She glanced at Siban. "I've been waiting for this."

Siban shook his head and then gave her a little shove toward the dragon.

She pushed her sword into its sheath, and avoiding the curved talons, stepped onto his thigh and climbed up his flank. The scales appeared smooth but to the touch the texture was rough and held her footing. Once on his back, she did as she'd seen Jade do, and gripped the spiraled horns. Her heart beat faster as she braced herself for the dragon's launch.

This time he spread his wings halfway and pushed off the ledge. They nosed downward, the cold wind rushing over them, before he fully extended his wings and looped upward. Joyous laughter rolled out of her when Luc banked steeply to the right and glided so close to the wall she felt as if she should draw in her feet.

She closed her eyes and let the freedom flow through her. Though their journey to the other side took only a minute, it would forever remain as one of her favorite memories.

"That was incredible." She patted the dragon's neck. "If we get out of this alive, perhaps you will take me flying one night."

The dragon purred again and then transformed back to Luc, his leathery scales shrinking to reform his clothing. "At last, somebody who appreciates my skillful flying."

"You mean somebody who is as daft as you are," Jade said.

"I've heard it said you must try something twelve times before you like it," Ravyn said.

Jade glared at her. "It will be a cold day in the Abyss before I willingly climb on that beast again."

"Careful, sister." Rell stepped back to allow an incoming dragon to land. "This just might be that day."

Since the ledges were not large enough for four dragons to land on at once, Rhys, Gregory, Trace, and Luc had to transport in shifts. The process went fairly quickly and for once, nothing unexpected happened.

Once each of the Shields had transformed back to a Bringer, the group congregated at the head of the path. Instead of a narrow, treacherous path along the ridge, they were now heading into a tunnel. The blackness within was so thick no light penetrated beyond a few feet inside.

"Lovely," Juna said, sticking her head inside. "Another dark, dank tunnel."

Gregory rolled his wrist forward and produced an orb of light in his free hand. "If you are able to control the fire, I suggest producing an orb to not only light the way, but as a first line of defense." He circumvented Juna and moved into the cave. "There should be no shortage of Bane presence from which to draw your power."

Rell's fingers tingled and vibrations skittered along her arms and prickled in her palms. The sensation was new and she wasn't sure what would happen if she allowed the power to pool.

Exhaling, she gave over to her Tell's desire. A tiny blue spark crackled weakly in her hand. She refocused her concentration, letting her Tell fuel rather than force the energy. The orb grew stronger. It took a full minute, but in the end, she held a brilliant ball of spinning white light in her palm. "I did it." Unlike the fire of the Shields, her glimmering orb was not made of fire. If they got out of here alive, she would practice to see what new powers this ability held. She turned to show Siban and she scowled. His flared more brightly. "Show off."

"You inspire me." He waved his sword toward the tunnel. "After you."

Rell started to open her mouth, but bit back her retort when she saw Icarus watching her and Siban. His expression was guarded, as if expecting one of the Bringers to hurl the orb of light at him. "Would you like to go first?"

A sneer turned up the corner of his lip. "No, thank you. I will follow behind."

Rell didn't know if that was a good decision. The best choice would have probably been to have Icarus lead the group. His presence might delay an attack from the Bane, but she certainly understood his reluctance.

The tunnel wound for what seemed like forever. The light from their orbs illuminated the passage a few yards ahead and then the tunnel fell into blackness. If there was an attack awaiting them, the only warning they'd have would be from the increased gnawing that heralded the Bane's presence. The menacing itch had increased as they'd headed deeper into the caverns and with Icarus so close behind, it took a concerted effort for Rell to not constantly scrub her arm and try and sense other dangers beyond the big demon on their heels.

The tunnel turned to the right. At the end a pinpoint of light glowed. Their pace slowed, Gregory growing more cautious the closer they drew to the opening. Would this lead to yet another trail or had they finally arrived at their destination?

A clawing sensation traveled up Rell's back. She rolled her shoulders, trying to ignore the warning. At the entrance, Gregory stopped for a few seconds and then proceeded into the light. From where Rell stood she saw a wide expanse of rock, and when she stepped out of the tunnel, panic welled up inside of her. They'd arrived.

Before them rose two gigantic doors, reaching thirty feet at least in height. Intricate carvings covered the wood, but Rell stood too far away to make out the images. However, the two Demon Bane standing guard in front of the doors sent ripples of fear through her. Their wings spread across the front of the exit. The spears they held reached three feet above their heads and were tipped with heavy iron points. Thick horns spiraled upward from their heads and gold rings adorned their ears, while gold bands encircled their biceps and ankles. They wore leather breastplates studded with gold and at the center was the symbol of the Summoners. Unlike the other demons she'd encountered in the Shadow World, these Bane emanated power and much like Icarus, they were horrifyingly beautiful.

Their yellow gazes remained focused on the group, but they did not move to stop the Bringers' approach. Rell searched the ceiling and sent her Tell into the dark recesses that could easily hide more Bane, but nothing besides the guards registered.

"Why do they not attack?" Juna asked.

"They guard whatever lies beyond the doors." Gregory was quiet for a few seconds. "We must get past them."

Rell's orb pulsed in her hand, growing to twice its size. The other Bringers lifted their swords, readying for a fight, but still no attack came. Icarus exited the tunnel and moved to stand next to Gregory. He said nothing, only stared.

At his appearance, the guards looked at each other, as if at a loss to understand why one of their own was with the enemy.

But the demons quickly recovered their emotionless mask and continued to guard the door.

The Bringers and Icarus approached cautiously and when they were about twenty feet from the door, the demon's lowered their spears, pointing them directly at Icarus and Gregory.

"I will speak to them," Icarus said, striding forward without waiting for Gregory's response. He stopped ten feet in front of the guards. "I wish to see Vile."

"You are not welcome here, Banished One." The guard lowered his spear several more inches, bringing it to chest level.

"Those who travel with the enemy are not permitted into the Sanctuary." The second demon took a step forward, as if to do battle.

Seemingly undaunted, Icarus did not move. "What is the Sanctuary?"

Neither demon spoke. Rell's heart pounded. Tremors danced along her skin, wanting to be released. A few of the Bringers shifted nervously. Rell sent out her Tell, trying to sense what lay beyond the doors, but it was as if a barrier blocked out any effort to scan beyond the guards.

She noticed the sentries' skin. Every inch was covered with tattoos and she could only guess that they were Summoners as well.

A heavy *thud* and loud creaking issued from the doors. The guards remained in place but glanced at each other. With aching slowness the giant doors began to swing inward, the grinding of the hinges reverberating off the walls. Icarus took several steps back, but did not rejoin the group.

Blue light and icy wind poured from between the expanding crack. Shivers rippled along Rell's skin, making her colder than she had been, if that was possible. A glistening expanse of black floor extended down a long walkway and at the very end a thick wall of pulsing blue ice rose up behind an enormous throne. On the seat sat the Demon King.

"Let our visitors in." Vile's voice sprang from inside. "After all, they've had a long journey."

The guards snapped to attention, lifting their spears and taking their places on either side of the entrance again.

"Come in," Vile said. "I've been expecting you."

The Bringers exchanged glances. Icarus did not turn to consult the others about what to do, but strode forward. Rell looked at Siban. She wanted to take his hand, but showing preference to him could mean his death if Vile decided to teach them a lesson. Whatever waited inside could possibly kill her. But it was the realization that even if she survived, Siban might not, that took her breath away. Always their arguments had been about her safety. What would her life be like if he didn't make it?

She looked at him. "Don't die."

He inhaled and nodded. "You either."

The group walked forward. Every nerve in Rell's body felt ultrasensitive. She tensed when they passed the guards, expecting them to attack from behind. When they didn't, she relaxed slightly—until they entered the Sanctuary.

Her mouth dropped open at the sheer magnitude of the hall. Obelisks of black stone soared from floor to ceiling, their smooth surfaces glimmering with bits of silver and iridescent blue. Between the pillars, blue flames as tall as Rell burned in giant hearths. No heat radiated from the fire. If anything, the blaze seemed to suck the warmth from the hall.

But it was the army of Bane that nearly stopped Rell in her tracks. A single demon stood in front of each obelisk. Much like the guards outside, these demons were beautiful but terrifying. Each wore the breastplate with the Summoner's symbol emblazoned on the front, but these sentinels wore skirts of what looked like rectangular gold plates hinged together with rings. Beneath the skirt their legs were clad in leather and each was adorned with the same gold bands around their biceps.

It was as if she'd walked into her worst nightmare, trapped beneath the earth with the creatures that had turned her life into years of living desolation. She shifted the sword in her hand, gripping the hilt more firmly. The weapon gave her comfort but she doubted it would be much use against so many of the Bane/Summoners.

They walked along the wide path, making sure to stay away from the deep gorge that opened between the walkways of each black obelisk. Towering stone sculptures of Bringers dwarfed the end of their path, each statue bearing the mark of the Summoner.

As they approached the throne, Rell's eyes settled on the wall behind Vile. Her hand snaked out to grab Siban's arm. When he looked at her, Rell flicked her head toward the towering blue ice. "The Bringers."

He sucked in a breath. Frozen in their peaceful state were the Bringers they'd been searching for. Level upon level, the exhibition was like a horrific sculpture that climbed and disappeared into the darkness above.

Siban leaned toward Magnus and pointed. "The Bringers."

Quickly the message traveled through the group, each reaction equally as appalled as Rell's had been. How could they possibly free them from the ice wall that reached a hundred feet or more above them?

"I see you've bested my illusion traps." Vile said, watching their approach. He sat regally on his throne, as if he truly was a king. "And I see you've brought my son. Now that is a surprise."

Icarus stopped several yards from the throne, causing the group to halt a few paces behind him. "Am I?"

Vile cocked his head. "Are you what?"

"Your son?" Though asked as a question, Icarus's words

held no inquiry. He seemed to have accepted the Bringers' explanation.

"Clever boy." Vile leaned forward, resting his elbows on his knees. "How did you figure it out?" His gaze slid to the group. "No doubt your new friends helped you to this conclusion." When Icarus didn't reply, Vile stood. "I like to think I was more than just a father to you."

"Yes, warden, kidnapper, tormentor." Icarus took a step forward. "Why?"

Vile raised his hands in the air. "Why? For revenge of course."

"Against whom?" Gregory asked.

"And who do we have here?" Vile's gaze leveled on him, a wicked smile spreading across his face. "Another surprise, I think." He pointed a talon at Gregory. "Your eyes give you away." He lowered his arm. "But how, when I made sure the only heir to the throne would be Icarus? Perhaps you are the son of that whore who started the Bane war." He folded his hand in front of his chest, his voice taking on a simpering tone. "Please, King Arron, help my people."

Gregory raised his sword, directing it at Vile's chest. "You will not speak so about my mother."

Vile laughed. "You are in my realm now. None dictate to me."

While the Demon King's attention was directed at Gregory and Icarus, Rell searched the hall. Craning her neck, she looked upward. A tiny sliver of light, barely visible, glowed hundreds of feet above. Perhaps it was an escape or maybe just another illusion.

"You spoke of revenge," Icarus said. "Against whom?"

"My brother." A sneer curled Vile's lip. He paced in front of the throne. "Harlin thought to imprison me as he did our mother simply because we were Summoners." His pacing stopped and he glared at them. "He feared us. We were stronger, more powerful than the other clans. My brother ambushed all the Summoners and locked them in the Abyss." His sneer softened. He lowered his voice to a whisper. "But I begged for my freedom, told him I would live out my days in a warded prison if he would do me the kindness owed to a brother and not sentence me to an eternity of torment as he had our mother." Vile's laughter ricocheted around the cavernous hall. "And he believed me."

"How did you escape?" Icarus posture was stiff, his stare boring into Vile.

Though his wings were folded, Rell could feel the rage pouring from him. She shielded her mind, trying to block out the intense flow of emotions threatening to overwhelm her. Siban reached for her. Instantly their connection calmed the chaos swirling through her. She twined her fingers with his, no longer caring if their joined hands revealed their love for each other.

"I didn't escape, my boy, I was never imprisoned." Vile slid onto the throne and folded his hands over his stomach. "An illusion. Another Summoner took my form and my place." He shrugged. "After that it was simple."

"Simple, how?" Gregory moved to stand next to Icarus. "And why take my brother."

Icarus's gaze settled on Gregory for a few seconds before returning to Vile.

"Harlin was vain and told no one of his acquiescence to imprison me in a warded cell. I bided my time, watching Arron grow incensed with my brother's treatment of the humans. I knew it would only be a matter of time before he took action and overthrew Harlin. The Summoners aided him in his fight, though he never knew this. We were still outcasts and imprisoned in the Abyss for all your father knew. Our presence had to remain a secret." He pointed to Icarus. "That's where you came in. You were just an infant and the apple of your father's eye. Fortunately your mother died giving birth to you, leaving your raising to wet nurses. When I had you kidnapped, I thought Arron would die of heartbreak. He nearly did." His expression turned dark. "Then the human bitch arrived pleading for his help with the Bane."

"But you are the Bane," Juna said. "How is that possible?"

Vile cocked his head. "You look very much like your mother."

Juna took a step forward, raising her hand, but Rhys captured her wrist, holding her in place. "Where is she?"

Vile waved a hand toward the wall of ice. "Let's just say she's been my guest for quite some time now."

"Have you killed her?" Ravyn joined the line. "Or have you made her Bane?"

"Neither." The Demon King's brow furrowed. "I would never hurt Phillipa. I love her."

"Love her?" Ravyn shook her head. "You are incapable of love."

"Do not pretend to know me, girl." He stood and strode to the wall of ice, stopping next to a woman, who Rell could now see bore a striking resemblance to Juna and Ravyn. He stroked the smooth surface near the woman's face. "I have loved her for an eternity." With surprising gentleness, he kissed the ice covering her cheek. "And she would have loved me too if not for your father." He let his hand slide down and away from the wall. "He lured her away with promises of happiness and a family."

"Which they had." Meran moved to stand next to her sisters. "But you destroyed that."

"Yes, I did." Vile walked to stand behind his throne and laid his arms on the back, resting his chin on them. "Now she will be with me forever. And you will join her."

"Over my dead body," Juna said.

"Oh, you may try to free her as you did the girl." He shrugged. "But I'm sure you've already discovered that a body is of little use without the soul."

"I beg to differ with you, Uncle." Icarus stepped back and looked at Rell.

Siban released her hand and with slow steps she walked forward. Vile's gaze drove into her and for a fraction of a second she was positive uncertainty and fear flashed in his eyes. He straightened and skirted the chair.

She stopped next to Icarus but didn't look at him, keeping her eyes on Vile and her grip tight on her sword. "Remember me?" Her words sounded much braver than she felt. "Daughter of Bowen Kendal?"

"But how?" The demon's gaze tracked along the gathered Bringers. "This has never been done."

Nobody spoke, all unwilling to reveal the healing ritual that had restored her.

"Perhaps my brother wasn't as much of an idiot as I believed." Excitement edged Vile's voice. "I'm sure you will share your secret with me eventually—after you've experienced my methods of persuasion." He pointed at Siban. "Ask the dark Bringer. I'm sure he remembers all too well the pleasures of being my captive."

Rell turned to look at Siban. Even if she hadn't felt his rage, his hard expression would have revealed his barely contained anger. She wanted to go to him, to calm him as he had done for her so often since they'd begun their journey. Giving in to the urge, she approached him and placed her hands against his arms. At first he didn't look at her, his gaze fixed on Vile. She released her Tell, letting it flow over him, willing it to drive away his pain. Slowly he lowered his eyes and after a few seconds, he nodded.

Before she could shut the barriers of her mind again, the screaming she'd heard in the tunnel erupted, the howls of anguish exploding in her. She stumbled but Siban caught her. With great effort she slammed her mental barriers and the cries ceased. A sensation of lies swamped her before she successfully blocked it all out.

"Ah, I understand now." Vile tapped his finger against his chin. "It was you who released him. That was a miscalculation on my part. I can see that now." He settled back on the throne. "I'd thought to drive the Bringers from hiding by turning a helpless girl. I knew they'd find out, but I hadn't counted on the girl being a warrior."

The words he spoke fueled Rell's determination to never fall under Vile's control again. She would die, fall on the immortal weapon by her own hand, before she would allow the Bane to take her.

"I think there are many things you have miscalculated, Uncle." Icarus spread his wings, sending the Bringers scattering.

Vile laughed again. "Do you mean to battle me, Icarus—or should I say Icarus Drake Stewart from the House of Cameron."

"I know only Icarus." He crouched. "You took the rest from me long ago."

Vile stood, spreading his wings, their barbed tips pointing forward. "You will lose, nephew. I have taught you all you know, but not all *I* know." The sentinels in front of the black obelisks moved forward. "And you and your friends will replace my comrades in the Abyss."

"You cannot open the Abyss, so your threat is mute," Icarus growled.

"Oh, but I can." He smiled, baring his fangs. "Now that you've so generously brought me the Trilation."

The three sisters glanced at each other and then lifted their swords. "We will never open the Abyss."

A knowing smile spread across Vile's sharp mouth. "We shall see."

CHAPTER NINETEEN

Icarus launched himself at Vile at the same time the Demon King attacked. The two demons clashed in the air, ripping at each other's flesh.

Siban grabbed Rell and spun her to face the back of the room. "Stay close."

"Protect each other's back for as long as you can," Gregory shouted. "Juna, take your sister's and try to free the Bringers."

"How?" She crouched next to him, ready for the attack from the encroaching Bane.

"You're the Trilation. Use that." He stepped in front of her. "We will hold them off as long as we can."

"I hate to break this to you, but we don't know what we're doing," Juna argued.

"Come on." Meran grabbed her sister's tunic and pulled Juna toward the wall of ice.

Siban shifted his attention to the imminent attack. Unlike his time imprisoned within the Shadow World, he was at full power and ready to fight. Anger rolled through him, igniting his Tell. Tremors raced through him and pooled into his hand. "Use whatever Bringer powers you have!"

"I plan to," Rhys said.

Before their eyes he shifted to a black dragon. Siban pulled Rell with him, barely dodging the spiked tail of the dragon.

Rell produced a glowing ball and hurled it at the nearest Bane. The demon waved his hand, sending the orb to crash against the wall. Chunks of rock erupted, leaving a giant hole. "It's not working."

Siban thrust his hands forward, and again the Bane repelled his attack. The black dragon roared, spreading his wings to shield them from the demons. The beast opened its mouth and loosed a stream of fire that spread across the line of Bane.

A few were caught in the attack, their screams horrific and piercing. Most launched themselves into the air, narrowly avoiding being incinerated.

"Don't mind if I do," Luc said. He shifted into his golden dragon. The powerful legs of the creature bent and pushed off, sending its body into the air after the escaped demons.

Rhys joined him.

"I will remain here and fight. Our attack will be stronger if we don't put all the Shields in one place," Gregory shouted.

Those on the ground created a circle, their backs to the inside and released a volley of fire and energy balls at the demons that engaged in the fight on the ground.

Icarus and Vile slammed into the walls, sending chunks of stone falling down. Siban dove out of the way and barely missed being struck by a hunk bigger than his head. Though they tried to keep their formation together, little by little the Bane drove them in different directions. Rell managed to stay next to him. Siban opened his Tell to her and she to him. Together they worked as a single unit, attacking repeatedly, fueling each other's fighting instincts.

A demon landed in front of Siban and slashed at him with its deadly talons, raking his chest. Fire burned along the gashes and blood seeped through his leather tunic. He stumbled backward and knocked into Rell, falling to the ground.

"No!" She spun and as the demon's talons snaked out to finish the job and impale Siban's chest, she trust her hand out. Without thinking, she shouted some ancient words of power. The demon froze.

Siban struggled to his knees, one hand pressed to his chest while the other gripped his sword. How Rell was immobilizing the demon he didn't know, but questions would wait.

"Stab him!" Her hand began to shake and sweat beaded on her forehead. "Hurry."

Siban drew back the Immortal sword and thrust it forward, piercing the center of the Summoner's symbol. Rell released her hold and staggered backward. Siban pulled his sword free. He gained his footing and caught Rell around the waist. They needed to get away from the demon. Despite the pain searing his chest, Siban pulled her toward a huge carved statue.

The demon convulsed several times. A black shadow formed behind it. Rell slapped her hands over her ears when the wails once again erupted. Thunder rumbled, sending vibrations along the ground like the ones in the passage near Vile's chamber. The statue they stood behind rocked, the giant stone scraping along the black floor.

Siban yanked her back against the wall. The cries grew louder. The black shadow behind the demon grew wider and denser. Wind rushed through the hall with a furious blast, pelting them with debris. Wrapping his arm around his face and covering Rell with his body, Siban shielded them from the punishing shards of rock.

The statue swayed more violently, the base lifting from the ground. With a groan, the monolith toppled forward, crashing against the ground. Siban looked over his shoulder at the demon he'd slayed. Hands extended from the interior of the black hole, grabbing the Bane and pulling it slowly inside. The demon fought their clawing grip but couldn't break free and disappeared within. A rumble rocked the ground and the black hole disappeared.

When he released Rell, he dropped to the ground again. Weakness shook his muscles. He touched the blood running down his chest and reached a hand toward her. "Rell."

"Siban." She eased him to the floor and looked around. "Jade!"

Darkness tinged the edge of his vision. He fought his weakening state. If he died, who would protect Rell?

Suddenly Jade was there, her hands pressed hard against his chest. He coughed, tasting blood in his mouth. None too gently, Jade shouted the ancient healing words. Sparks of heat raced along the gashes. Her voice grew louder. Like stitching a wound, the skin around his injuries drew together, meshing into long, angry, red welts.

Strength returned and his vision cleared. After another few seconds, Jade released him. "There, now be more careful."

His body hummed with energy and though he didn't need their help, Jade and Rell drew him to his feet. Before he could thank Jade, Ravyn screamed, drawing their attention.

"Go help Gregory," Rell said to Jade.

Rell and Siban raced across the hall to the wall of ice. The three sisters battled two Bane. Ravyn hurled balls of fire, while Juna drove them back with her sword. Jade joined the fight, grabbing one of the demons by the arm.

White light flowed from her and into the creature. Ravyn gripped its other arm, sending fire along the demon's skin. The creature yanked, jerking the two women forward. Meran shoved both hands against its chest and released golden light into the center of its body. The demon shrieked and convulsed but the three women held tight.

"Move!" Juna rushed forward. They released their hold and with a hard thrust, Juna buried the sword into the demon's chest. She pulled it free and leveled a kick at the symbol, sending the demon toppling into the deep gorge.

Rell faced the other Bane and again lifted her hand, holding it in place. Not waiting this time, Siban rammed his sword through the Summoner's chest and continued to push the Bane backward until it toppled into the gorge to join the demon that Juna had slayed. The familiar rumble of the Abyss as it claimed more prisoners rippled through the chamber.

Jade turned to Rell. "When did you learn to do that?"

Rell shrugged, her eyes wide. "It just happens."

"Well done," Jade said.

"There's too many of them." Ravyn nodded toward the end of the hall. Two more demons filtered through the open doors. "We can't free the Bringers and fight."

"You concentrate on them." Siban wiped his hands against his pants and repositioned his sword. "And we'll protect you."

"How are we going to get out of here?" Meran asked. "The door is blocked and we can't carry them all the way back through those tunnels."

"There's a light above. It might be an opening." Rell pointed to the ceiling. "At least some of us will be able to get free."

Nobody spoke for a few seconds, then Juna said, "Come on, sisters, let's find out if being the Trilation is worth more than opening the Abyss."

The three set their hands against the ice and closed their eyes.

"Doesn't it burn?" Jade asked.

"No," Ravyn said. "It's cold but doesn't burn."

The fight above them drew Siban, Rell, and Jade's attention. Vile and Icarus remained locked in a deadly battle, each demon tearing at the other and delivering unforgiving blows.

"Why don't the Summoners use fire?" Rell asked.

"Maybe it's not their power." Siban watched as a demon engaged Rhys's dragon. Its attacks were punishing but not deadly. Rhys easily defended himself. Trace had also transformed and though he fought several Bane, they didn't attack as one. "It's almost as if they are baiting us."

"Perhaps Vile has given them orders not to kill us," Jade said.

Rell shook her head. "Something doesn't feel right."

"I thought the same thing." Siban looked to where Magnus, Gregory, and Brita defended themselves. "Watch, the Bane attack halfheartedly, as if they're only trying to keep them occupied."

Ancient words flowed from the three sisters and a low hum vibrated along the ground.

"They don't approach us." Jade pointed to a line of Summoners beyond Gregory. "They line the far end of the hall but don't move. They're just observing."

"But why?" Rell glanced upward and then back to where the other Bringers easily held off the Bane. "Perhaps it's a trap of some kind."

"Not a trap." Siban faced the three sisters. "A diversion."

A loud *crack* sounded from the wall of ice. The images of the frozen Bringers wavered and were replaced by dark figures. Fingers scraped along the inside of the wall and anguished cries filtered through the ice. Another crack sounded, followed by a thunderous roar.

"Stop!" Siban raced forward and yanked Ravyn's hands from the ice. "Those are not Bringers."

"What are you talking about?" Juna's hands remained on the ice. "Our mother is inside."

"Look." He pointed to one of the dark figures. Its body slithered along the inside. For a fraction of a second an eight-pointed star pressed against the ice. "The Summoner's symbol."

A small fracture appeared in the structure and traced a disjointed path upward. The three sisters stumbled away from the wall.

"This isn't a wall of ice," Meran said. "It's the Abyss."

"He tricked us into opening it." Juna turned and sprinted toward Gregory, shouting at them.

Siban grabbed Rell's hand. "Come on!"

The five of them raced across the black expanse behind Juna and engaged the demons Gregory and the two others had been fighting.

"We have to get out of here." Siban swung his sword at the closest Bane. "Get the dragons."

A low groan radiated from the Abyss and the walls vibrated. Tremors undulated across the floor, sending the fighting Bane running toward the entrance of the hall.

"I'm going to help drive back the Bane from above." Gregory spun, transforming to a dragon and launched into the air.

"Maybe we can stop the Abyss from opening," Meran said.

"How? We didn't even know we were opening it to begin with." Ravyn turned to Brita. "Do you know?"

The Tell shook her head. "We were not given that information, but as the Trilation you should be able to project what you want."

The three sisters joined hands again and turned toward the fracturing structure. They closed their eyes and raised their hands.

"They're coming back." Magnus crouched, readying himself for the new wave of Bane sweeping toward them. "It looks like they mean to stop the Trilation."

"And I mean to stop them." Rell looked at Siban. "Let's vanquish these bastards once and for all."

"You read my mind," he said.

The first wave hit, bringing three demons to one Bringer. Siban hacked at the Bane, sending energy balls as quickly as he could manifest them, with little effect.

"Use your Tell," Brita shouted. "Concentrate your powers into your attack."

Siban let the barriers of his mind crumble. His Tell rushed through his body and down his arm. Energy pooled in his hand as he drove back one of the demons with his sword. When there was a brief lull, he sent his intentions into the orb and hurled it toward his opposition. It sped across the hall and blasted into a Bane. The demon exploded into a million glittering sparks, but another demon quickly took its place.

Wind swept through the hall and the glittering bits began to swirl, gathering into a violent vortex. The fiery sparks spun, sucking several of the Bane into it as it swept along the hall. With a violent roar, the vortex rammed through the floor, opening a giant gash in the floor and disappeared.

More Bane converged and again the Bringers attacked with a barrage of fire. Slowly they gained ground, forcing the demons back. Another crack rented the air and a loud groan rumbled from the Abyss.

"It's not working." Ravyn's voice raised above the cacophony of battle. "What do we do?"

"Look," Meran yelled.

Siban chanced a glance. From the ceiling thousands of imps crawled down the cavern wall toward the Abyss. He spun, hurled an orb and stabbed a charging demon with his sword. Another vortex formed, spinning toward the opening of the hall. The Bane fled, trying to avoid its path.

"What are they doing?" Juna shouted above the roar.

With a reprieve in the fighting, the Bringers turned to watch the imps. Their black bodies clung to the wall of the Abyss, covering it. The wails from within grew, as if angered by the creatures' interference.

"I think they're helping," Rell said.

"No!" Vile's bellow resonated through the hall. He dove toward the gathering imps, but Icarus landed on top of him and spun, sending his uncle crashing into one of the towering statues.

Vile slammed into the stone, decapitating the sculpture, and dropped to the ground. Quickly righting himself, he sent a blast of fire at the imps. Their squeals of pain filled the hall, the smell of their burning flesh billowing to choke Siban.

He coughed and covered his mouth with his sleeve. "We need to get out of here."

"What about the Abyss?" Ravyn asked.

"There's nothing to be done about it now." Magnus waved at the battling dragons. "Pray that the imps know what they are doing. If not, I'm sure we'll know about it soon enough. Best that we're not here when and if it opens."

One by one the dragons landed. Siban shoved Rell onto Luc's back along with Jade. Juna and Brita climbed onto Gregory, leaving Siban to ride Rhys and Magnus on Trace. He held out his hand to Meran, but before she could reach for him, Icarus swooped down and plucked her from the ground. The demon shot skyward toward the light at the top of the hall.

Ravyn transformed, but before heading toward the opening, she laid a wall of fire between the Bane and the escaping dragons. Luc shot into the air and Siban breathed a sigh of relief that Rell was on her way to safety. Gregory launched next, then Trace, and finally Siban and Rhys took to the air.

Vile paid them no heed, his attention focused fully on the Abyss and the imps. With their king not in pursuit, the other Bane seemed disinclined to continue the fight.

Above them the light grew. Icarus and Meran burst through

the opening first, followed by Ravyn, Luc, Gregory, Trace, and finally Rhys. Sunlight bit into Siban's eyes when they broke free from the dark interior of the Shadow World. He gasped, breathing in the sweet air of freedom.

CHAPTER TWENTY

Wind dragged at Rell's hair, the rays of the sun spreading over her the higher the golden dragon climbed. Compared to the icy interior from which they had just escaped, outside felt like a summer day. Jade wrapped her arms around Rell's waist and crushed the air from her as Luc glided down the slope of the mountain to where they had left the horses when they had entered the Shadow World.

She craned her neck to look behind them and sent up a prayer of thanks when the only others who followed them were members of their party. Perhaps the Sanctuary had collapsed or the Bane were too busy trying to counter the unexpected invasion of imps. Rell inhaled deeply, just thankful that they'd all gotten out alive.

The exhilaration of flight and narrowly escaping Vile's trap made her want to shout to the open air. A roar erupted from the golden dragon, reverberating against Rell's legs. Jade yelped and clutched her tighter. Rell laughed, unable to suppress the multitude of emotions swirling through her.

An answering roar erupted behind them. Rell craned her neck to see the black dragon banking around the mountain with Siban on its back. Her heart soared. She scanned the sky, mentally counting the Bringers and the dragons. All had escaped. Overcome with gratitude, she closed her eyes and sent up a heartfelt prayer of thanks to the Sainted Ones.

Their course dipped lower to drift a hundred feet above the trees. Because the clearing was small, the dragons circled, waiting for their turn to land. After Gregory had shifted back to human, Luc banked steeply to the left, eliciting another yelp from Jade, and alighted in the center of the clearing. It took a few seconds before Jade relinquished her punishing grip around Rell's waist. On shaky legs, Jade crawled off the dragon's back. Rell hopped from her place at the beast's neck, to its haunch, and then onto the ground.

Though he took longer than Gregory, eventually Luc shifted back to Bringer and walked to Jade, wrapping her in a protective hug. "It's all right. We're safe."

Jade wrapped her arms around Luc's waist and pressed her face into the crook of his shoulder. She didn't speak, only held him close for a good minute.

Obviously Rell was not the only one who was grateful to be alive. Rhys's black dragon circled. The Bringers on the ground moved into the trees to allow him to land. With a mighty down stroke of its wings, the dragon hovered a few seconds and then settled in the clearing.

Her heart beat faster at the sight of Siban on top of the powerful beast. He looked every bit the warrior. His gaze leveled on her, intense and serious. She swallowed and took several slow steps toward him. Without breaking their gaze, he rose, jumped from the dragon, and strode toward her.

Her pace quickened and she nearly threw herself into his arms. He scooped her up and crushed her to him. "We made it." His words whispered against her cheek. "Barely, but we made it."

She nodded and lifted her head. Despite the gathering crowd of Bringers, she twined her fingers in his mass of chocolate-brown locks and pushed his head toward hers to kiss him. Their mouths met and she let out a little whimper as the reality of what they'd just gone through hit her. They'd entered the Shadow World, and though they hadn't accomplished their mission, they'd learned so much more than they'd previously known. On a personal level, she and Siban had faced their nightmares and survived.

"Is everybody all right?" Gregory stood in the center of the clearing. Blood ran from a large gash on his forehead, his gaze traveling over each member of the group. "Does anybody need healing?"

A *thump* from above sounded, and though they had been the first through the opening, Icarus and Meran were the last to land. The demon flared his wings and settled a few yards from Gregory with Meran clutched to him. The demon's embrace loosened and his gaze lingered on her for a few seconds longer than felt natural.

Rell thought it looked as if Icarus released her with great reluctance. Meran's hands slid from around his neck and drifted down his chest before she stepped away. The demon watched her, his yellow stare swirling to silver, making him look almost human. Icarus watched Meran the same way Siban used to look at her when she was a demon. Good, if they planned on saving his life, he would need something or somebody to fight for.

Meran's eyes never left Icarus. "Thank you. You saved my life."

A strange expression flittered across Icarus face, one Rell had never seen the proud demon display—humility. "It is I who am in your debt." He lifted his head to stare at the group. "I do not know what it all means for me, but I am grateful for the knowledge of who I was."

"Are," Meran said. "Vile has never been able to fully take away who you are and I will do everything in my power to help you find your way back to us."

His eyes leveled on her. "Again, I am humbled by your generosity, but I fear there is little that can be done to mend what Vile has broken."

Tears burned in the back of Rell's eyes at his declaration. She stepped away from Siban and walked to where Icarus stood. "These Bringers"— she held out her arm, indicating the entire group— "welcomed me as one of their own. Even as a demon they gave me shelter and protection. Though I couldn't see it at the time, they did everything in their power to save me." She lowered her hand and turned to look at Siban. "I want to believe it is never too late, Icarus."

Siban glided forward. "Perhaps I've been wrong about you, Bane."

Icarus tipped his head and peered down at him. "You were wise not to trust me."

"Probably, but Rell is right. You deserve to know who you are."

"You are my brother." Gregory stopped in front of Icarus. "For far too long you've toiled alone." He shook his head. "No longer. Whether you want it or not, we will not abandon you."

"Remember when you asked me if being human was good?" Rell asked.

Icarus inclined his head.

"To live without the darkness is like lifting blinders from your eyes and unchaining your soul to let it soar free, unfettered by the desolation." She smiled. "It is good, Icarus, very good, and I wouldn't give it up for all the treasure in this world."

"Your words fill me with. . .hope. But I'm hesitant to give them too much weight. We are not the same, Rell. I have lived as a Bane for a thousand years and much of the stain on my

soul was of my own doing." He straightened and looked at his
brother. "Will you return to the manor?"

"Yes." Gregory paused. "Will you join us?"

"No." Icarus extended his wings. "There are things I must
take care of."

"You're not going back in the Shadow World, are you?"
Meran asked.

"I have had enough of my uncle's treachery." He shook his
head, the long black mane swishing against the edges of his
wings. "When I am finished I will find you."

With one last glance at Meran, Icarus launched himself into
the sky and banked to the south.

Meran shook her head and looked at the group. "I can
hardly believe what we've discovered."

"A thousand-year-old mystery," Rhys said. "One that I'm
sure involves many of our kin."

"I'm sure you're right," Brita said. "Hopefully we'll be able
to discover what exactly happened."

"Vile's journal should give us some clue." Gregory sighed.
"Unless he staged his chamber knowing we'd discover the
diary."

Magnus leaned his back against a tree. "I grow weary of
these deadly games."

"Unfortunately, it seems Vile does not." Rhys draped his
arm around Ravyn's shoulder and pulled her into the crook of
his arm. "It's more important than ever to protect ourselves
and those we love from what Vile has in store."

"I agree, but first we need to recover from what we just
went through." Jade walked to Gregory and placed her hand
near the cut on his forehead. "You need healing. What was it,
a talon?"

"Yes, after the Bane began fighting in earnest, one of them
caught me across the head. I'm lucky I only received this."

"I'll say." Jade closed her eyes and whispered the ancient words of the healing chant.

Besides her transition back to Bringer, Rell had never seen her sister's powers at work. The air around Jade and Gregory shimmered. Thin threads of green-and-white light flowed from the surrounding trees and swirled around his head, dancing in graceful circles around the two of them.

Vibrations skittered across Rell's skin like tiny butterfly wings, bringing with it a feeling of tranquility and oneness with the forest and all living things. Like her Tell, Jade's Redeemer powers were an entity in itself. Rell smiled. For the first time she saw Jade as a powerful Bringer and not the little sister she'd wronged thirteen years ago.

The healing only took a minute and when Jade removed her hand, no evidence of his injury remained. She turned. "Anybody else?"

One by one, Jade, Ravyn, and Meran worked through the Bringers healing them. Some bore only a disheveled appearance as evidence of the battle, but the women took no chances, not wanting to risk any internal bleeding.

When Jade's light entered Rell's body, it burned away most of the aches and fatigue, but didn't touch the desolation being in Vile's presences had left in her. "That will have to do for now." Jade removed her hands. "It will last us until we get home and can fully heal."

"Thank you." Rell smiled and rotated her wrist, amazed that the ache where she'd been struck by a chunk of falling stone was gone. "That feels much better."

• • •

Siban led the small mare to where Rell and Jade sat. Jade's glare cut to the animal. A sigh heaved from her. "Will this torture never end?"

Rell gave her a sympathetic pat on the back. "No."

"Thank you, Esmeralda. Your empathy is underwhelming." Jade's eyes darted around the clearing, as if looking for a place to hide. "Here comes Luc with my mount."

"You just faced down several Summoners, the Demon King, and rode a dragon. I think you can handle a horse," Rell said.

Jade scowled. "You're beginning to sound like Mother."

That made Rell smile. "I will take that as a compliment."

Rell mounted her horse, taking the reins from Siban.

"If we're ready, let's mount up." Gregory pulled his horse to the front of the line. "I think it best if we go as far as Illuma Grand today." He glanced at the sky. "We've probably four hours of sunlight and I'm sure we could all do with a rest before pushing on to the manor."

When nobody disagreed, Gregory urged his stallion forward and back along the path they had traveled. They felt no hint of the Bane, nor did they meet another person on the trail. The hum of bugs and the song of birds indicated their only companions. The farther they traveled from the Shadow World, the more relaxed Rell became. Though the battle was nowhere near over, at least tonight she'd be able to sleep peacefully. Grabbing every precious moment in life was a lesson being thrust at her more and more.

Just when she thought she understood the workings of her life, something would change. It was a chaotic existence, where friends became foes, cowards became heroes, and a demon could become a king.

The time seemed to pass more quickly than when they had traveled toward the Shadow World and they arrived at Illuma Grand just after nightfall. Once again they were received in front of the palatial structure by several men dressed in gray. The Bringers gave their horses over to the stable hands, with instructions to feed and water the animals well.

Rell couldn't help but notice that the gazes from the mixed bloods had changed. No longer did they look upon their arrival wide-eyed, as if the group was some exotic and strange animal prowling the halls of Illuma Grand. Now, respect and eagerness burned in place of fear. Beatrice had obviously been spreading the word.

Inside the hall, an older woman, dressed not in gray but blue velvet robes greeted them. Her gown was conservative but still spoke of wealth. She executed a graceful curtsey. "Sir Gregory."

He returned her welcome with a low bow. "Lady Tobin, you are a sight for weary eyes."

Her worried gaze traveled over the group. "I can see things are not well." She folded her hands in front of her. "And that you were not able to rescue my grandson?"

Gregory gave a slow shake of his head. "No, my lady, we were unable to locate those taken by the Bane."

"Well—" She blinked quickly a few times and sniffed. "I'm sure you did all you could, and from the looks of you, it was no easy journey."

"That, my lady, is an understatement," Rhys said. "May we beg lodging for the night?"

"Of course." She waved a young man to them. "See to rooms for our guests. Put them in my wing."

"Yes, Lady Tobin." The young man's gaze skated over them, his mouth silently moving as he counted each one of them. "Right away."

With that he turned and jogged across the hall and down the west corridor.

"After you freshen up, I hope you will join me for dinner." She lowered her voice. "I would very much like to hear of your adventure and your opinion about the rising danger of the

Bane."

"We would be honored, my lady." Gregory gave a quick bow and held her gaze. "I trust Lord Bagita will not be in attendance."

"No, he will not." Lady Tobin's mouth pinched in a sour expression. "I think it's time somebody put that man in his place."

"My lady, I believe you are just such a person," Gregory said.

The young man Lady Tobin had sent to prepare their rooms returned. "Your chambers will be ready in a few minutes if you'd like to follow me."

"We will dine in my private dining room at eight o'clock. My chamber is the last one at the end of the west hall."

"Thank you, my lady. I look forward to our talk," Gregory said.

"As do I," she replied.

"If you'll follow me," the young man said again.

Lady Tobin watched their departure. Though Rell had never met the woman, her heart went out to her. With her missing grandson and the problems brewing within Illuma Grand, life for the woman could not be easy.

Exhaustion swamped Rell, a yawn pulling at her. Suddenly she was very tired and wanted nothing more than to lie down. The young man indicated a group of rooms and then left, letting the group divide the chambers between themselves.

Siban opened the closest door and pulled Rell inside. She went willingly. The furnishings in the room were sparse and utilitarian, though after her time in the Shadow World, she would never turn her nose up at a comfortable bed.

"Lie down."

Rell waved him away. "I'm fine, Siban. You don't have to hover over me."

He walked to her and gently grasped her shoulders. "I'm not hovering, I'm tending."

She smirked. "Is there a difference?"

"Most definitely." He eased her toward the bed. "Hovering implies unnecessary worry." The back of her knees butted against the bed, setting her off-balance. She sat and Siban knelt in front of her. "Tending means that I am doing what needs to be done to make sure a member of my party stays healthy and unharmed."

It was impossible not to laugh at his serious expression. "All right, comrade, I'll let you *tend* to me."

"That's a good soldier." His fingers glided down her arms and he laid his palms against hers. "After I finish, you may tend to me."

She tipped her head toward him. "You're very generous."

"I know," he said. "Now close your eyes."

"But I want to watch you."

He smiled. "All right." Siban stood and picked up a pitcher. Tipping it, he let the water pour into the matching basin. He set the water beside the bed and dipped a linen cloth into the liquid, squeezing out the excess.

The rag was cool against her head. With gentle swipes, he cleaned the grime from her face. She couldn't take her eyes from him. Thick black lashes rested against his cheeks and his skin had darkened from the sun. He was beautiful inside and out. What he had seen in her when she was a demon was still a mystery to her. But now she understood how the strength of one person's love could save the other from near death. There was nothing she wouldn't do for him. No risk she wouldn't take. No foe she wouldn't battle to keep him safe. When they practiced using their Tell, they had glided side by side, connected but still separate. Now they were one, their souls merged.

When he was finished, Siban tossed the rag into the basin

and lifted her fingers to his lips. He gently kissed their tips. "I want to ask you something."

"What is it?"

Several seconds passed before he spoke. He seemed to struggle for what he wanted to say. "I love you."

"And I love you." She smiled, certain there was more to come.

"Rell, I want to be with you always."

Her throat tightened. "What are you saying?"

His hazel eyes locked with hers. "I want you to be my wife, Rell. Will you marry me?"

Stunned by his question, it took a few seconds for her to find her voice. She'd come too close to losing him in the Shadow World. There were so many things to consider, but the one thing she knew was that she didn't want to be without him. She nodded. "Yes."

A wide smile stretched across his mouth. White teeth gleamed and if possible, her love for him grew even more. She wrapped her arm around his neck and pulled him to her. Their mouths connected, sending a jolt of heat through her. Their tongues twined around each other and she shifted, attempting to drag him onto the bed with her.

Siban groaned and broke the kiss. "There are many other things I'd rather do right now, but we need to wash up and get ready for dinner."

Rell gave him her most devilish grin. "Maybe we can feign illness."

Siban sat back and shook his head. "Unless you're lying in a pool of your own blood or have a hole the size of a boulder through you, illness is unbelievable."

She scrunched up her face. "Damn."

"Come." He stood and pulled Rell to her feet. "Wash me so we can meet with the others."

"If I wash you, we'll never make it."

"Good point." He pulled his tunic over his head to reveal an expanse of golden skin. Rell smoothed her hand over his chest and trailed her fingers lower. He caught her hand. "You are being very uncooperative." He kissed her hand again. "I promise after we find out what information the good Lady Tobin has for us, I will let you touch me all you want."

"I like the sound of that."

"Not as much as I do," he said.

CHAPTER TWENTY-ONE

Lady Tobin's private dining room was far more opulent than
Rell's room. It seemed nobility and rank had its privileges,
even among the Bringers. From what she could see, Council
members possessed far more material wealth than the others
who lived and served at Illuma Grand.

"I hope your accommodations are adequate," Lady Tobin
asked.

Rell turned to see the older woman watching her. "Very
nice, thank you."

"My husband made his fortune as a merchant before he
died." She smiled, as if guessing Rell's thoughts. "When I was
widowed I moved to Illuma Grand to be with my daughter and
grandson. Most of what I owned was given to the needy. The
rest I brought here, hoping to reestablish myself."

"It's very lovely." To hide her guilty reaction, Rell locked
her hands behind her back. "I'm sorry about your husband."

Warmth seeped into Lady Tobin's smile. "Thank you, my
dear. That's very kind of you to say." She indicated a chair at the
table. "We're not all like Lord Bagita. Most of us on the Council
truly want what is best for the Bringers." With a flowing grace,

she sat in the chair next to the one she'd motioned to. "I will admit though, that it seems we've been remiss in our duties."

Rell took the seat next to Lady Tobin. Siban joined them, sitting on the other side of Rell.

"My lady, I am not one to judge the actions of others," Rell said. "I am realizing more and more that most people do the best they can with what they believe to be true."

"Wise words." A look of contemplation crossed Lady Tobin's face. "You remind me of somebody."

"She is Bowen Kendal's daughter," Gregory said, taking his place at the table.

The woman's eyes widened. "But I thought Bowen only had two daughters." Her gaze slid from Jade, who had just entered, back to Rell. "It was my understanding the oldest had been killed along with her father."

"Not dead, my lady." Siban covered Rell's hand with his, folding his fingers around hers. "But nearly as good as."

Lady Tobin's eyebrows lifted. "I would very much like to hear the story."

The remaining members of their party took their places at the table.

"I am afraid there is much to tell." Gregory glanced at the gray-clad women and men who had begun delivering dishes of food to the table. "But perhaps we should enjoy this delicious meal first."

"Perhaps that is best." She looked toward the door, drawing Rell's eyes as well. "Beatrice." A wide smile spread across Lady Tobin's thin lips. "I hope you don't mind, but I invited her to join us. She and my grandson are betrothed and I have taken her into my confidence."

Jade waved the redhead toward the chair placed next to her and then glanced at the older woman. "As have we."

Again Rell was struck that Jade's friendship with Beatrice

was not something new. This time the idea made her smile. It was good that she and her sister were finding their places in the world.

Two more trips brought an abundance of food Rell didn't believe their party could consume. One of the men set a bowl of roasted potatoes next to her. His arm briefly brushed her hand and instantly the feeling of mistrust invaded her. She glanced at the man. His gaze leveled on her for a second, but then he turned and quickly left the room. Unsure what the vague feeling meant, she kept the experience to herself. Too many other things needed to be discussed right now. She would talk to Siban about it later. It would come as no surprise if Fromme had spies working within Illuma Grand. They'd already found a Splinter within the walls, so why not spies?

The meal was like nothing Rell had ever eaten, even before being turned Bane. Delphina and her mother were excellent cooks, but the sheer elegance of the meal they dined on made her feel like royalty.

"Oh, sweet Sainted ones." Ravyn reached across the table and grabbed two figs off a large platter of fruit. "I adore these." She bit and chewed slowly, her eyes sliding shut.

"I never get tired of watching you eat figs," Rhys said to Ravyn.

She opened her eyes and winked at him, continuing to chew.

"Nor do I." Luc plucked a fig off the plate and held it out to Jade. "Your turn."

Jade leaned toward him, taking the fruit from him. "You first."

Magnus snorted and shoved a large chunk of pork into his mouth. "Please, not here," he said around his mouthful of food. "I'm trying to eat."

Lady Tobin stood and ushered the servers from the room.

"That will be all for now. I'll ring when we've finished." She followed them to the door. The man who had given Rell an uneasy feeling glanced toward the table, his departure slower than the rest. "Run along, Edgar." With a gentle but steady push against his shoulder, she herded him out the door. "You wouldn't want to keep Lord Bagita waiting."

Edgar's gaze jerked to Lady Tobin for a second before he pulled himself taller, lifted his chin, and marched down the hallway.

She clicked the door shut and turned to them, shaking her head. "I'm certain we'll be getting a visit from Fromme very soon. Edgar is his snitch and I'm sure he's off to report to him about our dinner." Disregarding etiquette, she settled back on her chair and rested her elbows on the table. "We can speak freely. Tell me what you've discovered."

All eyes turned to Gregory.

"I'm afraid the situation is grave, my lady." He pushed away his plate and leaned forward in his chair. "The time for discretion and secrets is at an end. We found the Abyss."

Lady Tobin gasped. "Here on Inness?"

"I'm afraid so. It gets worse," he continued. "Vile tricked Juna, Ravyn, and Meran into opening it or at least weakening it."

She collapsed against the back of her chair. "But how did he accomplish such a feat."

"By casting an illusion so the Abyss appeared to contain the missing Bringers," Juna said. "We thought we were freeing them, when in reality we were opening the Summoners' prison."

"An illusion?" The older woman shook her head. "I thought only the Summoners possessed such power?"

"That is true." Gregory's gaze leveled on her.

"What are you saying—that the Summoners still exist?" She looked down the table for confirmation and then back to

Gregory.

"That is exactly what I am saying, Lady Tobin. I won't sweeten the situation. The reality is that Vile controls a large clan of Summoners."

Beatrice's voice came from the other end of the table. "But why would the Summoners agree to work with the Bane."

"They didn't agree to work with the Bane," Jade said. "They *are* the Bane."

"Saint's help us." Lady Tobin pressed her hand against her chest. "Please tell me this isn't true."

Inhaling deeply, Gregory straightened in his chair and then slowly exhaled. "Vile, the Demon King, was once Ander, King Harlin's brother. The story is long and convoluted, but suffice it to say that Ander, along with many other Summoners, escaped imprisonment and fled to Inness, where they have been plotting for more than a thousand years."

"And what of the Abyss now? Has it been opened?" Beatrice asked.

"We don't know." Ravyn toyed with her linen napkin. "We tried to reverse what we had started, but I don't know how successful we were."

"I believe, at the very least, we weakened the wards." Juna took a drink of her wine and swallowed. "I fear we may be looking at a Summoner invasion soon."

"What can be done?" A note of panic laced Beatrice's voice. "We need to prepare."

"Agreed," Gregory said. "There are many other issues we need to take into consideration though. Things best not discussed here. First and foremost, we must begin to build our forces."

"But how?" Lady Tobin asked. "The residents of Illuma Grand have no powers."

"They will," Luc said.

"I have always thought you different than the rest of us, Sir Gregory. As I look at each one of you, I see the marks of full power." She narrowed her gaze. "When I first met Ravyn, she had no Tell mark."

Her unasked question hung in the air.

"I am to be first," Beatrice said into the silence. She pointed at Juna. "She promised if I rallied those who wished to fight, I would be brought to full power."

"It seems there has been much going on under my nose, even with those I love." Lady Tobin turned her piercing stare back on Gregory. "So is that it? Have I heard all the important issues so that I might decide my course of action?"

"Nearly," Gregory said.

She leaned back in her chair as if expecting more grave news. "What is it then? I doubt you can shock me any further."

"I am King Arron's youngest son." He straightened in his chair. "And we have found my brother, the heir to the Bringer throne."

Her eyes widened to the size of silver ducats. "I stand corrected; you have shocked me."

"Well hold on to your bodice, Lady Tobin, because he isn't finished," Luc said.

She heaved a heavy sigh. "Where is our reigning king now?"

"I should think he's flying over some sleeping village," Luc mumbled.

Jade elbowed him in the arm.

Lady Tobin squinted. "I don't understand. Please don't tell me he was taken by the Bane as well?"

"Of a sort, my lady. It turns out the heir is Icarus, Vile's second-in-command," Gregory said. "And my half brother."

Before she could reply, the doors burst open and Fromme Bagita, along with two other people stormed in. "What is the purpose of this clandestine meeting?"

Lady Tobin covered her shock at Gregory's announcement by plastering on a benign smile. "The purpose was to eat food, Fromme. I've offered our guests lodging and refreshments, as is my right."

Deceit and anger swamped Rell, the emotions rolling from the man and woman standing behind Lord Bagita. Too tired to deal with their reactions, she strengthened her mental shields.

"I doubt that is all that goes on here," the rat-faced man said.

"You're right, Deputy Master Byrnes." Gregory pushed away from the table and stood. "We are discussing how best to deal with the Bane threat."

"Not you, too," the woman standing next to Byrnes scoffed. "Haven't we had enough of that nonsense from Lord Blackwell?"

Rhys slowly stood, his expression darkening. Despite having seen him as a dragon and having trained with him at the manor, this was the first time Rell had ever seen him appear truly menacing. "I grow tired of your poisonous words, Lady Grimes." His gaze shifted to Fromme. "While you three plot for power over the Bringers, the Bane lay siege to Inness."

"So you would have us believe." Fromme puffed out his chest. "But we are not sheep who will blindly follow you on your crusade against an imaginary foe."

"There is not an ounce of my being that cares whether you believe me or not, Lord Bagita." Rhys stepped away from his chair and paced around the table. "But I will not allow any more Bringers to be taken by the Bane while you plot and deceive your way to a throne that does not exist." He stopped a foot from the three intruders. "And I will not stand by while you sell immortal weapons to the highest bidder so you can line your pockets with gold."

"How dare you accuse me of thievery," Fromme blustered.

"Do you know who I am? My brother is a Superior in the Order of the Saints. For your false accusations I could have you thrown in prison for the rest of your life."

With a quick flourish of his hand, Rhys pulled his sword from his sheath and pressed it against Bagita's neck, grabbing the man by his fur collar to hold him in place. Fromme screamed, his eyes and mouth rounding in fear. All those at the table jumped to their feet, but didn't intervene. Lady Grimes squealed and jumped back, knocking into Deputy Master Byrnes.

"I have watched you bleed our people dry," Rhys gritted out. "I have endeavored to guard our people while you turned a blind eye to those who have gone missing. I allowed you to question Ravyn as if she was some kind of criminal." He leaned in, bringing his nose close to Fromme's. "But that ends now."

"Rhys." Ravyn's voice cut through the tension. "He's not worth it."

Tension stretched through the room while everybody waited to see what Rhys would do. Rell glanced at Siban, but his gaze was fixed on the scene near the door, as if concentrating more than would be natural on Lord Bagita. She opened herself up to Siban, trying to sense what his Tell sent him. The impression ran deep, layer upon layer of deception. Her instinct urged her forward, away from the table.

Rhys lowered his sword and backed away. Fromme huffed and repositioned his weighty robe on his shoulders, scowling at the group. Rell walked four more steps and stopped, staring at the man, not knowing why she needed him to see her, but trusting her Tell that there was a purpose.

"What are you staring at, girl?" Fromme asked.

"Lord Bagita?" Meran said, drifting away from her chair to stand next to Rell. "Have you been introduced to the newest member of the Bringers?"

First he looked at Meran, his expression tightening. He stared at her for several long seconds. "Ascendant?"

She smiled. "Well, I used to be. But I have given up that title so that I might join in the battle against the Bane."

Shock registered on the three intruders faces. "But you were of the highest order. Most beloved by your followers," Fromme said. "Why would you give up such an esteemed position to join—" He waved a meaty hand toward the group. "Them?"

"I like to think the impending war is a higher calling, my lord." Though spoken softly, her answer left no doubt of where her loyalties lay. "But I didn't mean me. Have you met Esmeralda Kendal?"

Bagita looked at Jade and then back to Rell. He searched her face. "But you were killed."

"Not killed, just turned Bane," she said in a flat tone.

"Preposterous," Lady Grimes said, inching up behind Fromme.

Brita moved to stand on the other side of Rell and took her hand. "Perhaps you should show him."

Confused, Rell looked at Brita. "Show him?"

"Like Magnus showed you," was the woman's explanation.

Could she project her experiences to somebody else? She'd never tried, but Magnus had told her it was a Tell trait. The need to show Lord Bagita everything she'd gone through swamped Rell. She reached and gripped his wrist. He tried to jerk away from her, but she held tight and closed her eyes, concentrating on the night her father had been killed.

Images flowed through her mind. She felt Brita's Tell within her, guiding her in projecting the visions to Fromme. Sounds of fighting rang inside her head. The urge to break her hold nearly overwhelmed her, but Brita kept her grounded. Fire blazed before her eyes, their home going up in flames and her father's body lying lifeless on the ground. Then they were there. The Bane swarmed the area. She ran, but was plucked off the ground by a demon. Faster the images came. The Shadow World—the winged demon sucking out her soul. Her screams and then darkness.

Rell opened her eyes and stared at the man before her. His face had gone white, frozen in an expression of horror. Brita released her hold and stepped away. Slowly Rell lowered her hand. "I do not lie."

His head shook with denial, his body trembling from the scenes that had been her life. "It wasn't supposed to happen like that." He continued to shake his head. "He was only to get the documents."

"What documents?" Luc stepped forward. When Fromme only stared at him with wide eyes, he said again, "What documents?"

"No, this is another trick." The man began backing up. "It cannot be true."

Turning, Bagita fled out the door, muttering his denial of what he had seen. Lady Grimes edged toward the door and with a flourish, spun and followed Lord Bagita down the corridor. Rell leveled her gaze on Byrnes. "Would you like to see?"

He scowled at her, sniffed, lifted his nose in the air, and followed his friends out the door. Meran closed the door behind them and turned. "That was effective."

Siban wrapped his arm around Rell's waist. His touch instantly calmed the torrent of emotions that had surfaced when she'd relived the night she'd been turned Bane. "What did he mean, 'He was only to get the documents'?"

"I think we finally know who had a hand in the night Luc lost them gambling," Ravyn said.

"Had a hand in it?" Rell turned and looked at Luc. "It was all staged?"

He swallowed several times, his lips pinched into a tight line.

"Yes. Ravyn picked up on it right after I discovered you'd been turned Bane." His mouth relaxed. "It doesn't matter. I shouldn't have been so careless, Esmeralda. None of what happened to you would have occurred if I'd been more responsible."

Jade laid her chin against his arm but said nothing.

The guilt he still carried was evident from his expression. Yes, she'd been through the worst, but it had all happened for a reason. Jade's words came back to Rell and she said them aloud, "If everything that has occurred happened to bring us to this point now, then I would relive it all again."

"You can't mean that," Luc said. "You've lived a nightmare."

"And out of that nightmare I found Siban." She slipped her arm around his waist. "And you found Jade, and Gregory has found his brother." An understanding of the events in her life crystalized before Rell. "Because of what I went through, we might be able to heal Icarus, open the Mystic Arch again, and vanquish Vile and the Summoners." She pressed a fist against her heart. "Our lives have been intertwined from before we were born. The Bringers, this group, are like the threads of a rope, twisted, one life crossing over the other." Her gaze skated over each one of them. "I, for one, will die trying to make right what should have been amended a thousand years ago." She looked back at Luc. "If you need my forgiveness, then know you have it."

For once he seemed speechless, but from the look on his face it appeared she had lifted a burden he'd long carried. He walked to her and stopped. She looked up at him and saw that his eyes glistened with unspoken emotion. With slow movements, as if savoring the moment of freedom, he drew Rell toward him and hugged her. He pressed his mouth to a spot just above her ear. "Thank you."

She smiled against his chest and returned his embrace, squeezing him tightly. After a second they released each other and she stepped back, cocking her head to the side. "I'm really glad we didn't kill you."

He nodded. "Me, too."

"Well." Lady Tobin clapped her hands together once and shook her head. "Let me see if I have this correct." She pointed to Rell, her hands still pressed together. "You are Bowen's daughter, but were turned into a Bane, but somehow these wonderful Bringers healed you."

"Yes." Rell repressed a smile at the woman's exasperated expression.

"Your brother is still a Bane," she said to Gregory. "But there's great hope of healing him as well."

"Correct," the Bringer said.

"Vile is actually Ander. The Summoners still exist and are getting stronger. My grandson is still somewhere in the Shadow World." She paused. "And I don't even think I want to know what that business with Fromme was all about."

Luc turned to her. "It's probably best."

"Well then." She let out an abrupt sigh. "What do you need from us?"

All eyes turned to Gregory. "Gather the Bringers who wish to serve. Send them to Jacob Le Daun's manor. For now we will post out of there. His home will be easy to patrol and has already been warded. If most residents of Illuma Grand are willing to be brought to full power, then we will move our command back here. Inform the Council of what has transpired." He exhaled. "Prepare for a war."

CHAPTER TWENTY-TWO

Never had there been a more glorious sight than Le Daun Manor. A subtle vibration hummed along Siban's skin when they passed through the warded boundaries. The sensation sent the tension he didn't know he'd been holding from his body. They were home and safe.

A shriek from the front door erupted. "They're back." Delphina stuck her head back inside the manor. "Lord Le Daun, they're home."

In a matter of seconds, Delphina, her children, Jacob, Odette, Okee, and a woman Siban didn't recognize spilled onto the front landing.

Gregory stopped the line of horses in front of the steps and dismounted. The rest of the party followed suit.

"You are a sight for sore eyes." Jacob descended the steps and clutched Gregory's arm. "We were beginning to fear the worst." He shuffled down the line, touching each one of the Bringers and stopping when he got to Luc to pull him into a crushing hug. "I'm so glad my fears were unfounded."

"It's good to be home, Father." Luc returned the hug and didn't pull away until Jacob released him. "But the situation has become much more perilous."

"Now is not the time to share the unsettling details, my son." Jacob's gaze slid over his shoulder to the unfamiliar woman on the steps."

"What is she doing here?" Jade asked.

Siban looked at Rell for explanation.

"She is the Splinter we found coming out of the Council Chamber." Rell's hand strayed to the hilt of her sword. "You'll forgive us, Fatima, if we're a little leery of your motives for being here right now. Listening to the Demon King's lies and fighting his private army puts one in a less than trusting mood."

Silence blanketed the group, all eyes turning toward the Splinter, waiting for an answer.

She shifted nervously and wrapped an arm across her torso to drape her orange shawl over her shoulder.

"Give the woman a chance to speak." Jacob climbed the first step. "I think you'll find what she has to say very interesting."

"Not here." Juna looked to the sky. "After we've tended the horses we'll come inside. We can discuss matters there."

"I agree," said Gregory. "Vile's spies are everywhere."

"Very good." Jacob turned to Delphina. "Could we get refreshments, my dear?"

"Of course." Delphina turned to go inside.

"I would like to assist—if you will allow it," Fatima said.

"I'll take any help I can get when it comes to this lot." Delphina bustled inside with Fatima gliding gracefully behind her.

"First Ravyn adopts Delphina, and now it appears the Splinter has taken Juna up on her offer for aid." Rhys smirked. "It seems you sisters have a penchant for collecting strays."

"I haven't collected any strays," Meran said, turning her horse in the direction of the stables.

Luc snorted. "Perhaps you're forgetting about your

banished demon who lurks somewhere beyond the wards."

Meran sniffed and lifted her chin an inch. "Icarus is not my demon. He's Gregory's brother."

Jacob's mouth dropped open, his eyes leveling on Gregory. "What's this about Icarus?"

"Yes, it appears the heir to the Bringer throne is a Bane," Gregory said.

"Well, you know what they say." Luc slapped him on the back. "You can't pick your family."

"Thank you, Luc." Gregory tugged his horse forward. "That's not very comforting."

After the horses had been taken care of, the Bringers assembled back in the Great Hall. Siban took his place next to Rell and slid his hand onto her knee. Her hand slid over his and curled around his fingers.

They'd been out of the Shadow World for a little over a day and now that they were back at the manor and some of the worry over their situation had calmed, his mind turned to more enjoyable activities.

Last night had been a true test of his self-control. To let Rell sleep after that dinner had taken every shred of willpower he could muster. But they'd both needed it and he'd promised himself the next time he made love to her it would not be rushed. They'd yet to share an entire night together when more pressing matters hadn't invaded their thoughts and put them on edge. Tonight he would share with Rell the full experience of what happened between a man and a woman.

Siban shifted his attention to the problem at hand, a Splinter among them. Instead of taking his place at the front of the table as he usually did, Gregory scooted onto the end of the wooden bench next to Magnus. Siban couldn't help but notice that the man looked tired. He couldn't blame him. What they'd gone through in the Shadow World was a lot to contend with but to find out that your brother had been a Demon Bane for the last thousand years must be difficult to reconcile.

His thoughts turned to Icarus. What was to be done about him? Though his opinion about the demon's motives had changed after he had saved Rell and confronted Vile, Siban still didn't trust him. From his time in the Shadow World and the torture inflicted upon him, he'd tasted the strength of the darkness that Bane used to control those they dominated. But his respect for Icarus had increased. If the demon could truly be healed, he would have accomplished the impossible—keeping the suffocating black evil at bay for a millennia.

The Bringers drank deep of the ale Delphina and Fatima had delivered, waiting for Gregory to speak. Jacob presented two stools for the women to sit on.

"I've got things to do in the kitchen," Delphina said, waving away the offer.

"Sit." Jacob gripped her arm and gently led her to the stool. "This concerns you as well."

She glanced at the Bringers as if asking permission.

"He's right," Rhys said. "You and your children are part of our group and fall under our protection. As such you deserve to know where things stand and what to expect."

Delphina smoothed her hands down the front of her skirt and sat next to Fatima. The two women exchanged worried glances.

The rest of the Bringers took their places at the table but didn't speak, waiting for Gregory to begin.

He released a soul weary sigh. "First, Jacob, please introduce our new guest and explain why we now seem to have a Splinter in residence."

Before Jacob could speak, Juna cut him off. "I'll do the

honors." She sat across from Gregory, but turned her body to face the woman. "Her name is Fatima. She has a child. We caught her sneaking out of the Council Chamber when we stopped at Illuma Grand on the way to the Shadow World. She said she had been invited there to dance for Fromme Bagita, but in reality she was sent there by Vile and Sha-hera to search for immortal weapons, which she did not find." Juna's tone was matter of fact. She cocked her head to the side. "Did I leave anything out?"

Fatima held her gaze for several seconds before lowering her eyes to her lap. "You left out that I no longer wish to serve the Bane."

"Why not?" Rell asked. She tapped her index finger with a steady beat against the wood of the table. "Why should we believe you?

The woman toyed with the fringe on her orange shawl. "I know you can read me." She tapped her chin, indicating Rell's Tell tattoo. "There are enough of you to know whether or not I am lying when I say I no longer serve Sha-hera and Vile."

"And again I'll ask, why?" Rell said.

Fatima took a deep breath. "After you found me at Illuma Grand, I began to think about what you said—that Sha-hera would take my child anyway no matter what I did for her."

"At the time you didn't seem to believe me." Rell's tapping stopped. "What changed your mind?"

"She came to me again." Despite the intense stares of the Bringers, the woman didn't quell under their scrutiny. "This time her orders were more—demanding."

Gregory cupped his hands around his mug and leaned forward, his gaze narrowing. "What did she want you to do?"

"She demanded that I gather the Splinters from my clan, and said I should send messengers to other clans. They are to occupy cities around Itta, Alba, and Faela."

"For what purpose?" Juna asked. "After what I've seen in the Shadow World, Vile doesn't needs the Splinters to battle for him."

"I don't believe Sha-hera speaks for Vile any longer. She seemed angry, saying we were to report only to her." Fatima shook her head. "Then she told me that I, along with the women of my clan, were to travel north and meet her at the boundaries of the Frost Lands, a town called Pillager's Peak. That's when I realized the price she demanded I pay for her protection was too steep."

"The Frost Lands?" Rhys asked. "What purpose would she have there?"

"I asked, but all she said was that I should ask fewer questions and to make sure I was at Pillager's Point in three weeks' time." Fatima was silent for a few seconds, her hand still toying with the fringe on her shawl. "But before Sha-hera left she said something about Vile's precious cargo."

Furtive glances ricocheted between the Bringers.

"And she did not say what this cargo was?" Gregory asked.

"No." Fatima smoothed her hands over her knees. "I was too scared to push for more information. But when I got back to camp I gathered our belongings and my daughter and traveled here." She lowered her gaze to her lap again. "When I danced for Fromme, I was able to—coax information about the Bringers from him. That's how I knew to come here."

"Very resourceful," Meran said. "And where is your child now?"

"Upstairs playing with Hayden." Delphina smiled at Fatima. "The two get along like mutton and gravy."

Gregory glanced down the table. "What say you? Is she telling the truth?"

"Yes." Juna's gaze slid from Fatima to Gregory. "As far as I can tell."

Next he looked at Brita. She nodded but didn't add further remarks. His stare leveled on Siban. "What is your impression?"

Everything Fatima said rang with truth and no vibrations of dishonesty registered against Siban's Tell. He, for one, was willing to trust her at her word—for now. At the risk of more conflict with Rell, he spoke what he felt. "Her words ring with truth."

Gregory nodded and leveled his gaze on Rell. "You seem more skeptical than the others, Rell. It is important that we are united in decisions that affect us all. What do you think about what Fatima has said?"

"I am living proof that one can make poor decisions, grow to regret them, and endeavor to make amends." Rell swirled her finger in a circular pattern on the table but didn't look up. "But I also know the treacherous nature of the dark entities that give the Splinters their powers." She lifted her head, her gaze locking with Fatima's. "So though what you say feels like truth, know that I will be watching you and will expect lies. But most of all, know that I will be the first to run you through with my blade if you do lie to us."

The room was silent for a few seconds, the tension taut. A slow smile spread across Gregory's face. He nodded and looked back at Fatima. "It appears you are to be trusted for now. If you fight and serve with the Bringers, we will protect you to our dying breath."

Fatima stared at the group. "I have never had anybody willing to die for me."

"It is a great responsibility," Rell said. "Do not take it lightly."

"I won't." The Splinter inhaled. "My child is the most important thing to me. I will do whatever it takes to keep her safe. And whatever it takes to keep her from growing up in the same world I did."

"A child is a strong catalyst," Brita said. "Sha-hera knew this and she used it against you." She bestowed one of her soul soothing smiles to Fatima. "You've made the right decision coming here."

"I believe it, too." Fatima stood. "That is all the information I have for you. If it's all right, I'd like to go check on Aurora."

"Of course." Gregory stood, watching her depart. When the click of her footsteps had faded, he turned to the group. "It seems we are picking up some unexpected allies."

"One," Juna said. "There is no telling if Sha-hera has made other contacts among the group." She rested her elbows on the table. "I doubt the Splinters as a whole would be open to aiding us."

"I agree," Meran said. "Fatima seems the exception in a community of black magic doers. Even if her priorities have not been straight before Sha-hera's demands, I feel they are now."

"I'm curious as to what the precious cargo is that the demons will be transporting." Rhys looked at the group. "What are the chances it's the missing Bringers?"

"My thoughts exactly." Jacob picked at the rough edge of the table. "But why the Frost Lands?"

Luc let out a frustrated grunt and shook his head. "Your guess is as good as mine, but rest assured, Vile has a purpose."

"Gregory?" Rhys turned his attention to their leader. "Are there other Bringers from your party in the north?"

"Yes." He braced his hands against the table and leaned in. "Near Pillager's Peak, as a matter of fact. I had several establish themselves there among the people, but from their reports, the land is desolate and nothing travels beyond the border towns."

"Which would be perfect if Vile wanted to hide something there," Ravyn added.

"True, but he has hundreds of miles of caverns where he

could keep the Bringers and we'd probably never find them."
Jade shrugged. "Why go to all the trouble of moving the
Bringers north?"

Gregory was silent for a few seconds, his gaze leveling on
Brita and then Magnus. Siban opened himself up to the three's
silent exchange. They suspected something, but he couldn't
decipher anything further. "You suspect something?" Siban
looked back to Gregory. "What is it you're not telling us?"

He sighed. "There is a rumor of a place far beyond the
boundary of the Frost Lands. It is said to be watched by
sentinels."

"Bane?" Juna asked.

"I don't know." Gregory straightened and paced a short
path in front of the table. "But from the tales, this place was
once a portal." He stopped and looked at them. "It's called the
Threshold."

"I've never heard of it," Rhys said.

"Only those who came from Bael would have heard of it,"
Magnus said. "Though even there it was part of legend."

"Is it another portal into Bael?" Meran asked.

"Not necessarily." Gregory began pacing again. "It is said
that the Threshold can open into thousands of different worlds."

"Why hasn't Vile tried to use the portal?" Siban asked,
growing frustrated as more questions arose. "Or has he?"

Gregory shook his head. "Not that I know of. The Threshold
is said to be dangerous. The laws of time and physical space do
not apply near the portal."

"Meaning?" Siban sat forward. If he was going to risk his
life yet again, he wanted all the details of what they would be
facing—if that was even the plan Gregory was edging toward.

"We have little knowledge of the place." Brita looked at
Gregory, as if asking permission to proceed. He gave a single
nod, and she turned her attention back to the group. "Time

is linear within our world. We are born, live a long time, and then die. Events happen in order, cause and effect. But near the Threshold time is warped. Events fold in on each other, creating chaos and power rifts."

"Lovely," Luc said. He smoothed his hand across the table. "And I'm assuming that is where we are headed?"

"Until now, we had hoped it was a legend, and even if it wasn't, that the Threshold remained hidden." Brita folded her hands in her lap. "But if Vile is moving toward the Frost Lands, then we can assume the Threshold exists and that he knows of it."

Luc dropped his forehead to the table and groaned.

His reaction mirrored how Siban felt. He leaned an elbow on the table and massaged his temple, trying to ward off the growing headache. "I can sense how perilous this journey will be."

He lowered his hand and looked at Gregory. "That's what you're proposing, correct? To travel beyond the boundary into the Frost Lands in search of the Threshold and the Bringers?"

"I think we should consider the fact that Vile has access to another way into Bael." Gregory paused. "Or many worlds. He needs to be stopped."

"And we need to find our mother once and for all." Juna stood. "I'm in. When do we leave?"

"It's not that easy, Juna." Ravyn pinned her sister with a glare. "You can't rush headlong into this battle. We need to prepare—have a plan."

Juna opened her mouth to retort, but Gregory gripped her upper arm, drawing her attention. "She's right. It's not only the Threshold that is perilous. The land beyond the boundary towns is riddled with dangers."

"I've heard tell of white, fanged animals bigger than a horse," Jade said, her eyes wide.

Luc lifted his head and glared at her. "You almost sound excited."

"I'm not scared." She rubbed his back. "I've got my dragon to protect me."

"Your dragon would rather stay here and quell the Splinter invasion," he grumbled.

Juna pulled her arm free of Gregory's clutch. "We've got to move fast. Fatima said they were to be there in three weeks' time. That leaves little time for talk."

"For once I agree with Juna," Magnus said. "I say we gather provisions and head out as soon as possible."

"Your enthusiasm is encouraging, but first we must decide who is going. There are other tasks besides this journey that require completing." He looked at Brita and Magnus. "I'll need you two here at the manor." When Magnus opened his mouth to protest, Gregory held up his hand, stopping the warrior. "You will need to bring those who travel from Illuma Grand to full power." Magnus pressed his lips together but didn't argue. "It is imperative that I have two people I can trust. You know the ritual and I have no doubt that you can prepare the new recruits for battle."

Magnus stroked his beard, but his brow remained furrowed. "You wish us to command the new recruits?"

"You and Brita have seen more combat than any one of us. Your knowledge of battle tactics is unparalleled."

Siban couldn't help but feel that though the things Gregory said were true, he was using thinly disguised flattery to gain compliance. From the look on Magnus's face, it was working.

"If and when the need to move to Illuma Grand arises, I need somebody who will do it without hesitation," Gregory continued. "You are an extension of me and I trust both of you completely."

"Well." Magnus lowered his hand to rest against his knee.

"Perhaps you're right. You will need a seasoned warrior to run things in your stead."

"Two seasoned warriors." Brita arched a brow at him.

"Yes, of course, two seasoned warriors. We accept."

Siban repressed a grin, realizing that Gregory was a master of manipulation.

"What about the rest of us?" Rell asked. "What are our duties?"

Again Gregory was quiet for a minute as he regarded each of those gathered, assessing where they would be best used. He pointed to Trace, Odette, and Okee. "Travel east, south, and west. Tell the others of our quest and about the Summoners. I will write up orders tonight for you to deliver to the captains in the areas. You are in charge." Gregory turned to the remaining seven. "We will travel north to the Threshold."

Siban released a silent sigh, his halfhearted hope of he and Rell receiving a less dangerous mission dashed.

"I can have my ship ready by tomorrow's evening tide," Rhys said. "We can get more provisions at my home in Alba."

"Excellent." Gregory looked at Rell and Siban. "I recall mention of a wedding."

Rell had told Jade and Ravyn about Siban's proposal. Not surprisingly, the news had traveled quickly through the group.

"We had hoped to wed after our return from the Shadow World," Siban said.

"Though we won't be able to stay long, the Dragon's Inn is on our course northward." Gregory held out his arms and smiled. "I think we could all use something to celebrate."

"Your mother and I found a lovely gown among Lord Le Daun's items. It turned out just beautiful. We worked two solid days on it before she left. It will be perfect for your wedding." Delphina stood. She bustled toward the stairs. "I'll need to fit it to you, but I can have it ready by the time you leave."

Rell turned to Siban. "It looks like we're going to have a wedding."

"Finally, you'll be all mine."

"As if I wasn't already." She leaned into him and gave him a quick peck on the lips.

He cupped her head and drew her to him, not satisfied with the brief kiss.

"Please tell me we're not going to have to watch them paw each other all the way to the Frost Lands," Luc said.

Siban broke the kiss but didn't look at Luc. "If you're lucky."

Laughter rippled through the crowd and Siban kissed Rell again. Even though their wedding a few days away, he had no plans of waiting until their wedding night to show Rell what it meant to be truly joined with somebody she loved. If previous events were a glimpse into their future, there would always be some threat looming, just waiting to disrupt their lives. Taking advantage of opportunities when they arose was Siban's new motto and he had every intention of taking advantage of the peace tonight.

CHAPTER TWENTY-THREE

The door clicked behind Rell. Resisting the urge to cast a glance at Siban, she walked to the bed and then pivoted, wrapping her arm around one of the tall wooden posters. "Are you tired?"

She prayed he wasn't. Siban slid the bolt across the door and slowly turned. Her heart skipped a beat and a flush of heat rushed through her. He looked determined and far from weary.

"No, I'm not the least bit tired." He walked toward her, his fingers drifting down the front of his torso. He started unbuttoning his vest. "Are you?"

Her eyes watched the graceful movements of his fingers as he unhooked one button at a time until it opened. She shook her head. "No."

With a roll of his shoulders, the vest slid down his arms and caught on his right hand. He pulled the garment free and tossed it on the chair near the fire. "What do you want to do?"

Next he undid his sword and tossed it on the chair. His attention shifted to the leather cord at the neck of his tunic. "Perhaps you'd like me to tell you a story?"

She continued to watch him, her mouth growing drier with each inch of tan flesh he exposed. "Not in the mood."

With one seamless movement, he lifted the shirt over his head and added it to the pile on the chair. "Perhaps you'd like me to sing you a song. Maybe the lullaby my mother sang me when I was a child?"

"That might put me to sleep." She pushed away from the bed and walked to him. Her fingers itched to feel the smooth skin spreading across his sculpted chest. She stopped so close she could feel the heat radiating from his body. "And the last thing I want to do right now is go to sleep."

"Hmmm." He reached for her belt and unhooked her sword from around her waist, lowering the weapon. The metal of the hilt clanked when it settled on the stone floor. With his right boot he scooted the sheath toward the chair. "Then, my lady, I am at a loss as to how I'm going to keep you entertained tonight."

She let her hands drift over his chest and down the sides of his body. Taut muscles rippled under her touch. "I'm sure you'll think of something."

He smiled and lifted his hands to pull at the lace of her tunic. His fingertips brushed against her décolletage, sending skitters of pleasure across her skin and making her nipples tighten. "Your faith in my abilities warms my heart."

She ran her hands over his hips and around his back to palm the tight globes of his ass. "You've not disappointed me thus far."

He gave a decisive groan. "Then best I not start now."

He brushed his lips against hers. She tilted her chin upward to meet his mouth's caress. While he gently laid siege to her with his lips and tongue, his talented hands divested her of her tunic and undershirt.

Though the fire had been stoked in the hearth, the air in the room held a nip of chill, which he quickly chased away.

His skilled fingers found their way to her breast. Taking her nipple between his thumb and index finger, he gently squeezed. A moan escaped her and she leaned into him, loving the intense shocks of pleasure that spiked at his touch. Her tongue slid along his and when she pulled closer his arousal pressed against her stomach.

He broke their kiss and lowered his lips to her other breast, drawing her nipple into his mouth. He suckled, continuing to stroke and roll her other stiff bud to a tight peak.

Rell threaded her fingers through his hair and arched her back, welcoming every divine lave of his tongue. "We still wear far too many clothes," she panted.

"Let's see what we can do about that," he said against her breast. Siban knelt and kissed his way down her stomach. Never halting his sweet assault against her skin, he effectively rid her of her boots, pants, and woolen hose.

When she was completely nude he stood and kicked his boots free and liberated himself of his remaining clothes. Her gaze took in the perfection of his body. Each muscle defined and each tiny white scar beautiful. Dark brown curls fell to just below his chin and his hazel eyes glimmered bright against his tan skin.

He moved back to her and wound his arms around her waist, lifting her and capturing her mouth again. She opened to him, snaking her arms around his neck and pulling him close. She wrapped her legs around his waist and though his cock pressed against her, he did not push to enter her. His mouth slanted over her, his tongue taunting and teasing her as he shuffled backward.

When he reached the bed, he stopped and knelt again, setting her on top of the duvet at the edge of the mattress. With a tug, he untied the binding holding her hair and worked the braid with his fingers until her hair hung in long, loose stands against her back. After another minute of glorious kissing, he pulled away and looked at her. "I'm going to give you a lot of pleasure tonight."

She smiled and brushed her fingers through his hair. "I have no doubt."

"Lie back." His gaze burned bright, sending waves of excitement through her. When she began to scoot further onto the bed to allow for his body, he placed a hand on her knee. "Right here. Lie back."

After a second of hesitation, she did as he asked and waited for him to join her. But instead of climbing on the bed, he moved forward to kneel between her legs. The shock of being so exposed to his gaze caused her to tense. She lifted her head and looked at him, unsure about what was going to happen next or what she was supposed to do.

A wicked smile creased his mouth. "Just lie there and enjoy."

She did as he asked and closed her eyes, trying to keep her embarrassment at bay. Her body flinched when the warmth of Siban's breath brushed against the inside of her thighs and he pressed a soft, moist kiss against her skin. Rell gasped at the intimate feel of his mouth on her.

Gliding upward, he slid his tongue along her thigh and gently blew. A shiver ran through her, which was in direct contrast to the heat building between her legs. His mouth drew closer to the sensitive place that ached for his touch. His fingers stroked her curls and slid along her lips, opening them to his touch.

Rell gasped again and arched when the tips of his fingers brushed her clit. "Siban."

"Shhhh." His gentle encouragement soothed her maidenly alarm but did nothing to clear the confusion of wanting more but not knowing exactly what she yearned for.

Before she could reply, his tongue slipped along her lips and laved her clit. Rell's eyes popped open and her back arched off the bed in response to the unfamiliar pleasure of his caress. His arms wrapped around her legs, his hands gripping her thighs to keep them open. She released several shallow breaths and tried to relax, letting her knees fall wide.

Again he touched her with his mouth, stroking her most private area with his tongue. It had been one thing to have him take her against the wall face to face, but this kind of lovemaking was like nothing she'd ever heard of. In the Shadow World, the demons she'd seen fornicating were rough and unyielding, never gentle in the way Siban touched her now.

The need to see him tugged at her. She lifted her head. Instantly her desire soared. The vision of Siban between her legs, loving her with his mouth, ignited emotions that ran the gamut from modesty to wanton voyeurism.

He lifted his eyes, and they burned into her. She shouldn't stare, but what she wanted was to look her fill, watch every splendid stoke he delivered to her. Siban released one of her thighs and reached up her to caress her breast as he continued to lick her. The air left her body as the sensations mingled, driving her higher.

Becoming bolder, Rell lifted to rest on one elbow and give him better access to her breasts. He continued to hold her gaze, his mouth working her while his fingers plucked at her nipple. Unable to resist, she lifted higher, let her knees fall open, and twined her fingers in his hair. Prickles of pleasure pooled between her legs. Her grip in his hair tightened, and she lifted her hips in response to each stroke of his tongue.

Then he released her other thigh, his hand disappearing from her sight. When she lifted her hips again, he slid a finger inside her, filling a need she didn't know she had. Sweet torture. Every caress and lick drove her toward the climax she knew awaited her. Another finger dipped inside her and Rell's body rose from the bed. She pulled his mouth closer, desperate to find her release.

First his tongue would flick against her sensitive bud and then he would suck, his gaze never leaving her. A low growl hummed against her, telling Rell he very much liked the pleasure he was giving her. Faster his tongue flicked and his fingers pumped, ratcheting her beyond control. She dropped back to the bed and dug her heels into the duvet, riding his mouth until her body exploded.

She convulsed with each lick as he continued to torment her until she finally released her hold on his hair and lay panting on the bed. Siban lifted his head and rose, crawling onto the bed to cover her with his body.

Rell twined her arms around his neck and dragged his mouth to hers. She could taste herself on his lips, could feel his desire pressing between her thighs. She opened her legs wide and reached between them, shifting to guide his cock into her. There was no hesitation this time when he slid inside, filling her.

No words were spoken, only quiet breaths from Siban as he slowly pushed in and withdrew. His fingers twined with hers and slid them along the duvet until her arms were above her head. Again he tilted his hips and slid deep into her.

"You feel so good, Rell. Just like I'd always imagined you would be. Slow, tight."

He released her hands and shifted to his knees, bringing Rell with him into a sitting position. Her legs hugged his on either side. She wrapped her arms around his neck, liking the freedom the new position afforded her. When he pushed into her again, she lifted his languid thrust and then lowered her body back onto his cock.

"That's nice," he whispered.

He gripped her rear end and he began to guide her up and down, keeping rhythm with his pace. Each time he entered her, his expression tightened and relaxed when he withdrew.

"Rell." Her name slipped from his lips and his pace quickened.

Sparks of pleasure spiraled through her. Her whimpers mingled with his name each time he plunged into her and buried his cock. "Siban."

She gripped his shoulders to keep her momentum and rhythm constant. A moan flowed from him and he pumped several more times, drawing her toward her release. Another push and her body shattered into a thousand pieces. She cried out, her nails digging into his flesh and her head tilting forward to push against his shoulder.

Suddenly Siban's body went rigid and he buried himself one final time, holding her hips tight against him as shudders racked his body. A cry tore from his lips but quickly died, strangling in his throat as his climax washed over him. He held her against him, his hips undulating under her while his body trembled with its release.

CHAPTER TWENTY-FOUR

Preparations were minimal for their journey north. Besides weapons and clothing, they packed nothing else. Rell's wedding dress was the only exception. Because they would be traveling in Rhys's ship, the crew was taking care of food and preparing their cabins. Once at Alba they would be staying at Rhys's home, Alba Haven.

Flutters of excitement skittered through Rell's stomach. She'd never traveled farther north than Faela. Probably because she'd spent the last thirteen years hiding from most everybody, the thought of traveling and seeing the world as a woman appealed to her. The prospect of meeting Willa's family was another subject all together.

Rhys, Luc, and Siban left for the ship at first light. Delphina had insisted on going as well, saying she needed to prepare the ship. Dozens of voyages had been successfully undertaken without her supervision. But no more. The woman seemed to have appointed herself overseer of their comforts. As far as Rell could tell, none of the Bringers were complaining.

It was late morning and Rell only had one more thing to do before they left. The warded area of the manor vibrated along her Tell, though she couldn't see the wards, they felt as strong as ever. She sent her awareness beyond the boundary, searching for the familiar void. She supposed she could have just shouted for Icarus, but the fact that he had never openly revealed himself to the others while at the manor, made her restrained. Better to treat him with caution than as one of their own—yet.

Her Tell skated across a black void. Instantly she recognized it. "Why do you lurk when you know I'm searching for you?"

A twig snapped and he glided from the woods. His reptilian eyes peered at her, but he appeared less tense and predatory than usual. He stopped a yard from her on the other side of the ward. "Habit I suppose."

"I wanted to tell you that we journey for the Frost Lands." She waited for his reaction, but when he said nothing, she continued. "We believe Vile is moving the Bringers there."

"Yes, I believe this as well."

She flinched. "You know this already?"

"I overheard Sha-hera speaking to the Splinter." He flicked his horns toward the manor. "The one that now resides within."

Rell reminded herself to never underestimate the demon. He seemed to see and know most everything that went on, though he wasn't forthcoming with the information. She'd kept many of her questions to herself when Gregory had shared the legend of the Threshold with them. Gregory had told her to explain their situation to Icarus. "Icarus, what do you know of the Threshold?"

He shook his head. "I've not heard of it before. What is it?"

"I'm not exactly sure. Gregory said it is another portal to other worlds and that they thought it was only a legend."

"Is this the place you travel to?"

"Yes. I think Vile has known about the Threshold for a very long time."

Icarus tipped his chin downward, sticking her with his gaze. "What else do you believe, Rell?"

She cleared her throat, not completely sure she should share her suspicions. "I believe if Vile has kept your human body it would be there. Supposedly the Threshold is very dangerous. From the maps Gregory showed us, we'll be journeying far beyond the border towns and deep into the Frost Lands. You must admit it would be the perfect place to keep something he wanted no one to find."

He was quiet for a second and then nodded. "Perhaps."

"Will you follow?" She didn't say join us because she knew the demon would not and that it would be impossible to provide cover for him in populated areas.

"There are situations I must check on here first."

Panic welled inside her. "Don't go back into the Shadow World, Icarus. It's too dangerous."

His brow furrowed. "I do not think I will ever become accustomed to your concern. I cannot promise you that." He seemed at a loss for word for a second. "But…I promise to be cautious. I have no desire to be imprisoned in the Abyss."

"All right." She relaxed slightly and looked over her shoulder when the jangle of the carriage sounded on the cobbled drive. "I have to go. We sail on the afternoon tide."

"Rell?"

She turned back to him. He took a deep breath and looked at the sky, not meeting her eyes. "If you find my body and I am not there—" His gaze tracked to her face. "Will you bring it back for me?" He swallowed hard. "Even if it's to be buried."

"If it is there, we will do everything in our power to bring it home." She took a step toward him. "Everything, Icarus."

He pursed his lips and gave a single nod. Rell knew him well enough to understand the action was his thank-you—silent, but genuine. Without another word, he strode back into the woods, and she turned and sprinted across the grounds back to the manor.

Rell, Jade, Ravyn, and Meran climbed inside the carriage. Juna refused the offer of riding within and rode her horse alongside. Trace drove the carriage and Jacob squeezed in beside Jade, leaving the three other women to cram onto one seat.

Rell found the ride to town uncomfortable. The carriage bounced and rolled, continually tossing her from one side to the other. However, her sister seemed unusually happy to be riding in the carriage instead of mounted on top of a horse. It was funny to see Jade so animated about the chance to sail again. For the entire ride, she and Ravyn retold the tale of their adventure with the Bane and how they'd single-handedly saved nearly all the crew. Though Jade had recounted the incident after it had happened, at that time Rell had been more concerned about killing Luc than in the actual magnitude of what the two women had done.

The carriage lurched to a stop. Jacob opened the door and stepped out. Noise swelled around them and the smells of the harbor invaded the cab. Jacob extended his hand, offering each of them assistance. Seagulls cried overhead, swirling and swooping to pick up pieces of fish and garbage thrown in the water by the fisherman. Shouts from the crews aboard the ships rose above the constant clatter and dock noises.

Like an encroaching storm, the swell of people pushed against Rell not only physically, but inside her mind. She strengthened her mental barriers and unlashed the small trunk on the back of the carriage that contained the gown Delphina had made her. The quicker they could be underway, the quicker she would be able to relax.

Traffic flowed around them but the many gawking stares made Rell feel out of place. She looked at her group and couldn't help but smile. What an odd sight they must be, five women dressed in pants, and tunics, all displaying impressive weaponry.

Juna dismounted and tied the reins of her horse to the back of the carriage. Mounts would be provided once they reached Alba so Jacob would return hers to his stables. From what Ravyn said, Rhys had plenty of everything to go around.

"Safe journey." Trace remained on his horse, his focus shifting to Rell. "And happy wedding."

The two sentences were more than she'd heard the man speak at one time. "Thank you. Safe journey to you as well."

He dipped his head toward them but said nothing more.

"Let me carry that, my dear." Jacob reached for her small trunk.

"I can manage." The box weighed very little and she couldn't bring herself to let anybody else carry it. "But thank you."

He smiled. "All right then. Let's go find Lord Blackwell's fine vessel."

The five women and Jacob walked along the dock until they came to a beautiful black-and-red ship wedged between two larger sailing vessels. The ship bobbed, the water sloshing between the hull and the pier they stood on. The railings gleamed in the afternoon sun. Rell shielded her eyes to look up. Several men she'd never met before scurried around the deck and up the rope ladder preparing to get underway.

"Rell!" The thunder of tiny feet pattered behind her.

She turned and nearly dropped the trunk when a small boy barreled into her and wrapped his arms around her legs. "Hayden, have you been getting us ready for sea?

"Uh-huh." He tilted his head back and smiled up at her. "Lord Blackwell said I can steer the ship when we're at sea."

Red tinged his chubby cheeks. Since she'd returned home, the boy had nearly stalked her every move. Being around him gave her yearnings she never thought she'd have—for a baby. She smoothed her hand down his back. "Then we're in good hands."

She released the boy and he sprinted away from her, disappearing around the corner of the captain's cabin.

"This is it." Ravyn stopped beside her. "I haven't seen the repairs to the deck yet."

Jade leaned toward Rell. "She blasted a big hole in it. Rhys was *not* pleased."

Ravyn stopped and glared at her. "I saved their lives from the Bane, didn't I?"

"*We* saved their lives." Jade cocked a brow. "A rescue I sometimes curse myself for when Luc becomes a pest."

Rell and Juna smirked and followed her up the gangplank. From what Rell could see, the deck looked good as new. No huge hole graced the spot where Ravyn stood, dragging her foot across the wood.

"You can't even tell." She looked up, grinning.

All activity stopped, the crew turning at once to stare at them as if they'd never seen women before. The good mood fled from Rell, unease replacing it. These men were unfamiliar to her and she didn't know what to expect. Within the Bringer group she was an equal, but in the world of humans women had their place.

A tall man with a gold earring dangling from his right ear approached. He slid the dirty hat from his head and clutched it to his chest. "Lady Ravyn." He gave a quick bow and turned to Jade. A smile spread across his stubbly mouth to show a missing front tooth. "Lady Jade." He crumpled the hat. "Don't know if I'll ever get used to calling you that."

"Zeek," Jade said. "It's so good to see you again." She stepped to the side. "This is my sister, Rell, and Lady Ravyn's sisters, Lady Meran and Lady Juna."

Juna face scrunched up as if she'd just heard a distasteful joke.

The man's eyes rounded as he took in each of the Bringer women. "Gah, I feel plenty safe now with five of ya onboard."

The tension melted from Rell. Obviously these men, at least Zeek anyway, had no problem with women.

"It's good to see you again." Ravyn waved to the men on the rope ladder. They smiled and waved back. "Let's hope this is an uneventful trip."

"I second that." Jade walked farther onto the deck and turned back to Zeek. "What are the chances of me getting to knot a few knots and tie a few ropes off?"

"We've got a small crew this trip, so all help is welcome." Zeek squashed his crumpled hat back on his head and ambled toward Jade. "I doubt you'll be needing me to show you the ropes again, eh?"

"Ah, Zeek." She pointed a finger at him. "You're still as funny as ever."

He blushed under her praise, his gapped grin widening. "Finally, somebody who appreciates my humor."

"Don't encourage him."

Rell glanced up to the naysayer. A short, round man scrambled down the rope ladder and landed lightly on the deck. He wore garish striped pants that came to his knees and black boots that looked a size too big for him. From what she could see, he had all his teeth but his head was bald as a baby's butt.

"Gem, charming as ever." Jade tilted her head and propped her hand on her hips. "Have you lost weight?"

He patted his stomach. "I have lost a pound or two; thanks for noticing."

Rell watched her sister charm the men on the boat, amazed by the ease with which she won them over. Perhaps if she'd never been turned Bane, she would possess some of the charms of a lady, but the woman she was now preferred silence to flattery.

Siban exited the bridge and half climbed half slid down the stairs. "We're about to get underway." He pointed to the glassed-in area above. "Would you like to watch from the bridge or bow?"

"Bow, as long as it's safe." Her heartbeat quickened at the thought of being near the front of a moving ship. "I don't know how to swim."

"Me either," Gem said, gripping a thick rope and pulling. "Can't stand getting wet."

It didn't take her Tell powers to confirm what he said. His smell did that for him.

"We'll try to keep you out of the water." Siban gave her a dazzling smile. "I'll come join you once we're underway."

She cast a glance around the deck when she reached the top. Jade stood among a group of men, talking as if they were old friends. Maybe they were. Again she realized how little she'd actually known about Jade's life outside of the Shadow World.

Rell joined Ravyn at the bow.

"I love this ship." Ravyn looked over her shoulder. "I think Jade does too."

"Yes, she's seems at home here."

Ravyn laughed. "Are you excited about your wedding?"

"Yes." Rell looked out over the water. "Also scared and unsure."

"Why unsure?" Ravyn turned to the side and rested her arm on the railing, looking at Rell. "You love Siban, right?"

"That is the one thing I'm not unsure about." She met Ravyn's stare. "Why haven't you and Rhys wed?"

A chuckle slipped from Ravyn. "The subject hasn't come up yet." She turned back to the sea. "I think we're both waiting until the battle with the Bane is over."

Rell nodded. "That's why I'm unsure. So much is undecided. What if I get with child?"

"Would that be so bad?"

"I'm not my mother, Ravyn. She was always there for Jade and I." Rell frowned. "Until I took that away. What kind of mother would I be?"

"A wonderful one." Ravyn placed a hand on Rell's shoulder, forcing her to look at Ravyn. "One who would fight to the death to protect not only your child but your husband." She smiled. "I think you and Willa are more alike than you think."

Her words warmed Rell. She could feel Ravyn's conviction, that she truly believed what she said. "I would like to believe that."

"Then do." Her hand slid from Rell's shoulder. "I think it's time that Rhys and I stop waiting until the world is safe." She sighed. "That may never happen and I'd hate to die before making a true life with him."

"A double wedding then? I'm sure my mother would love that."

"Uh, no." Ravyn's eyes rounded. "I said we'd talk about it. In the meantime, we'll enjoy your and Siban's wedding."

She laughed and turned back to the water. It was amazing how their talk had lifted the majority of Rell's doubts. She loved Siban. Life without him would be as bleak as when she was a demon. There was no sure thing in these tumultuous times, but she wouldn't let the Bane steal anymore of her happiness. Not looking at Ravyn, she said, "Thank you."

Obviously understanding, Ravyn said, "You're welcome."

The two women stood together, enjoying the launch preperations. Ravyn explained different things about the ship, keeping their conversation light. Ropes were untied and tossed over the side of the boat onto the dock. With a loud *flap*, a single sail unfurled. The ship creaked and drifted backward out of the slip. The crew scampered around the deck and up the ladder, while Rhys manned the wheel, steering the vessel away from the pier and into open water.

More sails opened. The wind caught the material, snapping it to a tight billow. Waves crashed under the bow and the ship dipped down and then back up. Once all the sails had been unfurled, the ship sliced through the water, moving faster than Rell ever had in her life.

Siban left the bridge and maneuvered the steps to the deck. He joined her at the bow and slid his arm around her waist. It was a perfect moment in an imperfect world.

Meran approached. "Is this your first time on a ship?"

"Yes." Rell leaned out to look at the water. "The sea is so black."

"Deep and cold too." Meran smiled, as if what she said wasn't incredibly troubling. "If you don't get seasick, you'll sleep more soundly than you ever have. The rocking of the boat will lull you to pleasant dreams."

"And if I get seasick?" Rell asked.

Meran's smiled turned tight and she patted the side of the ship. "You might want to sleep near the railing."

"I haven't been sick myself," Ravyn said, "but I hear it's highly unpleasant."

"Well—" Rell thought for a moment, assessing her stomach. "I feel fine so far."

"Good," Siban said. "That's a very good sign."

She suspected he was placating her, but let it go. "So what do we do now?"

"Wait." Ravyn pulled her cloak around her and leaned her head back to drink up the sun. "We should arrive in Alba tomorrow afternoon."

"Sounds—wonderful."

And it did. The lack of danger was exactly what Rell wanted. To sleep soundly, rocked by the sea, was a type of tedium she considered a gift. There would come a time, too soon, to be sure, when she'd wish for such boredom. She was certain of it.

CHAPTER TWENTY-FIVE

Their time on the sea was uneventful and as much as she had craved the monotony of the travel, when they finally arrived in Alba, Rell was ready to get off the ship. Perhaps danger was in her blood. Inactivity, though important sometimes, was not something she wished to experience too often.

The din from the crowded dock swelled up above the bow of the boat. Rell leaned over the side and watched the people scurry about. The pier stretched as far as Rell could see. Ships bobbed lazily in the water, their sides scraping and bumping against the dock when a ship eased into a slip, disrupting the water.

"It's really something, isn't it?" Ravyn leaned her elbows on the rail and stared down at the people. The brisk afternoon breeze buffeted her black locks and she gathered the thick mass in her hand to hold it in place. "I remember the first time I saw the port. I couldn't believe there were so many people in one place."

"It's daunting being around this many people." Rell squinted and rubbed her forehead. "I feel as if they're all trying to crowd inside my head."

"Keep your mental shields erected. I'm still not very good at letting a little bit of information in at a time." She smiled. "Don't tell Rhys. He's been trying to teach me for quite a while now, and I dare say he'd be disappointed in me."

An unladylike snort escaped Rell. "I doubt that."

Jade joined them at the railing. "What are you talking about?"

"We were just watching the crowd." Ravyn pointed to a legless man near a barrel on the dock. "See that man down there?"

Rell followed her finger and nodded.

"Look at the pile of rags behind him."

Rell held up her hand and squinted against the afternoon sun and Jade leaned forward against the rail. At first the pile looked like discarded clothing, but with closer scrutiny a pair of ragged boots could be seen peeking from the heap. After a few seconds the boots moved.

"He's got legs. But how does he appear legless?"

"Ingenuity. The blanket over his lap hides his folded legs."

Jade shrugged. "A person needs to survive."

The loud cranking of the gangplank being lowered behind them drew their attention. The three women turned to watch the crew preparing to disembark. From observing the men, Rell could tell that they'd sailed together for enough time to know the routine and work together. That was something she could appreciate now that she was Bringer.

Delphina's voice could be heard ordering Hayden away from the gangplank. Rell made note of just how much work a young boy could be and squashed any bits of longing for a child that surfaced.

Siban exited the bridge and took the steps two at a time, hopping the last two to land on the deck. He strolled toward them, obviously happy to be home again.

"Once the gangplank is down, we'll be ready to disembark." He bent and picked up the small chest at Rell's feet. "We'll be walking, so I'll carry this."

"Is it far?" Not that it mattered. Walking would be nice after standing around for a day.

"It's a bit of a trek," Ravyn said. "Mainly because Alba Haven sits at the top of the hill."

Rell looked up, but all that could be seen were tall walls of what looked like a fortress. She pointed. "We're going up there?"

"Yes." Siban walked toward Rhys and Luc, who waited near the exit. "It's very beautiful and very safe."

"Well—" Ravyn's gaze cut to her. "If you stay within the walls, it's safe. All of Alba Haven is warded. Outside of the wall is quite another story."

"I'll remember that." Rell stepped closer to Siban.

"Don't worry, you're more than a match for any of the vagrants loitering about the gates of Alba Haven," he said.

Once they were all gathered, Gregory quickly surveyed the group. "Are we ready?"

"I believe so." Rhys moved to the front of their party. "There was no time to send word ahead to prepare for horses, so we'll have to walk to Alba Haven. I'm sure we won't encounter any trouble."

Besides Faela, Rell had never been in a large city, and even then it had been with her parents when she was very young. Excitement skittered through her as she descended the gangway. People fanned back, allowing their party to pass. She had to admit, they were an impressive group. By some unspoken consent, each of the Bringers were dressed in black and outfitted with their weapons.

Luc and Ravyn each wore a harness that ran from their right shoulders to just below their ribs. In the casing rested an

immortal dagger for quick retrieval. Though Rell still wore her
sword at her side, Siban had chosen a sheath that sat firmly
against his back. By reaching over his head, he was able to
grip the hilt and pull the sword free to drive it downward for
immediate attack. Once they reached Alba Haven and before
they left on their journey, Rell planned on rigging her sheath
to sit the same way. Though she'd grown used to the constant
tapping of her blade against her leg, she would prefer to have
the weapon secure when she pulled it from the sheath.

As they made their way along the dock, the creak of ropes
and ships knocking against the pier mingled with the slosh of
water and the clatter of carts. The odor of fish, both fresh and
rotting, hung in the air along with the smell of oil and wood.
There were so many people, all bustling to some place or
another.

A woman's high-pitched laugh rose from somewhere
behind her, but Rell didn't turn. From the docks they followed
the flow of the crowd and wound their way past the large gates
of the city. People flowed in and out through the opening.
Wagons, horse riders, and those walking merged into a giant
congested river of people. The constant breeze kicked up
swirling vortexes of dirt. Rell lifted her arm to shield her face
from the biting sand. When the wind died down, she brushed
her hand across her cheeks in an unsuccessful effort to remove
the grit. Compared to the open sea, the overcrowding of the
city was stifling.

Siban touched her waist. On one shoulder, he balanced the
small trunk. His eyes continually scanned the area for what she
assumed was trouble.

"The end of days is near!" A dirty man in a robe shook
his finger in the air. "The flying scourge will bleed our lands of
blood and spirit!"

Rell's steps slowed to watch the proselytizer.

The man's watery eyes leveled on the group, narrowing in on the three sisters. "A legion to lead us. Three to triumph."

Juna stopped and stared for a second. "Is he talking about us?"

"His name is Malachi," Siban said. "I used to think he was a crazy old monk, but after everything that's happened—"

He let the rest of the statement hang in the air.

"Let's get settled first," Rhys said, starting forward again. "I think it would be a good idea to have a talk with Malachi later."

"Agreed," Gregory said.

"Angels!" Malachi's eyes widened, his hands folding in prayer against his chin. "Do not forsake us."

"He said the exact same thing to me when I first arrived." Ravyn gave a little shudder. "It's very disconcerting."

"I'll say," Meran mumbled. She placed her hand against Gregory's back and pushed him forward. "Let's not linger."

Something about the man's intensity tugged at Rell. Though at first glance he appeared to be just another doomsayer preaching at the city gates, what he said struck a chord in her. She let her Tell ghost over him and touched the familiar taint of darkness. She refocused on the course before her but the monk continued to plague her mind.

He'd definitely been touched by the Bane somehow, but he didn't possess the thick presence like Siban and she had experienced. Perhaps his faith kept him protected. She glanced back one more time. He still followed their progress, his hands remaining pressed against his chin in prayer.

Thoughts of the monk slipped away and were replaced by the bustle and life within the heart of the city. Shops crowded together on the narrow streets, their wooden signs hanging above the door, announcing their wares or services. People loitered in doorways, some brave enough to ask for money. Several cowered away from the group and rushed back inside the dark shelter of the rooms beyond the doorway. Woman leaned out of windows above the shops, waving and propositioning men passing by. Some were successful. Those who were not, stooped to exposing themselves, hoping to lure the men upstairs.

Fall had already touched Alba. Small fires burned next to many of the vendors whose stalls were set up in the city's center. Perhaps it was the exhilaration of their trip and the excitement of arriving at Alba Haven, but Rell was not cold.

Their course circled to the right, consistently climbing in a spiral. The narrow crammed streets of the marketplace gave way to homes. Modest at first, the dwellings grew in grandeur. None were as elegant as Jacob Le Daun's manor, but did speak of wealth. About two-thirds of the way up, the buildings took on a rundown feel. Again, people lounged in the doorways of what looked like abandoned buildings.

Eventually Rhys stopped before a massive gate. He lifted the iron knocker and pounded, the sound echoing against the buildings surrounding them. They waited.

Siban leaned toward Rell. "I used to man the door. Nobody had to wait this long."

Rhys turned his head, smirking. "Would you like your old position back?"

Siban was quiet for a second, as if contemplating Rhys's offer, and then sighed. "No, it appears I have been ruined for sedentary duty."

"We all have, I think," Luc said. "Pity."

The grinding of a bolt drawing back dragged against the inside of the gate door. A chain clattered and the moaning protest of the iron hinges groaned when the long door began to inch open. Rhys waited until there was enough room to pass and then proceeded inside.

Rell stepped into another world. A cobbled path led off in different directions. Arches framed the walkways with simple but beautiful stonework. To her surprise, women carried folded blankets and baskets of fruit down one of the walkways. A man, who looked like a solider, led a horse toward what were probably the stables.

From behind the now-closed gate, a man appeared. "Lord Blackwell. We were not expecting you."

"Geoffrey." Rhys grasped the man's forearm. "We didn't have time to send a messenger ahead."

Rell noticed that he didn't add that he hoped they weren't inconvenienced. From what Siban had told her, Rhys was the lord of Alba Haven and the people who lived within its walls were under his care and protection.

"I'm sure Nattie will be quite happy to see you." A smile played at the man's mouth. He turned to Ravyn. "Lady Ravyn, it is good to see you again." He squinted, his eyes drifting to her Tell tattoo. "It appears much has happened since you left us." His gaze scanned the group. "I can't wait to hear the tale."

She patted his arm. "And what a tale it is."

"Take one of the other men and go to the city gates. There's an old monk preaching the end of the world. Bring him here," Rhys said. "If he's unwilling to come with you, tell him the angels wish to see him."

The man's eyebrows rose in question. "Angels, my lord?"

"He'll know what you're talking about." Rhys turned and headed toward the largest arch. "And after that I need a message sent to The Dragon's Head Inn. Tell them we'll be arriving tomorrow night."

"Very good, my lord. I'll take care of it." Geoffrey called from behind him. "By the way, is it?"

Rhys stopped and looked back at him. "Is it what?"

"The end of the world?" The man's tone held no hint of mirth.

"Let's pray not." In silence, Rhys led the group through the main arch and into the bailey.

Meran's steps slowed. "Either I have gone round the bend, or I'm seeing spirits."

Rell stared in the direction Meran pointed. "I don't see anything."

"I see them as well," Ravyn said. "Alba Haven is full of ghosts. You'll get used to it. I believe that's part of being an oracle."

"I'm fairly certain I will never get used to it." Juna skirted the edge of the walk, as if putting as much room between her and the unseen spirits. "Ever."

Two black doors loomed ahead of them. Shiny brass bands embellished the dark wood and glinted in the sun. Gripping the handles, Rhys pushed the doors open and strode in. The breath hitched in Rell's throat as she tried to take in the expansive and magnificent foyer. Above her the ceiling soared, arching like the sky. A beautiful mural spread across the ceiling, the painting a detailed depiction of the night sky.

"Ah, it's good to be home." Siban inhaled. "It feels like it's been forever."

Never, in all the hours they'd spent together in the Shadow World, had he spoken of Alba Haven's beauty, only of missing his home and the delicious meals. It was hard to place Siban in these surroundings. She'd only known him in the dank caverns or Le Daun's manor. Suddenly she realized how little she truly knew about Siban's life. Only that his family had been killed and his sister now sat in silence, cloistered in a distant abbey. A few nights ago he'd spoken of a lullaby his mother used to sing. But that was as much as he'd shared. He knew everything of her, but she knew nothing of his life beyond being a Bringer.

"Rhys!" The woman's shout caused the entire group to turn toward a door at their left. "Thank the Sainted Ones, you made it back safely."

A tall thin, extremely beautiful woman closed the distance between them. Her gray hair was plaited into a long braid and swung when she walked toward them.

"Nattie." Rhys met her halfway across the foyer. Instead of hugging him, she gripped his biceps and held him at arm's length and looked him over from head to toe. He didn't resist. "You are a sight for sore eyes, Nattie."

"As are you." After a minute, she pulled him to her and squeezed. "We haven't heard anything since Siban left." She released him, but didn't lower her hands. "Is everything all right?"

"For now, yes." He shook his head. "There is much to tell."

They walked toward the group. Nattie's gaze immediately targeted Ravyn among the crowd. "And you." Instead of hugging her, Nattie gripped her chin and twisted her head left and then right, scowling. "And what is this?" She tapped Ravyn's Tell tattoo. "You didn't get drunk one night and have that done as a jest, did you?"

A brilliant smile spread across Ravyn's face, her blue eyes dancing with delight. A sense of love surrounded the group, sending warmth through Rell. Nattie seemed to be an important member of the household and obviously Ravyn cared for the woman very much.

"That would have been much easier." Ravyn gripped Nattie's hands and pulled them away from her face. "Come, let me introduce you." She tugged the older woman toward the group. From the way Siban stared at Nattie, he cared a lot about her as well.

"Of course you know Siban and Luc." Ravyn waved toward the two men.

"Nattie, you're looking as lovely as ever." Luc stepped forward and kissed the woman's hand.

She yanked it away. "I see you're still as much of a scoundrel as ever."

"Actually, I'm not." He straightened and reached for Jade, pulling her forward. "Nattie, I'd like you to meet Jade." He draped his arm around her shoulder. "I love her."

"Love her?" Nattie's gaze bounced between them and then settled on Jade. "How did you manage that one?"

"I tried to kill him," Jade said matter-of-factly and held out her hand. "Seemed to really win him over." She smiled. "I've heard many great things about you, Nattie."

"Well, I haven't heard nearly enough about you." She took Jade's hand in hers and was about to cover it with her other hand when she stopped. Slowly, she turned Jade's palm to face up. "My, this group is full of surprises."

"You have not heard the half of it." Luc pulled Jade to him and stepped to the side to make room. "This is Jade's sister, Rell. She used to be a Bane, but we healed her." Nattie's mouth dropped open and she moved to speak, but he cut her off. "Oh, that's not the most amazing part." He gave one of his charming half smiles. "As a Bane, she was the one who helped Siban escape the Shadow World, and they are to be married."

The woman held up her hands, but seemed unable to speak. Rell smiled, not knowing what to say to this overpowering woman.

As if sensing an opening, Ravyn moved to stand beside Meran and Juna. "And these two are my sisters. Juna is the oldest, and Meran is the youngest." She twisted to the left. "And this is Gregory. Until he crossed through the Mystic Arch, he was the Bringer King, which means his brother, who was kidnapped as a baby is still alive and here in Inness." Ravyn paused. "Unfortunately he's a Demon Bane, but we're working on that."

Nattie snapped her mouth closed and narrowed her gaze on the group. "You're trying to kill me with all of this, aren't you?"

"You'll get used to it," Delphina slipped in.

"And of course..." Ravyn ushered the woman and her children forward. "This is Delphina, Serena, Hayden, and sweet baby Jenna."

Nattie eyed the group suspiciously. "You Bringers too?"

"No." Moving forward a few steps, Delphina extended her hand. "Lady Ravyn took us in and I tried to tend this lot when we was in Faela."

"It's quite a task, isn't it?" Nattie said.

Delphina nodded. "I see you're a woman of great understanding in this matter. Perhaps you could give me a few pointers."

Appreciation glinted in Nattie's eyes. "Indeed I can." She glanced back to Rhys. "And you're going to tell me everything that has happened so far."

Rhys leaned in and kissed her on the cheek. "We will give you the whole story at dinner, though I doubt you'll be happy to hear it."

"I suspect you're right." She sighed. "Well, go find your rooms. Your chambers have been ready for some time." She looked at Delphina. "You and the children come with me. I've got a lovely pot of tea brewing and freshly baked honey and biscuits." Nattie turned and strode toward the kitchen, calling over her shoulder. "Rhys, I'll leave you to showing the others where they can sleep."

"Of course." He smiled and shook his head. "It's so good to see you again, Nattie."

With a dismissive wave, she disappeared through the archway.

From Nattie's bossy demeanor, Rell got the impression that she ruled Alba Haven, and unless Rhys intervened, Nattie's word was law.

Siban's arm slipped around her waist. "I'll show you my quarters."

A thrill rippled through her. This would be the first time she'd see where Siban had lived during his dark days after escaping the Shadow World. She wondered what other things she'd learn about the man she'd fallen in love with during the most tumultuous time of her life.

CHAPTER TWENTY-SIX

Instead of heading up the spiral staircase that had handrails fashioned into dragons, Siban lead Rell to a door that sat behind the stairwell, partially hidden. Beyond the door the hall was a comfortable width, not narrow as she expected. Small, arched windows illuminated the walk along an extension that connected whatever was at the end to the main building.

Siban slowed. A door carved with vines and flowers stood before them.

"These are my chambers." He reached for the forged handle and settled on the metal. He turned to her. "Outside of Rhys and Nattie, nobody has ever been inside." He smiled, almost as if he was embarrassed. "Until now I've never wanted to share it with anybody."

"I'm glad you've chosen me," Rell said, her interest piqued.

He pressed his thumb against the latch and pushed the door open. What she expected was a dark and sparse room. When he opened the door it was as if he'd opened up a passage to another world. On three walls glass reached from floor to ceiling and sunlight lay bands of white gold across the stone floor. The forth wall was solid stone. A huge hearth stretched from the center outward, taking up a third of the wall.

She stepped inside, surprised by how warm the afternoon sun made the room. "It's an atrium."

"Yes. Rhys let me stay here after I returned." He followed her inside. "The glass helped me to not feel closed in and the vibrations of the plants soothed the darkness."

A tree grew in the center of the room and beneath it sat Siban's bed. The canopy was draped in green chiffon, with a border of darker green velvet around the bottom edge. A thick duvet of the same green velvet covered the mattress and the head of the bed was piled high with sumptuous pillows.

Rell circled the tree and the bed, running her hand across the top of the soft material. "It's beautiful."

He smirked. "I've spent many a sleepless night here."

"And hopefully you'll spend many more." Her hand drifted up the poster and she leaned against it. "But this time I'll be here to get you through those hours."

"I think I'd like that very much."

She gave him a coy smile. "As would I."

Her gaze continued around the atrium. Among the plants sat a large wardrobe. Vines grew over the top, making it blend in as if part of nature. Stone paths branched out from the middle of the room and between them grew various plants and flowers. Two white butterflies flittered among the late-season blooms. Each piece of furniture blended so well within the living vegetation, that Rell wouldn't have been surprised to see a bird perched in the tree.

A large table near the window caught her eye. Bottles and glazed clay dishes sat in neat order and a glass filled with paintbrushes rested on a smaller table. Sheets of paper lay spread in orderly disarray on the top. She turned to him, her brow crinkling. "Do you paint?"

"Yes." He joined her at the table and lifted one of the

pieces of parchment. "I stopped for a while but had begun again before I left for Faela."

The garden beyond his window stood out in striking detail. Though the flowers were now fading with the onset of fall, Rell could imagine exactly what the lovely garden had looked like when in full bloom.

"It's beautiful." She touched a bright red poppy. "I feel as if I can almost smell them."

He pulled another sheet from under the pile, looked at it, and after a few seconds handed it to her.

"Oh, Siban." She set the garden painting aside and gingerly took the picture from him. "It's me." Indeed it was—had been—her. The image was of her Bane form, the familiar features so defined it was as if Rell the demon still lived upon this page. She followed the curve of the tiny horns with the tip of her finger. Her eyes were almond-shaped, but they were human, not reptilian like the rest of the Bane. "You've made me beautiful."

"You were beautiful to me." He stood behind her and stared down at the picture. "I must have drawn your image a hundred times over the last year. When I would wake from a bad dream I'd get up and sketch your image as I remembered you." His hand caressed her upper arm. "Thinking of you always drove the nightmares away."

She set the picture back on the table and turned to him, winding her arms around his neck. "Thank you for sharing your world with me."

He bent and kissed her, the contact gently brushing her lips. "Thank you for giving me back my world." They kissed again and then he released her. "You realize these are our chambers now. You can change them however you'd like."

"I wouldn't change a thing, Siban. It's perfect exactly how it is." She paused and looked around. "Except for maybe another wardrobe and a chair of my own so we may sit by each other."

"You're too easy to please." He took her hand and led her to the windows. "These can be cold during the winter, so I will have drapes fashioned." Tugging her behind him, he walked down the path to the left, seemingly excited about the prospect of redecorating the atrium. "Perhaps an area for your interests." He stopped and looked at her. "What do you like to do? Do you sew?"

She cocked an eyebrow at him. "Do I look like I sew?"

His gaze tracked down and back up her body. "Thankfully, no."

"How about—" She released his hand and stepped onto a circular area about twelve feet in diameter. "A sparring field."

"You wish to do battle in our chambers?"

"I like to think of it as training." She spun and imitated slashing with her sword.

On her downward swing, Siban caught her arm. "How about instead of a sparring field we turn it into a nursery?"

Rell blinked several times, her arm growing slack. "You want to have children?"

"I want to have children with you." He drew her to him. "Don't you?"

Did she? With the way her life had been she'd never even given it a thought. What kind of mother would she be? "I don't know." She laid her hands against his chest and stared into his eyes. "If I did, I would want them with you."

"Then that's all we need to know now." A sweet smile spread across his face. "We've still much to do before I could feel comfortable bringing a child into the world."

A sigh escaped her. "Speaking of which, we should probably get cleaned up and go see what the plans are."

"Yes." His mouth captured hers and his tongue swept inside, sending a thrill through her that made her want to lock the door and ignore the world for a few hours. But the kiss was brief. "Let's go see what's stewing within Alba Haven."

She sighed again and let Siban guide her out of their magical chambers.

Loud voices emanated from what was obviously the kitchen. Pots and pans clattered, Nattie's commands rising above the noise. "He has missed you something terrible. Squawking for hours on end."

Rell entered the kitchen to see Ravyn and Rhys sitting at a long wooden table. Perched on Ravyn's shoulder was the most beautiful bird she'd ever seen. Brilliant red-and-orange feathers flowed like fiery lace down its tail and bright golden eyes peered intelligently around.

"I've missed him too," Ravyn cooed, feeding the bird bits of bread from her hand.

Mesmerized, Rell slid into the seat across from her. "What's his name?"

"Beacon." Ravyn stroked a finger along the bird's head. "I found him in the market place before I left for Faela."

The content smile on Rhys's face as he watched Ravyn and the bird warmed Rell. He truly loved her. That much was obvious.

"What kind is he?" The urge to stroke the bird itched at Rell's fingers. "I've never seen his like."

"He's a Firebrand." Ravyn looked at her. "Would you like to hold him?"

"Could I?" She was standing before she finished the question. Rell skirted the table and straddled the bench to face the bird on Ravyn's left side. "He's so beautiful."

A low gurgle purred from the bird's throat.

"I think he likes you," Rhys said.

"Hold out your arm." Ravyn turned on the bench and touched her forearm with Rell's. "If he's in a good mood, he'll climb onto you."

With rocking steps, Beacon scooted down Ravyn's arm and onto Rell. "He's heavier than he looks." Rell stroked his head and her eyes widened. "And so warm."

"That's the Firebrand in him."

"Have the children seen him yet?" Rell asked.

"Oh yes." Nattie chuckled. "Delphina had to carry him out of the kitchen when I was showing them to their chambers." She sighed. "It's nice having young ones at Alba Haven again."

As Rell caressed the bird's soft head it settled on her shoulder and nestled against her hair. Perhaps because she'd once had wings herself, she connected with Beacon on a level deeper than animal and human.

The rest of the group entered the kitchen. Instantly the women crowded around Rell and Ravyn, oohing over the beautiful bird.

"Really, the fuss you make over that bird." The harsh tone of Nattie's words was tempered by the adoring look she gave Beacon. "He's such a bother when you're not here."

"I'm sorry, Nattie." Ravyn winked at Rell. "We'll take him with us on our next journey."

"To the Frost Lands?" She thunked a jug of wine onto the table. "I should say you won't. That bird would freeze to death before you even reached the boundary." Next she shoved a tray of goblets next to the wine and gave a long-suffering sigh. "I guess I could take care of him while you're gone."

"Thank you, Nattie, that's so kind of you." Ravyn's expression was serious, but humor laced her words.

"Well, I'm a kind person," Nattie said.

"That's a matter of opinion."

Rell turned to see a little man with exceptionally large feet shuffle into the room. His hair was sparse but his eyes sparkled with intelligence and mischief.

Rhys rose. "Jaspar, it's great to see you."

"It is great to be seen, my lord." The old man descended to a low bow and slowly rose again. "I hear you've had quite the trip."

"Quite." Rhys took his seat again. "And what has been happening at Alba Haven while I've been gone."

"Naught but Nattie's blustering, my lord."

Nattie harrumphed, but said nothing further, keeping her attention on the task of peeling potatoes.

Jaspar shuffled to the table and lifted a goblet of wine from the tray. "I believe Geoffrey has fetched what you requested."

A few seconds later loud voices wafted in from the outer hall, giving Rell the impression that Jaspar either knew of the monk's arrival or he was a Tell.

"Where are they?" The monk's voice grew louder. "Where are the angels?"

"I guess that means us," Ravyn said.

The three sisters stood and formed a line in the center of the kitchen, waiting for the monk to arrive. When he saw them, his eyes widened and drifted to the ceiling. With folded hands, he inched toward them, and once he stood a foot away, he lowered to his knees and kissed each one of their boots.

Juna rolled her eyes, but Meran watched him with eyes of a woman who was used to her followers adoration. When he sat back on his feet, she bent and grasped his arm. "There's no need for such formality within these walls, Brother."

The monk struggled to his feet, his eyes never leaving her face. "I thought I'd not live to see the arrival of the angels." He covered Meran's hand with his. "You are here to save us."

"Come, sit." Ravyn indicated the bench at the table. "Have some ale. You must be thirsty."

"Thank you, my lady. You're generosity humbles me." He took the goblet from her and downed the contents in one gulp, giving his lips a satisfying smack afterward. "Excellent, just excellent."

Rell looked at Siban, raising her eyebrows in question. At the city gates Malachi had seemed irrational, but now the man appeared as sane as she was.

"Brother Malachi," Rhys began, "we're very interested in what you were saying by the gates." He picked up the pitcher and refilled the good Brother's goblet. "Can you explain your prophecy?"

"A legion to lead us." He directed his cup at the women. "Three to triumph."

"Yes, exactly," Juna said, taking a seat. "What exactly do you mean by legion?"

"I am only the messenger, my lady. I do not labor to understand." He took another long draw of the ale.

"Well—" She scowled. "That's convenient."

"However," Malachi interjected, "I do know from where the prophecy comes." He waved his hand at the ceiling. "One such as you painted the sky."

"Could you elaborate a little bit, Brother." Juna leaned forward and rested her palms on the table. "Who do you mean one such as us?"

The monk turned over his palms. Though there was no sun emblems tattooed on his palms, all gathered seemed to know what he was talking about.

"A Bringer painted the mural in Alba Haven?"

"Yes, to mark the beginning of the end. When the planets align, the scourge will bleed our land of blood and spirit."

"If one wanted to take that literally," Rell said, "it sounds like the Bane plan on turning a lot more people into minions."

"The Bane! The scourge," Malachi shouted.

Meran laid a gentle hand on the monk's shoulder. "Do you know who painted the mural, Brother Malachi?"

"He who wrote the word. He who spread his protection."

Malachi took another drink and swallowed. "The scourge steals our souls and puts them in a pretty box so he can take them out to taunt and play with."

"Do you mean the Demon King?" Siban asked.

"Yes, yes, vile, vile creature."

"Is the pretty box you're talking about the Abyss?" Juna asked.

The monk shook his head vigorously. "No, the pretty, cold box holds no sinners, only saviors."

"The captured Bringers?" Luc asked the group instead of Malachi. "And the ice.

"Where is the pretty box, Brother?" Ravyn's voice was gentle, but the compulsion she used brushed against Rell with surprising force.

"The box is cold and hidden." He held out his glass for a refill. "None dare travel to find it."

"Is it…" Siban paused, his gaze leveling on the monk. "In the Frost Lands."

"Yes, where the snow never melts." He brought the goblet to his mouth but didn't drink. "But it's dangerous there. Those who seek never return."

"So Vile has, or is taking, the Bringers to the Frost Lands. We had figured that already." Juna heaved a heavy sigh and thunked back against her chair. "What else can you tell us, Brother Malachi—anything that can help us?"

He stared into his drink for a few seconds and then lifted his head to look directly at her. Rell was struck by how intelligent and focused his gaze seemed, as if a veil had lifted and he was suddenly cognizant. "My Brothers guard the entrance to the Threshold. Be warned, they are not gentle of nature like me. Travel beyond the boundary city." An instant later his eyes glazed over and he focused again on his ale and muttered into his cup, "The angels are here."

"It's almost as if he has brief periods of lucidity." Meran turned away from the man. "As if something is blocking his memory."

"Perhaps if we tried to heal him he would remember more," Jade said.

"It's worth a try, but we've had a long day, and we have an early start tomorrow morning." Gregory turned to Rhys. "Would it be possible to lodge Brother Malachi here tonight? I think he might be a good addition to our party."

"Of course." Rhys watched the old man lay claim to the rest of his drink. "I think you're right. He may still have information for us."

"I'll send somebody to ready a chamber for him." Nattie set down her knife and bustled out of the kitchen.

"After dinner we should turn in early." Gregory took a seat at the table. "We'll need to be on the road by dawn."

"Maybe we should go to bed right now." Siban yawned unconvincingly. "I'm rather tired."

"For the love of Saints," Nattie said, walking back into the kitchen. "Let the poor girl eat before you work up her appetite again."

Rell blushed, mortified at being the center of their attention.

"You'll get used to it." Ravyn said, taking Beacon from her. "Just be thankful Nattie hasn't woken you up in the morning." She leaned closer. "Lock your door if you have one."

"The bigger the bolt the better," Rhys added.

"Don't listen to them, Rell. The whole lot of them are a bunch of liars." When Nattie went back to peeling potatoes, Ravyn gave a conspiratorial shake of her head. "I saw that."

Siban leaned toward her. "I hope you won't be too tired after we eat."

"Too tired for what," she whispered.

A wicked smile spread across his lips. "Dessert."

A warm flush crept up her neck. "I'm fairly certain that whatever dessert you have in mind I will not be too tired for."

CHAPTER TWENTY-SEVEN

They departed Alba Haven at sunup. Rhys led the party on Sampson. The black horse appeared very happy to be outside of Alba Haven and reunited with his rider.

Most of the city's inhabitants still slept, but a few shop owners were out, sweeping the filth of the previous day's business away from their doorstep.

Rell yawned and rubbed her eyes. More than anything, Siban wished they were still in their bed under the tree, making love.

A loud braying erupted from Malachi's donkey. Probably from having to pull the small wagon and its load of children, Delphina, and Malachi.

"My thoughts exactly, Penelope," the monk said. "There's a foul feel on the breeze this morning."

"That's last night's ale coming back to greet you, Brother Malachi," Luc said.

"Not so, my lord." Malachi turned in his saddle. "I had but two mugs before dinner"

"But," Luc continued, "how many did you have after we retired?"

The old man blustered what sounded like another denial, but he didn't actually form the words.

Quiet conversation flowed between the riders as their course wound downward toward the city gates. For Siban, the feel of the morning was anything but foul. Though later they would journey on to the Frost Lands and no doubt danger, today they traveled toward Rell's family and his and Rell's wedding.

She glanced at him and smiled, as if sensing his mood. Her expression mirrored his. Within the next two days they would be wed, barring any unforeseen interruptions.

The line exiting the city was sparse, but already travelers from the surrounding villages were pouring into Alba. Beggars had already claimed their spots along the wall. Dirty children squatted, sleepy-eyed and yawning. Normally they swarmed the travelers, begging for coin, but in this early hour the children were just waking up.

A man in rags sitting with a woven basket gave a weak wave to Malachi when he passed. The monk returned his greeting and then turned his attention forward, toward the mountains. A sense of self-importance rolled from Malachi. Perhaps now that the Bringers had brought him into the fold, the monk finally felt like he had a purpose in life. Siban thought about the man's life. Each day he'd stood at the city gates, predicting the world's doom, and each day he had been treated as an old man who had gone insane. Now that the Bringers had given his prophecy credence, Malachi's behavior had become less erratic.

Outside the city walls the land opened to an expansive and barren plain. Ruts cut deep into the hard packed earth from the constant flow in and out of the city. People carried baskets strapped to their backs, their wares piled high inside. Brightly painted wagons rumbled past them. Some were completely enclosed like those of the nomadic Splinters. Some were two wheeled and open, being pulled by their owners.

They traveled across the plains and entered the pass. Narrow walls surrounded them and the group thinned to a single-file line. The air grew cooler than out on the plains but the mountain blocked the wind. Slender waterfalls plummeted from above the rise and splashed onto flat slabs of slate at the base, causing a fine mist to hover within the pass. More wagons and people on foot passed them on their way to Alba. It looked like it would be another busy day at the market.

At the top of the pass the ground leveled out. A river ran along the trail and when the sun shone high in the sky the party stopped to partake of provisions Nattie had packed for the journey. Siban found a spot near the river for him and Rell. Most of the party joined them, letting the horses drink and graze while they ate.

"I can see no matter where we stay, we'll not go hungry." Rell pulled chicken wrapped in an oil cloth from her pack. "How Nattie stays so thin is a mystery."

Siban reached for a chicken leg. "She too busy ordering everybody else around to eat."

Rell added several chunks of hard cheese and a half a loaf of round bread to their pile. "It looks as if she's given each of us a feast."

Jade plopped down beside her and flinched. "I'll never get used to riding. Good old-fashioned walking is what I prefer." She began rifling through her own pack. "I'm starving."

"How long until we get to the inn?" Meran dropped her pack next to Siban and squatted. "Is it much farther?"

"A few more hours."

"Thank the Saints!" A loud groan squeezed from Malachi when he lowered his round body to the ground. "I've not ridden Penelope this much in years. Though she does appear to be faring better than I."

"I promise you'll have a comfortable bed when we arrive at Dragon's Head, Brother." Rhys knelt by the river and washed his hands before joining them. "It's the finest inn north of Alba."

"I'm a bit nervous." Jade took a bite of bread and chewed.

"Me, too." Despite Rell's outward calm, Siban could sense her trepidation about meeting their new and numerous family members. "There's just so many of them."

"You'll love every one of them," Ravyn said.

Jade swallowed. "What are they like?"

A grin spread across Ravyn's mouth. "They are very exuberant."

Rell frowned. "That's not very reassuring."

"Once you've met them you'll wonder why you were ever nervous." Ravyn pulled a chicken wing apart. "Then you'll never want to leave the inn. It's a magical place."

Siban looked at Willa's daughters. "Rhys has only spoken well of your family. I'm sure they'll welcome you with open arms."

"I hope you're right," Jade said, and then took another bite of bread.

From that point on they spoke of lighthearted things, each seeming to only focus on the positive and not weigh down the first part of their journey with foreboding and the what-ifs of what awaited them at the Frost Lands. The small reprieve from doom was welcomed by Siban. He'd rather live in the present and focus on the good things around him.

After packing up their meal, and a joint effort to reseat Malachi on his donkey, they mounted the horses and continued on their trek. The sound of the sea grew louder, its roar their constant companion until they exited the trees onto rolling plains. The sea stretched out to their right, its undulating water crashing against the shore in a continuous assault of waves.

Small rocks and boulders lay strewn over the open plains

but the trail was clear. On the other side of the grasslands they entered a forest. About a hundred yards in, the taint of Bane prickled against Siban's skin.

Rhys pulled the line to a stop, twisted in his saddle, and directed his question at Siban and Rell. "Friend or foe?"

The familiar sensation signaled Icarus's presence, but Siban turned to Rell to confirm his guess.

"I believe its Icarus." She paused. "But we should make sure."

Rhys nodded.

"Call to him," Siban said.

Rell cleared her throat. "Icarus?"

A second later the heavy down stroke of wings sounded and Icarus landed on the trail in front of them. The horses reared and instantly Siban sent his Tell out to encompass the riders, and soothe the animals. The horses calmed.

"We wanted to make sure it was you who followed us and not another Bane," she said.

"You have not been followed." His muscular body blocked their path. "I've not felt another Bane from the time I left the area Faela."

The thought that no demons followed them delighted Siban, yet made him uneasy. For the last month the Bane had seemed to be growing bolder. Why limit their activity now? Since they were moving north, surely their party should be encountering more demons. For the first time having Icarus near gave him comfort.

"We journey as far as the Dragon's Head Inn today," Gregory said. "Be warned, the area around the inn is warded. I wouldn't want to see you injured by attempting to approach."

Icarus tipped his head. "Your concern is touching, brother."

Siban couldn't tell if the demon spoke truthfully or was being facetious. He glanced at Rell. A trace of a smile played around her lips. Siban relaxed slightly, trusting her mood to be an accurate indicator of the situation.

"I will be near." Icarus flared his wings. "If you need me."

With a graceful leap, he launched himself into the air and disappeared above the canopy of the trees. Siban hoped, for all their sakes, that Icarus had their best interests in mind.

. . .

The rest of their journey was pleasant and uneventful. Near sundown they rounded a bend and were greeted by a myriad of smells and sounds.

Ravyn turned to Rell. "The inn."

The smells from the cooking fire and the evening meal blended with shouts and laughter, bringing with it a comfort she'd not felt for thirteen years. A flutter of excitement skittered through Rell and her palms began to sweat despite the cool, late-afternoon air. In a few minutes she would meet her mother's new family.

She glanced at Jade, who sat with a stiff spine in her saddle. More than ever, Rell was grateful for her sister. They'd been through so much together and now, when they were about to meet their half brothers and sisters, their connection only felt stronger. No matter what, she and Jade were Bowen and Willa's daughters. No matter what, they would always stand united.

More shouts erupted when they rode into the courtyard of the inn. Rell's eyes widened as a mob of redheaded children ran toward them. Geoffrey sat on the porch, having successfully delivered the message of their arrival.

"Bless the Saints," Jade said. "There are so many of them."

"My thoughts exactly." Rell pulled her mare to a stop and slowly dismounted.

Siban moved to stand beside her, his presence giving her strength during what was turning out to be a nerve-racking event. Then Willa was there, exiting the front door of the inn and running toward them. Rell and Jade walked forward, their pace picking up as they closed the distance toward their mother.

She wrapped them in a ferocious hug and laid kisses against first Rell's temple and then Jade's. "I can scarce believe you're here." Releasing them, she took a step back and beamed at them. "I've been near sick with worry about all of you, but when Geoffrey arrived early this morning and told us the wonderful news, I thought I'd burst with happiness."

"We are just as happy to be here."

The butterflies in Rell's stomach eased a bit. Ravyn was right; her new family was more welcoming than she could have imagined.

A short, round man, with a ring of red hair waddled toward them. "Welcome, welcome."

Surely this was not Orvis, the man who had fathered ten children and made her mother fall in love with him? Rell slid a questioning glance to first Jade, then Willa.

Through tight lips her mother whispered, "Orvis."

"That's Orvis?" Jade asked, echoing Rell's thoughts.

"That, my daughters, is Orvis." Laughter tinkled from Willa. "He is the complete opposite of your father, but bless his heart, the man is everything I need."

After embracing Rhys and exchanging greetings, Orvis sidled to where they stood. "Let me see." He pointed at Jade. "You favor your mother, so you must be Jade, and that makes you Esmeralda."

"Correct—sir." Rell wasn't sure what she was supposed to call him. He wasn't their father, and yet Orvis felt too familiar. She floundered for appropriate conversation. "Your inn is lovely."

"Please, call me Orvis. After all, we're family." He rested his hands on top of his ample belly and smiled. "Come, you must meet the rest of our clan."

Willa looped her arms through her elder daughters', guiding them toward the horde that had gathered around the party and were lobbing one question after another at the group.

"Line up," Orvis barked. Instantly the children fell into a vague semblance of a line, each one wearing a large grin. "Starting from the oldest to youngest—this is Willie."

A ginger-haired young man gave a quick bow.

"Elizabeth is my oldest daughter." Orvis stopped and gave them a sheepish grin. "Besides you two, of course."

"Of course," Jade said with a quick nod.

Though Orvis was their stepfather, Rell didn't know how she felt about him calling her his daughter. Somehow it felt disrespectful to her real father. She let the comment go and refocused on his introductions.

"Mary, Matilda, Maxwell, Genevieve, Jamie, Gareth, Audra, and finally, little Sarah."

In succession, each child either bowed or curtsied. At the end of Orvis's introduction, they all stood staring, as if waiting for her to say something.

"It is so wonderful to finally meet you," Jade said, thankfully taking the lead. "Mother, you didn't tell me how handsome they all were."

The line of children giggled and preened at Jade's pretty words.

Rell struggled for something clever to say, but nothing brilliant came to her. "I agree, you are all fine-looking young men and women. How lucky we are to have you as brothers and sisters."

The words felt awkward to say. It had only been a few weeks since she'd gained her humanity back. Sweet words still didn't come naturally to her. Hopefully, in time, some of the old Esmeralda would return. Being around this group she would be forced to talk and be kind, whether she wanted to or not.

"Come inside for refreshments." Orvis held his arms wide. "The entire inn is at your disposal."

Willa guided them forward. "Once he heard about the wedding, Orvis kicked everybody out."

"He didn't have to do that for us."

"Yes he did." Her mother gave her arm a squeeze. "Tomorrow's wedding ceremony will be a family affair. No uninvited guests welcome."

"Tomorrow?" Rell pulled Willa and Jade to a stop. "So soon?"

"It is my understanding that you'll be traveling north as soon as possible." Willa started forward again, tugging Rell with her. "By the Saints, you will have your wedding."

"Yes, I guess you're right." She didn't want to hold up the party, but the idea of getting married tomorrow sent her stomach into a riot of nausea inducing tumbles. "Is that enough time?"

"We've been planning the event since I got back. The girls are giddy with excitement and Geoffrey delivered your dress safe and sound. All we needed were the bride and groom, and here you are."

"Yes, here we are." Rell glanced at Siban, who looked as uncomfortable as she was.

"It will be wonderful. I promise," Willa said.

Four of the children gathered the reins of their horses and led them away. Obviously it was a task they'd done quite often. Sampson went willingly, leading more than being led by the oldest boy.

Inside, the group was swept into the great room and seated at the tables near the hearth. Food and drinks began arriving almost instantly. Siban took a place near Rell at the table, his usual spot at her side had been usurped by the youngest of the girls. She gave him an apologetic smile, but he seemed highly amused by the situation.

Sarah and Audra sat on either side of Rell, pelting her with questions about her wedding. Though Rell's answers were short and to the point, the girls seemed not to notice. And if she didn't explain something in enough detail, the children would simply rephrase their question and ask it again.

They beamed at her as if she was the most amazing thing they'd seen in their lifetime. After several minutes of their interrogation, Rell began to relax. The two girls were sweet and open. Their immediate acceptance of her melted any remaining doubts she had about her new family.

Laughter echoed through the room as the other children entertained the rest of the Bringers with their questions and stories. While the children were there, talk revolved around issues that didn't involve their journey north or the battle brewing between the Bringers and Vile. When only Willie and Mary remained and the other children had toddled off to bed, their discussion turned to more serious matters.

Gregory told of their journey into the Shadow World, leaving out the part of Icarus being nearby, and when he finished with his tale, nobody spoke for a long time. Even though she had experienced it for herself, hearing their trials again made Rell tired.

"Well that, Sir Gregory, is quite a story." Orvis leaned back in his chair. "I, for one, will say an extra prayer of thanks for your safe return."

"Hear, hear," Willa said. "I only wish this brewing trouble would go away."

"We will do our best to make that happen," Rhys said.

"Hopefully not at the expense of any of your lives." Willa looked at her daughters. "I've only just gotten my family back."

Orvis placed his hand on top of hers. "We'll not lose them

so easily." He gave her a reassuring smile. "They are Bringers and your and Bowen's daughters. They're made of strong stuff."

"I know what you say is true, but I'm their mother. I can't help but worry."

"We'll be all right." Jade looked around the group. "There is none finer than these people. If any can vanquish Vile, it is them."

"Us," Luc corrected.

"Yes," Rell said. "We will vanquish him. We've already done so much in such a short time and all of us have so much to fight for now."

A murmur of agreement rippled through the group.

"We will do what we can here," Willie said. "You can count on us."

"Indeed we will," Orvis nodded. "Indeed we will."

Rell yawned at the same time Ravyn did.

"It appears our guests grow weary." Orvis rocked forward and stood. "Come, I'll show you to your rooms. The entire upstairs has been prepared for you."

Rell sent up a prayer of thanks. All she wanted was to undress, wash, and crawl into bed next to Siban. He obviously had the same idea from the way he snaked his arm around her waist and pulled him to her. She went willingly and laid her head against his shoulder.

"Oh, no you don't," Willa said, tugging Rell free from his grasp. "The bride and the groom are not to see each other on their wedding day."

"It's not our wedding day yet." Siban reached for Rell, but Willa laughed and pulled her away from his reach.

"If you sleep in the same room, you will wake and see her in the morning." Willa gripped Rell's arms and marched her toward a door near the hearth. "You will sleep upstairs, and she will sleep down here, where I can make sure you leave her alone."

Siban groaned. "I find that fiercely unfair."

The rest of the group laughed. Luc slapped him on the back. "Tough luck, friend. But just think, after tomorrow Willa won't be able to tell you what you can and can't do with her daughter."

Willa scowled at him. "If you have the faintest notion of asking for Jade's hand in marriage, Luc, I suggest you watch what you say."

He'd just taken a swallow of ale and choked at her comment. Rhys pounded Luc on the back. "You all right?"

Despite his fit of coughing, Luc managed to hold up a hand in surrender.

Rell went willingly, enjoying Siban's anguish over being parted. "I'm sorry."

He stood there watching her being led away from him, his eyes round and forlorn. Willa clicked the door closed behind them and turned with an evil smile. "It's always good to keep them wanting."

"I'll remember that." Rell fell onto the bed and stared at the wood beams running through the ceiling. "It's good to be here."

She sat up and Willa joined her on the bed. "It's good to have you here."

The room was small but cozy. A small fire burned in the hearth on the wall opposite the hearth in the great room. Rell smiled when she saw her wedding dress hanging in the corner. "I can't believe I'm getting married tomorrow." She looked at Willa. "I never thought such a thing would be possible."

"You are a testament that miracles do happen." Her mother brushed a lock of hair from her forehead. "You are my miracle." Willa wrapped her arm around Rell's shoulder and kissed her on the cheek. "Never doubt that."

"I won't." She gripped her mother's hand. "Thank you."

Willa furrowed her brow. "For what?"

There were so many things she wanted to thank her mother for, too many to say at once. "For everything. The Bringers gave me my body back, but you and Siban have given me a family again." Tears burned at the back of her eyes. She met her mother's gaze. "I still struggle with the darkness sometimes, but it's getting easier now that I have a place in this world and people who love me."

"We all feel like that sometimes, Rell." Willa stroked her hand. "But know that you and Jade are just as much a part of this family as any of us. There's always a place for you here, no matter what happens."

"Thank you, that means everything to me." Rell yawned.

"All right. To bed with you." Willa stood and walked to the fireplace to stoke the fire. "Morning will come quick enough. There's water in the basin or if you prefer a bath, I can draw that for you."

Rell shook her head. "I'm too tired. I'll wash up and bathe in the morning."

"All right, love." Willa walked to the door and opened it. "Sleep tight. I'll wake you in the morning."

"Good night, Mother." Rell watched her mother leave, feeling truly at peace for the first time in a long time.

CHAPTER TWENTY-EIGHT

Rell rolled to her side and stared out the window. Thin rays of sunlight streaked through the crack in the drapes. Tiny dust specks danced with what seemed like joy for the happy occasion. Today was her wedding day.

Rell stretched, extending her limbs along the warm, soft linens of the bed. Sadly Siban was not there to share the time before the activities of the day began. She smiled. Every morning after today, she'd wake up to him beside her. It was more than she had ever dreamed of.

The idea of getting up tumbled around her head for a few seconds, but instead she snuggled deeper into the pile of pillows, determined to get a little more sleep. This was her day and after everything she'd been through the past several weeks, she deserved to rest and not worry about routine or responsibilities.

A knock sounded at the door. Rell groaned and pulled the pillow over her head, willing the intruder to go away. The muffled *click* of the door sounded and the quiet squeaking of the hinges signaled that whoever knocked would not be deterred by her feigned sleeping.

"I know you're not asleep, so you might as well stop pretending."

Rell cracked open her eyes and glared at her mother. "One more hour."

Willa slid a breakfast tray onto a table and walked to the window. She gripped the edge of the curtains and threw them wide. "It's nearly noon."

Rell flung her arm over her eyes. "Noon? It can't be."

"It is." Willa walked to the large tub in the corner and opened a cabinet against the wall. "Eat first and then have a bath." She pulled on a lever, which let the water run free. "Are you nervous?"

Rell sat up and yawned. "No, why would I be nervous?"

"A woman's wedding day is very special and can be a little scary." Willa laid out a large bath sheet and smaller towel. "It's the time when she leaves her family and becomes a wife." After setting several bottles on a table near the tub, she moved to sit on the bed next to Rell. Willa brushed a stray strand of hair away from Rell's eyes and then cupped her cheek. "Then again, you've been away from your family for a very long time and you and Siban's relationship is not ordinary."

She covered her mother's hand with her own. "No, but it will still be a good marriage despite its—" She searched for the right word. "Its uniqueness."

"I believe it will as well." Willa lowered her hand. "So…" She gave a little shrug. "We didn't get much of a chance to speak last night. What do you think of your brothers and sisters? I know they can be overwhelming at times, but they really do mean well."

"They are a like a large litter of puppies, always busy and inquisitive." The thought of how they had argued over who would carry her pack brought a smile to Rell's face. "I think they're wonderful."

Tiny creases formed next to Willa's eyes when she smiled. "Good, because they are determined to help you get ready for your wedding."

"Really?" She sat and pushed the covers from her legs. "Well, I guess I'd better get my bathing done." She swung her legs over the side of the bed and stood. "I'm not sure I'll ever get used to having so many people around."

Willa rubbed her back. "You will when you have children of your own."

"Children?" Since she and Siban had talked about it at Alba Haven, the idea had lingered. "I don't think I'd make a very good mother."

"You, my daughter, would make one of the best mothers." Willa stood. "I fear for any who dare to hurt your offspring." She clapped her hands together. "Now, eat and bathe. I'll keep the horde at bay for another hour, but after that I can't promise anything."

"I have been warned." Rell watched Willa walk to the bathtub and shut off the water. Her nose tingling with the hint of impending tears. "Thank you again—for everything."

Willa smiled and glided to the door. "Thank you for coming home to get married, Esmeralda."

With that she quit the room, leaving Rell alone with her thoughts, a steaming tub of water, and a plate of food that smelled delicious. She made quick work of the latter two, picking at the plate of meat, cheese, and fresh bread while reclining in the steaming water. When she'd finished her meal and scrubbed herself raw, Rell stood and stepped out of the tub, wrapping herself in a large linen bath sheet.

A knock sounded at the door, and as she turned the door creaked open and Matilda stuck her head in. "She's up." Matilda pushed open the door, letting in a line of girls and women. "We're here to help you get ready."

Caught naked, with nothing but a sheet to wrap around her, sent panic racing through Rell. She pulled the sheet tighter and backed toward the wall. "All of you?"

"Shooo." Willa squeezed into the room, waving her hands. "At least let the girl get dressed in her essentials before you descend upon her like locusts."

The girls moaned and with slumped shoulders, scuffed out of the room, leaving Jade, Meran, Ravyn, and her mother.

"We'll let you get dressed," Jade said. Her smile belied her amusement at Rell's discomfort. "Call us when you're ready."

"I don't think I will ever be ready for that," Rell mumbled.

The door closed, but she waited a few seconds to make sure nobody would reopen it. When she was fairly certain it was safe, she dropped the sheet and slipped the long sheath that hung at the front of her dress over her head. Next she donned the thick robe Willa had provided and sat by the fire to dry her hair.

She blotted the ends with the bath sheet and sighed. It looked like she was not going to get out of her sisters' eagerness to be involved in her wedding preparations. Another sigh slipped from her and she stood, tossed the towel to the side, and walked to the door. Mustering her courage, she pulled the door open to reveal the six excited, freckled faces of her half sisters.

Rell inhaled. "All right, girls, I'm ready."

A cheer went up and they filed into the room, moving Rell to a chair in the center. Hands fluttered about her body and hair, combing through the locks. After the first few minutes Rell lost track of who was doing what to her and gave herself over to the ministrations of the young girls.

When they were finished, she didn't recognize herself. Flowers had been woven into her hair and the green wedding gown that Delphia had created made her eyes even greener. As she stared at herself in the looking glass she truly felt beautiful.

The lilting music of flutes wafted through the door. Rell stood at the entrance, her gaze fixed and unseeing on the people gathered at the front of the inn. A bouquet of fall flowers appeared in front of Rell, the red-and-orange bunch bright against the lively green of her gown. She reached for them with a shaking hand and took them from Jade.

"You look as if you're about to lose your luncheon," her sister said.

"I'm so nervous." Rell gripped the stems with both hands and looked at Jade. "I feel like something is bound go wrong, as if I don't deserve this happiness."

A sweet smile spread across Jade's face. She brushed her hand against Rell's cheek. "Trust me, this is the most right thing you've ever done in your life." She sniffed and squared her shoulders. "Now, it's time." Her eyes rounded with excitement. "Let's get you married to that dashingly handsome man waiting at the end of the path."

Rell swallowed hard. "I can do this."

"Of course you can," Jade said. "This should be the easiest thing you've done in the last thirteen years."

"You'd think as much, wouldn't you?" Butterflies tumbled in Rell's stomach.

Elizabeth gave a little tug on the gown's train, fluffing it to spread it in a wide arc across the ground. "You look beautiful, Esmeralda."

Though they only known each other for a day, there was an undeniable bond between her and Elizabeth. "Thank you for all your help today. My hair has never looked so lovely."

"Got five bratty sisters, each with a mass of locks that require more taming than a wild horse." She walked to stand beside Rell and tugged gently on the sleeve of her gown before smoothing the short brown fur to fall in one direction. "Had to learn quick or else they'd walk around looking like a bunch of hedgehogs." She smiled at Rell. "I've always been the oldest. It's nice having grown sisters, women more my own age."

"Yes, sisters need to stick together—always," Jade said, taking her place in front of Rell.

"So tell me, sister," Rell gave Elizabeth a conspiratorial wink. "Has Luc asked for your hand yet?"

"Shhht." Her sister turned and glared at her. "Let's not ruin the day."

Rell repressed a laugh and followed Jade out the door. Every so often the breeze would rustle the trees and send bright yellow leaves fluttering to the ground, as if in celebration of her and Siban's marriage.

The assembled crowd stood on either side of a path that had first been cleared and then strewn with the same orange-and-red petals of her bouquet. Smiles graced all her friends' faces and warmed her heart. They had battled together, and now they would celebrate together.

The freckled faces of her brothers and sisters beamed at her from the front row. Hayden's blond head stuck out among the sea of red curls. He raised his hand and wiggled his fingers at Rell. Tears welled but thankfully didn't spill down her cheeks. She blinked back the emotions threatening to overwhelm her and waved back at the little boy.

Orvis stood beside his children, wearing the grin of a proud father. Though she knew her mother had loved her father more than anything in the world, she certainly understood how the charming innkeeper had won Willa's heart. He treated her like gold and had given her exactly what she needed to fill what the Bane and Rell had taken from her.

At the sight of her mother, a lump formed in Rell's throat. Willa watched her, her pale blue eyes round and glistening. Tears were to be expected at joyous occasions, but seeing her mother truly happy made this day even more perfect.

Her breath caught when she saw Siban standing under an arch of vines and leaves. Never had he looked so handsome. Strands of gold and reddish-brown hair reflected in the afternoon sun. His trousers and boots were fashioned of dark brown leather and the shirt he wore beneath his coat was a paler shade of green to match her gown. Crafted from rich brocade and velvet, his waistcoat matched the brown of his pants. At his hip hung his immortal sword, but it was Siban's sparkling hazel eyes that held Rell's gaze.

She opened herself to him, drinking in the love that he sent flowing to her. In turn, she directed her joy at becoming his wife across the distance. His grin spread.

Both Gregory and Malachi stood at the arch, waiting to perform the ceremony. They would be wed both in the eyes of the Order of the Saints and the Bringers. There would be no disputing their union under any law.

A faint prickle of Bane skittered along Rell's arms. She searched the trees but didn't see Icarus. With the grounds of the inn warded, he'd not be able to get close, but she was certain he could see her. The demon was clever and if he wanted to view the ceremony, he'd find a way.

When they reached the arch, Jade stepped to the left and Rell took her place beside Siban. Instead of standing side by side, he faced her and removed the flowers from her grip, handing them to Jade. He twined his fingers with Rell's, drawing her against him and kissed her.

"We're not to that part yet," Malachi said.

Laughter rippled through the crowd. After another second, Siban broke the kiss. "Life is too short to put off the best things."

A murmur of approval flowed through the crowd. After all, most of them had narrowly escaped death and very soon would face more perils.

Gregory's voice rose above the din. "Today we come

together to celebrate the union between Esmeralda Kendal and Siban Gaspar."

Rell lifted her eyebrows in surprise. "Gaspar?" she mouthed.

He winked at her.

She supposed she should have learned his last name, but it had never seemed important. Lady Gaspar? Rolling the name around in her head, she decided she liked the new title very much.

"In the eyes of the Saints," Malachi said.

"And in the hearts of the Bringers," Gregory added, "do we join these two people in the most sacred of unions."

"As the Saints bestow their blessing on us," Malachi's normally watery eyes sparkled as he spoke the words. "So do we, with great joy, bless the union between Esmeralda and Siban."

"Do you both," Gregory said, "vow to honor each other, to pledge your hearts to each other through life, no matter what may lie ahead?"

"We do." Together they answered, Siban's fingers tightening around hers.

"Do you promise to keep faith in each other during times of trouble and to not stray," Malachi added.

"We do."

Though the monk's words were necessary to bind them, Rell couldn't imagine ever straying from Siban. He was her life, her heart, and if need be, she would die to make sure they had a future together.

Gregory spoke again. "Through the pressures of the present and the uncertainties of the future, do you promise to guide and protect each other?"

"We do."

Malachi folded his hands in front of him. "Then by the

power of the church, do I pronounce this couple wed."

"And," Gregory said, before anybody cheered, "do I, with rights bestowed upon me as a member of the royal house of James, also declare this couple wed."

Cheers erupted from their friends and family. Once again, Siban pulled her to him and kissed her, this time with no restraint.

Two months ago, Rell's existence had been consumed by revenge and darkness. Now, even though her life still held countless dangers, it bore untold happiness. She had more family than one person deserved and had a husband who loved her for who she was, be that Bane or Bringer. No matter what the fate of the world, on this day, all her prayers had been answered.

ACKNOWLEDGEMENTS

I want to thank Erin Molta for being an awesome editor with an eye for what I could no longer see the story needed. Thank you for your patience.

I also want to thank my alpha readers who suffer through the first draft of my stories and give me sage advice on what does and doesn't work. I appreciate you so much!

ABOUT THE AUTHOR

Boone Brux is a bestselling author. Her books range from high fantasy to humorous paranormal.

A former nanny, Boone has lived all over the world, finally settling in the icy region of Alaska, where she writes full time. Always looking for the next adventure, it's not unusual to find her traversing the remotest parts of the Alaskan bush. No person or escapade is off-limits when it comes to weaving real-life experiences into her books or blogs.

To read more about Boone, find her at www.boonebrux.com.

HEAVY METAL
By Natalie J. Damschroder

All Riley Kordek wants is a chance to figure out her new ability to bend metal's energy. When a hot guy who knows more than he should helps her escape attackers, she thinks she might've found someone who can lead her to answers.

When Sam Remington takes Riley to the Society for Goddess Education and Defense, the stakes rise beyond what either of them could have imagined. Riley uncovers a plot with disastrous ramifications not only for herself, but for Sam and the people he loves—and potentially every goddess in the country.

DEEP RISING
By N.R. Rhodes

In his nine-year stint with the CIA, Jared Caldwell thought he'd seen it all. But when his latest mission instructs him to apprehend the beautiful scientist Lana, who's allegedly linked to a devastating new form of warfare, he isn't prepared for the prospect of battling man-made tsunamis—or the misplaced feelings he harbors for his number one suspect.

But time is running out and Jared and Lana must work together to protect the mainland. As the heat between them—and the threat of mass destruction—rises there is more at stake than just their hearts.

DEEP IN CRIMSON
By Sara Gillman

Kidnapped by humans and raised in a research facility, Jett was taught to believe his own race of demons to be insidious and violent. Jett wants to bring his captor to justice, so he joins forces with the demon Guardians, and the demon child's older sister, Lexine.

Irresistible attraction grows between Jett and Lexine, but if Jett goes through the all-consuming process of becoming a Guardian, he may forfeit any chance they have of being together.

HEAVEN & HELLSBANE
By Paige Cuccaro

Someone's murdering angels and turning the half human, half angel illorum warriors against their angelic supporters. No one's more surprised than Emma Jane Hellsbane when she's called in to find the killers.

But when her own angelic mentor — and off-limits hottie — Eli is targeted, Emma takes it personally. Now Emma isn't just fighting off demons, rogue nephilim, and Fallen angels, but she's defending her honor as well.

It's all in a day's work as Heaven's ultimate bounty hunter.

WAKING UP DEAD
By Emma Shortt

When her best friend, Tye, disappears hunting for food, kick-ass Jackson Hart's 'head south to safety' plan looks like it's dead before it's even begun. But then she meets ex-mechanic Luke Granger, who offers her protection against the zombie hordes.

But the flesh eaters are getting smarter and the bunker is compromised, so Jackson and Luke travel for thousands of miles looking for other humans. On the way, they discover that even if flesh eating zombies are knocking down their door, there's always time for sex and even love.

MALICIOUS MISCHIEF
By Marianne Harden

For twenty-four-year-old college dropout Rylie Keyes, keeping her job means figuring out the truth about a senior citizen who was found murdered while in her care. The late Otto Weiner was not a liked man and his enemies will stop at nothing to keep their part in his murder secret.

Forced to dust off her old PI training, Rylie must align with a circus-bike-wheeling Samoan while juggling the attention of two very hot cops. She has no idea that along the way she just might win, or lose, a little piece of her heart.

CINDERELLA SCREWED ME OVER

By Cindi Madsen

Darby Quinn has a bone to pick with Cinderella. Burned one too many times by ex-boyfriends, she's sworn off love, Prince Charmings, and happy endings. Or at least she did… until she met Jake.

Charming, fun, and unwilling to give up on her, Jake doesn't fit any of the profiles Darby has created from her case studies of ex-princes-gone-bad. Finally presented with her own Prince Charming, Darby learns that sometimes the perfect love, like a perfect pair of shoes, is just within your grasp.